BEGINNINGS AND ENDINGS

He could have walked over to her and held her and made love to her, but he didn't. He couldn't. He didn't know who she was anymore. She looked like the sixteen-year-old girl with whom he had fallen in love eleven years ago, but instead she was the woman who had yelled at him in rage a month ago. He didn't know her.

Mark had to find the old Janet. To retrace the steps, then he could go to her. He wanted to go to her, to his Janet.

"Do you remember the first time we made love?" he asked without looking at her.

"Of course," she answered, tears flooding her eyes.

Mark looked at her then, his own eyes glistening.

"What were you thinking?"

"What?"

"What were you thinking when we made love? It was a big step and we never talked about it. What were you thinking?"

"I was thinking what I always thought when you touched me," Janet said very quietly. "I was thinking, I love you."

"Janet," Mark said emotionally. But he still couldn't move to her . . .

But he had to try. She had to try. No matter the cost. . . .

THE CARLTON CLUB

KATHERINE STONE

ZEBRA BOOKS
KENSINGTON PUBLISHING CORP.

ZEBRA BOOKS

are published by

Kensington Publishing Corp.
850 Third Avenue
New York, NY 10022

Tenth printing: April 1996   C

Printed in the United States of America

Part One

Chapter One

San Francisco, California
November, 1980

Dr. Leslie Adams gazed out University Hospital's eleventh floor picture window mesmerized by the magnificence of San Francisco at daybreak. As she watched, the pearl-gray sky became pale yellow. It was the kind of pastel autumn dawn that promised a soft muted sun. It would be a gentle sun, just warm enough to melt the thick layer of fog that covered San Francisco Bay like a plush down comforter.

Leslie knew the kind of fresh, crisp, exhilarating day it would be. A warm sun. A cool, but not cold, breeze. A day for light woolen scarves and rosy-red cheeks and mugs of hot chocolate. Leslie loved days like this. She had memories, lovely distant memories, of such days . . . a walk in a secluded pine-scented meadow . . . a wind-tossed ferry boat ride across white-capped water . . .

Leslie thought about the rich taste of hot chocolate as she curled her hands around her barely warm cup of over-brewed black coffee and sighed. The sigh was a little nostalgic, because of the memories, and a little wistful, because she would love to be out there today, enjoying the autumn briskness. But mostly it was, simply, a sigh of fatigue.

It had been a long, busy sleepless night; but she had made it, and her patients had made it. Everyone had survived. Now, finally, as the night's cold darkness yielded to the warmth of the new-day sun, the hospital was silent. At peace. Sleeping.

Mark would tell her that, even if only for an hour, she should try to sleep.

Mark. He had hoped she would have an easy night. That was what he was really telling her ten hours ago. . . .

"I have a feeling it is going to a quiet night," he said as he walked into the doctors' write-up area.

"Mark! Hi," she said looking up, a little startled, from the medical record she was reviewing. "What did—"

"I said I have a feeling it's going to be a quiet night," he repeated as he settled into a chair across from her. "Very quiet. No more admissions. No midnight fever work-ups or chest pain. . . ."

"Dream on," she said, laughing.

"This is a very strong feeling," he countered lightly. Then he leveled his dark brown eyes at her and added seriously, "Which means that Dr. Leslie Adams, intern *extraordinaire,* can get some sleep."

Leslie's eyes met his for a brief awkward moment, then fell, unable to hold his gaze. They both knew that, even if the night was quiet, Leslie wouldn't sleep. She wouldn't even try. I can't really sleep at the hospital, Leslie explained easily to anyone who questioned her habit of staying up all night when she was on call.

It was true. It *was* difficult to sleep at the hospital. The interruptions were frequent, and the hours when it was even possible to sleep were few. It was true, but those weren't the real reasons. The real reason was too personal, too superstitious, too silly to tell anyone . . .

Leslie believed that if she stayed awake, alert, keeping vigil over the patients in her charge, nothing bad would happen to them. Somehow her wakeful presence would protect them against the unknown, unpredictable catastrophes that could and did occur.

So, Leslie didn't sleep. She simply patrolled. A quiet,

serious sentry. A highly trained shepherd. Unobtrusive, but ever-present. It was illogical. *Silly.* But it was *working.* It felt right.

Doing what felt right was what Leslie had always done. At George Washington High School in Seattle, doing what felt right won her recognition as Most Inspirational and Most Likely To Succeed. Doing what felt right drew good-natured teasing from her friends about being *too* good, *too* perfect: predictable, reliable Leslie. They teased her at Radcliffe, too, when she chose biology over a Saturday night "mixer" or an organic chemistry experiment over the Harvard-Yale crew race.

The teasing was always gentle. They were her friends, after all. And no one begrudged Leslie her rules. She didn't try to impose them on anyone else, and she didn't expect anyone else to follow them. Her friends knew that Leslie's rules were just for Leslie, just the way Leslie had to do things.

Now, as an intern, she had to stay up all night, awake, alert, vigilant. It was the only way that felt right. It didn't make sense, she knew that, but it felt right.

Except when Mark teased her. Then she felt foolish. What if Mark guessed the real reason, her silly superstition? Mark was so rational, so logical. He would think it ridiculous. He would think *her* ridiculous. Mark, of all people—

"No plans to sleep?" Mark asked finally, interrupting the silence, sorry that he made her uncomfortable.

Leslie tossed the chestnut curls that fell into her sapphire-blue eyes and smiled bravely. "No plans to sleep. I have a feeling it's going to be busy."

Mark smiled. She could be so sensitive. And so proud.

"Any problems with your patients?" he asked.

"No. The patient I just admitted with acute asthma is already clearing. I'm just reviewing his old chart. Then I'll be all caught up," Leslie said, ready for the busy night to begin or for a long quiet night of patrolling.

"I think I'll go home, then," Mark said, standing up suddenly.

9

Go home. Mark's words caught Leslie by surprise. It was only seven. For the past month, because he no longer had a reason to leave—because he no longer had a *home*—Mark frequently spent extra hours at the hospital. Even when he could leave, when other residents were in charge, he often stayed to help Leslie with her patients or to review charts or to read journals.

It must be better than being alone, Leslie decided as she watched the new pattern emerge. It must be better for Mark to be here than to be alone with all the unanswerable questions that must be tormenting him. Not that the hospital really provided escape. Leslie saw the pain and sadness in his dark eyes, even though he tried to hide it. Even though he told no one, not even her.

She knew of course, because Janet was her friend. She and Janet talked about it all the time.

But Mark and Leslie never talked about it.

"Home," she echoed softly.

"If you don't need—"

"No," Leslie said quickly. "Everything's under control."

She sensed his restlessness as he leaned against the doorjamb waiting for her to say good-night. Restless, eager, full of anticipation, there was a glimmer of hope in the dark eyes where, recently, there had been none. Was Mark rushing off to see Janet?

No. Leslie would have known *that*.

Mark was leaving, eager, full of hope, to be with someone else, and just the thought of whoever she was made his eyes sparkle with life and happiness.

"Have a nice evening," Leslie said gaily, smiling above the ache that consumed her.

"You too." Mark smiled back. "Try to get some sleep."

He would have told her to try to sleep now, ten hours later, if even for an hour.

Had *he* slept, Leslie wondered as she took a swallow of luke-warm, bitter coffee. Where had he slept? And with whom. . . .

Stop thinking about him, she told herself sternly, forcing her thoughts away from Mark and back to the glorious day that was unfolding before her. This time as she gazed out the window she focused on the thick layer of fog that lay beneath the pale yellow glow of the autumn dawn.

Fog. It wasn't supposed to be there. It was November. This kind of fog—thick, opaque, smothering—was a summer phenomenon. Leslie had learned about the notorious San Francisco summer fog, four months before, the day her internship began. Four months. It seemed so long ago.

The department chairman had told them, the internship class of 1980–81, how delighted he was to have them in his internal medicine program. He *was* delighted. He looked at the bright, healthy, eager young doctors assembled before him. He knew they were among the nation's best. The internship class that listened intently to the words of their department chairman that day in June was a select group. And carefully selected at that.

They had all graduated at the top of their medical school classes. They had all been elected to Alpha Omega Alpha, the medical school equivalent of Phi Beta Kappa. The only question, a question the most competitive among them might ask a colleague, was, When were you elected to AOA? junior year? autumn of senior year? or, perish the thought, *spring* of senior year?

They had all spent the month between medical school graduation and the beginning of their internship preparing for the year that lay ahead. Some simply rested, knowing but not really believing the rumors of the exhaustion that would beset them (not *them*). Some traveled. Some got married. Some read—*reread*—textbooks of medicine. Some studied the "how-to" manuals for interns.

All framed their recently earned Doctor of Medicine diplomas. *None* spent any time dreading the year to come. The University of California at San Francisco was the internship they wanted. It was the ultimate trophy, the reward for their hard work. It was the best.

They were the best.

That June day, the day the internship started, they were

11

eager. *Ready*. The department chairman looked at them thoughtfully. He knew from years of experience that, as prepared as they were, as smart as they were, as eager and as confident as they were, they were *not* ready. They could not be adequately prepared for the year—the ordeal—that lay ahead.

He tried to tell them. He knew that they would hear his words, but they wouldn't understand. In a month he could repeat the speech, and they would look at him with their dark-circled eyes and gaunt faces and nod wisely. In a month they would understand. He wondered if any of them would remember that he had told them.

"Your internship is like our weather here in San Francisco," he said earnestly, his gray eyes serious.

They listened, politely, smiling. He was such a distinguished physician. They were so glad to be here!

"In the summer months we have fog. Oh, there are brief glimpses of sun and clarity, but mostly, it is foggy and gray and dismal at a time—summer!—when it should be just the opposite. That's what these summer months of your internship will be like. They will be foggy, confusing and grim."

The eager faces looked puzzled. Was he being funny?

"There will be questions you can't answer," he explained. "Problems you don't know how to handle. Patients you can't save. It is very different from, for example, National Boards. On National Boards there are clear questions with correct answers, and I know from your applications how well you all did on your Boards. . . ."

A titter of relief. *Good, he knows how good we are. But what is he talking about?*

"But *doctors*," he continued, "take care of real patients and lots of foggy questions without clear answers. There will be days when the shades of gray, like the fog, seem relentless. It's difficult because it is so different from what you expect. In summer you expect sun not fog. When you start your internship, having graduated top in your class, you expect to continue to have all the right answers."

He looked at them, knowing what they were thinking: I

12

do have the right answers. I *will* have. I always have had.

"But," he said pleasantly, "the fog of your internship will lift as predictably as the San Francisco summer fog vanishes. By mid-September the breezes will be fresh and cool, and the skies will be clear and blue. Your spirits will lift. Your confidence will be restored. You'll understand that shades of gray are part of medicine. Come September it will be smooth sailing."

It had been exactly as he predicted: a difficult, confusing, disillusioning adjustment. But it had also been just as he promised. By September, when the sun came out, the fog vanished and the skies were blue, they *were* adjusted. They knew they could and would make it. The exhaustion, the pressure, the energy required did not change.

But the fog had lifted.

Now, almost two months later, the fog had returned.

How would the department chairman explain it? A fog relapse. What could it mean? The interns have gotten too confident, too sure. Let the fog return! A *reminder.*

As Leslie toyed with the meaning, the *symbolism,* of the fog, she thought lovingly about her parents in Seattle. Her mother, a journalist, and her father, a professor of English at the University of Washington, could spend endless hours happily analyzing the symbols and metaphors and hidden meanings in their favorite books and poems. Leslie was their only child, the precious daughter who, despite the genes that should have made her a writer or a poet, was a scientist. Susan and Matthew Adams watched her grow up with proud loving amazement. How could *their* daughter prefer Galileo to Faulkner, volunteer work at the hospital to the Repertory's production of *Man and Superman,* science projects to novels and physics to poetry?

This November fog, Leslie decided finally, feeling truly the daughter of her literary parents, was *not* a professional fog. It was not a soupy signal that the lessons of shades of gray and uncertainty had been inadequately learned and needed remedial work. If it was a symbol at all, Leslie

13

concluded, it was a symbol of personal fog.

In the distance Leslie heard the comforting sounds of the hospital waking up, preparing for the new day. The elevators, silent and immobile all night, now moved constantly as they shuttled the rested day shift to its wards and retrieved the tired night shift. Leslie heard the rattle of breakfast carts being wheeled from room to room, the clank of the bedside scales, the quiet chatter of nurses' reports and the almost soundless footfalls of the morning blood-draw team in their rubber-soled shoes.

Even though Leslie heard the familiar reassuring noises that undeniably heralded the close of another night on call, her thoughts were not tranquil. She was thinking about the fog. The surprising dense fog outside the window. And the fog inside — the personal fog that had settled, firmly, around her. Again.

Again. It had been there in summer, all summer. But, like the San Francisco fog, it had vanished — had been *banished* by her — in September. It was back now, an enveloping unsummoned presence, because everything had changed. Because maybe it wasn't impossible anymore. Because she could dare to think about it. About *him.*

It wasn't really very complicated. One didn't need a degree in English to decipher the meaning of the mysterious fog. Even a scientist could make the correct diagnosis, Leslie thought wryly. Even an *intern* . . .

The diagnosis was simple: Mark David Taylor, M.D.

Chapter Two

The alarm sounded noisily, a too harsh intrusion on a pleasant but unremembered dream. Mark groaned and in one motion rolled over and depressed the alarm silence button. As he awakened, Mark realized two things. The first was that he was unusually tired, fatigued beyond the chronic feeling of being sleep deprived. The second realization was even more unusual. Unusual and startling

Mark realized that he wasn't unhappy. His first feeling, preceding consciousness by a few moments, was *not* the familiar aching sadness that had been with him for the past month.

For the past month. Ever since Janet had left him.

This morning's feeling was happy and eager and so energetic that it almost erased the fatigue. The feeling was new. Mark had never felt it before. Not even with Janet. Not even in the beginning. Not ever before.

As Mark's consciousness caught up with the vital feeling that had awakened the instant the alarm sounded, he remembered the cause of the feeling: Kathleen. And he knew why his chronic sleep deficit seemed more acute. Kathleen hadn't left until three. Only four hours ago she was still in his bed making him feel the way he still felt even after she was gone.

Kathleen. As he showered, Mark thought about her, remembering last night, astonished that he had only known her for a week.

As Mark recalled the events of the past week he resisted any attempt to put meaning to them. He was still reeling from Janet's angry words, still trying to make sense of Janet's condemnation of their marriage. Her condemnation of him. For the past month Mark lay awake at night, tired but unable to sleep, wondering how to save his marriage and what he would do if it wasn't salvageable.

For the past month Mark had taken his life one day at a time. In the few moments he had that weren't of necessity focused on his patients, he tried to make sense of what happened. He tried to understand the venom of Janet's words.

One day at a time.

And now there was Kathleen and the wonderful feeling that, for the moment, obliterated the anguish and turmoil about Janet.

One day at a time.

Kathleen.

One night at a time.

Mark met Kathleen on Halloween. Mark was on call on Halloween.

"You are always on call on Halloween," Janet might have said if they hadn't separated three weeks before.

Just as she said that he was *always* "on" on Thanksgiving or Christmas (which was also her birthday) or their anniversary or his birthday. It wasn't true of course. It was the luck of the schedule. He was *always* on call every third night, at least. Sometimes every other night. Sometimes those on call nights coincided with *real world* events like holidays and birthdays and anniversaries.

"Besides," he would have asked Janet, "what would we do if I was off on Halloween? Go to a party with my friends most of whom you detest?"

That—the way Janet felt about his friends, about medicine—was part of the news she had given him three weeks before.

"I hate your friends and I hate medicine," Janet had

said. Then she added quietly, "And I think you do, too."

By Halloween there was no Janet, and Mark didn't care whether he was "on" or "off" on Halloween. Or any other time for that matter. Except that Halloween meant craziness. Halloween was like a full-moon night, only worse. But since Mark was on call for the critical care units at University Hospital, he would probably feel very little of the Halloween impact.

The emergency room, particularly at San Francisco General Hospital, would be hit the hardest by the Halloween phenomenon. There they would see lacerations that were unusually long and deep and old and dirty because of the blood alcohol level of the victim. They would see broken bones, the result of the inevitable conflicts as the traditional Gays' Halloween Parade made its way along Castro Street to the jeers and taunts of macho "straights." They would see the drug fall-out from parties: angel-dust (PCP) "freak-outs," cocaine-induced headaches and palpitations and the age-old marijuana death paranoia made worse by the ghoulish costumes on fellow party-goers.

Halloween in the ER was the stuff anecdotes were made of. Anecdotes to tell at parties. To your friends. Medical anecdotes to tell medical friends. Everything Janet hated.

Mark was quite content to be on call for the critical care units instead of the emergency room. His admissions would be legitimately sick, uncostumed, undrugged and uncrazed by the Halloween spirit.

Mark was paged to the emergency room at ten P.M. on Halloween.

"We have a fifty-six-year-old woman with substernal chest pain," the harried resident told him, "radiating to her left arm, lasting maybe five minutes. Responded to nitro. Has chronic angina but this lasted longer. No EKG changes. Pain-free now. Probably just angina, but I'd like to bring her in as a rule out. It's a soft hit . . ." the voice trailed off apologetically.

A hit was an admission, any admission. A night with no admissions was a no hitter. A soft hit meant it might be safe to send the patient home, but . . .

Soft hits were fine with Mark. He believed in erring on the side of the patient. It was safest to admit the woman. Just in case.

"Sounds appropriate to me. I'll be right down to get her. Is it a zoo down there?"

"An unbelievable zoo."

"Listen, after I get her tucked in, if it's quiet up here, I'll be happy to come help."

"Thanks, Mark. That would be great."

Mark found that his patient, although sick, sane and undrugged, *was* in costume. At least her head was. The rest of her was already clad in a bland, standard issue hospital gown. She wore a white wig with perfectly curled ringlets and a diamond tiara. Marie Antoinette, or someone, Mark thought idly, noticing at the same time how lovely, gracious and regal-looking she was. She extended a beautifully manicured and lavishly jeweled hand to him.

"Hello, Dr. Taylor," she said, as if meeting him at a party.

"Hello, Mrs. Jenkins. How are you feeling?"

"Fine, now. Really. No pain. I probably could go—" she stopped abruptly. It was obvious to Mark that his elegant, gracious patient felt uneasy about going home. The soft hit became a hard one. She was worried. She felt sicker than she looked. The pain must have been worse than she described. Admit. Admit.

"No, we want you to stay," Mark said firmly. "You're completely pain free now?"

She nodded and smiled. A voice reached them from behind.

"Mother, I just spoke to Father. Oh, hello! Sorry!" she exclaimed, startled as she opened the curtain surrounding her mother's monitored bed to find that her mother was not alone.

She was completely in costume. She wore a gray and mauve, floor-length velvet gown studded with tiny pearls and cut low in front, revealing her round, full breasts. Her dark black hair was piled on her head and draped with pearls. Her dark-lashed violet eyes sparkled with surprise and pleasure when she saw Mark.

18

"Kathleen, this is Dr. Taylor, the CCU doctor. Dr. Taylor, this is my daughter, Kathleen."

"Hi," Mark said. She is so beautiful, he thought.

"Hi," Kathleen said. She glanced at her mother and was relieved enough by how comfortable she looked to spend a moment noticing her mother's doctor.

The usual clichés, Kathleen thought: tall, dark, handsome. Clichés, she mused. *Tall*. That was easy, a statement of fact. Kathleen embellished it a little. Mark was a perfect height. *Dark*. Completely inadequate to describe the dark brown hair that curled sensuously over his ears and onto his neck or the intense, thoughtful, serious dark brown eyes made darker by the blue-black half-circles under them. *Handsome*. Unbelievably, indescribably handsome, Kathleen thought. The whole dark, earnest, strong, romantic package.

Tall, dark and handsome. It didn't begin to do him justice.

"How's Mother?" Kathleen asked after a moment.

"Fine," Mark and Virginia Jenkins answered in unison.

"No evidence of any damage, but we're going to admit her for two or three days, just to be certain," Mark explained.

"As a rule out," Virginia Jenkins explained to her daughter.

Mark looked from beautiful mother to beautiful daughter and arched an eyebrow. A rule out was medical jargon, short for rule out myocardial infarction, heart attack. At some centers such an admission was called a ROMI. During the daily morning report at such centers the resident would say, "We admitted two ROMIs last night." In San Francisco the resident would say, "We admitted two rule outs."

Clearly Virginia and Kathleen Jenkins had been to centers favoring the rule out jargon and were familiar with it.

"Dr. Taylor walked in just moments before you did, Kathleen, so I haven't had the chance to give him my past history. I do have legitimate coronary artery disease," she explained to Mark, "confirmed by angiogram. It's not se-

19

vere enough to bypass. Yet. I'm followed at the Atherton Clinic by Dr. Brown. Occasionally my chronic stable angina acts up, and I get admitted as a rule out. Fortunately, I always *have* ruled out," she added firmly, a trace of worry in her voice.

Tonight's episode of pain was different, Mark thought. She's just not admitting it. Even to herself.

"You're an excellent historian, Mrs. Jenkins. I'll give Dr. Brown a call once we get you settled upstairs."

"We were at a ball at the Fairmont," Kathleen interjected. "We thought it best to come here rather than to drive all the way to Palo Alto. She usually gets admitted to Stanford Hospital." Kathleen was as polite and gracious as her mother. They didn't want to offend anyone, neither Virginia's usual physician nor Mark.

"You did exactly the right thing. We'll keep Dr. Brown posted and transfer you to Stanford Hospital in day or two if you like."

"If my enzymes are normal you'll just discharge me in two days anyway. So I might as well stay here."

Mark was a second-year resident. He was a year ahead of Leslie and was her supervising resident. As his intern, Leslie assumed primary care of all patients admitted by Mark on his on-call nights. Then they managed the patients together, Leslie as intern and Mark as supervisor.

The morning after Halloween, Leslie became Virginia Jenkins's intern. That afternoon the cardiac enzymes returned slightly elevated, and the electrocardiogram showed minor ST segment changes without Q waves.

"She's had a very small subendocardial MI. She probably had more than five minutes of discomfort even though she really insisted that was all. She was denying a little last night. I'm sure she'll give you the whole story, Leslie," Mark said to her. "No point pushing her because we have the diagnosis. But she needs to understand that whatever she felt and isn't telling us about is an important warning signal."

20

Virginia Jenkins did tell Leslie. It wasn't a confession. It was simply an amazed appreciation that the weakness she had felt all day long—weakness and heaviness without pain—was her heart.

Kathleen stayed in her mother's room as much as visiting hours would permit. Between visits she read in the waiting room. William Jenkins returned from New York at the news of his wife's hospitalization. He visited mostly in the evenings.

Mark decided that Kathleen looked even more beautiful in broad daylight, wearing soft silk blouses and tailored skirts and allowing her long black hair to fall free. Serene, understated, elegant beauty.

Mark and Kathleen saw each other several times every day. Sometimes they would just wave at each other, she sitting in the waiting room and he rushing off to rounds, the ER, the ICU or Radiology. Whenever he could, even for a moment, he would stop to talk. Each day Mark and Leslie met with Kathleen and her parents to discuss Virginia's progress and the plans. The Jenkinses took the news of Virginia's small heart attack calmly.

"It's a warning, Mother," Kathleen said, her voice a little shaky. "You push too hard."

It was decided that Virginia would remain in the CCU at University Hospital in San Francisco for several days. Then, if stable, she would be transferred to Stanford for the balance of her ten-day hospitalization.

During that time Mark and Kathleen learned few facts about each other, but they both knew that they felt good—happy—every time they waved, every time they talked, every time they even caught a glimpse of each other. The warm happy feeling persisted while they were apart, and it was renewed, strengthened, the next time they saw each other.

At eight o'clock the night before Virginia was to be transferred to Stanford, Mark found Kathleen in the visitors' waiting room. He was on call again but not very busy, not too busy to stop for a moment.

"Hi!" Kathleen smiled. Then a moment of worry flick-

21

ered across her violet eyes. "Is Mother . . .?"

"She's fine. Rock-stable. I just wanted to say hi. And good-bye. I may not see you in the morning."

"Oh," Kathleen said, frowning slightly. Then she added, "You certainly work hard. You're here all the time. It must be difficult for your wife."

Kathleen's eyes drifted toward Mark's wedding ring. It was a plain solid band of eighteen carat gold. Very traditional. Very married.

But he doesn't act very married, Kathleen thought.

Mark looked at his ring. He still wore it. His marriage wasn't *over,* just in trouble. Mark had no idea if he and Janet could ever recover from the angry words and the bitterness. It was too soon to know, too soon to predict. They were in a holding pattern. Since that afternoon in early October, he and Janet had spoken to each other, over the phone, a few times. Those conversations were slow, difficult and punctuated by painful silences and even more painful words. They agreed they needed time apart, time to let the anger and emotions cool, time to think. Then, maybe, they could try to work it out.

In Mark's mind the marriage wasn't over. He didn't even have a clear idea about what Janet thought was so wrong. Even though he had moved into a tiny apartment near the hospital, bought a new, albeit inexpensive, stereo and opened his own checking account, Mark had not removed his wedding ring. He hadn't even thought about removing it.

As he looked from Kathleen's sparkling violet eyes to the scuffed soft-gold ring given to him five years before by a woman he could barely speak to anymore, Mark wondered why he still wore it.

"We — my wife and I — are separated," Mark told the violet eyes, watching them widen at the news. Kathleen was the first person he had told. Mark assumed Leslie knew because Leslie and Janet were friends. But Leslie didn't mention it to him because Leslie wouldn't. And no one else knew. Until now.

"Separated?" Kathleen echoed softly.

"For about a month."

"A trial separation?" Kathleen asked.

"I wonder what that means," Mark mused. Until he had spoken this word, separation, he hadn't even put a label on what was happening to him and Janet. To his marriage. *"Trial* separation. Meaning let's try it, and if we like it we'll get separated often. Or . . ."

Kathleen laughed. It was a light, lovely appreciative laugh.

Mark shrugged and smiled. He hadn't been appreciated for a while. Not for Mark the person. Mark the man. And recently from Janet not even appreciated for his one indisputable accomplishment: Mark, the doctor.

"Does it mean," Kathleen asked finally, after their smiling eyes had met for a moment, "that you could come to a party with me?"

"Oh!" Mark was surprised, pleased. Now that what he and Janet were doing had a label—separation—it needed a definition.

It only took him a moment, but in that moment Kathleen added quickly, "Or would that be unethical because of Mother?"

"No," he said firmly, "and yes. Sure. I'd love to."

Kathleen nodded, smiling.

"But I don't have anything that's very Henry the Eighth."

"Louis Quatorze!"

"Oh, right. I knew that. I had you pegged as Marie Antoinette."

"We were just generic Louis Quatorze. I don't even like to pretend to be someone who got guillotined!"

"No." Mark shuddered.

"Oh, dear," Kathleen said suddenly.

"What?" Is she thinking of a gracious way to retract the invitation, Mark wondered uneasily.

"Well, there's no special attire, *but"*—she wrinkled her nose—"it is an engagement party. For my best friend. Would that be hard for you?"

"No," Mark said, relieved that she wasn't withdrawing the invitation. But, he thought, it might be hard. I don't know. I'll find out. Then he remembered a real obstacle. "When is the party? I may be on call."

"You're not! At least not by my calculations. It's this Thursday night. Day after tomorrow, You're on tonight, so every third would put you on again Friday. Is that right? Can you come?"

"That's right. Yes, I can come," Mark said, flattered that she had bothered to learn even that little detail about his life.

Thursday night, Mark thought. A party on Thursday night. Thursday night was a *school* night, or it had been, for Mark, from kindergarten through medical school. For *twenty* years. Then, for the past two years, as an intern and resident, Thursday night was still a work night. Or the night before a long work day. Not a party night.

Who had parties—engagement parties—on Thursday night?

He would find out.

Kathleen gave him her parents' telephone number in Atherton, and they agreed over the phone the next night that she would meet him at his apartment at seven-thirty. The engagement party was in a private home near the Presidio at eight.

Thursday evening Mark left the hospital at seven, rushed to his apartment, showered, shaved and was knotting his tie when Kathleen arrived promptly at seven-thirty.

"Hi," he said, dazzled as always by her appearance. Tonight she wore her black hair piled in soft curls on top of her head. Small tendrils escaped down her long ivory neck. Mark took her camel's-hair coat and silently admired the violet, silk cocktail dress.

"Hi. Am I early?"

"No, you're on time. I'm almost ready. I didn't get away from the hospital until seven."

"Was it OK for you to leave when you did?"

"Yes. Of course." Or I wouldn't have left, Mark thought. Janet knew that. Maybe Kathleen didn't. Except that Kathleen would, *should,* understand because her mother had been a patient. Kathleen would be outraged if a doctor

24

left her mother, if her mother needed him, simply because the doctor had a date with *her*.

Kathleen caught the sharpness of Mark's tone and turned her attention to his apartment in an attempt to divert the conversation. The apartment was terrible. It was so tiny. The living room, dining room and kitchen were all one area. The limited floor space was cluttered with unpacked cardboard boxes. The apartment was clean but sterile. The only sign of life or personality was a stereo balanced on cinder blocks, two speakers and a stack of record albums.

Kathleen couldn't think of one positive thing to say about the apartment, and Mark had been edgy about her last question. Perhaps if she looked at the albums. . . .

"It's pretty bad, isn't it?" he asked, his voice stopping her as she walked — it would only take a few steps — across the living room to the stereo.

Kathleen turned slowly and smiled at him. Her eyes met his.

"It really defines the concept of *trial*, doesn't it?" she asked lightly, her eyes sparkling.

They both laughed.

Chapter Three

Janet would have loved the engagement party, Mark thought. He was the only doctor there. The others, Mark deduced, were an intriguing mixture of attorneys, stockbrokers, market analysts, advertising and corporate executives. *Beyond* YUPPIE, Mark decided. These people, Kathleen's friends, were not struggling to get to the top. Despite the fact that none was over thirty-five, it was clear that they were already there. They had power and wealth and confidence.

None of them cared that Mark was a doctor, but all of them cared that he was Kathleen's date. *That* interested them. The men eyed Mark with curiosity, the women with frank admiration.

"My God, Katie, where did you get *him?*" The beautiful women, Kathleen's friends, asked her in front of him.

And behind his back, he heard them say, "When you're through with him, *please* give him my number!" and, "Is he married?"

His wedding ring! He still wore it. He had planned to take it off, at least for the evening. Or, *beginning* with the evening. He wasn't sure. But she had arrived and he had forgotten. Inertia? Ambivalence? Or something less significant like an overworked preoccupied resident who just forgot?

Mark listened with interest to the conversations of Kathleen's friends. They chatted about books and politics and theater and the stock market and sports and restaurants and vacation spots and real estate. Mark had little to add. He hadn't seen a movie since *Star Wars*. He knew vaguely that the Forty Niners were finally having a good season. Since he and Janet had separated, he started watching the late night and early morning newscasts, as much for companionship as for information. At least he was current on current events. Of course he read a lot, but in the past year the only nonmedical reading he had done was written before the twentieth century.

It didn't matter that Mark said little. He fit in anyway. Because he smiled appropriately and he was a good listener. But mostly Mark fit in, was welcomed, because he was with Kathleen. Kathleen was the queen bee. This was her group. These were her friends. They loved her, deferred to her. They liked, maybe envied, her date.

Mark realized how little he knew about her.

How old was she? Meeting her as he had at the bedside of her ill but youthful mother, Mark assumed she was young. Maybe twenty. But now as she talked knowledgeably about *Joanna,* the new musical to be introduced by Union Square Theater, Kathleen seemed older. She could be twenty. Or thirty. Or older.

Kathleen's appearance gave no clue. Her wrinkle-free, animated face changed age with the mood of the moment. She was older when the conversation was serious, and younger when she laughed or teased the bride-to-be.

What did Kathleen do? If she was twenty she was probably a student. But these were her friends. They weren't twenty, and they weren't students. They had influential, responsible, demanding jobs. Mark knew she had something to do with Union Square Theater, but he got the impression that it wasn't a job.

Mark noticed that no one asked her, "How's work?"

No one asked Kathleen many personal questions, except, "How is your mother?" and, gesturing toward Mark, "Who is he?" and, whispering, "What ever happened to Bill? I thought . . ."

Kathleen's annoyance at being asked personal questions

about Mark within his earshot was obvious. Her violet eyes scowled briefly at her inquisitive friends. They got the message. Mark was different. Kathleen cared about him. She brought him to the party because she wanted to be with him. It was a date, *their* date. He wasn't simply someone to show off to her friends.

Yes, they realized, Mark was very different.

As the evening wore on, fortified by champagne or Mark's smiles or both, Kathleen found the courage to touch him. Tentatively, she rested her slender, soft white hand with its delicate, purple veins on his arm, her perfectly manicured, tapered fingers wrapping lightly around his forearm.

Mark responded by putting his hand on top of hers. After a few moments he entwined his fingers with hers. Mark's large hand with its closely clipped fingernails — for percussion of chests and pain-free palpation of abdomens — dwarfed her delicate, exquisite one. Kathleen's hand was jewel-free, pure and white. Mark's hand, the hand that held hers and returned her squeeze, the hand that wanted to touch more of her, was not so pure. That hand was adorned with a band of gold.

"Let's go out to the terrace. It's cool but the view is so spectacular," Kathleen whispered to him after a while, after they had mingled with her curious friends long enough.

But there was no view. While they had been inside the fog had come. Dense, heavy, opaque fog. They couldn't even see across the terrace.

"Evening fog!" Kathleen exclaimed, "How unusual for November."

"Oh, well," Mark murmured, putting his arm around her. "Are you cold?"

"Not with your arm around me," she answered quietly, moving closer against him. "Do you want to leave? It's almost ten."

"Well, it is a . . ." Mark paused.

"School night?" Kathleen asked quickly.

"A school night. I hate to pull you away from your friends."

"This is the first of a million pre-nuptial 'do's for Betsey and Jeff. I needed to be here, of course, but we can leave now."

Mark wanted to leave, but it was not because he had to get some sleep. He just wanted to be alone with Kathleen. He was alone with her now on the terrace, and the moment, holding her against him, talking to her, was perfect. Too perfect to disrupt.

"Whose house is this?" Mark asked.

"Jeff's parents. We told them this party was for the kids only. They're spending the night at the Stanford Court. This party will go on until dawn."

Mark wondered if Kathleen would return here after she left him.

"These are your good friends, aren't they?" Mark asked, stating the obvious. He was working up to the tougher questions. How old are you? What do you do? Who are you?

"My best friends. My childhood girlfriends and boy— My very oldest, dearest friends. We've known each other since—"

"The Katie days?" Mark asked, wondering about the boyfriends. How many of these men had been Kathleen's boyfriends? How many had she slept with? Were any current boyfriends? Who was Bill?

Kathleen could have told him if he had asked. Six. Six had been boyfriends. Real boyfriends. Man friends. She could have told him. But she might not have.

Kathleen laughed, nodding.

"Since the Katie days, yes. The Katie days were good days. I had long, black braids and made a pretty good little Katie. Then came the preppie days. We all disbanded and regrouped for the holidays and vacations. Then I was Kit- and Kit-Kat," Kathleen hesitated, then said, "and *Kitzy!* Awful."

"You prefer Kathleen."

"I do."

"So do I," Mark said. Then he asked, "Disbanded from where?"

"What? Oh. From Atherton, mostly. Some, like Jeff, from San Francisco proper. We were—are—the Carlton Club Kids. The Carlton Club is a country club in Atherton. Terribly upper crust, you know," she said, giggling, with a British accent. "Anyway, we met there as kids, spent our summers there, riding our horses, swimming, playing tennis, going to parties and dances. Some of us went to school together, but mostly we were scattered among private schools in the United States and Switzerland."

"Rich kids."

"Oh yes," Kathleen said gaily. "You'd recognize the last names of about half the people in the house. Most of them work for, in other words *manage,* companies of the same name. Some have broken away completely of course and established themselves from scratch. Some aren't doing anything."

Mark got the distinct impression that Kathleen fell into that group. But he asked, "Do you work for the company of the same name?"

"Do you know a company with Jenkins in its name?" she asked lightly, turning in his arms so that she faced him. She looked into his eyes, her own flashing, smiling. Teasing.

"No," he answered, wanting to kiss her.

"Would you like to know what my father does?" she asked, her face close to his.

"Sure," he sighed as he felt her body pressing closer to his.

"He's the CEO—Chief Executive Officer—of an international computer and business machine company that I bet you've heard of."

"Oh?" Mark didn't care. He would kiss her. The fog made it all right. And Janet had left *him.*

Kathleen told him the name of the company as their lips met. Mark heard the name. The full effect would register later.

All he cared about now were her soft, warm hungry lips. And his. And the lovely body that pressed, molding perfectly against his. And the soft, silky hair that fell down her back as they kissed. Mark held her and kissed her, intoxicated by the smoothness of her skin, the gentle touch of her hands on his neck, the warmth of her mouth . . .

Until she began to shiver.

Mark pulled back.

"Cold?" he asked. Of course she was cold, he thought, in her sheer silk dress in the mid-summer's November fog. Despite his warm kisses and his arms around her, she was cold.

"I don't know," she said. Cold or nervous, she thought. Nervous? *Anxious?*

"You're shivering."

"I must be cold."

"Let's go in."

"Let's go in and leave."

"OK."

They drove in silence to Mark's apartment. He held her hand, releasing it only to shift gears in his vintage Volkswagen Beetle. The protected foggy mood had been disrupted by the harsh brightness inside the house and by the knowing glances of Kathleen's best friends. Knowing, slightly envious glances at their beautiful friend with her hair flowing sensuously down her back and her cheeks flushed. They *knew* why Kathleen and her tall, dark, handsome date were leaving so early. And they were a little jealous.

Kathleen's friends knew because they knew Kathleen. They knew Kathleen always got her way. Effortlessly. And they knew how much men wanted Kathleen. Always.

But as Mark and Kathleen drove in silence, holding hands, Kathleen didn't know. And Mark didn't know.

He knew he wanted her. He knew he wanted to hold her naked body against his, to kiss her, to make love to her.

Janet's words roared in his ears. "You don't even want to make love anymore. Maybe you *can't.*"

Mark wanted to make love with Kathleen. More than he had wanted anything for a long time.

And Kathleen wanted to make love with Mark, but it scared her. He scared her because he wasn't a Carlton Club Kid. He took everything so seriously. He spent his days and nights saving people's lives or watching them die. He wasn't

31

ready to give up on his marriage, and she could get hurt.

She had never felt this way—not quite *this* way—about anyone ever before.

"Would you like to come in?" he asked as he parked his VW behind her BMW. She could easily get into her car and return to the party or home or wherever Carlton Club Kids go at ten-thirty at night when the workers are sleeping.

"Sure," she said, shivering inside her camel's hair coat.

Mark's apartment was on the second floor of an old Victorian house which had been converted into apartments. Its occupants were mostly interns and residents because it was only a five-minute, albeit uphill, walk to University Hospital.

Mark held her hand as he led her up the stairs. He hadn't made a decision except that he didn't want her to leave. He heard his phone ringing as they approached the apartment. It would be Janet. He hadn't heard from her for a week. Not once, he realized, since he had met Kathleen. It could only be Janet. Leslie was on call, but she wouldn't call him on his night off. There were senior residents in the hospital to help her. It could only be Janet. He could let it ring.

Mark slowed his pace and opened the door only after the ringing had stopped. Once inside Mark unplugged the phone and turned to look at Kathleen.

"Probably Janet," she said, because she couldn't think of anything else to say. Because Janet *was* the issue, phone call or not.

"Probably. She knows I often disconnect the phone when I'm not on call," he said. "Would you like something to drink?"

"No, thank you."

Mark lifted the stack of four records that lay on the stereo turntable up the stem until they rested, poised, ready to drop one by one. Then turned on the stereo.

Neither spoke or moved until the needle met the record and the music began. In those moments Kathleen tried to guess, What will it be? Jazz? Blues? Rock and Roll? Waylon Jennings or Neil Diamond? Barbra Streisand or Beverly Sills? Mozart or the Bee Gees?

Those four records, obvious favorites, played and replayed, would tell her something new, something *else* about him.

Mark listened to the first few bars, adjusting the volume, then looked at her quizzically.

"Scheherazade," Kathleen said, smiling, gazing into his eyes.

"Very good," he said, walking toward her. "Do you want to take off your coat?"

Kathleen looked up at him and said softly, bravely, "I want you to take off my coat."

And my dress, she thought, shivering again.

Mark smiled. He kissed her as he unbuttoned the leather buttons of her coat. When he had it off he held her against him, kissing her, reaching carefully for the tiny silk-covered buttons of her dress. Patiently, he began to unbutton them with one hand, the other hand buried in her soft, tangled black hair, holding her head, pulling her mouth against his.

Finally his patience faltered.

"How many buttons?" he asked.

"Too many," she answered. "Chic but not practical."

"Maybe I'm hurrying too much?"

"I think we're both in a hurry," Kathleen said. "No time to think about it."

"I have thought about it," Mark said. He had made his decision.

"You have?"

"Yes. But, still, will you help me with these damned buttons?"

"With pleasure."

Mark's bed was a double-bed mattress without box springs that lay on the floor. The sheets were a slightly rough, cotton blend and the pillows were lumpy.

It didn't matter.

He held her lovely naked body against his slender strong one, kissing her, tracing paths all over her with his tongue, touching her, moving her, moving with her to the rhythm of the music he loved, whispering her name.

"Kathleen."

33

"Mark."

They smiled at each other with open eyes and closed mouths until the desire they saw in each other's eyes made them close their eyes and open their mouths. They moved together lost in the warmth of their bodies and the mood of the music and the strength of the passion.

"Oh, Mark!" she whispered urgently when the wonderful sensations began to crescendo.

"Kathleen." He felt her quickening breaths, the pounding of her heart and the rhythm of her hips. The force of her desire was as demanding as his own, under the cool silkiness of her skin.

After they made love the first time, his breathing slowed and he reluctantly moved off her so that she could breathe without his weight.

Mark whispered, *"Kitzy."*

"You'll pay for that!"

"Really? How?"

"I'll show you in a minute. After I recover." She rolled toward him and touched his hair. "Or should I go now? It's late."

"I don't want you to go." *Ever.*

"I have to go, sometime. My parents worry if I'm not home by dawn," she said, smiling into his thoughtful brown eyes. "OK, let's see how I did."

"You know how you did. Sensational."

"No. With name-that-tune. *Scheherazade.* Then *Sleeping Beauty.* Then *Swan Lake.* Then whatever's playing now. I recognize it, but I can't name it."

"Giselle. It's my ballet suite. Sort of the old standbys but my favorites," he paused, then he said, "I can't believe you were paying attention."

"Listening, yes. Subliminally. Paying attention, no. How could I? You had my undivided attention." *You still do. I want to do it all over again. And again.*

"If you promise that's true, I'll go turn the stack."

"It's true. The music is nice. Sensual." He could probably make the national anthem sensual, she thought as she watched him walk, naked, into the other room. Tall. Dark.

Handsome. *Naked*. The missing necessary adjective. It completed the perfect picture.

When he returned, she said, "This is for Kitzy. Hold still and enjoy."

"What?"

"Sensory overload."

"This will be punishment."

"You'll see. You have to hold still, and you'll want to move. You'll want to touch me."

"And you won't let me?"

"No. Never. Not after Kitzy."

"OK."

Kathleen did what he had done to her, kissing his entire body, tracing little circles with her warm, moist tongue and her velvet, soft fingertips over his nipples, along his thighs, between his thighs. She kept her body away from his, but her silky hair caressed his face, his chest, his abdomen and his legs as she moved, slowly, lovingly. As she kissed him in places that Janet never had. In ways that Janet never had.

When he wanted her, her whole body next to his, part of him, Kathleen came to him, eagerly, willingly. Because she wanted him, too. She didn't want to play games. Not with him.

At three o'clock she said, "This time I really am leaving."

She had tried, halfheartedly, at one. And at two. Each time she had gotten as far as the stereo, flipped the stack and, at his urging, returned to his bed.

"I don't want you to."

"I don't want to, but I have to. Besides, you're on call tonight, right?"

"Uh-huh."

"So, I'm leaving."

"OK. Not really, but OK." As she dressed, he asked, "How old are you, Kathleen?"

"Twenty-seven. How about you?"

"Twenty-seven."

She kissed him, a long, deep good-bye kiss.

As she turned to leave, he asked, "What do you do?"

"What you mean? What do I get paid to do?"

35

"Yes."

"Nothing," she said. "Absolutely nothing."

Mark was suddenly aware that his shower water had turned ice-cold, rudely interrupting his reverie.

Damned apartment, he thought. Although, despite its many other drawbacks, ample hot water had never been a problem.

Mark shivered as he returned to his bedroom. He glanced at his clock and learned the reason for the cold water. He had been in the shower for thirty minutes, lost in the magnificent memory of Kathleen.

The ice-cold water, the still-disconnected phone, the fact that he would be late for rounds — something he didn't tolerate in others — brought Mark abruptly back to the reality of his life.

As he rushed to get ready he thought about Janet. Now he had been unfaithful to her — something to add to the list, *her* list, of things he had done to destroy their marriage.

He had never been unfaithful before. Until last night, he had never even made love with anyone but Janet. Mark had only kissed a few girls, and they had been girls. He was sixteen when he met Janet, and after he met her there had been no one else.

Until now. Now he had been unfaithful to her. But was infidelity really an issue during a trial separation? Was it really a violation of the same magnitude? More new terms and definitions. More confusion.

More *fog,* he thought as he ran through the unseasonal, still-thick fog that lay in his path while he made his way finally, late, from the apartment to University Hospital.

As he breezed through the revolving door into the hospital's main lobby, Mark forced himself to forget about Janet and Kathleen. He had trained himself to do this. It was necessary. At work, he had to focus, without distraction, on his job, on his patients. The personal problems had to be put aside, banished from his thoughts. It was something else Janet complained about, his ability to turn his emotions off and on. His cool objectivity.

But it was something else that made him good at what he did, at being a doctor. It allowed him to give his patients undivided attention. Mark was certain that Leslie Adams had the same ability to disassociate the personal from the professional. Leslie was always professional, and she was very good at what she did.

Leslie Adams was the one woman he *could* think about in the hospital. Thinking about Leslie made Mark smile. He smiled then, despite the fact that he was twenty minutes late, as he ran up the eleven flights of stairs two steps at a time. Mark never used the hospital elevators. He was impatient with their slowness and knew the exercise, the only exercise he got, was good for him. In a thirty-six hour, on-call period, Mark traveled repeatedly between the eleventh-floor ward, the seventh-floor intensive care unit, the ground floor ER, the basement level morgue, the fourth-floor lab and the third-floor radiology suite. It gave Mark ample exercise. It showed. He was in good shape.

Leslie Adams, M.D., Mark mused.

She was a terrific intern. The best. In any other profession Leslie might have been considered compulsive to a fault, but not in medicine. In medicine compulsion was the key — compulsion balanced by good judgment — the ability to focus on the important and de-emphasize, but never *ignore,* the apparently trivial.

Too many interns couldn't see the forest for the trees. But not Leslie. She saw the big picture, but she compulsively paid attention to the details.

If she didn't know what something meant, what to make of a slightly abnormal lab value or a patient complaint that didn't seem to fit, she asked for help. For another opinion. For Mark's opinion.

"Mark," she would say, her brilliant blue eyes frowning earnestly at the patient lab data sheet. "Mr. Rolf's LDH is still elevated. It doesn't make sense. He's not hemolyzing, and his other enzymes are normal. I've checked all his meds, and none of them can do this. In every other way, he's improving . . ."

37

"So what's your plan?" Mark would ask, knowing that Leslie had a plan. But knowing, too, as good as she was, as solid as her judgment and instincts were, she was unsure of herself. It was something else that made her good. She listened, she learned and she asked questions when she didn't know.

Leslie Adams wasn't afraid of saying those three words that had been *verboten* in medical school: I don't know.

Leslie would make mistakes. They all would and *did*. That was the trickiness and vagary of medicine. But Leslie would never make big mistakes, never careless ones. Her mistakes would be slight errors in judgment due to inexperience or because she was fooled or misled by a symptom or sign or lab value that didn't fit and turned out to be important. Leslie's mistakes would never cause harm to a patient. They would be little errors that would damage her confidence, make her examine herself even more critically and remind her, if she would admit it, that she was human after all.

Leslie's compulsive, careful attention to detail would probably protect her from making the kind of mistake that was so serious it would drive her away from medicine. Even if she alone knew about it.

As Mark reached the sixth floor, he slowed his pace a bit. He was late, but everything would be under control. Leslie had been on call. Everyone would be safe and sound.

Mark shook his head slightly as he thought about her, the hospital watchdog, pacing the halls all night long, warding off trouble. He guessed that was the real reason for her sleeplessness, because she believed, somehow, it would help. She had to do it. It was part of her compulsion.

Mark also knew that Leslie's calm cheeriness, almost too much at times, was only a façade. It *had* to be. Inside she was a bundle of nerves, anxiety and fatigue just like the rest of them. She probably had the same critical opinions about her colleagues, the nursing staff, the call schedule and the soft hits that they all did. She just withheld comment. They were all critical, hypercritical, of themselves and of each other. They were all perfectionists at heart, suddenly confronted with the imperfect, imprecise, nonscientific realities of the practice of medicine.

Leslie and Janet were friends. Mark wondered what Leslie thought of him. Of course she knew what had happened between him and Janet. And why. Leslie probably had more insight into his marriage than he did. Did she think he was as despicable as Janet did? Probably. Compulsive, critical Leslie wouldn't be very tolerant of the sort of behavior Janet attributed to him.

But if Leslie felt only contempt for him as a human being it didn't show. In fact, in the past month, she had seemed almost sympathetic, as if she knew, understood, and didn't judge. Or was she just overcompensating because she felt guilty about her real *critical* feelings?

She probably doesn't think about it—me—at all, Mark decided. Leslie, the true professional.

As he rounded the corner onto the ward, Mark saw his team—two medical students and two interns, Leslie and Greg—circled around the chart rack. Mark saw Leslie before she saw him. She was looking at her watch and frowning, concerned but not annoyed.

Then Greg saw Mark and said, "Chief, ho!"

Leslie looked up quickly and smiled. Her sapphire-blue eyes sparkled with a look of relief above the dark circles, the tell-tale signs of her sleepness night.

Chapter Four

Janet Louise Wells was born at noon on Christmas Day, 1953. She was born in her parents' small, snowbound farmhouse five miles west of Kearney, Nebraska, and one hundred thirty miles west of Lincoln where six months earlier her future husband, Mark David Taylor, had been born on a hot humid day in July.

Janet was a perfect baby, then a perfect child, then a perfect teenager. Her cheerfulness and serenity were pervasive and genuine. Everyone liked her. It was impossible not to like the pretty girl with the spun-gold hair, clear, gray eyes and ready, flawless smile. Janet made friends easily because she smiled and was so pretty.

And because she shared her toys. Possessiveness was not in Janet's nature. Generosity was. She was noncompetitive. She threatened no one. Janet spent the first sixteen years of her life genuinely content with her life on the tiny farm, attending the small rural school, baking with her mother, sewing with her grandmother and playing with her friends.

And singing.

Janet loved to sing. No one knew how much she loved it. They heard her sing in the church choir and admired her clear, lovely voice. There were no music classes at her school, no choral groups, no band.

It didn't matter to Janet. She preferred to sing by herself anyway. She didn't need or care about an audience. In the late afternoon, after school and before dinner, she would run to the far corner of her father's cornfield, and she would sing.

Janet sang anything and everything. She learned the songs by listening to records and to the radio. She learned the tunes instantly and the lyrics after listening only a few times. Janet preferred musicals. She would sing every song in order. Telling the story. Living the story.

If Janet was possessive about anything it was her private time in the cornfields. Without it she would not have been so content. Or so generous. Or so happy.

On July 11, 1969, the day Mark David Taylor celebrated his sixteenth birthday, Harold Wells told his fifteen-and-a-half-year-old daughter and his twin thirteen-year-old sons that they were selling the farm, they had no choice, and were moving to Lincoln.

Janet entered Lincoln High School that fall as a junior. She left her class of sixteen students, her best friends in Kearney, and entered a class of three hundred students in which the groups and cliques had been firmly established since winter of the sophomore year.

Janet was an outsider because of timing and because of who she was: a country girl in a city.

Janet wouldn't have minded being alone, being an outsider, if she had been able to have privacy, but her new home was an apartment with no yard. She had no cornfields. She had no place to escape.

No place to sing.

Janet met Mark on the first day of school. If Mark hadn't been junior class president, and if he hadn't appointed himself in charge of orienting the new juniors, he and Janet would never have met. Mark's crowd, the achievement-oriented, scholar athletes and their aggressive, confident female companions would have been inaccessible, and probably unknown, to Janet.

There were twenty new entering juniors. Mark led them around the three-story, brick building through the cafeteria to the study halls, the gym, the student lounge and the library. Mark gave the tour cheerfully, enthusiastically, trying to make them all feel comfortable and welcome. But his mind was on Janet.

Mark had never seen eyes so clear or so big or so gray. Or hair quite so blond and silky. Or a smile so demure and beautiful.

"I'll show you to your home room," Mark said to her after the tour was over.

"Oh. OK. Thank you," she said quietly, her eyes meeting his directly without embarrassment.

Janet walked silently beside Mark, not fidgeting, not anxious, not even, apparently, trying to think of something to say. Mark found Janet's silence strangely peaceful.

Except that he wanted to find out about her.

"You're from Kearney?"

"Near Kearney."

"Do you like Lincoln?"

"No. Not really," she said calmly without breaking her stride.

Her words made Mark stop. Lincoln was his home. He *loved* Lincoln.

"You don't? Why not?"

Janet stopped when Mark stopped and looked up at him with her smoky gray eyes.

"No cornfields," she said. "I miss the cornfields."

"Lincoln is surrounded by cornfields!"

"I miss *our* cornfield," Janet replied simply.

Within two months, Mark had retrieved his class pin from Sara, a smart pretty cheerleader, and was dating Janet. Mark couldn't tell how Janet felt about him. He was used to girls flirting with him, teasing him and sending him clear, interpretable signals.

Janet sent no signals; but she always said yes when he asked her out, and she always seemed happy when they were together. Janet spoke little, smiled a lot and listened attentively when Mark spoke.

Being with Janet made Mark realize how hard he and his friends were trying. They were all trying to prove, beyond a doubt, that they were what they believed themselves to be: the best student, the best quarterback, the best actress, the best-looking or the best personality.

The Best.

Janet didn't try. She didn't care about being the best. Janet was Janet. And Mark loved being with her.

After a while he stopped trying to impress her. He didn't need to. She knew who he was, and she liked him.

Janet made things for him. He would find chocolate chip cookies in his locker. Or a hand-knit muffler. Or a handmade card, cleverly decorated, a thank you for a special date. Mark loved Janet's presents. They were reminders of Janet, of the peace and happiness he felt when he was with her. That peace, the peacefulness of being with Janet, balanced the relentless pressure of the rest of his life.

Pressure. Pressure to be the best. Pressure to be a doctor—to be the *best* doctor. Pressure not to disappoint anyone, especially his father, and pressure to live up to his magnificent potential.

Janet's life, briefly filled with an unfamiliar turmoil of its own when her family moved to Lincoln, became peaceful because of Mark. And because of her music. Janet discovered that although she no longer had her own private stage, her father's cornfield, the big city offered intriguing new outlets for her singing.

There were music classes. Janet took as many as her schedule would allow. And choral groups—Janet joined them all. The music teachers instantly recognized her talent. Raw, untrained talent. They were intrigued by the pretty, blond girl with the lovely, haunting voice.

The other girls in the school who sang and acted and vied for solos in the choral groups and for leads in the school musical productions promptly recognized Janet as a foe. She was another competitor in an already overcrowded, competitive group, a group in which everyone wanted to be the best.

Janet didn't want to compete, but she wanted to sing. She was unruffled by audiences and unflattered by the praises of the teachers.

The strong loveliness of her voice—so rich, so sensuous, so moving—amazed Mark when he heard her sing, finally,

43

in January. Always before, her singing engagements had conflicted with one of his many commitments.

Mark kissed her after the performance that night. It was their first kiss although they had been dating for almost four months. When Mark kissed her, Janet put her arms around his neck, stretched her fingers into his dark brown hair and pulled his mouth deep into hers.

After that they kissed often. Long, quiet, passionate kisses that filled Mark with great peace and made him forget, for a moment, the pressures of his life.

Mark wanted Janet to sing for him when they were alone.

"Find me a cornfield and I'll sing for you anytime."

Mark found a cornfield for them five miles outside of Lincoln. They found a private distant corner where they could lie together, holding each other, kissing each other, and where she could sing just for him.

Mark's competitiveness, his need to be the best, was so inbred that he couldn't stand to see anyone bypass a chance for success. A chance to be the best. A star. So, it was *his* fault that Janet auditioned for the lead in Lincoln High School's production of *South Pacific* that spring. It was her fault, because of her talent, that she won the part. As Nellie, Janet got to "wash that man right outta my hair," to be as "corny as Kansas in August" and to sing a lovely, romantic, moving duet about "some enchanted evening."

Janet was a sensation. The standing ovations, the rave reviews in the Lincoln newspapers, the sell-out performances were all testimony to her marvelous, captivating talent.

But Janet's success made some people squirm. Who the hell does she think she is? the girls who dated Mark's friends, who considered Mark one of *theirs,* wondered. It was amazing enough that the quiet, country hick could seduce Mark into leaving lively, vivacious Sara. "She has to be putting out!" they hissed. And now Janet had virtually stolen the lead from another one of *them*.

It was too pushy. Too nervy. Didn't the country girl know her place?

Janet's success also made Mark's parents squirm. From the beginning they hoped this unfortunate *liaison* would pass, that Mark would outgrow Janet's country naiveté or get bored with her passivity. As the months passed, they were afraid he wouldn't. For the first time in his life, Mark countered their incessant plans for his future with plans of his own.

"Won't it be wonderful when you finish your residency and return to join your father in practice? You'll probably want to live nearby. In the country club, maybe."

Mark had been hearing plans like that for years. Usually he made no comment, silently acknowledging his parents' words with a taciturn nod. Now, because of Janet, he had plans of his own, and his parents didn't like what they heard.

"Janet and I are going to live outside of town. In the country. I won't mind commuting."

That made his parents squirm. As they watched their maybe-future-daughter-in-law prance around the stage in skimpy outfits, they squirmed even more. It was all so undignified. So improper.

Of course they hadn't minded watching Sara Johnston, daughter of Lincoln's best general surgeon, leading cheers at the football and basketball games. They wouldn't have minded having Sara as their daughter-in-law. In fact, that was what they had planned.

Janet detected the Taylors' disapproval of her almost immediately.

"Why don't your folks like me?" she asked. She did not say, "I don't think your folks like me," or, "I wonder if . . ." Janet asked, as a matter of fact, why they didn't like her.

"They had plans for me and Sara," Mark said. "Daughter of leading surgeon and son of leading internist, himself destined to be the leading internist. That sort of thing."

The best with the best, Janet mused.

Janet didn't like Mark's parents, either. She knew, although she and Mark never discussed it, that his father was the driving force behind Mark's obsession with success and achievement. Janet resented Dr. Taylor for it. She resented the pressure on Mark.

Mark loved Janet's performance in *South Pacific*. Janet loved it, too. She learned that she loved something more than just the singing. She loved performing. She loved the audience. She loved sharing her talent and her joy.

During the last month of their junior year in high school, Mark was elected student body president and give Janet his class pin and his letter sweater. And he kissed her breasts for the first time.

They lay in their cornfield on a balmy spring night, softly lighted by the vernal moon. They had kissed, without talking, for an hour. Slowly, Mark lowered his hand over her blouse, then gently slipped his fingers between the buttons, touching her soft skin. Then he carefully unbuttoned a button, trying to sense her reaction, hoping she wouldn't resist, knowing he would stop if she did.

Janet didn't resist. She moved closer to him. She helped him unbutton her blouse and unfasten her bra. Then she lay beneath him, her naked chest silhouetted in the spring moonlight.

Mark looked at her beautiful cream-colored breasts — young and fresh — waiting to be kissed, gently, roughly, every way, for hours and hours. Wordlessly Janet pulled his soft lips to her round, warm breasts.

A year later, after they had both been accepted to the University of Nebraska in Lincoln, after Mark had been named class valedictorian and after Janet had triumphed as Maria in the school production of *The Sound of Music,* they made love for the first time.

They had never discussed it. They had spent the past year holding each other and kissing each other. Bare chested. Nothing more. But that night, in their secluded cornfield under the same springtime moon that had shone on them a year before, Mark removed all her clothes. Then his. He watched the clear, gray eyes that squeezed tight for a brief moment as he entered her, then opened, smiling, as she wrapped her legs tightly around him and moved quietly, quickly with him.

"I love you," he told her afterwards. It was the first time

he had told her that. He repeated joyfully, "I love you, Janet."

"I love you too, Mark."

During the four years at the University of Nebraska — home of the Cornhuskers — in Lincoln, Mark lived in the Phi Delta Theta fraternity. It was the same fraternity his father had pledged. Mark got A's in all his courses. He took the required pre-med courses: biology, physics, inorganic and organic chemistry and calculus. But he majored in English. Mark's favorite course was English literature.

Janet lived at home. She performed in all the University musical productions. She earned A's — and one A plus — in her music, dance and acting classes and B's and C's in her other classes. Janet took typing and secretarial skills classes because they seemed practical. Her favorite class was dance. The music courses added little, except exposure, to her natural singing talent, but the dance classes taught her something she didn't know, something she needed to know to win the roles she wanted. Janet was years behind the students who had started ballet at age five, but she had aptitude and energy.

Mark and Janet made love often, at least three or four times a week. Over eight hundred times before their wedding night, Janet calculated during a lecture on shorthand in the spring of her senior year. They didn't experiment in their love making. They made love in the same way, the traditional way, quietly, passionately, every time. They never talked about it. There was nothing to discuss. It was completely satisfying for both of them.

Mark and Janet were married two weeks after graduation. Mark's parents paid for the entire wedding because it *had* to be held at the Riverwoods Country club, and they *had* to invite four hundred guests. Janet's parents didn't belong to Riverwoods, and they couldn't have afforded a wedding of any size.

47

Janet almost balked.

"What will we owe them, your parents, in return for this?" she asked. Mark had already told her he would not, could not, accept his father's offer to pay for his medical school tuition at any medical school in the country. Mark's father wanted Mark to attend Harvard Medical School, but Mark only applied to one medical school, the one with the lowest tuition because of his state residency, the University of Nebraska in Omaha. Mark refused his father's offer to pay for his medical education because what if he, *they,* decided not to return to Lincoln to practice after all?

"It will put us into debt, Janet, but I can work the first two summers," he said.

"And I'll be working. We'll manage. I don't want you to take the money from your father, either."

In response to Janet's question about the debt for their wedding, Mark said, "We're doing *them* the favor. They want this social event, and we're agreeing to participate. I just hope you don't mind too much. Or your parents."

"It's such a terrible waste of money, but if I stand in the way of it they'll dislike me even more. If that's possible. All I want is to marry you and leave Lincoln."

During the weeks before the wedding, Janet was unusually quiet in the presence of Mark's mother. She wanted to avoid any scenes or unpleasantness. They had already had a confrontation about the rings. Janet stood firm on few issues because all she really wanted was Mark. The whole process was simply a means to an end.

But Janet stood firm about the rings.

"I want eighteen-carat gold bands. Plain and simple," she explained to her future mother-in-law.

"Eighteen carat is so soft! It loses its shine."

"I know, Mrs. Taylor. That's why I like it. It ages, matures, with the marriage."

Janet's parents wore eighteen-carat gold bands. Their bands were scuffed and battered, but still golden like their marriage that had weathered the trials and joys of their twenty-five years together. Janet hoped her marriage to Mark would be as durable, as wonderful despite the hardships, as her parents'. Janet wanted bands like theirs. For luck.

Janet won that battle and secured her victory by quickly ordering the rings. They were engraved with their initials, the date and a single word: *Always*.

Mrs. Taylor persisted. An eighteen-carat gold band could be overlooked if the diamond was set properly.

"Have you and Mark chosen a diamond? You should probably get one of at least a carat."

"Diamonds are so expensive!" So frivolous, Janet thought, at a time when they knew they would be going into debt. Even if money wasn't an issue, Janet wouldn't have wanted one.

"We'll buy it for you. Or lend Mark the money to be repaid on your twentieth anniversary. Or"—Janet watched Mrs. Taylor almost choke on the next words—"you could have my mother's diamond. I'm sure she would have wanted Mark's wife to have it. It's almost two carats, emerald cut, flaw—"

"No, thank you. No diamond. Really, I'm just not the type."

Not the type is right, Mrs. Taylor thought. Not Mark's type. Not our type. And she won't let us make her better.

"With just the two plain gold bands," Mark's mother persevered, "it looks like a *shotgun* wedding. You know, dear, like you *have* to get married."

"We do have to get married, Mrs. Taylor," Janet said as she leveled her eyes, steel gray and serious, at her future mother-in-law's startled, blinking ones. Janet added, softly, carefully, "We have to get married because we love each other."

Chapter Five

During Mark's first two years of medical school, Janet worked as a secretary-receptionist in a neurosurgeon's office all day and had dinner ready for Mark when he got home from his afternoon classes. Mark spent most evenings at the library or in the anatomy lab, and Janet spent her evenings performing in community theater productions. She and Mark arrived home about midnight, made love and fell asleep.

During Mark's third and fourth years when he was on the wards, doing clerkships, being on call with his team, his schedule was erratic and unpredictable. If Janet was gone in the evenings, she might go for days without really seeing him. Janet decided to stop performing. It was an easy decision. She wanted to be with Mark whenever she could. Still, she missed it.

On March fifteenth of his fourth year, Mark learned that he matched for an internal medicine internship at the University of California in San Francisco. It was his first choice. Two months later, he learned that he would graduate from medical school with highest honors.

Two weeks before graduation, Mark's moodiness, the moodiness that would ultimately drive them apart, first surfaced.

Janet had seen glimpses of it in high school, when the pressure got too great, and his father talked about Mark hanging out his shingle below *his,* and when Mark told her how much he enjoyed his English classes.

But in high school and in college and until the final weeks of medical school, Mark's moodiness had been infrequent and curable. Janet could cure it. Mark would come to her, kiss her, hold her and make love to her. He would feel better.

The moodiness that began six weeks before his internship was different. It didn't go away so easily. It seemed more resistant to her love. For the sixteen months between the end of medical school and the day that Janet told him she had to get away from him, the moodiness increased until it became a dark constant presence. And it was aggravated by fatigue and pressure and his compulsion to be the best.

Mark immersed himself in medicine.

Even though he hates it, Janet decided, finally, after endless months of watching his torment.

She was convinced that Mark hated medicine, even though he did it well, even though he was the *best*. When she suggested to him, gently, carefully, that he didn't like what he was doing, Mark became incensed. He loved medicine, he answered swiftly. Didn't she know that?

No. She knew just the opposite.

So Janet hated medicine for him. She hated every part of it: the sick patients, the relentless call schedule, the arrogant, competitive residents (his *friends*), the compulsive personalities. Janet hated it for both of them. And, little by little, because Mark was on the other side, because he was one of *them,* because he defended *them* and *it,* Janet began to hate him, too.

It tore them apart because they both hated it, but Mark wouldn't admit it.

And because she couldn't comfort him, love him, out of his moods anymore.

Mark arrived home at four o'clock that Sunday afternoon, October fifth, fifteen months after his internship had started. He hadn't been on call. He had just been in the hospital since early morning making rounds with his team. He had slept eight hours the night before. Janet knew. She had watched him sleep as she lay awake, tormented, trying to decide what to do.

Talk, she decided. Talk to him when he was rested. She watched him sleep. He would be rested.

Janet paced, herself exhausted, until she heard him return.

"Hi," Mark said absently as he walked in the door and past her. Preoccupied, as usual.

"Mark?"

"What?" he snapped, startled.

Usually she just left him alone.

"We have to talk."

"About what?" he asked suspiciously.

He, they, had declared a moratorium on discussions about whether he really liked medicine. That had been six months ago. They hadn't discussed it since.

"Our marriage."

"Our *marriage?*"

That was a new topic. They had never discussed their marriage. What was there to discuss?

"OK," he said tentatively.

"It's in trouble, Mark," Janet said carefully. It's over, she thought. But, maybe, she was wrong. Maybe he could make her change the way she felt. If he really cared. If he really loved her.

"What do you mean?"

"I mean we don't have anything to do with each other anymore."

"Come on, Janet. We're together every second that I'm not at the hospital."

"We're in the same house. We're not together."

"This is ridiculous. I have no idea what you're talking about. I'm too tired—" Mark started to leave the room.

"Goddamn you!" Janet shouted.

"Janet!"

"Listen to me, Mark, *please*. I hate this. I hate our life. I hate that you never touch me anymore. I hate your friends and medicine. And I know that you do, too." Janet held up her hand to stop him from interrupting. "You just won't admit it. I cannot live like this."

"Like what?"

"Hating the man I married. Not knowing you. Not being able to touch you. Having you pull away when I try. Not being able to talk to you. Not being able to comfort you."

"*Comfort* me?"

"Oh, Mark," Janet said softly as tears filled her gray eyes. "You don't have any idea what I'm talking about, do you?"

"No," he said honestly, his voice tired, "I don't. I can't believe that you hate me, Janet."

"I do, Mark. I'm really afraid that I do," Janet said as the hot tears spilled onto her cheeks. I love the man I married so much. But this other man, this man I don't know . . .

"I love you, Janet," he said weakly, almost mechanically.

"Do you, Mark? When was the last time you touched me? I'm sure you don't know. It was four months ago. You used to want to make love with me all the time. Now all you care about—pretend to care about—is medicine. You don't even want to make love anymore. Maybe you *can't*."

"Janet!" Mark's shock was quickly replaced by anger. "You knew this wouldn't be easy. You knew that these years would be hard, the hardest. That I would be tired. That I wouldn't feel like making love every night."

"Four months, Mark."

"But nothing else has changed—"

"Everything else has changed. I could live with you forever, never make love with you again, if I believed that I made a difference to you. That I was part of your life."

"You are. You do."

"No. I used to be. But not anymore. You've shut me out. You are moody and angry and unhappy, and you won't share it with me."

"I am not."

"You don't even know," Janet said sadly, defeated.

"I am tired. This is hard work. That is all."

"No."

"Yes," Mark sighed. "Janet, this is so classic. This is why

doctors' marriages fall apart. This is what happens. Don't let it happen to us."

"I'm not complaining about your call schedule or that you fall asleep during dinner or that you work on Christmas. That isn't what this is all about."

"But you *do* complain about those things."

"I *note* those things. They are annoying, but they don't end marriages. At least they wouldn't end mine."

"End?"

"End, Mark. You are not listening. I don't believe that you love me anymore."

"I do."

Janet sighed. Mark hated medicine and said he loved it. What did it mean when he said he loved her? He probably didn't even know.

"I don't feel loved."

"That's your problem," he said coldly.

"Maybe it is. When you don't feel loved, when *I* don't feel loved, I begin to hate myself. Look at me, Mark. I'm fat. I've gained twenty pounds in the past six months."

Janet had always been slender, fit. When she danced, she had no fat on her sleek, trim body. Twenty pounds didn't make Janet less beautiful, but it made her feel terrible. She was enveloped in a heavy thickness which, more than anything, was an ever present symbol of how unhappy she was.

"You look fine." Mark's tone reflected annoyance. He was tired of this conversation. He had other things to worry about. What was Janet's problem?

"Mark," she said finally, standing in front of him, trembling with rage and frustration. "Listen to me, damn you. I am leaving you. I cannot stand being with you anymore. I cannot stand hating myself and hating you."

"I don't believe you."

"Believe me."

Janet went into the bedroom and returned almost immediately with two heavy, obviously packed, suitcases.

"Janet—" Mark stood up.

"I have to leave, Mark. I am suffocating."

"Where are you going?"

54

"I have reservations at a motel tonight. It's near. I can take a taxi. Tomorrow I'll find an apartment near the office or on a bus line. You need the car."

Their rented house on Twin Peaks was on a bus line. It was an easy commute for Janet to the real estate office where she worked as a receptionist.

"Janet, don't leave. Can't we talk about it?"

"We've just been talking about it, and it's obvious that we can't talk. We can't communicate. We can't even agree on what has happened to us."

"Nothing has happened to us," Mark said firmly.

"You see!" Janet yelled in frustration. "Nothing has happened except that I hate you and myself and I'm leaving."

They stared at each other, glowering, for a moment.

"I'll leave," Mark said finally, angrily.

"No, why?"

"Because this is your home. You fixed it up. I couldn't stand being here without you. And I couldn't stand being blamed for hurting you even more by displacing you from your home," he said acidly.

"*Our* home."

"Not anymore apparently. Will it ever be again, Janet?"

"I don't know, Mark. I hope so."

He tossed the car keys at her, too hard, too fast. They hit her hand then the floor.

"Get out of here for an hour, will you, so I can pack in peace? Then bring the car back and I'll leave."

Janet called Leslie later that night.

"He's gone, Les," Janet said, tears streaming down her cheeks.

"Gone?"

"I was going to leave but he insisted."

"Oh, Janet, I am so sorry."

"It's what I thought, what I was afraid, would happen."

"I know. But still . . ." Leslie hesitated. "Do you want me to come over, now?"

"Yes. If you're not too tired."

55

Leslie met Janet at the Department of Medicine party held in mid-July at the Yacht Club. By then, three weeks into her internship, Leslie had worked daily—twenty-four hours a day—with Mark. She had worked with him, talked to him, laughed with him, and already, she had *fallen in love* with him.

Leslie was curious to see the woman whom Mark had chosen to be his wife, the woman Mark loved. Leslie hadn't expected to like her, not *really*. But as she and Janet talked that night, and as they spent time together over the summer when Mark was on call, they became friends. Good friends, caring friends, friends in spite of the fact that Janet was Mark's wife. . . . Because, despite her friendship with Janet, Leslie's feelings for Mark didn't change. They just remained hidden, deep in a part of her that no one would ever know, where they belonged.

"I love your house!" Leslie said the first time she visited Mark's and Janet's rental on Twin Peaks one evening while Mark was working.

From the outside the small house looked like every other little box on the block—square, bland, off-white stucco—but inside it was cheery and cozy and unique. Janet had made it that way, decorating it with quaint pretty pictures of country scenes and with colorful, intricate needlepoint pillows and hooked rugs that she had made.

"It's so homey," Leslie said, genuinely impressed. Mark must look forward to coming home, she thought. Leslie paused in each of the five rooms. She spent the most time in Mark's study, the second of two bedrooms. In it hung his diplomas, his Alpha Omega Alpha certificate, a huge red and white Nebraska Cornhuskers banner, their wedding picture and dozens of other photos of their life together arranged in a beautiful, colorful collage.

"Mark David Taylor, M.D.," Leslie observed, studying Mark's medical school diploma. "M.D.T., M.D. Kind of catchy. Mark never uses his middle initial."

"He probably doesn't want to be reminded," Janet said

with surprising coldness. "I'm sure that Mark's father, Dr. Taylor, had M.D. on his mind the moment Mark was born and pronounced male."

"Oh!"

"He's not a nice man, Mark's father," Janet said distantly, wondering what role Mark's father was playing in Mark's moods and in the destruction of her marriage.

"Oh."

Leslie spent time, when she was off and Mark was on, exploring San Francisco with Janet. And she spent the time when she was on working, *being*, with Mark. Admiring him . . .

One night in August she said to him, quietly, almost under her breath, "You know so much. It's so wonderful."

She might as well have said, "You're so wonderful."

Mark laughed.

"Leslie Adams, you are suffering from the intern-on-resident crush syndrome!" he said amiably.

Leslie blushed. Then, as she thought about what she had said—What if he guesses how I feel about him?—she turned pale.

"Hey, Leslie, I'm flattered," Mark said quickly, sensing her uneasiness, unaware of its cause. "Not many people think I walk on water. It makes me feel good. I plan to enjoy it while it lasts. Next week when you start working with Adam Russell you'll have a crush on him—all the facts he knows—and forget all about me."

For a moment, Mark wanted to tousle her chestnut curls and erase the troubled look from her large, serious blue eyes. But, instead of touching her, he smiled. It worked. Leslie smiled back. A tentative, awkward smile. But a smile nonetheless.

Oh Mark, she thought, I don't have a crush on your medical know-how, even though it's spectacular. I have a crush on *you*. And it's not a crush.

Leslie quietly ached for Mark, wanting him, dreaming about him, knowing that he was happily married to the woman who was becoming her closest friend. Sometimes Leslie was tempted to tell Janet. They would laugh about it. Janet would say gaily that, as much as she liked her, Leslie couldn't have Mark. He was taken.

But Leslie didn't mention it. It wasn't something she could laugh about. Not yet.

Janet wouldn't have laughed, either. She was suffering, aching, too. She knew that her marriage—which had been decaying for over a year—was now, finally, in its death throes.

By the time the summer fog lifted, by mid-September, Leslie's mind was clear on the subject of Mark. Leslie had made it clear, had forced herself to admit the impossibility, the silliness, of her feelings for Mark. Mark was a wonderful man. He was married to, in love with, a wonderful woman.

It was clear. The fog was gone. Now maybe she could tell Janet about it. And they could laugh.

On September twelfth Janet made a cake—a fabulous cake decorated with evergreen trees and snow-capped mountains in honor of Leslie's home in Seattle—for Leslie's twenty-sixth birthday. As Leslie watched her friend serve the almost-too-beautiful-to-eat cake, she was tempted to tell Janet about how she felt—how she *had* felt—about Mark.

But Janet spoke first. Janet told Leslie about her marriage to Mark. About the marriage that she believed was over.

Leslie listened, quietly, her heart pounding, her mind spinning. *Don't ask me for advice, Janet. I don't even know if I can be impartial. I care about him too much.*

Not that Mark showed a flicker of interest in *her*. He praised her. He told her she was an excellent intern, and he teased her, gently, about her compulsive behavior. Mark treated Leslie the way an older, wiser brother treats his little sister. Teasing, fond, a little protective.

Even if Mark was free, even if his marriage to Janet was doomed to fail, it didn't mean he would fall in love with Leslie.

Leslie shuddered. Janet *was* her friend. That was the reality. The rest was fantasy.

Leslie had to help Janet. She had to help her save her marriage. Leslie listened in amazement and disbelief to what Janet told her.

Janet told her that Mark hated medicine.

"Oh, no, Janet. Mark doesn't hate it. Not any more than we all do. We all hate being exhausted and cooped up and feeling our lives passing by. We all feel that we're missing something during all those hours we spend in the hospital. It's a natural feeling. It's something we talk about."

"I think he hates it more than the rest of you."

"I don't see it, Janet. I really don't. And I work with him. Mark's a wonderful doctor. The best."

The Best. The words hit Janet like a knife. Of course Mark was the best.

"He's so moody and irritable," Janet continued.

"Mark? Not at work. Oh, he gets annoyed like we all do when we get inappropriate admissions or when the blood-draw team says they can't find a vein or when the X ray misses the area of pathology altogether. Our work situation is full of frustrations."

"You don't think he's sullen or angry?"

"No. But I haven't actually worked with him, on the same team, since mid-August. Maybe something has happened—"

"No. It isn't new. It's just getting worse. It's been going on for over a year." Janet started to cry. "Maybe it isn't medicine, after all. Maybe what he really hates is coming home to me."

"No, *Janet*. Mark talks about you all the time. Things like, 'Here are cookies Janet made for the team' or 'Janet says we all should read *Heartsounds*' or 'I told Janet I'd be home by eight. I'm going to try.'"

Janet shook her head, still crying. She knew what Mark was like when he got home. It didn't help to hear that he seemed all right at work. It made it worse.

"I can't live with him anymore, Leslie. Not feeling the way I do. Not living the way we do."

"*Talk* to him, Janet. Mark is a reasonable, gentle, kind man," Leslie said softly.

Janet's wet gray eyes opened wide.

"I admit it, Janet. I think Mark's terrific," Leslie said truthfully. Then she added, "I think you both are."

Two and a half weeks later after Janet and Mark had their talk and Mark had left, Leslie sat once again in her friend's kitchen.

"How did you leave it?"

"What? Oh. We think for a week. Then we talk again next Sunday night. Go from there."

"It will probably work out."

"Not unless he suddenly gets some insight. We're a million miles apart. Or maybe I'm just crazy," Janet said grimly.

"You're not crazy. You're not inventing this unhappiness. It's real. I just hope you two can work it out," Leslie said, realizing how much she meant it.

Mark and Janet belonged together.

Chapter Six

The November fog lasted through the weekend, thick in the morning and evening, clearing during the day. It had resettled by the time Mark left the hospital at six Saturday evening. To him the outside world hadn't changed a bit since he'd rushed to work, late, thirty-four hours before.

The phone was ringing when he entered his apartment. It was Janet.

"Hi, Mark."

"Hi."

"I think we should meet and talk." It was the first time in their five week separation that Janet suggested they see each other.

"All right."

"Can you come to dinner tomorrow night?"

"Not dinner. After. At seven. OK?"

"OK."

After he hung up, Mark called Kathleen. Her father answered.

"Hello, Mr. Jenkins," C.E.O. of . . . unbelievable, Mark thought. "This is Mark Taylor. How is Mrs. Jenkins?"

"Very well, thank you. They're going to turn her loose, to use Kathleen's phrase, next Tuesday."

"Great. Uh, is Kathleen there?"

"No, sorry. She's away for the weekend. Due back Monday evening. How did you like the party Thursday?"

"Very much. A little out of my league, but everyone was

very nice." The nicest part was making love to your daughter, Mark mused.

"The Carlton Club Kids are their own league. Kathleen said you really held your own."

"Oh, she did? Well . . ."

"Shall I tell her you called?"

"Please. Have her call me if she wants to."

"She'll want to."

"Give my best to Mrs. Jenkins."

"Sure will. Thanks, Mark."

He is such a nice, low key man, Mark thought. A nice, low key C.E.O. of one of the world's largest and most powerful corporations.

Mark arrived at Janet's, at his and Janet's house, promptly at seven.

He drew a sharp breath when he saw her. She looked exactly the way she had looked when they met eleven years before: thin, wide-eyed, young, trusting. In five weeks Janet had lost all the weight she had gained. Maybe more. Her slender face made her huge gray eyes seem even larger. Her gaunt cheeks gave her a haunted, haunting look.

"You look great," he said.

"Thanks." She smiled. "Come in."

"Thanks."

"Do you want some coffee?"

"Sure. Please."

How long can we keep this up? she wondered. The careful politeness.

They sat in the living room. It looked the same. Janet had done nothing to move him out. His possessions and her possessions. *Their* possessions. Mark noticed with surprise that Janet didn't wear her ring. Mark still wore his, although he might, *would,* have removed it before his date with Kathleen. If he had remembered.

Had Janet been dating? he wondered. Had she made love with someone else, too?

"You look just like you looked the day we met," Mark

said finally, gently.

"Do I? I feel better now. About the way I look."

"How about everything else?"

"I don't know. How do you feel?"

"I still don't understand," he said slowly. "Maybe I have been more distant and preoccupied. I didn't realize we hadn't made love for four months."

"You were so moody at home. Leslie says you're not that way at work."

"Leslie? We shouldn't get her in the middle of this," Mark said with an edge to his voice.

"I know. I *agree.*"

"I don't think I'm moody at work or at home."

"There are days when you come home and don't even speak to me. At all. And when I try to touch you, you pull away."

"Not many days."

"Many, many days. Day after day. Night after night."

They sat in silence for a long time, an eternity of thoughts and memories and questions without answers.

He could have walked over to her and held her and made love to her, but he didn't. He couldn't. He didn't know who she was. She was the woman who had yelled at him in a rage a month before, but she looked like the sixteen-year-old girl with girl with whom he had fallen in love eleven years ago. She was the woman, not the girl. He didn't know her.

He had to find the old Janet. To retrace the steps. Then he could go to her. He wanted to go to her. To Janet. To his Janet.

"Do you remember the first time we made love?" he asked without looking at her.

"Of course," she answered, tears flooding her eyes.

Mark looked at her then, his own eyes glistening.

"What were you thinking?"

"What?"

"What were you thinking when we made love? It was a big step and we never talked about it. What were you thinking?"

63

"I was thinking what I always thought when you touched me," she said very quietly. "I was thinking, I love you. I love you."

"*Janet,*" he said emotionally. But still he couldn't move to her. He looked at his hand and the scuffed, eighteen carat gold band he had worn for the past five years. "Why aren't you wearing your ring?"

"Because the ring is a symbol of you, of us. It means we're together. I have to feel how it would be without you. To feel the loss."

"How does it feel?"

"Awful. Empty. Sad." A small part relief, she thought. She didn't want to think *that,* but it was there. In her mind. In her heart. A part of the way she felt.

"So we should try again."

Janet nodded, crying.

"No?" he asked, confused.

"Yes. But it's still too soon. We are here, crying because we can remember how much we loved each other eleven years ago, but we can't even touch each other now."

"But we both want to try, don't we? I do," Mark said.

"Yes."

"I have clinics in December."

"*Clinics?*"

"It's new. To give everyone a break. Nine to five on weekdays. No night call. No weekends. No holidays. I'll be off for Christmas, for your birthday. Should I move back in then? In three weeks?" Mark asked carefully.

"OK," Janet said believing it would never work. Not now. Not in three weeks. Not ever. But they had to try. She had to try. Maybe she was wrong.

Kathleen called Tuesday night.

"I learned something about you," she began.

"Kathleen!"

"Yes."

"What did you learn?"

"You told me you went to the University of Nebraska in

64

Lincoln, right?"

"Yes."

"Then, what I learned is that you're a cornhusk."

"Cornhus*ker!*"

"No, those are the other guys. You're a cornhusk. Or you have a corn—"

"Kathleen, it's not even close to what you think it is."

"I know, but it sounds like it should be, doesn't it?"

"I don't think you can discuss such things over public airways."

"Wireways."

"*Any*ways."

Silence.

"So, you rang?" she asked, finally.

"I did. To thank you for Thursday."

"You're welcome."

"And," Mark hesitated, "I was going to ask you out . . ."

"But?" she asked, disappointed.

"A new development in the trial separation."

"Oh."

"A trial reunion."

"Is she there?"

"No. We don't start until December first."

"Oh. *Strange.* In the meantime?"

"In the meantime, I just have to think about it." I can't see you Kathleen, Mark thought. I can't.

"What *do* you think?"

"I think it's an eleven-year relationship. We meant for better or worse when we said it five years ago. We have to give it every chance. That's what I think. What I want."

"Oh," Kathleen said quietly, her voice and confidence a little shaky. Damn. Mark's wife was so lucky to have him. "Well let me know."

"If you don't hear from me, you'll know."

By December fifteenth both Mark and Janet knew their marriage was over. They both knew they had tried, maybe too hard, to resuscitate something that was dead.

Neither really understood what happened. Each understood it from his or her standpoint, but they couldn't agree. They couldn't make sense of it. They tried to talk patiently, but hit impasse after impasse.

At first the frustration erupted into rage.

Later it was replaced by sadness and grieving.

They spent hours reminiscing, remembering the beginning, the happy times. As they talked the memories became vivid, but they could not force the remembered joy and love into the present.

They made love once. Afterward they held each other and wept. They cried for the love that somewhere, somehow, was lost forever.

"How could it have happened to us, Janet?" he asked, bewildered.

Janet just shook her head, but the lyrics of a song, the song that summarized it for her, taunted her. She wanted to sing it for him; but it would just make him angry because he didn't believe her interpretation of what had happened, and it would anger her that he didn't believe her.

But, it was how she felt, had always felt. Every lyric.

If I can make you smile . . .

If I can fill your eyes with pleasure just by holding you . . .

Ah, well, that's enough for me,

That's all the hero I need be . . .

It *had* been enough, she knew, because there had been a time when she could make him happy, when she could fill him with peace with a touch or a kiss. It had been enough for her; she would never have wanted more, but somehow she lost the ability to comfort him. Her presence didn't matter anymore.

Whether Mark loved her any less, or whether his own torment, the torment he still denied, had become greater than the power of her love, she would never know.

They were left with no feelings. No stir of love. Just a present numbness and an aching pain and sadness for the lovely memories of the past — memories of love and passion and feelings that were gone. . . .

The second week, their last week together, they filed for divorce and started to divide their property. The actual process of dividing their possessions was too painful to do together. It brought back too many memories: their wedding pictures, the hand-knit mufflers, the quilt for their bed, the souvenirs of happy times.

Janet agreed to pack the boxes for both of them after he left, but she needed to know what he wanted.

"Do you want the fine china or the everyday?" The four-hundred-guest wedding had left them with complete sets of the china patterns that Mrs. Taylor had insisted they choose.

"I don't care."

"Stainless or silver?"

"I don't *care*," Mark snapped, then repeated gently, "I really don't care, Janet."

"Is there anything you do want?" she asked finally.

"The Cornhuskers banner," he said impulsively. Then he wondered, *am* I really thinking about Kathleen? Certainly not *consciously*. He had focused only on Janet, on *them*. He had tried so hard.

But something within him, something subconscious, made him want the banner. He didn't want it for himself. He wanted to show it to Kathleen.

It all made him very sad.

For the first Christmas in years that Mark could have celebrated his wife's birthday with her, Janet flew home, alone, to snowy Nebraska. They both knew that the well-greased wheels of uncontested divorce in California were moving efficiently, inevitably toward dissolution of the marriage of Janet Wells Taylor and Mark David Taylor.

Mark, alone in San Francisco on December twenty-third, decided to call Kathleen.

"It's Mark."

"I recognize your, er, husky voice," she said, barely able to breathe. If you don't hear from me, you'll know, he had said. And now she was hearing from him.

67

"Cute Kitzy."

"So?"

"We are getting a divorce."

"Are you OK?" He didn't sound OK.

"Yes. It's hard. Sad."

"Do you want to talk about it?"

"Not really. Nothing to say. It's over."

Good, Kathleen thought. She didn't want to nurse Mark through the recovery period of a failed marriage. She wasn't interested in an event by event rehash. She had seen friends be helpful and sympathetic only to have the finally rehabilitated ex-husband spread his newly strengthened wings and find someone new, someone who didn't know quite so much about his weaknesses and his past mistakes.

Kathleen also knew that recently divorced men usually needed affairs with a number of women—a sexual spree— before even considering a serious relationship. Kathleen had slept with enough recently freed husbands. They were a drearily manic bunch.

Kathleen almost told Mark to call her in six or eight months when he was ready for the serious relationship, but she couldn't. Maybe Mark would be different. He was already so different from all the others.

"Kathleen, are you there?"

"Yes. Was it my turn to speak?"

"Uh-huh."

"OK. Hi. There. Now it's your turn."

"I have something to show you."

"I know. It *is* something."

Silence.

"Sorry," Kathleen said. This wasn't really her usual style. She didn't like it. He didn't like it. Kathleen the perfect lady. But Mark made her silly and giddy. And sexy.

"When can I see you?"

"Anytime. Except it's the holidays, isn't it? Do you have plans for Christmas?"

"I can't do a family Christmas, Kathleen," Mark said quickly, apologetically. "It's very nice of you. How's your mother?"

"Well. A hundred percent. Taking it easy. I didn't really mean family Christmas, though you would be welcome. I meant the Carlton Club Kids Christmas Celebration."

"That's not Kathleen's Carlton Club Kids Christmas Celebration, is it?" Mark teased.

"You've heard of it!" Kathleen teased back.

"Of course. Who hasn't?" Mark sensed the feeling, the Kathleen feeling, pumping into his body. He wanted to see her. "What is it?"

"Well, around here, the Atherton Mansion Gang—"

"Atherton Mansion Gang?"

"That's the folks. They aren't as alliterative as the Kids. Anyway, the AMG celebrates Christmas on Christmas Eve with present opening early Christmas morning. The rest of the Christmas day and evening are boring. As kids we hated Christmas night. So, we invented the Celebration. It's our biggest party of the year. It has grown as we have. Now it's held on the top floor at the Fairmont."

"And you don't have a date?"

"Not if you say no."

"It's fancy, isn't it?"

"Yes," Kathleen admitted. "It really is. Black tie. Tuxedo. The whole bit."

"I haven't worn a tuxedo since—" Mark stopped.

"Your wedding."

"Right."

"You probably don't have time to go tuxedo renting, do you?"

"No . . . listen, Kathleen, maybe we could see each other—"

"No, please, Mark. I really want you to come. The Kids have been asking about you. What I was going to say was, if you give me your size I'll get the tux with all the trimmings and bring it to you."

"Nothing crazy, Kathleen."

"No! The Celebration is when we all try to out-gorgeous each other. It's lots of fun. Photographers snapping souvenir portraits. It usually makes the society page of *The Chronicle.*"

"No," Mark said firmly. *I don't want that.*

"OK. We can avoid the press." *Maybe just a private photograph? As a memento?*

"OK."

"When shall I come to your apartment? Are you working on Christmas?"

"No, the whole day off." It was nice that Kathleen understood that doctors worked on Christmas, and that the idea didn't seem to bother her.

"Oh. You don't want to come down here for lunch? My parents would love to see you."

"No. Thank you."

"Well. The dust begins to settle about noon. I could be there by two. I could bring turkey and cranberry sauce. . . Is that too early?"

"No." *Now would be fine. Can't you come now?* "That's great. When is the party? The . . . er . . . Celebration?"

"It starts at eight, but it's best not to arrive until at least nine-thirty."

After he hung up, Mark thought about how many times they could listen to his four ballet albums, in bed, between two and nine-thirty. He didn't give a damn about turkey.

After she hung up, Kathleen had a similar thought. *Scheherazade, Sleeping Beauty, Swan Lake, Giselle.* Then *Giselle, Swan Lake, Sleeping Beauty, Scheherazade.* Then . . .

Chapter Seven

By mid-January Mark had collected the boxes Janet had carefully packed. His half of the memories. Mark didn't need, couldn't use, any of the furniture. The divorce was all but fact, simply waiting for the required number of days to elapse.

Kathleen saw Mark every third night. She always saw him on the night before he was on call. It was the night he was the most rested. It was also the night he needed the most sleep. On those nights Kathleen was always in his apartment when he arrived home, and she forced herself to leave his bed by two in the morning.

Sometimes if he wasn't too tired on the night following his on call night, if he got home in time, he would call her, and she would come to him.

"I think I should get an apartment in the city," Kathleen announced to her parents one morning at breakfast. At that moment Mark was running his second code of the day, trying to resuscitate a patient who had had a cardiac arrest.

"Are you moving in with him, dear?" her father asked bluntly.

"No." Because Mark hadn't asked her. It was too soon. Mark needed his privacy. His private time.

"Then why?"

"I want to be able to spend the night with him. All night," she said. *So I can fall asleep and wake up in his arms. So I don't have to leave him in the middle of the night.* "I don't want to have to worry about you worrying that I've crashed somewhere between here and there."

Kathleen's morality was not an issue. Only her safety and her happiness. She was twenty-seven years old and lived in her girlhood room, in her own wing of the mansion, because it was more splendid than any apartment. And because she enjoyed being with her parents.

Kathleen had complete freedom, but she had never wanted to spend the night with her other men. Not all night every night. Mark was different.

"Just let us know where you'll be, dear. Leave Mark's number with us. We know you are safe with him."

Neither parent had seen Mark since Kathleen's mother's hospitalization, but their memories of him, of his kindness, were strong and clear and enduring.

By the end of January, with Mark's permission, Kathleen had purchased a box spring to put under the mattress, four feather pillows to replace the lumpy ones and two complete sets of Laura Ashley sheets with matching comforters. She bought five live plants for the living room and hung the red and white Cornhuskers banner over the bed, even though it clashed with the pretty, delicate Laura Ashley patterns.

Mark stored the boxes of memories in the attic of the building.

Little by little, guided by Kathleen's stylish eye, the apartment looked better. Better, bigger, comfortable. Theirs.

"It still needs a face lift," Kathleen said one night. "A coat of paint in the living room. Some pictures . . ."

"Who's going to paint it?"

"I am. If that's OK. Some day when you're on call, so it can air out. OK? Please?"

"Sure," Mark said, putting his arms around her. "If you want to."

At ten in the morning on February fifth, Janet climbed the stairs to Mark's apartment. She had never been there, but Mark had given her the address. She carried a small box that contained the last of the memories and mail that hadn't been forwarded. It was nothing of great value. She could leave the box outside his apartment door.

One last detail. Janet was moving out of the house—their house—in a week.

She didn't even call to tell him. She didn't want to speak to him. Too painful. Nothing to say. Janet chose a time, ten o'clock on a Thursday morning, when she knew he wouldn't be there. She knew he was working on the wards at San Francisco General Hospital with Leslie.

Janet was surprised to find the door to Mark's apartment wide open. She saw drop cloths and smelled paint. She assumed it was the landlord. She walked into the apartment. As long as the door was open she might as well leave the box inside.

"Hello?" she called.

"Hello!" answered a surprised female voice.

Janet walked farther in and almost collided with Kathleen. Kathleen had been expecting Betsey, who was coming to watch, *only*, the painting process.

"Oh! Hello," Kathleen said. She had no idea that she was looking at Mark's almost ex-wife.

But she recognized the face.

"I'm Janet. I have a box of things for Mark."

"Janet. I'm Kathleen. I'm a friend of Mark's. I offered to paint his apartment."

Kathleen recognized Janet's face immediately. How could she forget it? It was *her*. She hoped Janet wouldn't recognize her. There was a chance she wouldn't. Kathleen looked so different today, in her painting clothes, than she had the day before.

But Janet did recognize her.

"Aren't you? Didn't—"

"Yes."

The day before, the Board of Union Square Theater had auditioned the finalists for *Joanna*. The finalists had been selected after two grueling weeks of auditions in front of choreographers, directors, producers and cast members of other Union Square Theater productions. Kathleen was a member of the board, and the board had an advisory say in the final selection.

Joanna was such an important production. Such a risk. It was the first original musical Union Square Theater had done—a musical opening not in New York on Broadway but in San Francisco on Geary. It was a landmark event for the theater. They all knew that *Joanna* had potential, great potential.

But they had to choose exactly the right cast.

Janet was there as a finalist. She was the only amateur who had survived to the finals.

J. Wells. Kathleen remembered the name on the roster, the name of the woman with the haunting beauty and the lovely, clear, soulful voice.

It was Kathleen who had suggested that they audition J. Wells for the lead not just for the supporting cast. Janet had overhead the suggestion. She knew who made it. Now she knew more about the sophisticated young woman with the jet-black hair and violet eyes.

"You're Mark's wife?"

"His ex-wife. Almost. I guess you know."

"I didn't know who you were yesterday. Different—"

"I'm using my maiden name."

Different name. Different woman.

True, Mark had never told her anything about Janet, but Kathleen had allowed herself to imagine a large, unsophisticated farm girl. Pretty, plump, uninspired. It was a comforting image.

Kathleen had left the audition thinking about the remarkable walk-on who had mesmerized and captivated them and who they hoped would captivate audiences in San Francisco and maybe even in New York. Who was the intriguing, beautiful woman with incredible talent and the huge gray eyes? Kathleen had wondered.

Now she knew.

"You were wonderful," Kathleen said.

"Thank you."

"You've heard, haven't you? The decision?"

"No. They said they would call sometime today," Janet answered quickly, eager to leave. She couldn't stand seeing Kathleen in Mark's apartment. Kathleen obviously belonged there. Janet was the outsider. Janet had to leave. It was too painful.

But Kathleen had something to say to her.

"They were supposed to call you at nine. You got the lead, Janet. You stole it right away from all those seasoned professionals. You deserve it. You were the best."

The Best. How Janet hated those two words. But she wanted the part—*any* part—in the musical. She had to start singing and performing again. Her sanity depended on it.

Janet eyed Kathleen skeptically. The lead?

Her skepticism was well founded. It seemed highly unlikely that a complete unknown would be selected as the lead. The concept of introducing a new musical was innovative enough. But an unknown musical with an unknown lead? It was so risky. Too risky. Janet couldn't imagine that anyone would be willing to take the risk.

But Janet didn't know Ross MacMillan. Ross took risks and converted them into phenomenal successes. When Ross founded Union Square Theater in 1976, everyone said it would fail. San Francisco didn't *need* another theater. Now theatergoers rushed to get season tickets and eagerly awaited announcements of Union Square Theater's upcoming productions. They were never disappointed.

Ross MacMillan took risks. They really weren't risks with Ross at the creative helm; they were opportunities. He knew what was possible, and he took what was possible and made it into something spectacular.

Ross MacMillan was thirty-three years old and looked like he should be on stage rather than behind it. But as crowd-stopping as his looks were ("Wasn't that Robert Redford?"), his ability to mesmerize an audience through his genius as a director was even greater,

Ross MacMillan was a Carlton Club Kid.

And Ross MacMillan was ultimately responsible for the decision to cast Janet Wells as the lead in *Joanna*. The board was advisory. It was his decision.

"Where were they supposed to call you?" Kathleen asked Janet.

"At work. But I don't go in until noon on Thursdays."

"Call there. Right now. When I left the theater yesterday you had the part. I think it would be best for you to check before you leave. . . ." *Because this is about the worst possible scenario.*

Kathleen gestured toward the phone, realizing too late that beside the phone, beautifully framed, was the stunning portrait taken of Mark and Kathleen at the Celebration. A magnificent, romantic picture. Their private memory.

Janet saw the picture, recoiled for a moment, then dialed her office. There was a message to call Ross MacMillan at Union Square Theater. Janet memorized the number and dialed the theater.

"Really? I won Joanna?" *The* role. The role that would make or break Union Square Theater's innovative experiment. Janet's heart pounded. "Yes, I'll be there at eight Monday morning. Yes. Thank you, Mr. MacMillan."

After she replaced the receiver, Janet paused for a moment to look at the photograph. When she turned to Kathleen, her usually calm, gray eyes were stormy with emotion. Janet tried to smile.

"It didn't take him long, did it? Or—" Janet stopped. Was she looking at the reason? The real reason? Was Kathleen the reason for Mark's moodiness and detachment? Was she why Mark didn't touch Janet? How long had they been together? A year? Fifteen months?

"Janet," Kathleen said, blinking back her own tears. She realized now what a great loss it had been for both of them. She knew now why all that Mark had said about his failed marriage to Janet was that it made him sad. Why he still, quietly, grieved. "Mark and I met *after—after* it was over— and it has taken him a long time. It will take him a long time. Believe me, Janet."

"I have to go," Janet said, walking toward the door. She stopped, just before she reached it, and turned, tears running down her face.

"Will I see you again? I mean, through the production?"

"There will be a few parties."

"Don't . . . could you please—does he have to come with you?"

"No. I'll come alone. Or not at all. It's *your* show. You're the star."

"Thanks," Janet sniffed. "I really thought I was doing better."

"I can't think of anything worse than what you're going through right now, can you?" Kathleen asked, hopefully.

"No," Janet smiled, barely. "Oh. Would you—could you see that he does see the show?"

"Of course he will," Kathleen said, her own violet eyes glistening.

Mark would be so proud of Janet.

After Janet left, Kathleen sat, numb, immobile, for an hour, wondering for the thousandth time if she should just leave him alone, let him recover. Leave him alone and then hope that Mark, once healed, would find her again.

Mark never even mentioned Janet. Or his grief. He barely let it show. Only when he thought Kathleen wasn't watching. But what about the times when she wasn't there? What about when he was alone? Kathleen wondered.

How would she tell Mark about today, about meeting Janet?

Betsey found Kathleen in a lump in the kitchen when she arrived. Kathleen didn't tell her what had happened. They spent the afternoon chattering about nothing and listening to records while Kathleen painted.

Mark didn't call the next night. He probably got home too late, Kathleen decided. But the questions thundered in her brain. What if Janet had called him and told him what had happened? What if it brought them back together?

Mark would let me know, Kathleen thought.

The next day, the every third night that was theirs, Kathleen arrived at the apartment carrying three framed pictures for the newly painted walls. Two pictures were unoriginal, but they were Kathleen's favorite scenic posters of San Francisco. The first, bright and fresh, was a sleek, shiny sailboat with a multicolored spinnaker gliding across the shimmering blue bay. The second, soft and romantic, was a twilight silhouette of the city with a spring moon and a single star. The third picture was original. Made just for Mark.

It was a photograph—enlarged to a top-quality two-by-three-foot print—of a brick mansion with white marble pillars surrounded by perfectly manicured, emerald-green lawns and brilliant, exquisitely tended gardens of roses and lilacs and azaleas. The mansion and its luxurious grounds made an undeniable statement about wealth, taste, heritage and privilege. Chiseled into the marble and brick near the entrance were the words: The Carlton Club.

Kathleen smiled as she hung the last picture. It was perfect. The picture, the matting, the frame.

She hoped he liked it.

She hoped he liked her. Still.

Mark called at six. He sounded tired but normal.

"ETA one hour, OK?"

"Sure. Bad day?"

"The usual. But things are slowing down. A sick GI bleeder, but Leslie's here tonight. She's got it under control," Mark said lightly.

Kathleen had the distinct impression that Leslie was within earshot of Mark. Kathleen liked Leslie. She had been so gentle with her mother. Just as Mark had been.

Mark appeared an hour later. He was obviously happy to see her.

"I want to take a shower before I touch you. And I want to touch you. So I'm taking my shower now, all right?"

"OK," Kathleen answered, kissing his lips briefly as he passed.

"You did a great job of painting," he said.

Kathleen followed him from the entry area to the bathroom door. It was a matter of a few feet.

"Thanks. Wait until you see today's improvements!"

"Can't wait. Do you want you join me in here? After I

wash off a few layers of blood and germs. . . ."

"No thank you," Kathleen said, watching him undress. "I have to keep an eye on dinner."

She looked at his white resident's pants, truly splattered with blood, and said, "You are careful, aren't you. Mark? About the blood. About hepatitis? And the new one, *AIDS?*"

Mark was a little surprised that Kathleen knew that hepatitis was transmitted by blood and even more surprised that she had heard about AIDS. AIDS, Acquired Immune Deficiency Syndrome, was new. It had only been recognized in North America recently. San Francisco had a substantial share of the cases, and the rumors were just beginning that spread might be through blood products as well as sexual contact.

"Blood splashes on clothes don't do any harm. It's needle sticks, splashes in the eyes, mucous membranes. We're careful about those." Mark was talking about the transmission of hepatitis.

"Have you—do you—take care of patients with AIDS?" she asked.

"Of course," he said. Mark had two patients with AIDS, both dying, on his service right now.

"Does it bother you? The pictures I've seen—it looks awful."

"It *is* awful." The worst, he thought. "It doesn't bother me to take care of them. What bothers me is that it's killing young men, men my age, and we don't know what causes it, how to treat it, how to stop it. . . ." Mark's voice, through the sound of the shower water, was angry.

"But if you know so little about it, and it's so awful, doesn't it bother you that you might catch it?" Kathleen persisted.

"I'm a doctor, Kathleen," Mark said with an edge to his voice. "I take care of sick patients all day, every day. There is no reason to think that you can catch AIDS by taking care of patients. Not if you're careful. Not if you take the usual precautions. And I *am* careful."

"I have to go check on dinner," Kathleen said, suddenly,

realizing that the tone of his voice, sharp and intense, made her uneasy.

After she left the bathroom, as he lathered himself with soap for the third time, Mark thought about his patients with AIDS. They were young men wasting away—fighting because they were so young, had been so healthy, had everything to live for—and inevitably dying of the lethal mysterious new disease. He wondered if there was a *best* way to die. A warm, peaceful, quiet death . . .

Mark didn't know what was the best, but he knew that AIDS was one of the worst. They all knew it. It was the disease they all didn't want to get.

They were very careful.

When Mark rejoined Kathleen after his long shower, he looked refreshed and untroubled. He wore khaki slacks and an oxford shirt, open at the collar, with sleeves rolled halfway up his pale but finely muscled forearms.

He noticed the pictures immediately.

"They are wonderful, Kathleen," he said. Then, moving closer to the picture of the brick mansion, he asked, "What's this?"

"Look closely. The pillar on the left."

Mark leaned forward and read aloud, "The Carlton Club."

"I had to get something to counterbalance the Cornhuskers' banner."

"Maybe we should put this above our bed. It goes much better with feather pillows and Laura whoever sheets."

Our bed, Kathleen thought, a rush of joy pulsing through her. She said softly, "Ashley."

She thought of saying, No, the Cornhuskers' banner captures the spirit of the—*our*—bed. But it wasn't true. Their lovemaking was everything, all moods, Cornhuskers to Laura Ashley, uninhibited sport to proper Carlton Club. Laughter and quiet tenderness. Lust and romance. Adventure and tradition. Everything.

During dinner Kathleen told him about her meeting with Janet.

"I assumed she left the box at the door and that you

80

brought it in when you came to paint."

"No."

"Oh."

Silence.

"Mark, do you remember the woman I told you about? The amateur we auditioned on Wednesday for *Joanna?*"

"The one you thought was so sensational? The one who got the lead over all the pros? Sure. I remember. Why?" he asked idly.

"Janet," Kathleen said quietly.

"Janet?" Mark asked. Of course Janet, he thought. That's what she had done in high school and college—stolen the leading roles from the pros. Not because she cared about being the best. Just because she needed to sing.

Mark blinked back a sudden mist in his eyes. Then he said, his voice husky, "Good for her."

After a few moments, he asked, "Did you know that on Wednesday?"

"No. Not until I met her, here, yesterday. She used—is using—her . . ." Kathleen hesitated.

"Maiden name?"

"Yes."

"Was she thrilled?" he asked, knowing that she had to be but that it might not show.

Kathleen only remembered the tears and Janet's hurt, comprehending expression as she looked at the photograph of Kathleen and Mark.

"I'm sure she was," Kathleen said.

The conversation shifted. They talked about nothing of importance. They talked less than usual. Mark was quiet.

Later, as they got ready for bed, he asked, casually, "Will there be parties for the production? Ones you'll need to attend?"

"Yes. I told her you wouldn't be at any of them. I probably won't be, either. It's her show. OK?"

"Yes."

A few moments later, he said, "I want to see the show, though."

"I know. She wants you to."

81

That night they made love in a new way. In the oldest way. The most chaste way. First they kissed for a long time. Just kissing, just their mouths. Their hands and their lips didn't explore. Then he entered her and they moved, together, united, entwined. Slow, rhythmic, leisurely lovemaking. Wonderful romantic lovemaking.

Kathleen had no idea that was the way that Mark and Janet had made love. Only. Always. Hundreds and hundreds of times.

Over the next two weeks there were periods when Mark was distant and preoccupied. Kathleen didn't know the cause. It could have been because of Janet. That would make sense. Or it could have been because of the death of both the AIDS patients within hours of each other. Mark had been there. He had watched them die. Helpless. Unable to prevent the inevitable.

Perhaps it was the long telephone conversation with his father. Mark asked Kathleen to wait in the bedroom, but she heard bits, angry tones she had never heard from Mark before. When she decided the conversation was over—when she heard only silence from the other room—Kathleen joined him. Mark didn't even acknowledge her presence. He had already retreated to a corner of the living room and was reading *The Adventures of Sherlock Holmes*. Kathleen picked up the book that lay on the end table, *Ulysses* by James Joyce, and tried to read, too.

She couldn't read, couldn't concentrate. Finally, she gave up and simply watched Mark, absorbed in his book, oblivious to her stares.

"This isn't good," she whispered after over an hour of silence.

Mark looked up at the sound of her voice, startled, almost disoriented.

"What did you say?"

"I said, this isn't good."

"What isn't?"

"You shutting me out like this."

Shutting me out. Janet's words. Now Kathleen's words. Mark put his book down and went to her side.

"What do you mean?" he asked gently, with concern in his voice.

"I mean you had a horrible conversation, I assume, with your father, after which you withdraw completely and behave as if I'm not here and never existed."

"I'm *sorry.* I didn't realize," Mark said. "What *should* I do?"

"I don't know. How about saying, 'My father is such a bastard. Kathleen, do you mind if I just escape into the streets of London with Holmes for a while?' "

"That sounds easy," Mark said with relief.

"Except I don't think you're even aware when you are doing it."

"Have there been other times?" Mark pulled her close to him, gently, worried.

"In the past two weeks, several. In the past two months, a few."

"I honestly wasn't aware."

"I know." Kathleen believed him. He would know if he paid attention. It was probably an old bad habit. Kathleen wondered how Janet had felt about it, assuming it wasn't all simply because of Janet.

"So what should I do?"

"Pay attention. I don't need to know what's bothering you, unless you want to tell me. I just need to know it's not me."

"It's not you, never you," he said, kissing her.

"Then do I have permission to point it out when you're doing it? In case you don't know?" So you'll learn, she thought.

"Yes! Kathleen. I don't want to shut you out."

"And you won't snarl?" she asked, kissing him back.

"I don't snarl," he said softly.

"Oh yes, you do."

The next week was better. Mark's need to retreat into a

book or lose himself in dark troublesome thoughts was not less, but he good-humoredly announced his moods and his intentions. Kathleen respected his privacy and struggled with *Ulysses* as she waited for the mood to pass. It always did. It was always gone before they went to bed.

"You probably understand *Ulysses,* don't you?" she teased one night as she lay beside him. "I didn't really get it when we studied it at Vassar, although I think I got an A on the paper I wrote about it! I still don't get it."

"It's one of my favorites. A masterpiece."

"Can we pick our way through it sometime? Word by word?"

"Sure. But not now," he said, nuzzling her soft round breast.

"No," she sighed, "not now."

By the third week in February, Kathleen realized that despite the new ground rules, which allowed her not to take his moodiness personally, Mark had too much on his mind. Too many things to resolve: Janet, his failed marriage, whatever it was with his father.

Mark couldn't build a new relationship until the residual feelings and emotions about his marriage were resolved. That would take time. And privacy.

Kathleen couldn't help him. He wasn't that kind of man, and she wasn't that kind of woman.

They could solve *their* problems—Mark and Kathleen problems—together, but she didn't want to help him with old problems. She didn't want the burden of Mark and Janet problems.

By the end of February Kathleen made her decision.

"Betsey and I have decided to take a trip."

"Without Jeff? Without the groom-to-be?"

"He'll survive."

"Where are you going?"

"Hawaii. The Mauna Kea Hotel on the big island. It's a favorite. Betsey and I go there every six or eight months—just the two of us—to talk, take stock of our lives and lie in the sun. We've been doing it for years."

"When do you leave?"

"Day after tomorrow."

"When do you return?"

"Betsey will be back in a week," Kathleen said. She hesitated a moment before saying. "And I'll be back in four months."

"Four months!"

"You're snarling."

"This is not a snarl. We've gone beyond snarl. What the hell are you doing, Kathleen?"

"I'm giving you, in the jargon of the day, *space*."

"Oh God. *Why?*"

"Because you need it."

"Really? You know what I need and I don't?"

"Don't get angry, Mark," Kathleen pleaded. "You're right. I don't know what you need. I know what I need and what I *think* you need."

"Which is?"

"I think you need time to resolve your feelings about your marriage."

"The marriage is over. Resolved," Mark said flatly. He looked into her violet eyes and repeated, gently, "It's over, Kathleen."

"You don't think about it? About what went wrong?"

"Yes, of course. But mostly in the context of not making, trying not to make, the same mistakes with you. With us."

Oh, Mark, Kathleen thought, I'll stay.

But her decision was firm.

"Besides," she said lightly, "you need to sow some wild oats."

"Sow some wild oats? You make me sound like a sixteen-year-old—"

"Cornhusk-*er.*"

"Kathleen, I'm twenty-seven, chronically tired, completely, deliriously happy to be with you . . ." Mark paused, then asked. "Do you really want me to sleep with other women while you're gone?"

"Yes!" No, not really, Kathleen thought, an ache settling in the pit of her stomach. Was the risk worth it? Sleep with them, Mark, she thought, but don't fall in love with them. Learn how special *we* really are.

"This is ridiculous."

Kathleen shrugged. "When was the last time you slept with someone other than me or Janet?"

"Never."

"Oh *no*. I'll see you in a year. Or two."

"Kathleen, you are reducing me to a nonthinking, unfeeling animal with irrepressible, insatiable urges. It's only a little bit flattering. It's mostly insulting."

"Mark," she began. I love you, she thought. I want you. Forever. This is the only way it can happen. She said, "Four months is a short time."

"A lot can happen in four months," Mark said grimly, recalling the last four months of his own life. He had lost the woman with whom he had planned to spend his life. He had fallen in — cared deeply about another woman. That happened so quickly that he hadn't had time to think. . . .

Kathleen is right, he realized. Four months is a short time, but it could make a big difference. It could give him, give them, time to be certain.

Mark held out his arms to her. Kathleen fell into them gratefully.

"Where will you be?" He pressed his lips against her shiny black hair.

"Lots of places. *Incommunicado*." Kathleen planned to be in Atherton between short trips like the one to Hawaii, but it was better if Mark didn't know that.

"Ah, Communicado. Lovely spot," he teased. Then he said seriously, "So the rules of this trial separation are that we don't communicate? And I make love with every woman I meet?"

"Something like that."

"When do you re-materialize?"

"After Wimbledon."

"Wimbledon? The tennis championships? You're going?"

"Of course," Kathleen said lightly in her best Carlton Club voice that implied, Isn't everyone? "I always do. My parents and I go. CEOs get wonderful center court seats."

"So you'll be back when?"

"A day or two after the finals. July eighth or ninth, I think."

"In time to be with me on my birthday?"

"Which is. . . ?"

"July eleventh."

"If you want me to."

"I want you to."

"What if you don't, by then?"

"Then I'll let you know."

Chapter Eight

Jean Watson—Mrs. Watson—was admitted to Leslie's service at University Hospital on April fifteenth. Before Leslie saw her new patient, she learned the details of her complicated medical history from Mrs. Watson's physician, Dr. Jack Samuels, a hematology-oncology specialist.

"She's the nicest woman in the world, Leslie. With a lethal disease. This hospitalization will probably be her last. We diagnosed breast cancer a year ago, positive nodes, negative estrogen receptors. We gave her aggressive chemo and haven't documented mets. Anyway, she was doing very well until a month ago when she presented with fatigue and bleeding from her gums. I did a bone marrow . . . she's aplastic."

"Not a marrow full of tumor?" Leslie asked.

"No. An *aplastic* marrow. Completely empty."

"Maybe it will come back."

"Leslie, she has no cells. Her marrow is completely wiped out. We've been supporting her with red cells, white cells and platelets all month."

"How about a marrow transplant? Maybe you could kill her tumor at the same time. Cure everything."

"I would love to transplant her, but we're already almost unable to cross-match her for blood transfusions. She consumes platelets as quickly as we infuse them. Immunologically, she'd be a nightmare to transplant. She would never survive."

"So she has an auto-immune process going on as well? Breast cancer, an aplastic marrow *and* an auto-immune syndrome?"

"Uh-huh."

"Maybe the tumor is making something, secreting some substance that is suppressing her marrow and making the auto-antibodies. . . ." Leslie mused.

Dr. Samuels looked at Leslie for a moment. He had heard about her. His colleagues raved about how bright she was. And pleasant. And compulsive. But he had never worked with her. He had noticed her, of course. It was hard not to notice the slender, drawn face framed in chestnut curls, the bright sapphire-blue eyes and the trim but voluptuous figure unsuccessfully concealed by her white coat. And the smile, sometimes tired, sometimes wan, was always there. Always retrievable.

They all noticed her, the entire faculty, and they talked about her, kindly wondering, Who is she? What does she do when she leaves the hospital? Does she have anyone waiting for her? Is she happy?

They hoped so. They liked her.

Now, talking with her, mesmerized by her fresh, natural beauty and her large, attentive, concerned blue eyes, Jack Samuels knew, felt, what they had been talking about.

Then Leslie suggested that the tumor might be secreting a substance. . . . *That* was what he thought. It would be extremely unusual. Reportable. Most interns, or even residents, would never have considered it.

"That's what I've been wondering, too, Leslie," he said.

"Does that mean we will be giving her more chemotherapy?" she asked.

"Maybe. I haven't decided. It's awfully hard to give chemotherapy that destroys the marrow to someone whose marrow you are trying to stimulate. Not to mention the trouble with supporting her with blood products."

"But if it is all due to tumor and we don't treat it. . . ." Leslie said quietly.

"I know. This is a tough one. Let's discuss it after you see her and review her records. Let me know what you think," he said, scarcely believing what he heard himself say. Jack Samuels had never, ever, asked for an intern's opinion on such an important decision. Of course, as a faculty member, he went through the usual rituals of involving the interns, engaging them in Socratic dialogue. He even listened to what they said.

But he had never before solicited an opinion.

Leslie simply nodded and said, "OK."

"I guess she's not on the floor yet. I was going to introduce you."

"I'll see her as soon as she arrives. Then shall I call you?"

"Yes."

"All right. Thank you, Dr. Samuels."

"Call me Jack, Leslie," he said, amazing himself again, but chuckling inwardly at how his wife, herself a physician, would diagnose what had happened. An acute, self-limited attack of middle age, she would say, laughing.

From Jack Samuels's description, Leslie formed a clear picture of what Mrs. Watson would look like: frail, exhausted, dying.

"Mrs. Watson?" Leslie asked with surprise when she saw the woman sitting in the bed assigned to Jean Watson.

Jean Watson sat cross-legged on the hospital bed. She wore a modest, fluffy, bright-yellow robe. Her hair was dark red, her face freckled, her eyes merry and twinkly and her smile broad. Her fifty-eight-year-old face, wrinkled and full of character, instantly sent the message that those fifty-eight years had been full, interesting, happy ones.

"Yes?" she chirped.

"Mrs. Watson, I'm Leslie Adams. I'm the intern who will be taking care of you."

Leslie usually introduced herself as Leslie Adams, intern, rather than Dr. Adams. It caused less distance.

Sometimes Leslie had to be firm about who she was and the authority she had. Then she was *Dr.* Adams. *The doctor.* Those times usually occurred in the San Francisco General Hospital emergency room with alcoholics, drug addicts and psychotic patients who were too drugged, confused or belligerent to pay attention to anything but her size, her fragile prettiness and her sex. Leslie had to tell them, clearly, directly, that she was their doctor. And that she was in charge.

But it wasn't necessary with Mrs. Watson.

"You're a doctor!"

"Well, yes," Leslie said patiently. "Interns are doctors."

"Dear, I know that. I was reacting to your age, not your rank. You look so young! I've been in hospitals enough in the past year that I know the entire hierarchy. I'm even up on the name change. Aren't you really an R-1?"

Leslie smiled. It was true. The term intern was officially being abandoned. They would all be residents—first year, R-1s; second year, like Mark, R-2s; and so on. The term intern might disappear, but the job description, the tradition of being an intern, the ordeal of the internship year, wouldn't change.

"A rose by any other name," Leslie said, laughing.

"Ah yes. I see."

It surprised Leslie that Mrs. Watson thought she looked young. Before her internship Leslie *had* looked young, but she felt she had aged so much in the past nine months. She felt older. She noticed little lines on her face, around her eyes, that she had never seen before. She knew she looked drawn and gaunt. She felt the tugging of her skin.

Mrs. Watson was the picture of health, of robust, genetically predetermined long life. Leslie learned, as she took Mrs. Watson's family history, that her parents had died at ages ninety-two and ninety-four.

"And never misheard a word or lost a thought in all those years," Jean Watson said proudly.

It wasn't until Jean Watson removed her fluffy yellow robe that the magnitude of her illness became apparent. Her body was ravaged—thin, wrinkled, missing one breast and blue-black with bruises because the low platelet count did not enable her blood to clot properly.

"I'm a mess, aren't I?" she asked, smiling wryly.

Leslie smiled back, unable to think of anything to say.

She was taken aback by the deathlike body attached to the lively, happy woman she was beginning to know.

"I think you need a central line, to minimize the needle sticks," she said, finally.

"A Hickman? I've had a few. They don't last long; they clot off in spite of my low platelets!"

Great, Leslie thought. Jack Samuels had forgotten to mention that problem.

"OK. Well, then, you'll just have to help me find the veins," Leslie said lightly, knowing how hard it would be, how fragile the veins must be, how over-used already.

"They're pretty bad," Jean Watson said.

"Well, I'm pretty good at starting lines in tricky, delicate veins," Leslie said cheerfully. She knew it would be tough — tough for Mrs. Watson — because it *hurt* to have needle sticks over and over, and because it was frustrating. It was a reminder of the body's betrayal. The body had betrayed the mind and the spirit. The body had gotten sick, weak. The body was going to die.

As Leslie watched Jean Watson's body die over the next few weeks, despite chemotherapy and plasmaphoresis and white cell, red cell and platelet transfusions, Leslie learned about the quick, lively, loving mind that did not want to die. Not yet. Not ever.

Leslie spent many hours with Jean, caring for her, talking to her. Each day she patiently and as gently as possible searched for veins. She started intravenous lines for the necessary transfusions and medications, and she withdrew blood to check the blood counts. Leslie watched the first few moments of each transfusion. Jean's immunologically primed body might have a serious allergic reaction to the blood products.

They talked. Occasionally about a possible vein to try, rarely about Jean's medical condition and mostly about their lives.

"Next time. Next life, I am going to have a daughter," Jean said one day.

"You have pretty wonderful sons," Leslie said, gently tapping a potential vein, trying to make it stand up.

"I do. I know. But five boys and no girls!" she laughed.

Leslie had met all five sons, all redheaded and freckle-faced, like their mother. All with merry eyes and smiles, like hers. After seeing the sons and their mother, Leslie expected that Mr. Watson would be redheaded, too.

But he wasn't. He had a full head of dark curly hair and dark eyes that had managed to skip his children's generation. Perhaps his redheaded sons would have curly-black-haired girls. Grandchildren, maybe granddaughters, that Jean Watson would never see.

Carl Watson was a kind, loving man. He and the "boys," as the Watsons fondly referred to their sons, visited Jean daily. The boys ranged in age from sixteen to thirty. During their visits, Leslie always heard laughter coming from Jean's room—light feminine laughs surrounded by a chorus of deep masculine ones.

Seeing the Watsons together, laughing, talking, loving, made Leslie think about her own parents. The weekly calls to her parents in Seattle began to last a little longer. Sometimes she called them twice a week. It was so comforting to talk to them, to hear their voices, to have her mother quiz her about her weight and her health and men.

The Watsons were so like Leslie's family. Close and loving. Except our family is lucky. At least we have been lucky *so far,* Leslie thought, wondering superstitiously how to insure the luck forever. The Watsons had done nothing wrong. Jean's illness was simply a tragedy. Senseless. Painful. Nobody's fault. No way to prevent it.

Luck. Fate. Divine will. . . .

Mark looked at the envelope for a moment. His name and address were hand-written, but the return address was engraved in dark blue script. Union Square Theater. On Geary. The handwriting looked like Kathleen's.

Mark opened the envelope quickly. Kathleen had been gone for six weeks. It seemed much longer.

It was Kathleen's handwriting. The envelope contained a note dated February twenty-seventh, the day before she left

for Hawaii, two theater tickets and an engraved invitation.
Mark read the note first:

*Hi! This note is to be attached to two excellent
opening night tickets to* Joanna — *yet to be printed —
and an invitation to the dress rehearsal party — yet to
be engraved — and sent to you in time for both events.
Assuming all has gone as planned, do with them as
you will.*

I am looking forward to your birthday.

Aloha,
Kathleen

Mark smiled as he read her note. It was a gentle reminder
of her energy and her humor. Not that he needed to be
reminded. He thought about her constantly. Missed her.
Wanted her.

But he knew that she was right about this time apart.

He did need the time and the privacy. He had to try to
solve the issues — the ones he could solve — like his real feelings about losing Janet. Sadness. Regret. But no urge to try
again, to try to go back. There was no place to go. That
place — the place in time where the love of Janet and Mark
had flourished — existed only in their minds, because they
could remember, and in their hearts, aching hearts, that
had lost the feeling.

Mark and Janet were over. Mark had to salvage the
lessons and move on. He had to try not to make the same
mistakes. Already with Kathleen he had repeated a mistake,
but Kathleen had told him. In time.

Mark needed this time alone to think of the other mistakes he had made, could make again, could avoid. But
what about the mistakes he didn't recognize? What if
Kathleen didn't recognize them either, until, as with Janet,
it was too late?

Mark knew there would always be the risk of mistakes,
of alienating someone he loved, because of his moods and
because of the other problem. The big, unresolved prob-

lem. The problem that Janet had recognized and he had denied, vehemently, angrily.

Only now, as he spent his nights alone and forced himself to think, did he realize that Janet had been right. Mark didn't like being a doctor. It was so simple and so complicated. It was what he had been destined to be. By his father. By his own inner drive. Something about being the best. . .

But Mark didn't like it. More than that, Janet was right, he *hated* it.

What was he going to do about it?

Mark didn't know. It was too hard to make decisions in the midst of a busy residency, he told himself. Maybe it would get better. That's what everyone said. It gets better. So far it hadn't.

And it had already destroyed one marriage.

Mark looked at the engraved invitation to the dress rehearsal party and checked his pocket calendar. He couldn't go. He was on call. That meant he would be off the next night, opening night. He could go to the opening night performance.

Mark looked at the tickets. *Two* tickets.

Kathleen, he thought, smiling. She was reminding him to take a date.

Even about that, his need to see other women, Kathleen had been right.

Without her, knowing that she expected him to see other women, Mark stopped resisting the advances that had begun the day his wedding band came off.

All he could compare it to was high school. That was the last time he had dated. In a way it was similar. Except the signals were stronger, clearer, more specific now. These women wanted to sleep with him.

Apparently none of them viewed him as marriage material. Kathleen's firm knowledge that just-divorced men make terrible husbands but enthusiastic lovers was shared by the women who approached him.

They wanted to have fun. They wanted to show him all the things he had missed while he was married. They had no illusions about falling in love. The ones who did, the ones who had secretly admired Mark for two years and who knew what kind of man he was, stayed away. Maybe in a year. When he was emotionally ready to try again . . .

Mark fell into the game easily. It was so simple. The stakes weren't high. No one got hurt, and it didn't jeopardize his relationship with Kathleen; it strengthened it. When she returned, before she returned, he would quit. Without regret.

Until her return Mark would play the game. It was a welcome escape from the problems that plagued him, an interesting, exciting diversion when the pressures became too great and the questions too unanswerable.

Mark rarely dated anyone more than three times.

Except for Gail.

Gail had made bold clear advances toward him since the first day of his internship. She saw his eighteen-carat gold wedding band and didn't care. Gail knew the turnover rate in physician marriages was about fifty percent, and she wasn't even particular about the marital status.

As head nurse in the coronary care unit, Gail knew a lot about reading cardiograms, interpreting arrhythmias and administering cardiac medications. Gail had been doing it for ten years.

Two weeks after Kathleen left, Gail called to Mark from across the CCU nurses' station. She held a cardiogram tracing. Her green eyes frowned.

"Mark, can you come here a minute?"

"Sure, what's up?"

"Look at this tracing. PVCs or APCs? I'm not sure."

Mark looked at the tracing briefly—it only took a moment—then looked at her with surprise.

"APCs, Gail," he said. He couldn't believe Gail would have any trouble making that determination.

"That's what I thought. Thanks." Her green eyes didn't leave his. "How are you doing, Mark?"

"I'm OK."

"Just OK?"

"Better every day."

Gail moved close to him and touched the belt that held up his loose white pants.

"No one is feeding you," she purred, her hand lingering.

"Gail!" he said, removing her hand, but not leaving as he might have done *before*. He was a little intrigued. He had lost weight since Kathleen left. More weight. And he hadn't seen anyone.

"What?" she asked, eyes sparkling, feigning innocent surprise.

"What?"

"Why don't you come over for dinner?"

In Gail's bed later that night, before they made love for the second time, she said, "I knew they were APCs."

"What?"

"I just wanted to get your attention."

"Under false pretenses?"

"Any way. Besides, you wanted me to."

He answered her with a kiss.

Yes, he thought, I probably did.

Chapter Nine

Mark decided he would go to the opening night performance by himself. It would be wrong to take anyone to see Janet's show. It would spoil it for him.

Mark also decided that he should let Janet know he would be there.

They hadn't spoken since early January when she called to tell him he could come to pick up his half of the carefully packed boxes of memories. Mark dialed their old number. It had been disconnected. A live operator provided him with the new number. It had a prefix Mark didn't recognize. It was a toll call. Janet had moved out of the city.

"Janet. It's Mark," he said quietly when she answered.

"Hello." Her voice sounded calm.

"How are you?"

"Fine. Good."

"Where are you living?"

"North of the city along the coast. I'm renting a small cottage. It's part of a large estate," she said with enthusiasm. She loved her new home and its private acres.

"Sounds nice."

"It is."

"How is the show?"

"Great, I think," her voice softened. "It's been wonderful. I have learned so much."

"Different from Lincoln High and Omaha Community?"

"In every way."

"I'm planning to come to opening night . . ." his voice trailed off as if he intended to add, if that's all right with you?

"Good. Kathleen got tickets. I haven't seen her at all. I thought she might come to some rehearsals."

"She's away until July."

"Oh." *Oh!*

"I'm coming alone, but I have two tickets so you'll spot me instantly. I'll be sitting next to the only empty seat in the house."

"I don't think I can see the audience."

"Not Lincoln High, is it?"

Janet always found him in the audience. Sometimes she watched him while she performed as if performing just for him.

"No," she said idly, thinking. Then she said, "Are you really going alone?"

"Yes."

"Why don't you take Leslie? I really want her to see the show. I don't know if she'll go on her own."

"I'd be happy to take her," Mark said immediately. Leslie would not invade his privacy. She would be there for the same reason that he was. Because of Janet. *For* Janet.

"Why don't you call her now? I know she's home because we just spoke. I spent most of the time trying to convince her to go to opening night. I think she wants to."

"I'll call her. What's her number?"

Janet gave it to him.

Before he hung up, Janet said quickly, as if she had to say it quickly or not at all, "Why don't you and Leslie come backstage afterward? I'll leave your names with the stage manager."

At work, Mark and Leslie called each other, paged each other, spoke over the phone frequently:

"Mark, I'm in the ER. This man is a lot sicker than advertised. Can you come down?"

"Leslie, it's time for you to go home. I have to be here all night. Give me the rest of your scut list and leave."

"Mark, Mr. Simpson just died."

"Leslie, the team is making cafeteria rounds in five minutes. Meet us there."

At the hospital, any time day or night, Mark and Leslie talked on the phone. Effortlessly. At the hospital. But as Mark dialed Leslie's home phone number he felt strange. He didn't know a Leslie with a home phone number, a Leslie outside the hospital.

Leslie probably knew every detail of his failed marriage. She almost certainly knew about Janet's meeting with Kathleen. Leslie knew Kathleen because she had taken care of Kathleen's mother. There was little doubt that Leslie knew a great deal about Mark's personal life, but she never mentioned it.

With this phone call, a call suggested by Janet because of tickets arranged by Kathleen, Mark was admitting that Leslie knew all about him.

"Hello?"

"Leslie. It's Mark." He never identified himself when he called her at work. She knew his voice. But now he almost said, It's Mark Taylor.

"Hi."

"I just talked to Janet, and we decided that you and I should go to the opening night performance and then meet her backstage afterward." Mark stopped, a little out of breath. This was ridiculous! At work, he didn't run out of breath when he gave her much longer orders — "Leslie, draw two blood cultures, three if you can, Gram stain the urine and sputum, hang a sed rate, get cardiology to see him stat, then, as soon as that's cooking — *before,* if it starts to take too much time — let's start him on naf and gent . . ."

"You have tickets?" Leslie had just called the theater. The show was sold out.

"Good ones. Kathleen's away but she arranged for tickets," he said. Why not just admit to everything? They both knew Leslie knew about the audition, Kathleen, everything. It was easier. It just felt strange.

"I'd like to go. It's April thirtieth, isn't it?" Only a week away.

"Right. And the next day I leave San Francisco General and return to University Hospital. As your resident on the heme-onc service I think."

"Yes."

"How's the service?" he asked.

Leslie told him in great detail about Jean Watson. By the time they hung up, after a typical at work conversation, they were both surprised and a little disoriented to find themselves in their own apartments instead of in the hospital.

Mark and Leslie had dinner, a light pre-theater soup and sandwich at the restaurant designed precisely for such a meal, *Le Souçon,* located directly across from Union Square Theater on Geary.

"You look pretty dazzling," Mark said finally, in a proud older-brother tone.

Leslie wore a black dress with sheer sleeves, tapered waist and slightly flared skirt. It was looser than the last time she had worn it. Every part of her was thinner, *thin.* Except her breasts. They were still full and round and ample, a sharp contrast of softness against her boney ribcage.

Leslie had piled her chestnut curls on top of her head, secured, barely, with a large gold barrette. She accented her large blue eyes with mascara and a suggestion of blue eye shadow and touched her full lips with soft pink lipstick.

So do you look dazzling, Leslie thought. Mark in a dark suit.

"Well, it's a different look than all white with stethoscope bulges and iodine stains," she murmured.

"You look very nice," he repeated.

Over dinner, Leslie asked, "Are you excited about next year?"

"Next year?"

"Being an R-3! It should be much nicer."

The R-3 schedule was better. Consultant services, less night call, no scut work.

"Yes, it should be," Mark said, distantly, then fell silent.

Leslie was taken aback. She had never seen this before, but she recognized it because Janet had described it so well.

"Sorry," he said recovering quickly, recognizing what had happened. I'm trying, Kathleen, he thought. I'm learning.

"Mark," Leslie began slowly. "If someone told you right now that you could never be a doctor in the United States — you know, some legislative decision banning all Marks from practicing — what would you do?"

Leslie watched his reaction and knew that Janet had been right all the time. Mark didn't want to be a doctor. Just the hypothetical question — the thought of not practicing medicine — made him smile, transported him somewhere else, to a happier place.

"I'd go back to school. Get a graduate degree in English. Teach English. Write maybe."

Mark's answer came quickly, confidently. He had thought about it. He knew what he would do. He knew what he wanted to do.

"That's what my father does. Both my parents actually."

"Really?"

"Yes. My mother is a journalist. Always writing. My father is a professor of English at the University of Washington." Leslie watched Mark's face, then added seriously, carefully, "I know my father would accept you in a minute as a grad student in his department. I know he would."

Mark started to say something then stopped. His expression changed and he shrugged.

"Just a pipe dream, Leslie. Maybe next life."

"This is the only life you can count on having, Mark," she said swiftly, surprising both of them by her urgency.

He smiled. A brotherly smile. A little sad. Then he asked, "What would you do? If no more Leslies could practice?"

"I don't know," she answered. It was a lie. Leslie knew exactly what she would do. She would pull up stakes and move to the nearest country that allowed Leslies to practice. No matter where it was.

But she couldn't tell Mark that.

Oh Mark, she thought. Don't do this to yourself! It's

102

hard enough if you want to be doing it. But if you don't even want it . . . the thought of going through an internship and residency, knowing that you didn't want to be a doctor, that your dreams lay somewhere else . . .

It made Leslie sad.

Now she knew that what Janet had said was true. It had probably destroyed his marriage, and it was probably, slowly, insidiously, destroying him. He hated what he was doing, and he wouldn't talk about it. He wouldn't even admit it.

Mark was the best doctor Leslie knew. *The best*. The words Janet hated. Mark hated what he was doing, but he was driven to continue and driven to be the best.

"*Hey* Leslie! What are you thinking?"

"I was thinking about you," she said honestly, looking into the dark eyes that made her tremble deep inside. "I was worrying about you."

"Don't worry about me," he said. "Come on, it's time to go to the theater."

Leslie and Mark watched *Joanna* from the best seats in the theater. The seats had been hand-picked by Kathleen who knew the acoustics, the lighting and the best view of the stage. Leslie didn't look at Mark. She didn't dare. She was afraid of the emotion she might see in his eyes — regret, pride, love, sadness — as he watched the magic and magnificence of Janet's performance.

Janet *was* magnificent. The entire production was magnificent, obviously destined to be the stunning success Ross MacMillan knew *Joanna* could be.

Mark and Leslie stood in the foyer of the theater during intermission. They were surrounded by the excited, enthusiastic chatter of the delighted theater patrons, but Mark was silent, somber in the midst of gaiety.

"Is this too hard for you, Mark? We could leave," Leslie said finally.

"The only hard part," he said honestly, "is thinking about the four years that she didn't perform — the years she

103

gave it up because I needed to have her at home."

"It's where she wanted to be," Leslie said. Unlike you, she thought, you're not where you want to be.

"Except I wasn't there. Not the way I should have been. I wasted four years of her life. I deprived her of doing what she loves."

"I'm sure Janet doesn't resent it," Leslie knew that Janet didn't resent it.

"I resent it for her," Mark said. Then he stopped abruptly and frowned slightly.

Out of the corner of his eye, as the door to the theater personnel area opened and shut, Mark caught a fleeting glimpse of a woman who looked like Kathleen.

I'm ready for her to come back now, he thought, knowing they still had over two months left to go.

After the performance, after the standing ovations for Janet and then the entire company, Leslie and Mark went backstage.

They didn't stay long; Janet was surrounded. They couldn't get near her. Leslie waved, smiled and shrugged, indicating that it was impossible to traverse the crowded area. Mark smiled and held Janet's gaze for a brief, awkward moment.

Janet returned the smile, then looked away. She was happy he had come, and she was relieved when she saw him leave.

She couldn't see him, talk to him, without aching, and he couldn't see her either.

Mark and Leslie drove to Leslie's apartment in silence. Mark walked her to the door.

"Thanks, Mark," she said.

"You're welcome. See you at eight A.M. for rounds."

Kathleen *was* in the theater, but she had no idea that Mark might have seen her. She had been in and out of town, pacing between Hawaii and Atherton, Bermuda and Atherton, New York and Atherton. She was restless about being away too long even though nothing would happen—

104

restless about being at home, waiting for the time to pass, not trusting herself not to call him.

Kathleen couldn't miss the opening night performance of *Joanna*. Ever since Ross MacMillan — her good friend and sometimes lover — had invited her to be on the Board of Union Square Theater, Kathleen had devoted long energetic hours to it.

Two years ago, Ross and Kathleen hatched the idea of opening a "Broadway" musical on Geary. They worked hard, convincing the board, finding backers, reading script after script until they found *Joanna* and, then, finally, assembling the perfect company.

Joanna was their baby.

Kathleen wasn't going to miss opening night.

Of course, she also wanted to see Mark. Even at a distance. And she wanted to see who occupied the seat next to his.

"This is all a little nuts, Katie," Ross said to her when she explained why she intended to watch the production hidden off stage.

"Maybe. But I am sticking to my plan. I just couldn't miss opening night."

Kathleen knew where Mark would be sitting. She had carefully selected the seats. Kathleen recognized Leslie and watched them both with increasing relief. Kathleen watched the way Mark and Leslie interacted — didn't interact — and knew that the relationship was platonic. Leslie was, simply, a friend of the family. The family that Mark and Janet used to be.

Kathleen relaxed and enjoyed the spectacular performance. Afterward she waited in the private theater lounge while Ross, who produced and directed *Joanna*, went backstage to congratulate his triumphant company. As he left, Kathleen asked him to notice if Mark was backstage and to observe his interactions with Janet if he was.

"You're not in third grade anymore, Katie," he said good-naturedly, smiling as he left.

Kathleen paced while she waited anxiously for Ross to return.

"So?" Kathleen asked the instant he reappeared forty-five minutes later.

"So everyone was absolutely ecstatic including the critics. It's a smash, Katie. We did it."

"So what about Mark? Was he there?"

"Jesus!"

"Ross," she pleaded.

"He was there for under two minutes. A curt nod at each other—Janet was swarmed, of course—from across the room. They looked uncomfortable. Not in love."

"Thanks."

"You're welcome. I'd be a little worried about the woman with Mark. She's gorgeous."

"I'm not worried."

"Good. C'mon, let's go to my place and celebrate."

"I *can't,*" Kathleen said, knowing then that the reason she hadn't slept with anyone in the past two months was because she couldn't. Wouldn't. Didn't want to.

Kathleen's other lovers had never interfered with her sexual relationship with Ross.

"I wish you had given me a little advance warning about this," Ross said amiably. They were good friends.

"I didn't know until right now."

"You are nuts, Katie, really nuts."

Chapter Ten

Jean Watson's condition deteriorated rapidly during the first week of May. Mark and Leslie and Jack Samuels discussed the options—new experimental protocols, different chemotherapy, transplantation—and came up empty. There was nothing more to do.

Jean's marrow showed no signs of recovery. It was almost impossible to transfuse her. She had started to have serious allergic reactions to blood and blood products. Because she had no platelets, she bled. Because she had few red blood cells, she was weak and anemic. Because she had no white blood cells in her bloodstream, no defense against invasion by bacteria, she had infections.

Still her mind and her spirit lived.

When Leslie made her seven A.M. rounds on May first, the morning following the opening night of *Joanna,* she found Jean propped up on her bed pouring over *The San Francisco Chronicle.*

"I've never seen reviews like these. Not from these critics. Your friend Janet! Well, they simply ran out of superlatives and space. I'm surprised they didn't spill over from the theater page to the front page—she's headline news!"

Leslie laughed.

"It was really marvelous. Janet truly *was* sensational. I

wish—" Leslie stopped short.

"You wish I could see it. So do I, my dear," she said in a matter-of-fact tone. Jean refused to feel sorry for herself. "But you can tell me all about it."

"I will. Don't worry. How are you feeling?"

"Bacteremic," Jean said simply. She knew the medical terms. Bacteremia meant bacteria in the bloodstream. Bacteria in a place they shouldn't be, but were, because she had no white blood cells, no defenses. Jean could tell when her bloodstream was contaminated. She felt a certain, indescribable but recognizable way. She asked as lightly as she could, "Who's in my blood today?"

"Klebsiella."

"The *E.coli* are gone?"

"So far."

Five days later two different bacteria, *Serratia marcesans* and *Pseudomonas aeruginosa* and a fungus, *Candida albicans,* all grew from multiple cultures of Jean's blood. Despite antibiotics her blood pressure dropped. She was in shock because of the organisms in her bloodstream.

There was nothing they could do, except make her comfortable.

Mark and Leslie were both on call the night Jean went into shock. It was a new on-call system. The R-1 and R-2 from the same team were on call together instead of on alternate nights. It provided better continuity of care, the schedule makers claimed.

Leslie preferred the new system because, apart from simply being with Mark, seeing even more of him, she trusted him the most medically.

At six in the evening, Leslie went into Jean's room. Carl was at her bedside. The boys had come and gone. They all knew she would die that night. The boys had already said good-bye.

Carl Watson held his wife's frail purple hand.

Jean's eyes flickered open when Leslie entered the room. "Leslie," she whispered, a slight smile.

"Hi," Leslie said and sat down.

Jean's eyes closed. After a few moments her breathing quickened. It was a physiologic response to the acidosis caused by shock.

Leslie and Carl watched Jean. Then Leslie turned to him.

"Are you OK?" she asked barely able to speak herself.

Carl's eyes glistened.

"I want to be with her, touching her, when she goes," he said, his voice shaky with emotion. "But I'm a little afraid."

"Do you want me to stay?" she asked.

"If you have time."

Time? Leslie thought. Do I have time to watch this lovely, beloved woman die?

Leslie switched her pager to the silent-vibratory mode. She would know if she was needed, but the beeper wouldn't sound.

Leslie took Jean's other hand. Was it her imagination or did she feel a squeeze as she took it?

Then they sat, silently, watching, waiting.

Leslie had never watched anyone die. She had *seen* patients die, but she had always been involved in trying to prevent the death. Even at the final moment.

She had never just watched.

After twenty minutes, Jean's breathing pattern changed again. Slow deep breaths. Final breaths.

It wouldn't be long

Leslie took Carl's hand, the hand that didn't hold Jean's, and held it.

When she did, they formed a circle. Jean's hands were held by her beloved husband and her dear Leslie, her surrogate daughter. The circle was complete when Leslie reached for Carl's hand.

Jean looked peaceful when she died. She simply exhaled one breath and didn't take another. It took Leslie a moment to realize that it was over.

Leslie and Carl didn't move after Jean died. They continued to hold Jean's hands and each others.

Leslie detected the warmth leaving Jean's hand. It made

109

her feel terribly empty and sad.

She didn't want Carl to feel it. He needed to remember the warmth. It would be too much for him to feel the warmth, the final vestige of life, leaving his wife's hand.

"Mr. Watson," Leslie began, a little firm, a little urgent. It was too much for her, too.

Carl looked at her, his cheeks damp with tears.

"She's gone," Leslie whispered, controlling her own emotion with difficulty. "Shall we go?"

Leslie pulled gently at his hand, the one she still held. Carl moved with her without resistance.

The hallway lights were bright, too bright. Carl and Leslie squinted as they emerged from the dimly lit room. Leslie signaled silently to the head nurse to let her know that Jean Watson had died.

All the arrangements had been made. After, *only* after Carl Watson left, the efficient, impersonal mechanics of the paperwork and red tape that accompanied death would be put into action.

Leslie walked down the hall with Carl to the visitors' waiting room. The boys were there. Leslie had assumed they had gone.

But, of course, they wouldn't leave. They waited for their father. To be with him. To take him home.

Leslie withdrew quickly. Carl Watson was where he needed to be. Five minutes before, her pager had vibrated. The telephone number indicated on the lighted dial was that of the emergency room.

Leslie dialed the number. Mark answered.

"Anything wrong?" he asked. Leslie usually answered pages immediately. Even this slight delay surprised Mark.

"Mrs. Watson just died. I was with Mr. Watson."

"Oh. Is everything OK?" Mark should have just asked the question that was really in his mind: Are you OK?

"Yes. Fine. What do we have?" Meaning, what does the admission you must be paging me about have wrong with him or her?

"We have a fifty-year-old man — Mr. Peterson — with liver cancer who has hepatic encephalophathy," Mark said.

110

It was the hematology/oncology service after all.

"I'll be right down."

Six hours and two admissions later, at midnight, Mark found Leslie sitting huddled in the doctors' write-up area staring out the window into the blackness. Mark closed the door behind him as he entered the small room.

He had been worrying about her.

"Leslie?"

Leslie spun around, surprised. Her blue eyes glistened, brilliant blue, wet with tears.

"Why did she have to die, Mark?" Leslie asked weakly. Hot tears spilled onto her cheeks.

Mark was beside her in an instant. Without hesitation he put his arms around her and held her, rocking her gently, stroking her dark curls.

"It was so sad," Leslie said finally, talking into his chest. "It was so awful, just *watching* her die. Not being able to stop it."

Leslie shook her head and began to cry again. Mark blinked back his own tears and whispered, "I know, honey. I know."

As Mark spoke his lips brushed against her soft chestnut hair.

Toward the end of May, on their second to last night on call together, Mark found Leslie sitting by the picture window on the eleventh floor.

It was five A.M.

"So this is where the Night Stalker lurks," he said, startling her.

Leslie spun around and suppressed a gasp.

He is so handsome! she thought.

Mark stood in front of her, his dark hair tousled, his baggy white pants pulled tight at his slender waist with an old leather belt. Instead of his usual oxford shirt and necktie Mark wore a blue, surgical scrub shirt. The deep V-neck

111

revealed a few dark, straight hairs on his bare, white chest. The short, loose sleeves showed his strong, sinewy, pale forearms. His white coat, his shirt and tie, his medical armamentarium, except for the pager which was clipped to his belt, were elsewhere—probably folded neatly in his on call room.

Mark stood in front of her, looking almost naked. Just Mark, a critical minimum of loose clothing and a pager. The bare essentials.

"Where she lurks when it's safe to stop stalking. When the sun comes up," Leslie said. Then she added a question, "Or do we have some business?"

"No. I just had six hours of uninterrupted sleep thanks to you. I'm wide awake. Rested. I decided to see if the rumors were true. If you really, in the eleventh month of your internship, still pace."

"This is why I do it, you know," Leslie answered a little coolly, her voice a little sharp. She gestured toward the view of sunrise over Golden Gate Park, the bay and the bridge. "It's so beautiful."

"I wasn't being critical, Leslie," Mark said quickly as he sat down across from her. His view was northeast toward Pacific Heights with its elegant condominium buildings shining in the new day sun.

"I'm a bit sensitive today, I guess," Leslie said.

"Why?"

"Because yesterday Greg signed out to me, at *noon,* to go jogging. His so-called stable service included two oozing GI bleeders and a leukemic with a temperature of one hundred four."

"Sounds like Greg," Mark murmured critically.

"Anyway, I nonverbally registered my annoyance," Leslie said, then hesitated. Maybe she didn't want to tell Mark about this after all.

Mark looked into her blue eyes. Eyes, he had learned over the past eleven months, that could deliver clear, specific messages. Eyes that could make direct blows. Remarkable dark blue eyes that weren't always so merry or cheerful. As the months passed, Leslie's always positive façade yielded occasionally to the pressures of fatigue and the realities, the frustrations and the lack of perfection she encountered. Leslie never said anything, never lost her temper, but her eyes effectively communicated annoyance, impatience, irritation and even censure.

Mark had never been on the receiving end of one of Leslie's glacial glances, but he had seen them delivered — ice cold, unyielding, uncompromising. Leslie could set her jaw and dig in with the best of them.

Mark hoped she would never look at him that way. He hoped that she would never have cause.

"I'm sure you did," he said. "So, what did Greg say?"

"He said," Leslie said slowly, looking out the window, embarrassed, "that I was strung so tight if he touched me I'd twang."

Mark started a laugh but suppressed it as he caught the shy, almost hurt expression in her eyes.

"It's sort of a cute remark, especially coming from an idiot like Greg."

"He's more than an idiot."

"How did his patients do?"

"Fine of course. By the time he jogged back two hours later, I had taken care of everything."

"So he's not such an idiot, is he?"

"I thought it was sort of an unfair remark," Leslie said.

"And untrue," Mark said, hesitating a moment. Then he added gently, carefully, "When I touched you, you didn't twang."

She had been so soft! A little wounded kitten cuddling into him for protection. As Mark held the boniness of her ribs, he felt the womanly fullness of her breasts, the soft warmth of her skin and the strong rapid pounding of her heart.

When you touched me, she thought as she stared at the shimmering sunlight on the azure bay, when you put your arms around me, I wanted to stay there forever.

Mark and Leslie sat in silence for many minutes, watching the new day begin.

At last Leslie decided to ask him. It was a risk. It could

113

make him mad, but she remembered the closeness of that night, the night Jean Watson died, the night he held her. She knew how much she cared about him—about what happened to him—even if it had nothing to do with her.

"Have you decided?" she asked.

"Decided?"

"To quit medicine," she said quietly. There. She had said it.

"*Quit* medicine?" Mark repeated, surprised but not angry.

Quit was as charged a word as *best*. Quit, something you never did. Best, something you always were.

"Yes. Quit."

"What made you ask that?"

"You told me the night we saw *Joanna* that you didn't want to be a doctor," Leslie said flatly, as if it were fact. They both knew he hadn't said *that*.

"I never said I didn't want to be a doctor," he said, amazed, thoughtful, but still not angry.

"No. But that's what I heard."

"Oh. Well," he began then stopped. When he spoke again, the words came slowly, tentatively, as if their very utterance might cause disaster. "Maybe I don't want to be a doctor."

The words were spoken and nothing terrible happened. Leslie's eyes, smiling, not shocked, met his.

"Maybe I don't," Mark repeated, his voice stronger. "I've never said that out loud before, Leslie. It's only been in the past few months that I've even begun to admit it to myself."

"So, are you going to get out?" she asked again.

"You make it sound so simple."

"It is simple. Hand me your pager. I'll turn it in for you."

"The mechanics might be simple, but the decision is not so easy . . . lots of complicating factors. I'm not even sure that I want out. There's a lot about medicine that I enjoy, that I would give up reluctantly. Would miss. Maybe I can find a niche that would allow me to practice medicine and . . ." Mark paused.

"And do what you really want to do?" Leslie added

quickly.

"And give me time to read. Write maybe."

"But you are thinking that you *might* quit, someday, aren't you?" Leslie pushed. Mark had to be desensitized to the word *quit*. A lot of angry people would shout it at him.

"I'm just beginning to think about what I can do. What I should do."

"You *can* do anything. You *should* get out. Now," Leslie said decisively.

Her tone took Mark aback. He looked at her and smiled. In the past month, working with her, making decisions with her, taking care of patients with her and seeing her enthusiasm, Mark had thought very little about quitting. It had been so pleasant.

"Is that what those crystal-blue eyes see for me in the future?"

"I'm not predicting what you will do," she said. Probably chairman of the Department of Medicine at Harvard, she thought. *The Best*. "Only what, for the record, for whatever it matters, *I* think you should do."

"Because you know I'm no damned good at this doctor business?" he asked, half teasing. He couldn't understand why Leslie felt so strongly.

"You know what I think about you. You're—" Leslie paused. There was no other choice. He was, and she had to say it—"the best."

Three nights later, their last night on call together, Mark was already waiting for her at the eleventh floor window when she arrived at five-thirty in the morning.

"I thought you went to bed at eleven," she said, her heart pounding. Why was he here?

"I did. I'm well rested. I wanted to talk to you," he said as he slid over on the plastic, turquoise couch with the blond, wooden handles to make room for her.

Leslie sat down, instead, in the chair across from him.

"You could talk to me, any time, during the day," she said.

115

"Not really."

Leslie knew what he meant. It was impossible to *talk* — about anything but medicine — while they were working. But this time, this quiet dawn time when everything was under control, when most house staff would be asleep anyway, this time was, somehow, different.

Leslie waited.

"I just wanted to tell you what a good doctor I think you are," Mark said. It sounded awkward. "Around here no one ever tells you when you're doing a good job. They just tell you when you've screwed up. I know you know I've felt this way since the beginning of your internship, but I wanted to tell you again."

"It sounds like you're saying good-bye," Leslie said quietly.

"I'm not. In fact I just saw the schedule. You and I will both be at San Francisco General in July."

"Oh! Well, then, thank you. It's been wonder—"

Mark held up his hand. "Enough! Neither of us is good at this."

Leslie smiled. Then she said earnestly but with a slight twinkle, "I know why you liked working with me this month."

"Why?"

"Because you've gotten lots of sleep."

"True. But that's not why—"

"Which you need," Leslie continued, "because of your active social life. Which, judging from the nurses is . . . uh . . . something."

"Oh. They don't really talk about it do they?" Mark asked, genuinely surprised.

"Mark, it's become a part of their daily report!"

Mark frowned. He didn't like the idea of being discussed.

"I'm not being critical at all!" Leslie said quickly. "No one is being critical. They all like you. Respect you."

"They *all?*" Mark asked soberly.

"Gail. Julie. *Gail.* Chris. . ."

"It doesn't seem right," he said. It was nobody's business. They shouldn't be talking about it. About his life and God knows what else.

"It's OK. Harmless. They probably discuss it around me more than anyone else."

"Why?"

"They assume, because I'm your shadow about every other month, that I know something. Which I don't of course," Leslie added.

"Know something like what?"

"Like if you're using them."

"They're using me."

"They know that," Leslie said quietly. She had heard more than she wanted to about Mark in their beds. Leslie hated hearing about it, but they sought her out looking for information she didn't have. Leslie added, "They seem to sense that there's a Kathleen out there somewhere and that when she returns the party's over."

"They're right," Mark said simply, deciding that the party was over now.

"Oh."

"You like her, don't you? You saw her quite a bit when her mother was here."

"Sure. When is she returning? Janet said something about July."

Janet.

"Is this a fact-finding mission?" he asked.

"No!" Leslie bristled.

"She's coming back in July. By the eleventh," Mark said quickly, pleasantly, sorry that he had offended her. He was annoyed that they talked about him, annoyed that they involved Leslie and sorry that she knew about him and them.

"You think this is all pretty strange . . . sleazy . . . don't you?" he asked bluntly.

Leslie shook her head slowly. Her eyes, sad and thoughtful and blue, met his as she said evenly, "This has all been such a hard time for you. For you and for Janet. There's no right, or wrong, way to deal with it. You just have to get through it. Survive it."

117

Yes, she thought it was sleazy—not that he did it as much as the fact that they talked about it.

"How is Janet?" he asked a few moments later.

"Busy with the show. We talk but I haven't seen her since opening night. She sounds all right."

Chapter Eleven

At nine o'clock on July ninth Mark dialed the telephone number to Kathleen's home in Atherton.

Kathleen answered.

"You're back."

"Just. An hour ago." In that hour, Kathleen had learned that there were no messages, no letters from him. Nothing to indicate that the plans had changed or to suggest that he didn't want to see her. "We decided not to stay for the wedding."

"The wedding?"

"Charles and Diana. You know. The king and queen to be. They aren't tying the royal knot until July twenty-ninth, and I had a birthday party to go to."

"You weren't really invited?"

"No," Kathleen admitted. "But of course we didn't try."

"So," he said gently, "How was it?"

Meaning the past few months. Kathleen knew what he meant, but she was euphoric. She could tell from his voice how much he wanted to see her. She could afford to tease him just a little.

"Fabulous! Did you watch any of it? The Connors-Borg semi-final was the best tennis ever. I'm sure that's why Borg lost to McEnroe in the final. He looked exhausted. McEnroe's great, of course. We'll probably be watching him for years to come. And Chris Evert Lloyd won—a major victory for twenty-seven-year-old women every-

"where."

"Kathleen," he said sternly, knowing she was toying with him. "How was it?"

"The longest, loneliest four months of my life. How about you?"

"The same. But it was a good idea. You were right."

"About everything?"

"About everything."

"Hmm. Did you enjoy opening night?"

"How did—you were there, weren't you?"

"I couldn't miss it. You didn't see me . . ."

"A glimpse. But of course you said you'd be away for four months," Mark's tone sharpened.

"I was away from *you*. Mostly out of town. But not the whole time. No."

"*Spying* on me?" he pushed, sharply.

"*No*, Mark. I saw you opening night. Period. Betsey couldn't believe I didn't drive by your apartment—she knows about my insatiable curiosity—to look for strange cars. I told her that all the cars around there are strange," Kathleen said lightly. Then she added seriously, "But of course that's not the point. The point was your time and your privacy. I don't want to know what you did. Or with whom."

As long as you come back to me, she thought.

"Good," he said, still edgy.

Kathleen was silent, blinking back tears.

"Kitzy, are you there?" he asked, finally, his voice softer.

"Yes."

"So?"

"So can we take it from the top? Starting with the longest, loneliest four months part?"

"Sure. Maybe we should continue this in person?"

"Do I get to see you before your birthday?"

"I hope so. I'm on call on my birthday."

"No. Mark, didn't you get promoted to an R-3?" she teased.

"I made the cut; but we're still on every sixth, and July eleventh happens to be one of them."

"Every sixth. It has a beautiful ring to it," Kathleen purred.

"It's all better, Kathleen. Everything's better. I'm going to enjoy this year," he said. Then he added gently, "We're going to enjoy this year."

"Good," she breathed.

Kathleen arrived at Mark's apartment the following evening with her arms full of packages.

"What's this?" he asked as he took the packages, filling his arms with them instead of *her*.

"Birthday presents and birthday cake," she said as she followed him into the living room. She noticed the champagne chilling in a mixing bowl filled with ice and the tray of cheese and crackers.

Kathleen smiled. Mark was planning what she had planned: a mature refined reunion, champagne and hors d'oeuvres and quiet conversation. They would spend hours telling each other about the past four months. And only after that would they . . .

Mark put down the packages and turned to face her.

"Hi," he said gazing into her violet eyes. He wanted to talk to her, laugh with her, hold her and love her. All at once. He was greedy for her. For all of her.

"Hi," she sighed. *How I have missed you.*

"Would you like some champagne?"

"Sure," she whispered. *I don't care. I would like you please.*

"Not really?" he asked. He walked toward her, smiling lovingly.

Kathleen trembled as he approached. She had dreamed of this moment for so long. That Mark would want her still. Her heart raced as she saw the desire in his eyes.

So much for a mature refined reunion.

They kissed as they undressed each other urgently, needing to be as close as possible as quickly as possible. Needing to feel whole, complete, again.

"Hi," he whispered into her shiny black hair.

121

"Hi," she breathed into his strong pale chest.

"I've missed you. Too much."

"Too much?"

"I need you now." *Right now.*

"I need you now, too," she whispered as he laid her down on the couch. She welcomed him onto her and inside her. Where he belonged.

"Kathleen," he whispered. "Kathleen."

"Do you think our relationship is purely sexual?" she asked, exhausted, giggling.

"No," he said firmly. "I know it's not."

Mark knew, because he had had several purely sexual relationships in the past four months. Kathleen knew the reason for Mark's confidence and was glad about it, but she didn't want to think about him with anyone else. Ever.

"Good."

"Are you going to move in with me? Live with me?" he asked her four hours after she had returned to his arms.

"Am I invited?"

"Yes."

"Then I will."

"Do we need a bigger apartment?" he asked, idly stroking her silky black hair as she nuzzled against his neck. "I mean your wardrobe alone . . ."

"I don't think I'll move all my worldly possessions," she said. Not yet. Maybe someday. She hoped. "Besides, Atherton is an easy commute. I have time to dash back and forth during the day. Visit my parents while you're working. This is a cozy place for us."

"You've made it cozy. What will you do all day, Kathleen? Won't you get bored?"

"After I run out of domestic things, I'll do what I do every day. Lots of different things. I won't be bored."

"What *do* you do every day?"

"Meetings, shopping, seeing friends, committees, projects. I keep very busy."

"You seem to. Oh, there's a party Saturday night at the

Yacht Club. Not as fancy as the Celebration, or any Carlton Club Kids' function, but a Department of Medicine tradition. I have to go to it."

Kathleen waited, wondering.

"OK?" he asked, finally.

"Do I go too? With you?" she asked weakly, unsure if he meant they both would go.

"Kathleen! Of course. Of *course."*

"Your friend Leslie doesn't like me," Kathleen whispered in Mark's ear, licking it briefly at the same time. They were dancing, moving slowly together, their long lean bodies draped comfortably together, swaying rhythmically. Mark and Kathleen didn't cling to each other. They didn't need to. The leisurely rhythm of their bodies, although chaste, revealed their true intimacy to anyone who was watching. Their bodies knew each other well.

People *were* watching. Many people. Gail, Julie and Chris watched with great interest. So this dark lovely creature with the violet eyes and aristocratic grace was their competition?

Good-bye, Mark. *Adieu.*

Leslie watched them in brief glimpses, too. She didn't want to, but it was impossible not to.

"Of course she likes you," Mark whispered back.

"No, she's glowering at me. Not glowering, actually. That's too strong. Just shooting ice-blue icicles my way."

"You're over-reading," Mark said, but he wondered. The messages of Leslie's eyes were always clear, exquisite, articulate communiqués, and Kathleen was a good observer. Neither woman was likely to get her signals crossed. He added, "She has no reason to dislike you."

Kathleen said nothing. She knew she was right. As the evening wore on Kathleen thought she learned the reason for Leslie's iciness. It wasn't that Leslie disliked Kathleen. Not really. It was just that Leslie cared so very much about Mark.

Kathleen wondered if Mark even knew.

No, she decided as she watched Mark speak with Leslie briefly as the party ended. He doesn't know.

"I think I should get a job," Kathleen told Betsey during lunch ten days later. It was the last week in July. They had spent the morning in San Francisco, buying the final pieces of Betsey's trousseau, and had returned to Atherton for lunch at the Carlton Club.

Betsey, her wedding only three weeks and one dress size away, picked at her watercress sandwich while Kathleen ate a seafood crepe.

"A job!" Betsey gasped. "For heaven's sake, why?"

"I think it makes Mark nervous that I don't work."

"But you do work. You're on a zillion committees, boards, charities. . . ."

"I know. But it all seems flighty to him. Frivolous."

"Kathleen, friend, you are flighty and frivolous. Except," Betsey added thoughtfully, "when it comes to Mark."

"I care about him," Kathleen said gently.

"I know. Does he know how rich you are? Does he know what your father does? Does he know your mother's maiden name? That would be an eye-opener: how many streets, buildings, squares, monuments and bridges in the Bay Area have the same name?"

"He doesn't know any of it. Except what Father does. Do you realize that I earn more in a month, from the trust from my grandparents, than Mark earns in *one year?*"

"You're kidding. I thought doctors—"

"Were rich? So did I. But I know for a fact that interns and residents get small salaries. Especially when you consider the number of hours they work. Doctors make good solid livings. Some surgeons, like neurosurgeons I think, make a lot, but they work *hard*. I can't believe how hard Mark and his friends work."

"So, not very many rich doctors? Just a myth?"

"No. Of course they make very good livings compared to other people who work for a living. But," Kathleen said soberly, "nothing compared to our wealth. I think doctors

124

are targets because they're identifiable. High visibility. Nobody even knows about us. Our names, as a family, appear every year on the ten, twenty or thirty richest lists, but nobody really knows that those families are composed of kids, like us, who are multimillionaires. We're hidden. We would really be targets if anyone knew we existed."

Betsey and Kathleen and their friends had been trained to keep low profiles because wealth had some very high price tags: kidnappings, ransoms, swindlers, drug dealers, gold diggers. No one looking at Kathleen or Betsey could guess at the wealth they represented. They looked like two young working women having lunch.

Except that they were having lunch at the Carlton Club. That was a clue. But they were safe there. They were safe with each other. It was why they stayed together. Why the Carlton Club Kids were all, still, best friends.

"Do you want to get a job?"

"No. Of course not! I am completely happy, and I'm already too busy."

"What would you do if you weren't rich, if you didn't have enough money to live on?"

Kathleen played with her seafood crepe for a moment before answering. Then her violet eyes sparkled, "I don't know. I guess if I couldn't find someone like us, which I couldn't because I wouldn't know *we* existed, I'd just have to go out and find some rich doctor!"

Chapter Twelve

"Hi," Mark said as he walked into the small lab in the intensive care unit at San Francisco General Hospital.

Leslie spun around, startled.

Everyone was a little on edge, watchful. The ICU was housing a very important, and very ill, patient. He was a police informant. He hadn't yet been able to tell his story. The people who wanted him never to tell it had already made one—very nearly successful—attempt on his life.

Everyone who worked in the ICU was on alert. Even though the patient was heavily guarded, the police were fearful of another attempt on his life. The police told them all to be on the lookout for someone who looked out of place, who didn't belong. Someone whom they didn't recognize. . .

But it was July. Half the physician staff was new. There were the interns, their eager faces just beginning to show the inevitable signs of strain and fatigue, and there were new residents, ones who had transferred from other programs. Then, there were fellows who had completed residencies elsewhere and had come to San Francisco for subspecialty training.

Leslie met new people every day. On her way to the lab just now, she had seen yet another new face. He was a handsome man with stylish blond hair, intelligent blue eyes and a long white coat signifying his status as a fellow. Probably the new nephrology fellow, Leslie decided. She knew a patient had just been admitted to the ICU for emergency hemodialysis. He smiled at her as she passed him. She returned the smile but didn't stop. She was carrying the blood gas she had just drawn. She would meet him later.

"Mark! Hi," she breathed. Then, as her edginess vanished, she teased, "Is this one of your nights? A cameo appearance?"

"Just you wait. You'll be amazed how quickly every sixth night rolls around. This is my fifth night on call of the year, and it's only July thirtieth."

"Well, it's my *tenth,* but who's counting?" Leslie countered lightly. Then, looking at his slightly tanned, less gaunt face and his relaxed brown eyes, she added, "You look good. Rested."

Happy, she thought. She realized that he hadn't been happy before, but she hadn't known it. It was only obvious in retrospect.

"I am. This R-3 business is just fine."

"You're on the infectious disease consult service, aren't you? Is it a good elective?"

"Very good."

"Anything new on AIDS?"

"Just that the epidemic is continuing with dramatic doubling rates. Most people think it will turn out to be a virus. Transmission probably like hepatitis B."

"Sexual transmission we all know about. Blood, too?"

"Probably blood. That's the rumor. Cases in hemophiliacs are being recognized."

"Huh."

"Nobody's sure, of course, but it would be a good time not to get a blood transfusion in New York or LA. Or *here.*"

"It's such an awful disease," Leslie said, then, focusing on the blood gas machine and the blood sample she had brought into the lab, she said, "Damn!"

127

"What?"

"I get so tired of people using this blood gas machine and not flushing it with heparin afterward!"

"Is it clotted?" Mark asked, moving beside her to inspect the decrepit machine and its slender plastic tubing.

"The clot can be worked out, but it's such a nuisance."

"Allow me, your friendly mellow R-3."

Leslie laughed.

"I'm a little snappy aren't I?" she asked.

"A little."

"Have you met my intern, Hal? Excuse me, *Dr.* Hal Rollins."

"OK, so Hal thinks he has a few answers," Mark said, laughing.

"A *few?*"

"All."

"You told me, almost precisely a year ago, that by this time this year I'd have an intern with a crush on me, padding obediently behind me, wagging his tail and drooling. Instead, I get Hal, who, by his own humble assessment, is God's gift to medicine."

"In a month he'll have a crush on you. When he learns how little he really knows."

"Grrr. This is his blood gas I'm running. His patient. Hal didn't think he needed a repeat gas, so . . ."

"So you're just quietly doing it? Not good, Leslie. You have to be tough."

"I have to make sure that the patients are OK, right? Top priority."

"Yeah. But you have to be tough with these little whippersnappers, too," Mark said firmly. "OK, give me the syringe. The clot's gone."

"My hero," Leslie said, still fuming at the thought of her intern. "Hal's the one who probably clogged it up."

"Oh," Mark said, looking at the label on the blood gas syringe that Leslie handed him. "This is from the fellow who turned state's evidence."

"*Tried* to," Leslie said. "Got shot before he gave them the key information."

"How's he doing?"

"I think he'll get another chance. Today he's much better."

"That's why the ICU is teeming with police."

"Uh-huh. What do they think, someone's going to walk in and shoot him again, in broad daylight, in the ICU?"

"That's *exactly* what they think."

"It could happen," Leslie said firmly. But it was what she and everyone else feared. It was why they were all so edgy, why they were all so watchful.

"It could. Anyone in a white coat could get in. Assuming he, or she, wasn't wearing army fatigues or carrying an ill-concealed submachine gun instead of a stethoscope. They'd just have to select a non-thug-looking psychopath—"

"Even thug-looking. Even battle fatigues—"

"Leslie, you really are in a charming mood tonight. Modern medicine hasn't come to that. I haven't spotted one thug, or one battle-fatigue-wearing intern, in this year's group. Maybe in the early seventies . . . but we're in a conservative era. Even Hal."

"Especially Hal. Those bow ties," Leslie said, laughing at last, shaking her head. "Bow ties!"

"OK. Here are your results," Mark said, reading the dials on the machine. "The pH is seven point—"

Three shots rang out. Then screaming. Shouting. Running. More shots.

Mark and Leslie froze.

"Stay here," Mark said, moving toward the door.

Leslie grabbed his arm.

"You stay here, too, Mark."

The door crashed open. A blond man, wearing a long white coat and carrying a black gun, entered and pulled the door shut behind him.

Leslie and Mark retreated to the far corner of the tiny lab.

"Don't say a word," the man hissed as he faced them.

When Leslie saw his face she gasped. It was the same man—the one who she had decided was the new nephrology fellow—she had seen moments ago. The man who looked like a board certified internist, not a thug. The man with the intelligent blue eyes . . .

The eyes were transformed now. They were wild, darting, crazed. *Crazy.* They were also a little euphoric, manic, triumphant. He had probably successfully killed his target, Leslie's patient. Now he only had to escape.

He was prepared to take hostages. Or to leave more victims.

He pressed his back against the door and leveled the gun at Mark and Leslie. He realized in an instant that there was no way out of the tiny lab except by the door through which he had entered.

The assassin grabbed Leslie's arm and pulled her beside him.

"C'mon, little nursey. You're comin' with me."

He jerked her toward him and held her, squeezing her arm until it ached. Then he put the gun to her head, pressing its cold barrel against her temple, and put his finger on the trigger.

"One peep and you're dead."

The room was silent except for the sound of their breathing. Outside, in the hallway, the shouting and footsteps had become distant. They were chasing the assassin out of the hospital.

But he was still in the ICU.

He's bleeding, Mark realized. The man had been shot in the leg. Large drops of blood splashed onto the linoleum floor.

Surely, Mark thought, he left a trail of blood leading to the lab.

Despite the silence from the other side of the door — too silent given the commotion that would be going on in the ICU in the aftermath — they must be out there. The police must know exactly where the murderer is.

They probably have the hallway sealed off, Mark decided. How many guns are pointed at the door? What if they decide to open fire, believing the man is alone in the lab? If they open fire, they will hit Leslie.

The man held Leslie in front of him, pressed against the

door. The gun was still pointed at her head. His finger was on the trigger.

Mark couldn't let it happen. Ten more seconds of silence, he decided, hoping it wasn't too much.

He counted patiently, evenly.

Nine. Ten.

"HEY!" Mark yelled and lunged at the startled assassin, who spun, the barrel of the gun leaving Leslie's temple and ramming, as he pulled the trigger, into Mark's chest.

"Mark!" Leslie screamed, rushing past the man who bolted for the door, opened it and ran into a circle of police. Trapped, he became frantic and started shooting, wounding two officers before he died.

"Mark, Mark," Leslie said, over and over, as she knelt beside him.

The bullet had created a gaping hole in Mark's chest. He gasped for breath. Despite the pain, he lay still. Afraid. In shock.

Bright red blood spurted from the wound and onto Leslie's face and chest as she hovered over him. Bright red blood. *Arterial* blood. He was losing blood quickly. With each heartbeat — and his heart was beating rapidly — another large spurt of blood left Mark's body.

He would bleed out, die from acute blood loss, very quickly. His strong young heart would pump harder and harder. Each pump more and more lethal.

Unless and until the hole in the artery was closed.

Leslie reached into the wound in Mark's chest with her left hand. She felt the hot blood pulsing toward her. She tried to determine the direction with the sensitive tips of her fingers, praying she would be able to reach the severed artery.

What if she couldn't find it?

What if her fingers wouldn't reach?

As Leslie rammed her hand inside his chest, deeper and deeper, she felt his shattered ribs and the sharp points of the broken bone tearing her own skin. She felt the warmth of his body, his hot pulsing blood and his lacy delicate lung moving, gasping against her hand.

"Leslie, let's get him out of here. Down to the trauma room."

The hall outside the tiny lab was now crowded with police, nurses, house staff, camera crews and reporters. The lab was too small for more than one or two more people. They couldn't take care of Mark there. They needed to get him into a big room with equipment and a trained trauma team.

"I have to —" Leslie said as her fingers finally reached the artery that was allowing Mark's life to bleed away. She gave her hand one final shove, stretching her fingers to the area of pulsation. With all her strength she pressed her fingers over the hot, slippery vessel.

The bleeding slowed.

"C'mon, Les!" The people in the hallway were getting anxious. They had no idea why Leslie wouldn't get out of the lab. Why she wouldn't move to let them get to Mark so they could take him to the ER.

"I'm tamponading an arterial bleeder," she said. "I have it now, so we can move him. But I can't take my hand away."

Until then they had only seen her back, her body hunched over Mark feverishly doing something. She turned slightly as she spoke. They saw her face, drenched in Mark's blood, and the red wetness of her chest.

They knew instantly she was right. They could all see how much blood he had lost. If she had the bleeding stopped, the top priority for all of them as they transported him to the trauma room was to protect her hold on the artery.

"Can we clamp it here, Leslie?"

In time, as soon as possible, Leslie's finger would be replaced by a metal clamp. Properly positioned, it would hold the artery closed until they could get him to surgery.

"I don't know. Maybe. I really have a good hold right now." Once she had the bleeding slowed, she had repositioned her hand, wedging the palm against the sharp bones of his broken ribs. She had a good, firm grasp of Mark's chest wall and of the severed artery.

"OK. Let's move him, then. He needs to be intubated as soon as possible."

The hole in Mark's chest did not allow him to breathe effectively. Each breath, each gasp sucked air in through the hole, putting pressure on the lung, preventing its normal expansion, making it collapse.

Mark was unconscious. He needed many things all at once. He needed an endotracheal tube, intravenous lines, blood, oxygen and surgery. One and a half minutes after they left the ICU lab, Mark was in the trauma room in the emergency room, intubated, with two intravenous lines. Blood work had been sent.

San Francisco General Hospital was one of the first and best trauma centers in the country. A team of trained doctors, each with a specific pre-assigned task, quickly and efficiently worked to give each trauma patient the best possible chance of survival.

The senior surgical resident was the trauma chief. During his six-month rotation as trauma chief, he never left the hospital. Dr. Ed Moore was already in the emergency room when Mark was shot, caring for a patient who had been stabbed in the thigh. Ed wanted to get the other patient stabilized so that he could devote his full attention to Mark when he reached the trauma room.

Ed Moore quickly moved beside Leslie.

"OK, Les," he said brusquely. Meaning, I've got him now.

Leslie looked at Ed and said calmly, firmly, "I have my finger on the severed artery."

Ed drew in a breath when he saw Leslie's bloodied face. "Hold onto it, Les. I'll get a clamp."

Ed eased the long silver clamp beside Leslie's finger. They couldn't see anything. It had to be done by feel. Leslie had to direct Ed.

"There," she said when she felt the cold clamp near the tip of her finger.

Ed opened and closed the clamp, taking a blind bite at the artery.

"OK. Let go."

133

As soon as Leslie released the pressure exerted by her finger, the blood, Mark's blood, spurted out at them.

"Damn," Ed sputtered.

Quickly Leslie pressed her fingers against the artery again. It was getting harder to maintain the seal. Her fingers cramped. The pain from the cuts in her own hand, cuts from Mark's broken, shattered ribs, throbbed in her palm. The new hot burst of blood made the artery even more slippery, more difficult to compress.

They tried again.

And again.

On the fourth try the clamp closed over the artery. When Leslie removed her fingers, there was no bleeding.

"Operating room in two minutes," Ed barked. "Where's the blood? I want two units—in him!—before we operate. And we're operating in two minutes."

With the endotracheal tube, oxygen and an attentive anesthesiologist managing Mark's breathing for him, Mark had regained consciousness.

Leslie saw Mark beckon to Ed. She had withdrawn to a corner of the trauma room as soon as the artery was successfully clamped. The energy and emotion that had enabled Leslie to act as quickly as she had now gave way to exhaustion and fear. Now that she was no longer an active participant, preoccupied with her task, she had time to think. And worry.

But Mark was in good hands. The best.

And he was talking! Leslie stood up straight as she watched Mark. Awake, alert, trying to communicate with Ed. Mark couldn't speak because of the endotracheal tube, but he clearly had a message. Leslie saw him gesture, saw them give him a pen and paper and saw him write something which he handed to Ed.

Leslie watched Ed's expression as he read what Mark had written. She watched Ed frown, then scowl. He began to speak animatedly, then angrily, at Mark.

Leslie couldn't hear what they said. The room was too full of other noises. It was filled with the sound of nurses and doctors and technicians making certain that Mark was stable, finalizing arrangements for the imminent transfer to the operating room and calling out laboratory results done on Mark's blood.

"The pO2 on the last gas is 280."

"Thanks! What's the pH?" the anesthesiologist asked.

"Seven point four."

"Great."

"His crit is twenty-eight."

A brief silence ensued, a break in the general hubbub.

"Did you hear that, Mark? Your crit is twenty-eight. And that's before rehydration. You've lost a helluva lot of blood," Ed Moore shouted, his voice especially loud because of the momentary silence in the trauma room.

Ed looked across the room at Leslie, at her blood-stained face and clothes. It gave him a rough idea — a grim idea — of Mark's blood loss, and he hadn't even seen the pool of blood in the ICU laboratory.

Leslie saw Mark's head move slightly from side to side. A clear negative message.

"OK, Mark, old buddy, I'll give it my goddamned best shot."

Ed walked toward Leslie and snapped to whoever was listening, "Where's Dr. T?"

Everyone was listening. Everyone had overheard Ed's last remarks to Mark. Everyone was wondering what had happened.

"Scrubbing," the head nurse answered, remembering that Dr. Moore had just asked a rather specific question.

"Good."

Dr. T., as they fondly referred to Dr. Jon Thomas, was the attending trauma surgeon. Dr. T. didn't scrub in on every case. It wasn't necessary. His trauma chief and the other surgery residents were highly trained. But Dr. T. came in for the critical cases. For cases like Mark.

Leslie was glad he would be there.

Ed stopped when he reached Leslie.

"If he's not a Jehovah's Witness, what is he?" Ed demanded.

"What do you mean?" Leslie asked, worried.

Ed shoved the crumpled piece of paper he held in his hand at her.

It read: *No Blood Tx*. It meant: No blood transfusions. It was written by Mark.

"He says he's not a JW, so what's his problem with receiving blood?"

Leslie shrugged. Then she remembered.

"AIDS," she whispered, almost to herself.

"AIDS? *Christ*. What's the evidence for that?"

"Not much, but apparently data is beginning to accumulate."

"Typical internist worrying, what *if*-ing. I have plenty of *hard* data about the mortality of Mark's type of chest wound, even given optimal management, such as blood transfusions. Leslie, this could cost Mark his life."

"Why don't you transfuse him anyway?" Leslie asked anxiously, knowing the answer.

"Because we have this in writing. Clear evidence that Mark does not want blood. Mark is conscious and sane, *legally* anyway. If he had whispered it to me, I might have misunderstood, or not heard it at all. But in writing, lots of witnesses. No can do. You know that."

"I know," she said weakly. Then she asked, "Can I talk to him? I could offer to give him my blood. Our blood has already intermingled. If I have AIDS, or if he does, the exposure has already happened."

As she spoke, Leslie held up her hand with her palm facing Ed. He knew that she had already been exposed to Mark's blood; it was all over her, but he hadn't realized until then how Mark could have been exposed to her blood. Reflexively, Ed reached for Leslie's badly cut hand and looked at it closely

"These are bad lacerations, Leslie," he said quietly.

Leslie shrugged. She would worry about her cuts later.

"So, you see, Mark's gotten some of my blood already," she said. "So could I talk to him?"

"Be my guest. He seems determined. What a fool!"

"Ed," Leslie pleaded gently, "please don't be angry with him."

"Hey, whoa, Les. I'm angry as hell at the guy. I also happen to like him. He's a friend. We go back two years and a lot of long, hard, on call nights. I'll try my best to save him," Ed said. Then he added sternly, "Even if I'd never met the bastard I would try my best to save him."

"Now you're angry with me," Leslie said grimly, realizing she *had* insulted him.

"No. I'm just angry. But don't worry. Being angry just pumps me up. I do my best operating when I'm a little mad," Ed said, briefly touching her shoulder on a rare patch of her coat that was white not red. "Hey, haven't you ever seen John McEnroe play tennis when he's angry? He always wins."

You have to win this one, Ed, Leslie thought as she watched him leave to go to the OR to scrub. You have to.

Then she walked over to Mark. His eyes were closed.

"Mark?"

The brown eyes opened. So much *pain*.

"Mark, it's Leslie. You need blood."

Pain and *fear*. Mark shook his head slowly, definitively.

"Because of AIDS?"

A slight nod, eyes closed.

"Mark, that is nonsense!"

Eyes opened, a trace of anger. But, mostly, pain and determination.

"Mark, what if I give you my blood? We've already—"

Mark's head moved swiftly to the side. *No.*

Ed was right. Mark had made his decision.

It's as if he wants to be allowed to die, Leslie thought suddenly. Mark *had* lunged at the assassin and into the gun. Now he was refusing live-saving, essential blood. Stop it, she told herself. It was just her own morbid imagination at work.

"Mark," Leslie said gently. "Shall I call Kathleen?"

Mark's eyes brightened for a moment, then faded. Joy then worry. He nodded.

"And Janet?"

A slight nod.

"Your parents?"

A strong no. Almost as strong as his refusal of blood.

"Gotta go, Leslie. OR's ready," the anesthesiologist said.

"Oh. OK. See you soon, Mark," she said.

"Are you going to scrub in, Leslie?" someone asked.

"What? Uh . . . no," she said. *No.*

Chapter Thirteen

Leslie followed Mark's stretcher out of the trauma room and into the glaring light of the television cameras. Leslie stared directly into the light, her blue eyes wide, blazing with anger and astonishment at the harsh intrusion. The rest of her face and her hair were covered with blood.

Beyond the cameras she saw her intern Hal. Leslie could not interpret the look on his face, but, remarkably, she felt a sudden closeness to him.

Leslie rushed past them all, down the hall, to the women's locker room. she removed all her clothes, her white jacket, her blue and white flowered shirt, her bra, her slip, her underpants and her nylons. All were stained red, red-brown, with Mark's blood. Leslie eyed the clothes helplessly. They were ruined, but she couldn't throw them away. Not yet. She couldn't throw away Mark's precious blood even though it was useless to him.

If only she could give him back some of his own blood!

Leslie couldn't throw away Mark's blood. She couldn't even rinse it out.

Slowly, carefully, Leslie folded the clothes and put them into her overnight bag.

Eventually she convinced herself that she had to wash Mark's blood off her body. It was even more morbid not to. She stood in the shower and let it wash off, her eyes closed shut so that she couldn't see how much of his precious blood was flowing down the drain. Leslie didn't scrub it off. She just let the water wash it away. Finally she dared to look at the water at her feet. It was clear.

Then Leslie got the soap and shampoo she had removed from her overnight bag and took a usual on call shower. It was a quick shower taken at a quiet time with the pager lying next to the shower stall on the tile floor.

The lacerations on Leslie's palm and fingers stung. As she washed they began to bleed. Her blood.

Momentarily mesmerized, Leslie watched her own blood swirl down the drain. Then she focused on the cuts themselves. Several were deep, but none extended down to tendon. The sensation and motor function in her hand seemed normal. They were probably too deep and narrow — true puncture wounds — to suture, but they needed attention. Sometime she would return to the ER, clean the wounds carefully with sterile solution, and ask one of the orthopedic surgeons to take a look.

Leslie had clean underpants, nylons and a blouse in her overnight bag, but she had no extra bra, no white coat, no skirt. She found a clean surgical scrub dress, a royal-blue, cotton dress with a deep V-neck and short sleeves. The dress was loose around her narrow hips and waist but snug over her bare breasts.

She would borrow someone's white coat or find an extra white coat somewhere to cover up her immodest outfit. Not that it mattered. Not that anything mattered except Mark.

Leslie walked out of the women's locker room and into the glare of the television cameras. They had followed her and waited.

"Dr. Adams," a reporter said. "Just a word, please."

Leslie stopped. She was too bewildered not to.

The cameras pointed at her. They focused on the damp chestnut hair combed hurriedly, before she left the locker room, with the trembling fingers of her uninjured hand. They focused on the brilliant blue eyes, and they focused on the ample, round breasts that strained against the too tight scrub dress.

She looks like an NCAA swimming champion, the reporter thought — damp, healthy, fit, excited — except her

140

breasts are too large for a swimmer.

"Dr. Adams, could you please tell us what happened?"

Leslie opened her mouth to speak, too stunned not to, but the question unleashed the memories. And her priorities. Her only priority was to find out about Mark.

"No," she said flatly into the camera. She leveled her clear blue eyes at the red light on the camera because the glare was less there. "No, I can't."

The cameras continued to roll as she sped away. They didn't have many words from Dr. Leslie Adams, but they had sensational color footage, before and after: before, the blood-soaked face and clothes; after, the clean, damp young woman, erotic and sensual in the ill-fitting scrub dress. Common to both sequences, captured in vivid color, captured as they delivered clear, eloquent non-verbal messages of astonishment, sadness, worry and anger, were those huge sapphire-blue eyes.

Channel Five had the best footage, but all the local stations had good shots. Good enough. They all ran the story on the shootings—the murdered would-be informant, the assassin, the wounded police officers and the critically injured resident—featuring the dramatic pictures of Dr. Leslie Adams. The segment was featured on every newscast on every channel for a full thirty-six hours.

All stations received a record number of phone calls.

After escaping the reporters, Leslie rushed to the operating room and went directly to the nursing station. The San Francisco General Hospital operating room was an active place. Cases were done twenty-four hours a day, seven days a week.

At that moment, Mark was one of four cases.

"How is he?" Leslie asked the head nurse, Gwen. Despite the other cases, Mark was everyone's primary concern. He was the most critical.

"So far, so good. They just started," Gwen said. Then, looking at Leslie, Gwen reached for a long white coat that hung on a hook on the wall. "Here. I don't know who this belongs to. It's been hanging here for at least three weeks. Whoever it belongs to, you need it more."

"Thanks, Gwen."

"We cleared out one waiting room for you and his friends and family. Waiting room B."

"Thanks," Leslie breathed. "I guess I'd better make some phone calls."

It was ten-fifteen. Leslie decided she would call Janet after the show. Leslie got Kathleen's parents' telephone number from directory assistance.

"Yes, Dr. Adams. Of course I remember you," Virginia Jenkins said. "You took such good care of me."

"How are you, Mrs. Jenkins?"

"Fine. Very well. No more angina even. They say I finally just clipped off the part of the narrowed artery that was causing the pain. So, I'm even better."

"I'm glad. Uh . . . is Kathleen there?"

"Oh, no, dear. She lives in the city. With Mark Taylor. Do you need their number?"

"Yes, please." Lives in the city with Mark. Virginia Jenkins sounded calm about it. Who wouldn't be? Leslie didn't know Mark's home telephone number. The page operator would have it, but Virginia Jenkins provided the number from memory.

"Thank you," Leslie said.

"Hi, babe," Kathleen answered the phone on the second ring. It was the time that Mark always called if he could. Even if it was to say he couldn't talk.

"Kathleen, it's Leslie Adams."

"Oh, Leslie. Mark's not here."

"I know, Kathleen. Mark's had an accident." Leslie's voice broke. Hot tears began to track down her cheeks.

"Leslie!"

"Mark is in surgery, Kathleen. He's been injured."

"Injured?"

"Shot."

"Shot! No. *No!* He couldn't be shot. How is he? Is he—"

"He's in surgery. He was shot in the chest. He was conscious before surgery. Not paralyzed," Leslie said. She gave Kathleen all the positive information she could think of. She didn't tell her about the blood. She didn't tell Kathleen

142

that if Mark lost one more drop of blood he could die. "Come to surgery, waiting room B, OK? Kathleen, take a taxi. It's much safer."

"Yes. I will. Leslie, are you with him? Will you be?"

"I'm here. Very near. In the OR."

Two hours later Mark was still in surgery, still alive. Janet, Leslie and Kathleen sat in waiting room B. It had taken the press no time to find the location. They had already established interest in the blue-eyed heroine who wouldn't speak to them. Then someone identified Janet, star of *Joanna,* San Francisco's hottest theater production, and their interest soared. No one recognized Kathleen or even asked her name. *That* was very lucky.

Leslie had to pass through the reporters to get into the OR to check on Mark. Each time it was an ordeal.

They all felt trapped. They sat, silently, each on one of the three couches arranged at right angles to each other against the pale yellow walls.

Aware of Leslie's problem with the eager reporters, Gwen began to deliver the reports so that Leslie did not have to leave the room. Still, it made Leslie restless. What if something happened and Gwen couldn't get away? *Because* something had happened.

"He hasn't bled at all," she said. "And they've ligated the artery. They had to remove his right lower lobe."

Kathleen and Janet gasped in unison.

"It's not a big deal," Leslie and Gwen reassured them.

"Why is he still in there?" Janet asked.

"Because there are lots of bone splinters. They are picking them out one by one. And because the wound was contaminated. They want to clean it thoroughly. They don't want to have to go back in. They're just being very careful. His vital signs have been rock-steady."

"What's his crit, Gwen?" Leslie asked finally, reluctantly.

"Eleven."

Oh my God, Leslie thought.

"What does that mean?" Kathleen asked, sensing Leslie's

143

concern despite her effort to appear calm.

"It's low," Leslie admitted. She didn't add that it meant he couldn't afford to bleed. Not even a little. If only I had gotten to the artery sooner, she thought, tormented, aching. If only . . .

"The press is a nuisance, eh? They're even quizzing *me* since they can't get at you," Gwen said on her third visit to waiting room B. "I've tried to get them to leave, but they sense my lack of authority. And, I think we may be coming face to face with a little chauvinism, ladies."

"I'm afraid so," Leslie said. "What we need is a chief of medicine." Or someone who thinks he is, Leslie thought. "Gwen, I can't dial out on this phone, can I?"

"No."

"Can it ring in?"

"The operator can connect to it."

"Would you page Dr. Hal Rollins? Then have him connected through to this extension?"

"Sure. Shall I page him stat?"

"No. Hal's pretty good answering his pages right away. It's one of his strong points."

While Leslie waited she remembered Hal's expression when she emerged from the trauma room. What was it? Certainly nothing she had seen before.

The telephone in the waiting room rang in three minutes.

"Hi boss," Hal said.

"How are things going, Hal?"

"Fine. *Nothing* is happening. It's like everyone—the whole world—is worried about Mark. It's weird. Tomblike."

Tomblike. A nice happy medical term meaning quiet. But not a good term to use tonight.

"Er . . . uh . . . quiet," Hal said quickly. "I heard that Mark's crit is eleven, and they can't transfuse him?"

"Uh-huh. Listen Hal, I need a favor."

"Shoo—" he began then caught himself. He had actually started to say "Shoot boss" like he always did, but he stopped himself, a little horrified. When he spoke it was in a voice that Leslie had never heard before, a voice to match

144

the expression she had seen earlier.

"Anything, Leslie," Hal said seriously. Then, before Leslie spoke, he added what had been on his mind. "You were really amazing. You really saved his life. You knew exactly what to do and you did it."

Leslie swallowed hard. Hal was complimenting her. He admired her. It had been admiration in his eyes. Leslie smiled slightly

"Thanks, Hal. Now here's what I need. I want you to come down to waiting room B. Identify yourself to the press as someone with authority. I don't even care if you lie to them. Just convince them to leave this area. Not the hospital, just this area. I don't want you to infringe on their First Amendment rights. Just get them away. OK?"

"Sure. *No* problem."

Leslie stood near the door, listening to Hal's speech, marveling at his confidence.

"Ladies and Gentlemen of the press. I am Dr. Hal Rollins. I represent the Department of Medicine. I am afraid we have a hospital policy about these waiting rooms, about who can be in this area. It's a conflict, First Amendment rights versus patient confidentiality, but I'm sure you'll understand that we have to protect our patients' rights. I assure you I will be the first to hear of any changes in Dr. Taylor's condition and will notify you immediately. If you would care to follow Dr. Rhodes to the cafeteria. . . . It's closed to the public at this hour, but the Department of Medicine has provided special passes for all of you. So, please, follow Dr. Rhodes."

Miraculously, they did follow Dr. Rhodes, the third year medical student who was carrying a fistful of yellow passes. Meal tickets. Probably Hal's entire supply for the month.

I misjudged him, Leslie thought.

Hal lingered outside the door until the press was out of sight, then he entered waiting room B.

"How'd I do, boss?" he asked, his voice a little less confident than usual, wanting Leslie's approval as he never had before.

"Fabulous, Hal. Truly. I'll see that you get all those meal tickets back. That was very generous."

"No *problemo*. I can get more. I have an in with the Department of Medicine secretary." The department secretary was the keeper, a notoriously stingy keeper, of the meal tickets.

Of course you do, Leslie thought. Typical Hal. But, still, she'd seen another side of him. And he of her.

She was grateful for what he had done, and he admired her for what she had done.

Five minutes after the press left, Janet stood up.

"I'm going to go."

"Janet!"

Leslie followed her into the hallway.

"I don't belong here, Leslie. I'm not helping him, and I'm preventing Kathleen from talking. Call me, please, as soon as you hear anything."

"I will."

Janet was right. Kathleen needed to talk. She started talking as soon as Leslie returned, but her words caught Leslie by surprise.

"Listen, Leslie, I know you don't like me. I know how much you care about Mark. But, believe me, I love him with all my heart. I really do."

"Kathleen, I—"

"And he loves me, Leslie," Kathleen continued firmly.

"I know that," Leslie said honestly. She had learned it that night. At least, she had admitted it to herself that night. She had seen the look in Mark's eyes at the mention of Kathleen's name.

Then Kathleen began to cry.

"Oh God, I wish he would quit medicine."

"What?" Apparently Mark had told her, and she didn't care. *Good.* "You wish he would quit—"

"Yes. He never would, of course. He loves it. He's committed to it," Kathleen sighed.

So she didn't know. Maybe there was nothing to know anymore. Maybe Mark had made peace with his inner conflict. Leslie remembered how happy, how relaxed he had looked tonight. Before . . .

"Why do you wish he would quit?" Leslie asked.

"Selfishness. So he would be safe. From the diseases. From getting shot. What is there about being a doctor that should put you at risk to get *shot?*" she demanded.

Leslie had no answer. Mark wasn't the first doctor to get shot. It happened. Angry patients, angry families, patients demanding narcotics, psychotic patients. . . .

"I don't know, Kathleen," Leslie said. Then she asked, curious, "You don't care if Mark is a doctor?"

"No! I don't care if he is anything or nothing. I just want to be with him," Kathleen smiled through her wet violet eyes, seeing a past memory or a future happiness. "If he wasn't a doctor, we would have more time together. Selfish. I'm selfish."

Their conversation was interrupted by Gwen who announced that they were beginning to close. Mark would be going up to the ICU in about twenty minutes.

Leslie and Kathleen slipped past the press assembled in front of the ICU. Hal was giving them an update, promising them an interview with one of the trauma surgeons as soon as the surgeon was free to leave Mark.

Leslie briefly introduced Kathleen to Ed Moore who was writing Mark's post-op orders at the ICU nursing station.

"He's OK so far, Leslie," Ed said. "But he still can't bleed. He has absolutely no reserve. We've already given him a blast of iron by vein."

So he can start making, remaking, red blood cells.

"You are a hero, Ed!"

"No, but we all gave it our best. And our luck has held, so far." Then he reached for her hand. The cuts were still unbandaged. Leslie hadn't had a chance to go back to the ER. Ed said gently, "You are the hero, Leslie. You saved his life."

"No," Leslie said, embarrassed, uncomfortable that Kathleen overheard.

"*Yes.* Here's the proof," he said examining her hand. "In thirty minutes, after we get him squared away here, you meet me in the ER. These wounds need attention."

"OK. Thanks."

There was some concern about allowing Kathleen in to see Mark. She was not family.

Leslie intervened quickly.

"Kathleen is his family. He needs her. They just don't happen to have the piece of paper and the blood test," Leslie said. Not yet, she thought.

"You'd make a good attorney, Leslie. Persuasive," the head nurse said. But the nurse allowed it mainly because of Mark. Anything to help Mark.

"Thank you," Kathleen said quietly as they walked toward Mark's room in the ICU.

"We kept the anesthesia pretty light. He's still out, but he should wake up soon," the anesthesiologist said to Leslie.

Leslie and Kathleen stopped at the door to Mark's room. The nurses were organizing the machines, lines, monitors, ventilator hoses and settings.

Mark lay still, motionless. So pale. A hematocrit of eleven made his skin white. Blue-white.

Leslie held back, knowing to wait for the nurses to get everything in order, to finish their necessary tasks. Leslie also held back because, as many times as she had seen ICU patients with lines and tubes lying motionless, it was always startling and a bit overwhelming.

Now the patient was Mark.

Kathleen did not hold back. She did not hesitate to move quickly toward the horribly pale, horribly still marionette who was Mark.

Kathleen smiled graciously as she worked her way around the busy, surprised nurses, careful not to disturb anything, ducking under tubes, stepping over cords, but aiming unerringly for the head of the bed. She had to get to a place where she could touch him, speak to him.

When she reached him Kathleen placed her head gently against his, temple to temple, and whispered into his ear.

"I love you, Mark. I love you."

Mark's eyes fluttered, and his hand, apparently lifeless until that moment, lifted off the bed and reached for her.

Kathleen caught his hand and held it. She whispered

again and again.

"I love you, Mark. I love you."

Leslie watched Mark and Kathleen for a moment, her eyes flooded with tears. Then she left to call Janet and to let Ed Moore take care of her hand. As she left, Leslie knew for the first time in the long emotional evening that Mark would make it. He had a reason to make it.

Kathleen was his reason.

Chapter Fourteen

James Stevenson flipped on the television's power switch. When Lynne was away, James drank his morning cup of coffee and smoked his first cigarette of the day in front of the morning news programs.

"After murdering his intended victim, the assassin hid in a small laboratory where two residents from the University of California's Department of Medicine were working. One of the residents, Dr. Mark Taylor, was shot. The other resident, Dr. Leslie Adams, pictured here. . . ."

James looked up instantly at the mention of Leslie's name, just in time to see the dramatic footage, artfully spliced. James moved closer to the television and turned up the volume. His pulse raced, and his mind spun as he watched the horrible, grotesque picture of her blood-covered face fade miraculously into the one of her just after she had emerged from the shower. Fresh, beautiful, sensual.

Leslie.

So she was here. In San Francisco.

She looked the same. James had seen that startled, bewildered look before—a similar picture, but a different time and a different place. That spring day, years before, her hair was damp, her face fresh from a brisk swim in the lake and her royal-blue tank suit clung to her the way the blue scrub dress did.

Leslie's raw, natural beauty. She didn't even recognize it,

at least not then, in high school, when her lovely face was framed by unruly chestnut curls and her soft voluptuous body was carefully hidden under cardigan sweaters and tailored blouses.

The silky unrestrained curls. The womanly figure. The blazing blue eyes. The full seductive lips.

Leslie.

How long had it been? James knew without thinking about it. Nine years almost to the day. It was that August, two months after graduation from high school, their accidental final meeting by the fountain at Seattle Center. Leslie, with her girlfriends, romping and giggling, because that's what they did in those carefree days. And James, holding Cheryl, kissing her, oblivious to Leslie's presence until Leslie, literally, ran into them.

"Oh! James!" Leslie had pulled up short, red with embarrassment, breathing quickly.

"Leslie. Hi," he had said, pulling away a little from Cheryl. But Cheryl didn't let go. "Uh, this is Cheryl. Cheryl this is Leslie. And Joanne. And Betty. And . . ."

A brief awkward final meeting. An uncomfortable ending to something that had never really begun.

Or had it?

A week later Leslie mailed a letter to him. It arrived with letters from Cheryl. For some reason James didn't notice it. Leslie's letter remained unopened and was stored in a shoebox with all the letters from Cheryl. Ten months later James discovered it. Opened it. Read it. It was too late for him and Leslie, but just in time for him. Just in time to change his life. Forever. For the better.

But Leslie didn't know. All she knew was that she had sent a letter, a letter that must have been terribly hard for her to send, that was never answered. Never acknowledged.

James hadn't seen her, talked to her, for nine years.

Now he knew where she was.

Dr. Leslie Adams. Department of Medicine. University of California at San Francisco.

James turned off the television, lit another cigarette and sat, without moving, except to light the next cigarette, and

151

the next, for hours.

"Hey you, Dr. Night Stalker," Mark called as Leslie walked past his hospital room. His door was open. It was five in the morning.

"Hi!" she whispered, peering into his private room.

Mark sat up in bed. The light was on. He was reading. He had been transferred from the ICU after a week's stay. This was his fourth morning on the ward.

"Are you busy or are you just prowling?"

"Prowling. There's no lovely view from this place, anyway. And it never feels peaceful."

"No calms between storms?"

"Just when you think you've hit a calm spot, you realize it's only an illusion. It's really the eye of another hurricane."

Mark smiled. Then he asked, "Where's Hal?"

Leslie sat down in the chair next to Mark's bed without answering.

"Leslie, where's Hal?"

"Asleep."

"Leslie, it was bad enough, but acceptable, for you to do this as an intern, but you do not stay up all night while your intern sleeps."

"I know," she said sheepishly. *But I do.*

"How *is* Prince Hal?"

"What have you been reading, *Henry IV?*"

"Very good."

"I was raised on this," Leslie said, gesturing to the stack of books, classics of English literature, next to Mark's bed. "At least, surrounded by it."

"Lucky," Mark mused. Then he asked again, "How is the crown prince?"

"Actually, he's better," Leslie said honestly, but understating the magnitude of improvement. Hal had gone overboard in the admiration department. She appreciated the quiet moments when Hal was asleep because then he wasn't trailing around behind her, admiring her. "Toning down.

152

Asking questions. He even has a bit of a crush on me."

"Good, I—"

"Told me so. I know. You were right. How are you?"

"Doing well. Retic—ing like crazy."

Reticulocytes—retics—were young red blood cells. Their presence in blood meant new red blood cells were being produced.

"And your crit is. . . ?"

"Twenty-four," Mark said proudly. "They are going to turn me loose to finish recuperating at home when I hit twenty-seven."

Home. To Kathleen.

"It still doesn't give you much leeway," Leslie said, looking at his pale white skin.

"You mean if I get shot again in the next few days? The re-bleed risk period is over."

"You are so lucky. You had the most uneventful, uncomplicated recovery in history."

"The reason I'm lucky is because you were there. Or so they say."

"I was lucky that *you* were there." *You saved my life, Mark.*

"That's nonsense. Anyway, I remember nothing between lunging at the guy and waking up in the trauma room. Are you ever going to tell me what really happened?"

Mark had asked her before, but Leslie always resisted giving details. She hated remembering. It was so personal, so private. It was so *intimate* to put her hand inside of him, deep into his chest, and, at the same time, it was so *impersonal* and anatomic. Like an autopsy.

"I told you. I put pressure on a bleeder."

"With one little finger?" Mark asked, holding up his hand, gesturing to hers. He knew what she had done. He had seen her hand. He had seen the scars on her palm, thick and uneven. Scars that would always be there.

"And after I stopped the bleeding," Leslie continued, ignoring him, "you went crazy and refused blood transfusions."

"I don't believe that decision was crazy."

153

"We'll never know. It turned out all right."

"Maybe we will know, someday, that it was the right decision."

Mark's telephone rang. It was six A.M. Leslie stood up and said, "Kathleen. I'll go."

"Stay put, Leslie. It's not Kathleen. It's probably a wrong number. Trunk lines crossed or something."

It wasn't a wrong number. It was Mark's father calling at eight A.M. from his office in Lincoln.

"Mark!" his father roared.

"Father," Mark answered flatly.

"Why in hell didn't you tell us?"

"I didn't want to worry you," Mark said, grimacing at Leslie. "It's just a flesh wound. How did you find out?"

"Sam Hall was at a urology meeting in San Francisco. He saw it on the news. When I ran into him in the hospital yesterday, he asked how you were and was surprised that your mother and I weren't in San Francisco."

"Oh. Well. You saved yourself a trip."

"Still in the hospital after ten days? That doesn't sound like a flesh wound. I want you transferred here."

"I'm going home in a day or two."

"Can Janet take care of you? Wouldn't it be better if you were here?"

Leslie couldn't hear Mark's father's words, but she heard Mark's tone and sensed the general flavor of the conversation, guessed what questions Mark was being asked.

Mark looked at her. He was a little embarrassed. Leslie stood up to leave, but Mark shook his head, covered the receiver with his hand and whispered to her.

"You don't have to leave, Leslie. Unless you want to. It's just about to get pretty ugly."

Then why don't I leave? Leslie wondered. Because Mark seemed to want her to stay.

"Janet and I are not together anymore, Father."

Leslie drew in a breath. It had been ten months since Mark and Janet had separated. The divorce had been final for months.

Mark smiled weakly at her.

"Not together?"

"Divorced."

"When did that happen?"

"Recently."

"When were you going to let us know?"

If Mark didn't let them know, no one else would. Certainly not Janet's parents. The Taylors had had no contact with Janet's parents after the wedding.

"Sometime. It didn't seem like an emergency."

"Not an emergency? Don't you know how happy this will make your mother? Delirious. It has been so hard for her, for both of us, thinking about you being married to that poor, gold-digging hick."

"Father."

"Mark, you know perfectly well she was beneath you. No good for you. It was so awkward. I'm just glad you came to your senses and left her."

"She left me. If it were possible, I would still be married to her. But it isn't."

"Well, however it happened, it's a blessing."

"It's a *shame,* Father."

"Your mother will be thrilled."

Mark closed his eyes and tilted his head back. The skin over his knuckles stretched tight as he gripped the phone. A vein stood out on his temple, and his jaw muscles rippled.

Leslie watched, horrified. So much pressure. So much rage. So much inner turmoil.

All he needs is an ulcer, she thought, a bleeding ulcer from the stress. It could kill him.

Leslie touched his shoulder with her hand. Mark looked at her, startled. Then he smiled, wanly, and patted her hand.

"I'm OK," he mouthed the words.

His father continued, "So, son, will you still finish up on time? On July first?"

"Yes. The residency director says I can be off for a month and still fulfill board requirements on schedule."

"Good. I think I'll have the shingle made up today. Maybe you would like to live at home now that Janet is gone?"

"Father," Mark said, staring into Leslie's blue eyes, gathering strength from their unquestioning support. "I'm going to do a cardiology fellowship starting July first. I'll be doing that for two or three years."

"When did you make that decision?" his father hissed.

"Recently."

"Mark, we don't need any more cardiologists in Lincoln. The town's teeming with them."

"Then, maybe, I'll just have to practice someplace else."

"You *wouldn't!*" It sounded like, You wouldn't *dare*. "After all our plans."

"All your plans, Father. I have to make my own plans."

"Your own plans? Goddammit, Mark, these are your plans. Have been for years."

"Then they've changed. A lot of things have changed."

"I can't believe it."

"Believe it."

"You little bastard. After all I've—"

White with rage, eyes clouded, muscles taut and skin damp, Mark slammed down the phone. Hung up on his father.

Leslie sat quietly, awkwardly, waiting for him to remember that she was there. She had taken her hand away from his shoulder. Mark was very far away.

Minutes later he looked over at her and smiled sheepishly.

"I'm getting some insight into the complications you mentioned," she said, remembering their early morning conversation three months before.

"Uh-huh."

"I think you made it pretty clear."

"Leslie, believe it or not, we've had conversations like this for years. He doesn't hear what I say, even when I say it like that. Until recently, one of these wonderful father-son yelling matches would be followed by a call from me, apologizing. Doing what he wanted me to do."

"Oh."

"But not anymore."

Good.

"When did you decide to do the cardiology fellowship?"

"Just in the last month. It's a little late to apply for next July."

"I know. I'm already starting on mine for the following July." Then Leslie added quietly, "Also in cardiology."

Mark smiled.

"We'll be seeing each other at cardiology meetings for years to come, won't we?"

"So where are you applying? They'd make a spot for you here I'm sure."

"I need to leave," Mark said flatly. They *had* offered to find a position for him, to create a place for him in their highly competitive cardiology program. "Peter Bent Brigham has an unexpected opening as the *New England Journal of Medicine* ads say. How about you?"

"Stanford's my first choice at the moment."

"You'll get in wherever you want."

So will you, she thought. But how about English graduate school, she wondered, looking at the volumes of Shakespeare, Faulkner, Joyce and Shaw beside his bed.

Leslie's pager sounded. She glanced at her watch. Eight-fifteen.

"Quarter past eight, Leslie. It's probably Hal wondering why you're late for rounds."

"I'm not late for rounds."

"You're not?" Morning rounds were always at eight.

"No," she said quietly. "We start at eight-thirty on nights after we've been on call."

"So Hal can catch a few extra winks?"

"So Hal can have a leisurely second cup of coffee. . . ."

"To wake himself up after the long night's sleep he gets because his resident had been up all night keeping watch?" Mark teased.

"Something like that. Really, Mark, Hal has improved dramatically. I'm whipping him into shape. In my own way. Anyway," Leslie said frowning at the digits on her pager, "it's the Department of Medicine office. May I use your phone?"

Leslie dialed the number without curiosity. Calls from the Department of Medicine office were common.

"Oh, yes, I do have a message for you," the secretary said. "Here it is. Ready?"

Leslie took a three by five inch index card and a pen from the left breast pocket of her white coat.

"Go ahead."

Leslie prepared to write but as she heard the message, her hand froze with the pen poised above the paper.

" . . . in his office all day," the secretary finished.

"I'm sorry. Could you repeat the number?" Leslie asked, her mind reeling.

James Stevenson would be in his office — an office with a local telephone number — all day. Would Dr. Adams please call?

"Huh," Leslie said after she hung up.

"What?" Mark asked.

"Oh. A voice from the distant, distant past. From high school. An old boy — an old friend," Leslie said, distractedly, before leaving to find Hal for rounds.

Friend. Boyfriend. What was James?

What *had* he been?

Part Two

Chapter Fifteen

George Washington High School, Seattle's largest public high school, drew its student body from two junior high schools, Benjamin Franklin and Thomas Edison. The merger of the students from the two junior high schools was not a blend. It was the creation of a stratified, two-class society: the haves and the have nots; the intellectuals and the hoodlums; the virgins and the hussies; those who would succeed and those who were destined to fail.

There were no railroad tracks separating the neighborhood whose teenagers attended Franklin from the neighborhood that sent its students to Edison, but there might as well have been. The separation was that distinct. The students who attended Thomas Edison Junior High lived on the wrong side of the imaginary tracks.

The main distinction between the two student bodies was environmental. Environment, not genes, segregated the two groups. The parents of Franklin students were university faculty, lawyers, doctors, bankers and college graduates. They raised their children on expectations of excellence, confidence in the child's ability, praise for suc-

161

cess and reward for accomplishment. They provided their children with an environment that encouraged talent, intellectual creativity and realization of potential.

The parents of the Edison students were no less intelligent than the parents of the Franklin students, but their goals were different: enough money to pay rent and buy food and clothes. They worked hard to survive, struggling to make ends meet. Their principal goal for their children was that the child graduate from high school without getting arrested, pregnant, addicted or killed. Their only hope was that the child would survive, relatively unscathed, to age eighteen, to adulthood, to the age of self-sufficiency.

The Franklin students were not intrinsically prejudiced against the Edison students. They were simply realistic. Likes attracted likes. Everyone was most comfortable, especially given the pressure of teenage society toward conformity, to be with his or her own kind.

But crossovers did occur. The faculty child, rebelling against his achievement-oriented parents, sought and found new friends in the beer-drinking, motorcycle-riding gangs from Edison. Occasionally a serious, thoughtful, academically motivated student from Edison would appear in the honors classes. He or she was welcome, a curiosity but a kindred spirit nonetheless, to join the Franklin group.

If the goals meshed, crossovers were permissible, even encouraged. The new blood in the group added interest and sometimes a new romance.

In this clearly stratified two-class system, James Stevenson found himself in No Man's Land. He had attended Edison, but because of his scores on the pre-entrance placement tests, James was assigned to the honors classes. Those classes were populated almost exclusively by the very best of the Franklin graduates. James did not share the goals of those students, but he did as well as they did, better even, on tests. James was as smart as the faculty kids, as smart as the kids with environmental privilege.

As smart as Leslie Adams and her friends.

They would have welcomed James instantly into their group, except that it wasn't clear that he wanted to be with them. James looked different, with his old faded jeans, his threadbare madras shirts and his black leather jacket.

James smoked. And drank. And swore. James rode a motorcycle. There was even a rumor that he had a girlfriend, a fourteen-year-old still at Edison, whom he *slept* with!

"He is a hoodlum," Leslie's girlfriends hissed.

"Not really," the boys in her group countered. "James set the curve on the last math exam, and he offered to help with the cerebral palsy bottle drive."

Part hoodlum. Although the actual proof was lacking. There was no evidence that James had ever broken the law—no real laws. He did smoke and drink and perhaps even have sex with a minor, but he didn't steal hubcaps or stereo equipment. He apparently was not involved with the rash of typewriter thefts from the school's third-floor typing class.

Part do-gooder. James joined in the altruistic efforts of the Franklin group. With them, James donated his time to community service. He helped raise money—through car washes and bottle drives—for the poor and disadvantaged. He tutored other students and worked in hospitals and nursing homes.

Unlike any student before, James apparently belonged to both groups. He was never committed, not totally, not uniquely, not in three years, to either group, and despite the divided allegiance, neither group sought to expel him.

James's friends from Thomas Edison had been friends since grade school. Most had known him since the day, at age five, when he changed his name from Jimmy to James. It had been James ever since. He insisted on it. As they got older, they called themselves the James Gang. They were secretly pleased that James, one of *them,* had successfully infiltrated the most elite faction of the Franklin group.

The boys from Franklin, the boys he met in the honors classes, were intrigued by James. They had to admire his brains—a critical factor—but they also admired his wildness, his lack of concern for authority, his nonchalance about drinking and smoking. And his sexual success. They were all at the age when they needed to experiment, to see how far the rules would stretch before they snapped.

James didn't worry about the rules, and he set the curves on the math exams.

James didn't seem to worry about very much.

Unlike the boys who accepted James on his terms, the girls, except for Leslie, rejected him.

"He's coarse," Leslie's friends said, wrinkling their noses. "And he's so strange-looking. He gives me the creeps!"

"I think he's interesting," Leslie said thoughtfully.

"Leslie! You have to be kidding," they giggled.

"No, I really think he is interesting."

Leslie also thought that James was very handsome, but she didn't dare tell them *that.* It was a matter of taste, anyway. There was nothing classically handsome about James. Nothing terribly aristocratic. No sign of privilege, environmental or otherwise.

James looked, Leslie decided, like a cougar. His dark green eyes were set wide apart in his face—cold, appraising, watchful green eyes. James's cheekbones were high and prominent above the hollow of his cheeks. His lips were thin, set in neutral, occasionally curling into a half smile. The inevitable cigarette dangled casually, erotically, from his lips, moving when he spoke, as if a part of him.

A cougar. Wild. Free. Untamed. And untamable.

James's thick black hair fell into his green eyes and curled sensually over his ears and down his neck.

At first James made Leslie nervous. He would watch her, the green eyes with the long black lashes calmly observing, squinting slightly as the smoke from his cigarette drifted into them. James never looked *pleasant* like the other boys. They were all full of smiles and winks and flirtations, trying to look sexy and provocative. James didn't try to look sexy.

James didn't have to try. The look was natural.

After a while James began to speak to her. They didn't have conversations. They just had brief and unexpected communications. Usually there was a message, indirect, a little hidden.

"The Macho Men are playing at the dance this Saturday," James would say. It was an announcement, not an invitation, but Leslie learned it meant that he would be at the dance. And that he wanted her to be? She didn't know.

She would go with her friends, and he would be there, wandering between the James gang and the Franklin group, watching her from the corner of his cougarlike eyes. He wouldn't dance. Not until the end. The last dance. Then he would ask her to dance. The slow dance.

"Rosemaiden?" he whispered one day as he passed her in the hallway. Rosemaiden was the award given to the girl voted Most Inspirational by the female student body. It was a yearly award. Leslie won all three years. It was an unprecedented accomplishment.

"Yes," she said weakly to his back as he continued down the hall.

James was entirely unpredictable. He appeared at some Franklin group parties and not at others. He usually arrived late and left early. He always arrived by himself and left alone. At the parties, James talked and joked with the boys, and he taunted the girls, Leslie's friends, because he knew they disliked him.

James always said something to Leslie. He never taunted *her*. Sometimes he teased, but he never taunted.

By senior year, Leslie had had four relationships with boys from her group. Boring, groping, silly relationships that weren't love or sex or anything but chaste attempts at growing up.

And, by senior year, Leslie had danced ten slow dances with James, had spent an entire quarter of a football game standing beside him—he had found her—saying nothing, had washed cars with him at a charity car wash, had seen him daily in honors classes at school and, in small cryptic pieces, had exchanged about two hours of dialogue with him.

But she thought about him *constantly*. She always felt his presence. The feeling made her anxious and uncertain. And eager.

One day in September of senior year, James caught up

with her after class. It was Friday afternoon.

"Done much deer hunting with bows and arrows?" he asked.

"No!" Then, curious, not wanting that to be the end of another unfinished, uninterpretable exchange, she asked, "Why?"

"Perfect weather for it. I'm going tomorrow."

"Oh." *Oh?*

"So, do you want to?"

"Yes," Leslie breathed, not certain about what he was asking or what she had agreed to.

"I'll pick you up at nine in the morning. I know where you live."

A date? With James? To hunt deer with bows and arrows?

Leslie and her parents waited for James to arrive. They waited in anxious silence, each preoccupied with specific worries about the date. Matthew Adams opposed hunting for sport. Period. It was not a debatable issue.

Susan Adams's finely tuned journalistic eyes and ears had deduced a great deal about the mysterious James. Over the past two years she had heard words like "wild" and "thug" and "scary" and "uncivilized" uttered contemptuously by Leslie's dearest friends. She had also heard her daughter's quiet protestations. Susan and Leslie were best friends. It was a friendship that had survived even the teenage "Oh *Mother!*" years.

Leslie had not told Susan about James. Not really. Susan had to guess, and she guessed that Leslie was intrigued with James because he was so different and that Leslie didn't, or couldn't, discuss her attraction because she herself didn't understand it.

Susan waited. A little worried. But mostly curious.

Leslie waited, too, her heart pounding, her mouth dry, *rehearsing* dialogue, planning topics. There weren't many topics. There wouldn't be much dialogue because James didn't talk. All she could think of quickly reduced to silly soliloquies on topics that wouldn't interest James. It was that or silence.

Maybe he wouldn't come after all.

At five minutes before nine they heard James arrive, his actual appearance heralded by the roar of his motorcycle.

Matthew Adams breathed a momentary sigh of relief. His original worries were allayed, but they were promptly replaced by much greater ones. They weren't really going hunting. Even though he noticed a single wooden bow, unstrung, carefully secured to the motorcycle, it was obvious the expedition was not serious. Hunters drove large station wagons, vans, trucks even. Large enough to carry the prey. Hunters did not go hunting with bows and arrows on motorcycles.

Motorcycles . . . the magnitude of the new worry rapidly surpassed the old one. Matthew did not want his daughter, his only child, riding on a motorcycle. It wasn't a rule. They had never even discussed it. There had been no need. None of Leslie's friends had motorcycles. *They* wouldn't.

Susan and Matthew prided themselves on being liberal, rational parents. Their relationship with Leslie was close and open. They both realized in the instant James arrived that all the previous parenting had been easy. Because Leslie had made no demands. She hadn't fallen in love, wanted to make love, wanted to stay out all night, wanted to drink or try drugs. Leslie hadn't wanted to do anything the least bit worrisome.

Susan and Matthew had discussed this day in the abstract. What they, as well-educated, intelligent, reasonable parents would do when their daughter began to explore, experiment, question. They would lie in bed at night calmly discussing what they would do. Issue by issue.

"What if she wants to try marijuana? Or LSD?"

"We discuss it with her. If she's really determined, we insist that she do it at home, so she's safe."

"What if she likes it?"

"Leslie is not an addict personality," Matthew said firmly.

167

"What about sex? Lots of teenagers have sex now. It's almost standard."

"Not with Leslie's group."

"Still . . ."

"If she did want to, which she won't, we'd talk to her about love and sex, and if she was determined, we'd make sure she knew how not to get pregnant."

"She knows that."

"What if she wants to live with someone?"

"In high school?"

"Eventually."

"When the time comes it might even be a good idea. But that's years from now."

It all sounded very easy, as they discussed it in the privacy of their own bedroom, with their virginal daughter safely sleeping two rooms away. They would be rational, they decided, confident that they could allow Leslie the freedom they knew she would need. When she needed it.

But now, looking at James's motorcycle, both were consumed by irrational emotion. A year before, Susan had done an exposé for the magazine section of Seattle's largest newspaper on the dangers of motorcycles. Susan explored the issues of helmets and the horrible, not quite lethal accidents . . .

"Mom. Dad," Leslie said sternly, looking at her parents, surprising herself and them.

"Why don't you take my car?" Matthew offered.

"No," Leslie said, starting for the door, planning to dash out to the curb, not noticing that James was already walking toward the house. *"Please!"*

It was a *please* that forced Matthew and Susan to look at the big picture, the picture of their daughter growing up and taking the risks necessary to mature without rebellion or repression. They glanced at each other and shrugged, weakly.

The doorbell rang. Leslie opened it.

"Hi, James," she said.

"Hi," he said, looking at her parents, expecting their disapproval.

"James, these are my parents."

"Dr. Adams," James said, extending his rough hand to Matthew.

How did James know to call him doctor? Matthew had a doctoral degree in English.

"Mrs. Adams," he said, nodding to her, but not shaking her hand.

In six months, Susan would complete her Ph.D. in journalism. Then she would be Dr. Adams, too. Leslie wondered if James would somehow learn about that, just as he had learned about her father.

Matthew was tongue-tied. The truly liberal, intellectual parent would say something like, "Great day for hunting" or "Nice bike" or "Have a nice *weekend*." All Matthew wanted to say was "No way. Not with my daughter."

Susan was tongue-tied for another reason. She saw, *felt*, instantly what it was that made her daughter so strangely silent about James. She realized, as soon as she saw him, that Leslie's attraction was more than intrigue. It was something much more powerful, more dangerous.

"It's a lovely autumn day," Susan sputtered, finally.

James frowned at Leslie for a moment, observing her light windbreaker and school-clothes quality blouse and V-neck sweater. At least she wore jeans.

"Do you have a warmer jacket, Leslie?" he asked.

"A ski parka."

"That would be better."

"OK."

All three members of the family turned to the closet, fortunately nearby, to get Leslie's parka. Susan laughed, lightening the tension a little.

James stood his ground, smiled awkwardly and considered Leslie's parents' reaction to him. A little disapproval, especially her father, but mostly just concern about their precious daughter.

I know she's precious, James thought. Don't you think I know that? Don't you know that I will be so careful with her?

James wondered, for a moment, if he should tell them

169

that, to reassure them. He decided not to. It offended him a little that they didn't know.

"Have fun," Susan murmured reflexively as they left.

"Oh boy," Matthew said, as he watched them getting onto the motorcycle.

"We're about to be tested?" Susan asked.

"I hope not. Leslie can't really be interested in him," Matthew said, confidently.

"You don't see it, either," Susan said quietly. Matthew didn't see it. Neither did Leslie's friends.

"See what?"

"What James has."

"Nothing!"

"Oh, no, darling. He has everything," she said, watching as James handed Leslie a helmet.

"Wear this," James said.

"OK," she said, trying to remember the current state law about wearing helmets. The law changed from year to year. It was an individual rights issue. The individual should be allowed to have a severe head injury if he so chose. Occasionally the state intervened. The state had to pay for the years — most of the victims were healthy teenagers — of hospitalization and care for the badly damaged victim. It was all in Susan's article. Leslie noticed that James wore a helmet, too.

It was probably law.

He got on. She got on behind him after he showed her where to rest her feet.

"Ready?" he asked.

She nodded, half shrugging.

But she wasn't ready. Her arms were at her sides.

"Hold on, Leslie."

Leslie looked around.

"Where?" she asked, finally.

"Put your arms around my waist and hold on tight. We'll be on the freeway. So you really have to hold on. OK?"

Leslie nodded and carefully put her arms around his waist. As soon as they started to move, her grasp tightened. It had to. And eventually she had to press her body against his back.

As the wind whipped against her face and she felt the warmth and strength of James, Leslie remembered her rehearsed dialogue, her planned topics and smiled. It was impossible to talk above the roar of the motorcycle and the sound of the wind. Before they reached the freeway, when they stopped at stop lights, they spoke briefly.

"Are you OK?" he asked above the sputtering of the motorcycle.

"Yes."

"Cold?"

"No."

"Let me know."

"I will," she said. How? She should have said how much she was enjoying it already. Exhilarating. The crisp autumn air. Touching him. She should have said she loved it.

But she didn't before they got onto the interstate, and after that they rode in silence for an hour.

They traveled east over the Lake Washington Floating Bridge across Mercer Island past Lake Sammamish. Beyond Lake Sammamish, the scenery shifted from urban and suburban to rural. At first there were farms, acres of green grass surrounding red and white farmhouses and alive with cows, horses, dogs and tractors.

After they drove through the village of Issaquah with its Swiss chalet architecture and single main street, the scenery changed again. They ascended into the heavily wooded foothills of the Cascade Mountains, gaining altitude, losing civilization, flanking themselves with dense forest and towering mountain peaks.

They exited off Interstate 90 at Snoqualmie, then rode along rutted country roads and finally turned onto a dirt road blocked by a gate with a large No Trespassing sign on it. Without hesitation James drove along a narrow path around the gate. The dirt road led deep into the woods. After about a mile James stopped and turned off the motor. He and Leslie got off the motorcycle, and James removed the wooden bow and quiver of arrows.

Leslie watched in silence as he strung the bow, using

171

considerable force to relax the bow and slide the string into the notch.

"Do you want to practice?" he asked. "That tree over there makes a good target."

"You've been here before?" Leslie asked. Of course James had been here before. One didn't simply drive past No Trespassing signs without a moment's hesitation unless he knew where he was going. Not even James.

"Sure. This," — he gestured expansively — "is all company property. This is where I spend every summer. Logging."

James disappeared every summer to work. Until now, Leslie hadn't known where. A logging camp. For Washington State's largest lumber company. It was a perfect job for James, Leslie thought. Outdoors. Untamed. A man's job.

"Oh."

"Have you ever used a bow and arrow?"

"No."

"I'll show you."

Leslie watched as James shot arrow after arrow. All landed within inches of each other in the trunk of a huge pine tree. It looked effortless, a fluid motion that was silent, except for the swish of the arrow as it left the bow and the soft thud as it hit its mark. Beautiful. Primitive. Natural.

"Want to try?" he asked finally.

"Yes!"

Leslie followed James as he moved closer to the tree.

"You should start from here," he said, handing her the bow and an arrow.

Leslie clumsily hooked the arrow into the bow string, then tried to level it against the strip of leather wrapped around the bow. She tried to imitate what she had seen James do, but she couldn't. The arrow wavered. She pulled gently on the bow string and met surprising resistance.

After a few moments, she looked at him and started giggling.

"Show off! This is really hard!"

"Takes practice."

"And strength. And coordination. It looked so easy

172

when you did it."

"We'll do it together," James said. He stood beside her and put his arms around her. His left hand wrapped over hers and held the bow. With his right hand James steadied the arrow and pulled back.

Leslie felt his strength and his closeness as he took her through the fluid motion, as a passenger, with him.

The arrow found its mark in the tree trunk in the center of the other arrows. Then James released her and walked to the tree to retrieve all the arrows.

He put the arrows in the quiver then looked at her seriously for a moment, as if about to say something.

The moment passed in silence.

"Let's go," he said finally. "Let's go find some deer."

"James . . ."

"What?"

"Can I be the hunter?" Leslie felt the same way about hunting as her father. The deer would be safe if she carried the bow and arrow.

"Sure," he said, half smiling. Then he added firmly, "But I don't kill animals for sport, either, Leslie."

"Then what are we doing?"

"Hunting. I thought the daughter of an English professor would know the meaning of the word." James paused. Then he said, "It means seeking or finding. Not killing."

"Like hunting for Easter eggs?" Leslie teased as the relief swept through her.

"Uh-huh," he said, refusing to be amused. He turned and started walking toward a path between the trees. "C'mon. Let's go."

Leslie followed, wordlessly. Finally she started giggling. James spun around.

"What?"

"I've just never hunted Easter eggs with a bow and arrows."

"Very cute."

"Thank you. So?"

"So I like to shoot arrows into tree trunks when I go deer hunting. OK?" James's voice had a slight edge for the first

173

time. Until then, the teasing had been easy and natural.

Leslie backed off immediately. She realized as she marched behind him through the dense underbrush that she had been teasing him as if she knew him. She had even wrapped her arms around his waist as if he were simply one of the other boys.

But he was *James*. As they walked on, single file, in silence, Leslie wondered if she had angered him. Or if he just thought she was silly.

Of course he thinks I'm silly, Leslie thought glumly. Silly and trivial. Leslie's mind searched frantically for future topics of conversation and found none.

The narrow path finally opened into a huge meadow. James slowed his pace as they neared the clearing. He turned to Leslie and put his finger to his lips. Leslie nodded meaningfully.

James saw the deer first and gestured to Leslie. She didn't see them right away. They were lost in the backdrop of the green-brown underbrush. When she saw them finally, as they came into focus separate and distinct from the background, Leslie gasped.

They were so beautiful. So free. There were three of them — two adults and a fawn — grazing peacefully, unperturbed, unaware, until the scent reached them, of the intrusion. . . .

The adults looked up in unison, alert to the danger, suddenly wary.

Leslie wanted to reassure them. We aren't here to hurt you! They stared at each other for a while, animals and humans, motionless. Then, almost in slow motion, the deer moved into the woods, disappearing into the brown-green maze.

"They are so beautiful! So graceful. So elegant. I like deer hunting," Leslie said. Thinking, after she said it, what a silly thing to say.

"It's beautiful even if you don't see any deer," James said as he sat down on a fallen tree trunk, laid down his bow and arrows and lit a cigarette.

"Yes," Leslie said, taking a deep breath of the delicately

pine-scented autumn air. She gazed up at the perfectly formed pine trees towering above her and the pale blue sky beyond. In a few moments the pine scent blended with the smell of cigarette smoke.

"Does it taste good?" Leslie asked.

"It's more than taste. It's warmth. Especially out here. It's like having your own bonfire inside you."

"I admit it smells good. Better here than in town." Leslie looked at the cigarette hanging casually from the corner of his thin mouth. She watched as the smoke curled around his face. His green eyes narrowed slightly. Leslie had watched her friends trying to smoke cigarettes in a sexy way, inhaling the exhaled smoke back through their nostrils, puffing smoke rings, holding the cigarette casually between their lips, practicing in front of mirrors. Most failed to look sexy despite the practice.

Leslie was confident that James had never practiced smoking in front of a mirror. His relationship with the cigarette was natural. And sexy.

"Haven't you ever even tried a cigarette?" he asked.

Leslie shook her head. *Silly little goody-goody me.*

"Want to?"

"Sure," she said bravely.

James took the cigarette from his mouth and handed it to her.

"It's easier to start with one that's already lighted," he explained. "Just inhale. Slowly and not too deep a breath."

Leslie felt the warmth inside her — it felt good — then the irrepressible instinct to cough. Then a warm dizzy feeling.

"Oh. Oh. Wow."

"Light-headed?"

"Yes. It's passing now. It felt sort of nice. What's that from?"

"Your brain was deprived of oxygen."

"No!"

"No. I guess it's the nicotine."

"It feels good. Is that why you smoke?" Leslie asked, deciding to take a second puff on the cigarette she held, non-sexily, in her hand.

175

"No. I don't even feel that anymore. I just smoke because I smoke. Are you planning to keep my cigarette?"

"Uh-huh."

"Great," James said, lighting a new one for himself. "This will make your parents like me even more than they already do."

"They like you!"

"Yeah. About as much as your girlfriends do."

Probably more than my girlfriends do, Leslie thought. It angered her that her friends didn't even try to conceal their contempt. She had always hoped that James hadn't noticed; but of course, he had, and it bothered him.

"They just don't understand you," Leslie said finally, weakly. She wondered if she should add, Not that I do either, of course. She didn't want to sound presumptuous.

"They understand that I am not one of their special elite group."

"But you are!"

"As a token. I fit in under that one all-important category. I do very well on exams."

"You set the curve," Leslie said quietly. "You're very smart."

"There are a lot of very smart people who don't do well on exams. There are a lot of people who are smart in ways that exams never test, but to your friends exams are the gold standard, the only measurement of worth and success."

Leslie watched the smoke curl up from her cigarette. Her second and third puffs had given her the same dizzy rush. She still felt a little light-headed. Or was the dizziness because of being with James? she wondered as she listened to him talk in long, articulate sentences, not the short phrases he used at school. Which one was the real James, she mused. James, fearless leader of the James gang? Or James, the reluctant but legitimate member of her group? Or was either the real James?

"That's not the only measurement of worth and success," she protested finally, weakly, knowing that it was a minimum requirement. Any other accomplishments, and most

176

of her friends had other accomplishments, were added to the firm, essential base of academic excellence.

"Let's say we all had no food, we were surrounded by deer and all we had were bows and arrows . . ."

"James, *I* don't use academic success as a measurement of worth!"

"I know. Emotionally, you may, a little, but rationally, you don't. But your friends do."

"They are your friends, too. The guys are. They envy you. They admire you. They can't believe how well you do without studying."

"I study," James said seriously, thinking about how he studied, or tried to study, in the afternoon between school and dinner. Before his father got home. Before the drinking and the fighting started. Before it became impossible to study. Then James would leave. Sometimes he would go to the library at the university to study in the silence there. Sometimes his parents' screams disturbed him too much to study. Then he would go find a party or a girl. Or drive ninety miles an hour on his motorcycle.

James studied when he could. It explained his late, unpredictable arrival at parties. Everyone assumed he had been with his other friends, *his* gang, but usually, he had been studying, somewhere. Or with a girl, somewhere. Or alone, somewhere.

James was aware that Leslie was watching him. He leveled his cougar eyes at her and said, "Anyway, your girlfriends are hypocrites. They prance around celebrating sweetness and light and goodness, but they cannot personally accept anyone who is the least bit different. They keep me away from you."

They keep me away from you. His words thundered in her slightly dizzy head and made her heart pound.

"Whaaaat?"

"Whenever I walk toward you, they close in around you. I feel like the *Titanic* heading into a field of icebergs."

Leslie giggled. "That's good. They'd love being called icebergs. But you're unsinkable, aren't you?" she asked, inwardly furious with her *friends*.

"No," James said, standing up. "Let's walk farther. Beyond the clearing, about a mile, there's a nice view of the mountains. Here, give me your cigarette butt."

Leslie handed the smashed cigarette butt to James. He put it, and his, in his pocket to dispose of somewhere else but not here.

"Smokey is my friend," James explained a little sheepishly.

Nice, Leslie thought. She was learning that tough wild James was really nice sensitive James, but she had always known that, hadn't she?

They walked for two miles. James led the way along the narrow fern-lined path through the woods. They stopped once to examine deer hoofprints.

"These are pretty fresh. A doe and a fawn. Probably heading toward the lake," he said.

Leslie nodded.

"Watch this," he said. He flexed the index and middle fingers of his hand and pressed them into the soft dirt, making an imprint that was almost identical to the deer prints. "Can you tell the difference?"

Leslie looked closely. There were subtle differences, but on casual inspection of the prints, the real and the fake looked the same.

"We make prints like these when we're hunting with people who think they have all the answers," James said, smiling wryly.

Like my friends, Leslie thought.

"We do? We trick them on purpose?"

"Yes we do."

Nice, James.

They reached another clearing, a large meadow with a close-enough-to-touch view of the Cascade Mountains, a range of jagged peaks of green, brown and granite, snow-capped in autumn just at the summit.

"Wow," Leslie said softly. Wow. Silly. It was so beautiful. Too beautiful for words.

She watched James light a cigarette and extended her hand toward him.

"You want another one?"

"Yes!" she said, watching as he extracted one for her. He eyed her skeptically. She interpreted his look as concern about her parents' disapproval and said, "My mother likes you."

"How do you know?"

"I can tell. And my father would like you if he knew you."

"Not if I turn his daughter into a chain smoker."

"You're a chain smoker."

"I know. It's a terrible habit," he said lightly. "Anyway, you're not the smoking type."

James held the match for Leslie as she inhaled, in puffs, imitating the way she had watched him light his cigarettes. The coughing followed immediately, along with the warmth and the dizziness. It made her feel a little bold.

"Does your girlfriend smoke?"

"My girlfriend?" James's surprise was genuine. "Who can you possibly mean?"

"Sophomore year. The rumor was that you had a girlfriend who was still at Edison," Leslie said carefully. *A fourteen-year-old whom you were sleeping with.*

"Oh. She wasn't my girlfriend," he said. Then he added, "I've never had a girlfriend."

"Never?"

"No."

"Are you going to, ever?"

"Maybe, I don't know. If I do it won't be a silly public event. Or a game."

Silly. That word again.

"Unlike the relationships I have? And my friends have? Is that what you mean?" She knew that was what he meant and that he was right, but it wasn't a major indictment. All they could be accused of was wanting to fall in love, and they changed partners frequently because they didn't fall in love. Because there was no magic. Because they were all just good friends.

They could only be accused of being silly. And of wanting something more.

"Who is your current boyfriend, Leslie?" James asked in an I-rest-my-case tone of voice.

"No one," she said defiantly, then inhaled clumsily on her cigarette. It was close to the truth. Her relationship with David had fizzled out quickly. They had nothing to say to each other and weren't, they discovered, sexually attracted to each other, either. But something was beginning with Alan. He was captain of the swim team and, of course, an honor student.

"Uh-huh."

"Why don't you want to have a girlfriend, James?"

"It's not necessary," he said automatically. He had no trouble finding girls when he wanted or needed them. James realized that he had shocked Leslie and regretted it. He added seriously, "It doesn't seem right to get involved with someone else, to involve them in your life, until you know yourself what you're going to do."

A long silence followed. Leslie watched the smoke curl slowly, gracefully out of her cigarette. She felt light-headed; but she was thinking clearly, and her thoughts made her dizzy.

All her boyfriends. She used them and they used her. They were all searching for something exciting. Taking not sharing. Wanting not giving. Greedy. Directed by their fine minds and not their hearts. They *knew* love was out there. They had heard about it, read about it, talked about it and never felt it.

Then there was James. He wasn't going to play the game, because it wasn't a game.

It wouldn't be a game, Leslie thought. Not with you and me.

James felt her stare and met her startled blue eyes with his cool green ones.

"What are you going to do?" Leslie asked, flustered, vaguely remembering what she had meant to ask before they had both fallen silent. "Where are you going to college?"

"Where?" he asked. His tone implied that a more pertinent question would have been, Are you going to college?

180

"I have applied to the University of Washington. I'll get in because of my grade point average. So I'll go there if I decide to go. I'll go for sure if we're still in Vietnam. I don't want to get drafted. My brother's in Vietnam."

"Oh. I didn't know that."

"Not the place to be."

"No." Not for someone who hunts for deer the way he hunts for Easter eggs. Not for *anyone,* Leslie thought. "What if you don't have to go to college?"

"I'll probably come back here to the logging camp. I could work my way up to foreman. I'm pretty smart. I do well on exams," he said wryly.

"Forever? Would you be a foreman of a logging camp for the rest of your life?" Leslie asked, trying to conceal her alarm and to suppress the thought that roared in her brain: What a waste! Leslie tried to suppress the thought because it was exactly what James resented so much about all of them. They had only one way of measuring worth and success.

"Life could be worse than being a planter of pines," James said firmly. "To rework Robert Frost a little."

Leslie's eyes widened. A planter of pines. Not a cutter of pines. Not a killer of pines.

"Don't look so surprised. We read some Frost last spring in English—"

"We picked *Mending Wall* apart, stone by stone."

"So I did a little outside reading. I like Frost," James said almost defensively. Then quickly steering the conversation away from himself, he asked, "Where are you going to college?"

"Radcliffe, *if* I get in."

"You will."

"I don't know. It's awfully competitive."

"So are you. Did you tell them you were a Rosemaiden?"

"I haven't told them anything yet. I'm mentally working on my personal statement. I have to decide pretty soon, though, because the application deadline is in a few weeks."

"Do you tell them what you plan to be when you grow

up?"

Leslie shrugged.

"What *do* you plan to be? An English professor?"

Leslie looked at him for a moment. She hadn't told anyone. Not even her mother. It was just the beginning of an idea, because she had always preferred science classes to English or history or art. She had been a volunteer, a candy-striper, at a local hospital for two years, and she loved it.

"A doctor," she said quietly.

"You'll be a good doctor," James said immediately.

"Thanks!" Leslie said, relieved, happy that James didn't seem disapproving or threatened. She added quietly, "I hope so."

Chapter Sixteen

Leslie expected things to be different with James after their day of deer hunting — a stronger bond, a new closeness — but as the weeks of autumn quarter passed, Leslie realized that nothing had changed. Nothing noticeable. The only change was the way she felt inside. Each day she left for school eager to see him, hoping for even a cryptic exchange and dreaming that someday there would be more.

Leslie could not forget the feel of her body against his. Each time she saw him, the memory that was always with her — as a muted, hazy warmth — became vivid, urgent, demanding. Uncomfortable.

Leslie wondered if James knew. She wondered if she should tell him.

She wondered if she would be able to suppress the urge to ask him to take her for another ride on his motorcycle. She wanted to wrap her arms around him, press against him and feel his strength.

It made Leslie uneasy to think that she might actually ask him. What if she wasn't able to resist? What if she really did ask him for a date? Unthinkable. Except she thought about it all the time.

That fall Leslie and James had the same study hall. James's assigned seat was behind hers, five rows back and three rows over. Still, Leslie managed to watch him in brief, surreptitious glances. Usually James spent study period staring out the window. Occasionally he flipped halfheartedly through his textbooks.

One day in November, James spent the entire hour working on a sheet of paper that lay on his desk. His concentration was intense. He didn't look up or pause. Leslie watched him work, watched him peer at the paper, writing quickly, frowning occasionally, erasing something, then writing again. Now she understood how he could get the best grades without apparently studying. He did study. He studied like this, in brief, intense, energetic spurts with absolute concentration.

Finally, shamed by her own staring—unnoticed by James but detected by several of her friends who arched skeptical eyebrows—and shamed by James's obvious diligence, Leslie began to work in earnest on an assignment for her honors French class.

When the bell sounded signaling the end of study hall, James and Leslie were both still working. The rest of the class had predictably stacked books and returned sheets of paper to inside pockets of folders a full three minutes before the bell was scheduled to sound. They wanted to waste no part of the five-minute break between classes with anything as mundane as reorganizing their school work.

Leslie was still neatly putting away her almost completed French assignment when James reached her desk.

"Here," he said. "This is for you."

He handed her a manila folder as he walked by her desk and out of the study hall.

He was gone before Leslie could recover from her surprise enough to say something. Not that she would know what to say until she saw the contents of the folder anyway.

Her hands trembled as she opened it.

James had not been writing an essay on the meaning of the moral wilderness in Hawthorne's *The Scarlet Letter*. Nor had he been solving an equation for the advanced mathematics class. Instead, James had been drawing a picture. For her.

It was a picture, a *perfect* picture, of the meadow he had shown her. Every detail was exactly as she remembered it: the tall pines, the long dew-covered grass, the fallen stump and the deer, across the meadow, looking startled and curious and regal. James had drawn it in pencil, in perfect, careful detail, perfect proportion and perfect shading. Even in black and white, the warmth of the autumn sun, the exquisite beauty of the deer and the towering majesty of the pines were eloquently, colorfully, conveyed.

James was an artist! Even through her untrained and prejudiced eyes, Leslie recognized James's talent.

He was a talented artist whose picture precisely captured a wonderful memory — *the* wonderful memory — that they had shared. James had preserved the memory for her.

James wanted her to remember.

Leslie's hands trembled even more as she carefully returned the picture to its folder and placed the folder inside her notebook. Then she rushed to her final class of the day.

Leslie did not hear one word of the lecture her history teacher gave on William Jennings Bryan although she feigned an expression of rapt attention. She resisted the almost irresistible urge to open her notebook and look at the picture.

She appeared calm and serious, but her mind raced. Why had he given it to her? Did anyone else know that he could draw? How could she thank him? *When* could she thank him? She had swim team practice as soon as school was out. She couldn't even try to find James because Alan was meeting her after class and walking with her to the pool. If only she would see James first, she could ask him to give her a ride to practice on his motorcycle. . .

Leslie didn't have a chance to look at the picture again until she got home that evening, *after* swim practice and *after* agreeing to go to the Homecoming Dance with Alan. When she finally looked at it again, in the privacy of her own bedroom, it was even more beautiful and more perfect.

Leslie decided to show it to her mother, her best friend. Even though she hadn't discussed James with Susan — what was there to discuss? — since the day she and James had gone deer hunting, Leslie sensed that Susan understood about James. Not that there was anything to understand.

185

James was there. A presence. Undefined but important to Leslie. Susan seemed to know that.

Susan was making garlic butter.

"Mother, look at this," Leslie said, carefully holding the picture so that her mother could see it but away from the butter.

Susan said nothing, but she quickly washed her hands in hot water and after they were clean and dry took the precious picture for closer scrutiny.

"This is very good, Leslie. What a beautiful scene. Even in black and white you feel the color and the life. Who did it?" Susan asked. She knew that Leslie hadn't drawn it but wondered who among her friends had this surprising talent.

"James," Leslie said softly. "It's where we went that day to look for deer. The three deer in the picture are the ones we saw."

Susan frowned slightly. She remembered how happy Leslie had been after the deer-hunting expedition and how, over the ensuing weeks, the happiness and excitement had begrudgingly faded. Susan knew that James hadn't called, that he hadn't asked Leslie out again. Leslie's disappointment was painfully obvious. It was obvious despite the fact that unlike all the other boys she had dated, had wanted to date, Leslie didn't talk about James.

Now her daughter's face was radiant again.

"Did he just give this to you?"

"Today. He drew it—or at least finished drawing it—in study hall. It is good, isn't it?" Leslie asked. Not that it mattered.

"Really very good."

"I thought I should frame it. To protect it."

"There's a good frame shop a mile from campus on University Avenue. We can take it there. I think a cream-colored mat with a forest green border might look good," Susan said, knowing that her own sense of color and art was excellent unlike Leslie's and that Leslie wanted her advice on this important project.

"Great. Maybe we could go there this evening? It's

186

Thursday night. They might be open."

"We can't have it framed yet. There is something missing from the picture," Susan said shaking her head.

"What?"

"His signature."

"Oh," Leslie said quietly. "Do you think he will sign it?"

"Of course," Susan said confidently. He had better sign it, she thought. He had better not be playing games with my daughter's heart. Susan's brief glimpse of James made her understand Leslie's attraction. James was different. Complicated. Sensual.

Susan understood it, but it made her uneasy as she thought about her uncomplicated and naive daughter.

"Of course he will sign it," she repeated firmly.

The next day Leslie found James during lunch period. He was leaning against the wall reading the school newspaper, *The Potomac*. During an almost sleepless night, Leslie had practiced a hundred ways to thank him and to ask him to sign the picture. No matter how she asked it he could always say no.

"James?"

"Hi, Leslie," he said folding the paper.

"It's beautiful!" she blurted out, completely forgetting all the carefully worded, sophisticated thank yous. She repeated, flustered, "Beautiful. Thank you."

"You're welcome," he said seriously. The green eyes looked pleased.

"I had no idea you could draw," she continued, frantically searching for lost lines, for a place in the carefully rehearsed script. But to no avail.

"It's a hobby."

"You're really good."

"Leslie, you're not really an art critic."

"I know," she admitted. Then, because she was still not thinking clearly, she said, "But my mother knows. She works with lots of commercial artists, collaborating on articles and so on—"

"You showed it to your mother?"

"Yes!" Leslie said a little defensively. "And she thinks it's

187

very good."

Leslie's eyes iced over for a moment. James caught the glare, smiled, then shrugged his shoulders. The iciness melted into sparkling blue radiance.

"Here's what else my mother says," she began, watching James's reaction. He looked curious. "She says we can't frame it—and it *has* to be framed—until you sign it."

"You want me to sign it?"

"Yes. Please," Leslie said quietly.

"OK. Sure."

Leslie took the picture, still protected in its folder, out of her notebook and handed it to James. She followed him into a classroom where he sat at a desk. In the lower right hand corner of the picture he wrote: *James 1971*.

"Thank you," she whispered when he handed it back to her.

"You're welcome."

They walked back into the hall. Lunch period was almost over. The hall was getting crowded.

"Are you going to the Homecoming Dance?" James asked casually.

Leslie's heart stopped. The Homecoming Dance was the mid-year prom. It was not like dances in the gym to which boys and girls went with their own groups. The Homecoming Dance was for couples only, with reservations in advance. A formal date. Was James asking her to go with him? Or was he just checking to see if she was going?

Leslie nodded slowly.

"With Alan?"

"Yes," she whispered.

James nodded as if confirming his suspicion.

"Well, time for class. See ya, Leslie," he said.

The only thing wrong with Alan, Leslie decided, was that he wasn't James, and since James had withdrawn again in the weeks after he had given her the picture, Alan would have to do. It made Leslie angry with herself, and with James, to wait for him to call night after night. She was angry because she waited and because James didn't call.

It was better to be busy.

Alan had transferred to George Washington from Lake Forest, Seattle's exclusive boys' school, during spring quarter of junior year. He had transferred because the George Washington swim team was the best high school swim team in the state. He wanted the visibility for college recruiters. Alan fit in perfectly with Leslie's group because of his grades and accomplishments. He held the Pacific Northwest record in the two hundred-meter free-style.

Like James, Alan brought interesting new blood to the group. But unlike James, all the girls wanted him. Alan dated most of them a few times. By fall of senior year, it was obvious to everyone that Alan was mainly interested in Leslie.

It was an inevitable match. In addition to the usual academic and environmental compatibilities — Alan's father was on the faculty in anthropology at the university — Leslie and Alan even looked alike. They both had chestnut brown curls and large blue eyes. They both smiled a lot and laughed easily. Because life was easy and happy. They both did what was expected of them. They *achieved,* they *accomplished,* and they did it cheerfully because it felt right.

Alan and James were friends, as much as James was anyone's friend. Alan had no idea about Leslie's feelings for James. It would never have occurred to him.

Leslie did not fall in love with Alan, but she liked being with him. It made her feel good that he cared so much about her. Alan told Leslie that he loved her. Leslie told him that they were too young to know what that even meant but that she *liked* him very much.

Leslie did like Alan very much. She liked everything about him: the way he looked, what he said, what he thought, the way he kissed her. Now, *finally,* after the groping, inept, insincere kissing and touching of previous relationships, Leslie actually wanted to be held and touched.

Sometimes when Alan kissed her, she pretended he was James.

On a Friday afternoon in mid-February James caught up with Leslie after their English literature class.

"We have to leave right after school if we're going to be on the ferry before the sun sets."

"We do?" she asked.

"Uh-huh."

"Why?" she asked weakly, stalling for time, making decisions, thinking about repercussions.

"Why what?"

"Why are we going?" She had made that decision. Whatever it was, she was going. With James.

"Because it's mid-February and the sky is blue and the mountains look like ice cream cones and you cannot waste a day like this. Not in Seattle."

It *was* a beautiful day. A sunny oasis in a mild but gray and drizzly winter.

"When do we leave?"

"Three-ten. I keep my bike in the parking lot near the gym."

"Bike?"

"Motorcycle."

"Three-ten," Leslie said as she left, her mind reeling, to deal with the repercussions.

As usual, Alan met Leslie at her locker after school.

"I'm not going to practice tonight," Leslie said, looking into her locker instead of at Alan.

"What? Leslie, why?"

"I just . . ." Leslie paused, searching for something that was technically the truth, "don't feel like it."

"Are you ill?"

"No."

"Cramps?" he asked softly.

"Alan!" That was too personal.

"Leslie I am trying to understand. We have a meet tomorrow, you know."

"Of course I know. I'll be there. My performance won't be worse if I skip this one practice. In fact it will probably be better."

"OK. I'll call tonight to see if you're all right."

"No, don't. I'm all right, really," she said, feeling guilty, unable to look at him.

"I'll see you tomorrow, then," he said. He kissed her briefly on the cheek.

Leslie smiled weakly. As soon as Alan left, she grabbed her books and dashed toward the parking lot near the gym. James was already there.

"I forgot that you always wear a skirt," he said, looking at Leslie's tartan plaid kilt. "I guess you can ride that way. Your legs may get cold."

"It's OK," Leslie said. *I'll press them against yours to keep warm.*

"What are these?" he asked, gesturing toward her armful of books.

"Homework!"

"Can't you leave them here?"

"For the weekend? James, you and I have a test on Monday in English lit," she said. Then she noticed that James had no books.

"Give them here, then," he said. He took her stack of books and balanced them in front of him on the motorcycle. Then he looked at her, handed her his helmet and said, "Hop on."

Leslie tucked the free folds of her skirt around her thighs, then wrapped her arms around James's chest.

James didn't take them in the direction of the ferry terminal in downtown Seattle. Instead he drove along side streets, finally stopping in front of a small dilapidated house with an untended garden and sagging roof. James turned off the engine.

"Home," he said simply. "I'll be right back."

James took Leslie's books and disappeared into the house. While she waited, Leslie studied James's neighborhood. The street was narrow, and the sidewalks and road were crisscrossed with grass-filled cracks. A battered car without a left front tire was parked across the street. The houses looked old and sad and forgotten. Leslie was deciding what it would take to fix up James's house—not that much, really, a little paint, a weekend of gardening, some

191

weed-killer—when he returned. Her books were gone, and he carried a motorcycle helmet for himself.

Without speaking they got back onto the motorcycle and sped off. It was almost rush hour. James avoided the freeway, selecting the more scenic route over University Bridge and along the shore of Lake Union on Eastlake Avenue. They traveled on Denny Way past the Space Needle to Elliot Way and the Puget Sound waterfront.

They drove past the wharf, the aquarium, Pike Place Market and several commercial piers before arriving at the ferry terminal. Their waterside route was lined by fishermen casting lines off the piers and by native Seattleites drawn to the typically summertime tourist attractions by the beauty of the February day. Kites floated above the blue waters of Elliot Bay, Ivar's sold more iced tea than clam chowder and the air was filled with sounds of laughing children and frolicking seagulls.

The ferry between downtown Seattle and Bainbridge Island arrived just as James and Leslie did. James pulled into the commuter parking lot which was mostly empty at that time of day on the Seattle side of the commuter route. He chained his motorcycle and the helmets to a metal post.

"Two one-way . . . er . . . round-trip tickets on the Bainbridge line," he told the ticket seller.

After the ticket taker collected two of the four orange-colored tickets from James as they walked onto the ferry, James handed the return-trip tickets to Leslie.

"Here. You can keep these as a souvenir. I bought them for you."

"We don't need them?"

"Not if we don't get off the ferry."

"Oh. So you're allowed to do that? Just ride back and forth on the ferry? Like sitting through multiple showings of the same movie at a theater. I've always wondered if that was allowed."

James looked at her with amazement and slowly shook his head.

"*Allowed* in a movie theater means that you can outglower the sixteen-year-old usher assigned to check the theater between showings. In my case, it's usually someone I've gone to school with since kindergarten. I don't suppose any of your friends would ever work in a movie theater."

Leslie shrugged, embarrassed. Her naiveté was showing.

"In the case of ferries you are *supposed* to get off. Most people take ferries to get to the other side anyway, but there are plenty of places to hide during the check between runs."

"Hide?"

"If you want to get off and hand the ticket taker those two tickets, you may."

"No. I want to hide," Leslie said, thinking, We *have* paid for the return trip. If anyone caught us — "If I hadn't been with you, you just would have bought a one-way ticket, huh?"

"Uh-huh."

Nice, James. Nice James.

They stood on the front deck of the ferry as it crossed Elliot Bay to Bainbridge Island. Bainbridge was a fashionable residential area inhabited by people who worked in downtown Seattle. They commuted by ferry, not by car. It was a peaceful, beautiful commute. They could read the morning newspaper, drink coffee and enjoy the dramatic seasons of the land, the water, the mountains and the sky. Sometimes a ferry broke down, or the winds were too strong and the waves too high to permit passage. Then, if they were lucky, they were stranded on the island to weather the storm in their Pacific Northwest homes.

Leslie looked at the Cascade Mountains to the east, the Olympic Mountains to the west and Mount Rainier to the south. The pristine white mountains sparkled in the winter sun. The rugged treacherous peaks were softened by the pink haze that heralded the end of the day. Elliot Bay glittered a deep blue, reflecting the sky above. So many days in winter the water was gray and cloudy, but today the waters were clear and blue, crested with feathery whitecaps caused by the gentle balmy breeze.

Draw me a picture of this, James, Leslie thought. Draw me a picture of the water and the islands and the mountains and the sky. Or a picture of the graceful strength of the

Space Needle. Or of the delicate white arches of the Science Center. Or of the sunny-day activity on the waterfront. Or of the powerful majesty of Mount Rainier.

Even if James drew her no pictures, Leslie would remember this day always. The memories were carefully, *indelibly,* etched in her mind. Memories of this glorious day in the city she loved. With James. Leslie would never forget it.

James stood close beside her without speaking. He, too, was mesmerized by the spectacle of the sunny day and the blue water and the beauty that surrounded them.

Too soon they reached Bainbridge Island. The ferry bumped gently against the creosote wood pilings of the ferry dock. James and Leslie watched the dock crew pull the ferry snugly into its berth with heavy ropes. As soon as the first car left the ferry boat, James said, "We'd better go."

Leslie looked at the deck. Except for them, it was empty. Everyone else had long since returned to their cars, eager to complete their commute and return to their homes to enjoy the sunset that was imminent and promised to be memorable.

Leslie followed him, silently, stealthily through the body of the ferry boat to the stairway at the stern. The stairway led to the car deck two flights below. At the bottom of the first landing James swung under the staircase into a storage space for life jackets.

It was dark. A few rays of natural light filtered through the slits in the staircase that formed the roof of the storage area. And it was small, just big enough for both of them to stand pressed against the stacks of orange life jackets.

Leslie started to speak, a sentence that would have flowed from a giggle, but James touched her lips with his finger.

Then she heard what he heard: footsteps. Efficient, official footsteps coming down the stairs. She held her breath. Her heart pounded. The footsteps slowed as they reached the landing. Then they sped up again, their rhythm restored as they took the second flight of stairs.

"The purser," James whispered as the sound receded.

"Does he check for stowaways?" Leslie asked, excited by this game, this adventure, this flirtation with harmless danger.

James nodded in the darkness. Leslie's eyes were accommodating to the dimness. She could see his face, close to hers, looking at her seriously.

"Now, what do we do if they find us?" he asked sternly. "Do we give them the tickets?"

"No, Bond. And if we think we're about to be caught . . ." Leslie paused. Then she added, conspiratorially, "We swallow them."

Leslie saw James's mouth curl into a smile.

They lapsed into silence. They had to be quiet and attentive. After a few moments, they heard the sound of cars being loaded onto the ferry.

"When. . . ?" she began.

"As soon as we hear a car door shut, near this stairway, we go."

Leslie nodded.

They listened. They heard doors shut in the distance, at the bow of the boat. Gradually the sounds got closer.

Then they heard the door that was their signal. Like the finely trained secret agents they pretended to be, they moved in unison out of the storage area onto the stairs and up to the deck.

When they reached the deck, Leslie said breathlessly, "That was fun!"

"Because you had the paid-for return tickets, which you never plan to use, in your pocket," James observed mildly as he reached in his pocket for a cigarette.

Leslie started to protest but considered what he said. It was probably true. She had had her fingers on the tickets in her pocket the entire time.

"A Rosemaiden to the core, I guess," she said with a sigh as she gestured toward his cigarette.

"It's not all that bad. You want a cigarette? Or have you quit smoking?"

"I keep trying," she said. They both knew that the only other cigarettes she had smoked had been that day months before in a meadow with him. "But it's gotten cold all of a sudden. I need a nice warm cigarette."

In the fifteen minutes it took to reload the ferry, while James and Leslie hid beneath the stairs, all signs of summer had disappeared. The sinking sun pulled its warmth with it and left behind a bitter, cold winter evening and a spectacular sunset. The sky glowed red and pink and yellow and orange. The skyline of the city twinkled in the foreground. The buildings reflected the sunset back toward the twilight sky from their huge plate-glass windows.

"Do you want to go inside?" James asked, handing her his lighted cigarette.

Leslie shook her head vigorously. Not for anything. It was too beautiful. She inhaled deeply, her lungs filling with warmth, then irritation from the unfamiliar smoke. She coughed and laughed.

Then she felt wonderfully dizzy and giddy. And a little unsteady. She held on to the painted green railing of the boat and closed her eyes for a moment against the chilling wind that had picked up force as the boat began to move.

She began to shiver.

Without hesitation James put his arms around her.

"You're freezing," he whispered. His cheek touched hers.

"Not if you hold me," she whispered into the wind, wondering if he would hear.

"I'll hold you," he whispered back. He released her for a moment to open his parka. Then he wrapped the parka around both of them, pulled her hands inside and folded his arms around her again.

Leslie felt his heart pounding, felt his lips brush her hair as the wind blew it into his face and felt his arms tighten around her as she pressed even closer. It was hard to breathe, but she didn't want him to loosen his grip.

The back of her head rested against his cheek. She was warm and secure. He made her that way.

But now he was cold. After a few minutes Leslie felt his jaw move. His teeth were chattering.

Leslie pulled free and turned toward him. She put her warm hands on his shivering, ice-cold cheeks.

"James," she whispered, feeling his cold skin, looking at his white and purple lips and cheeks. Looking into his eyes.

James wanted to kiss her then, but he couldn't. His lips were numb. He couldn't form words to speak. He couldn't even hold his cigarette with his lips.

Instead, he pulled her toward him, cradled her head against his chest and held her.

"Let's get some hot chocolate," he mumbled into her hair, his voice slurred.

"What?"

He put his arm around her and guided her toward the too bright lights of the ferry boat canteen. By the time the boat docked in Seattle, fortified by a mug of hot chocolate and a shared cigarette, they were warm again, ready for the cold ride home on James's motorcycle.

An old station wagon was parked in the driveway at James's house. James stopped at the curb but didn't turn off the engine.

"Shall I get off?" Leslie asked.

What is he doing home so early? James wondered. His father usually started his Friday afternoon drinking in a bar and often didn't arrive home until midnight, but he was home now. That meant trouble.

James hesitated.

"Leslie, I have to go in by myself. So, maybe I should just bring your books to the party at Larry's tomorrow night?"

How will I explain that to Alan? Leslie wondered. Why couldn't she go into James's house?

"I don't mind waiting out here. I'm not cold," Leslie said easily. She *did* mind waiting. James's neighborhood scared her, and she *was* cold; but it would be best to get her books now.

"You sure?"

"Yes."

"I'll be right back."

James wasn't gone long. Leslie thought she heard shouting from inside the house. Then she heard a door slam. James appeared carrying her books and an extra parka.

197

"Is everything OK?"

"Sure," he said not looking at her. "Here, wear this."

It was twenty minutes by motorcycle with James driving from his house to hers. Twenty minutes from one world to another.

In the final twenty minutes of a confusing, exciting, wonderful afternoon, Leslie had one last chance to touch him, to talk to him, to be alone with him . . . until when? Twenty minutes to try to decide if he really had wanted to kiss her when she touched his face with her hands. His eyes said so, but he didn't. What made him change his mind? Could she make him change it back? Should she ask him who owned the old station wagon and why there was shouting? Was he angry that she had made him go in his house to get her books?

Did I do something wrong, James? When will I see you again? Kiss me, James.

By the time they reached her house, Leslie's mind was exhausted. She knew she couldn't, wouldn't, question him. She didn't even care about the answers. She just didn't want him to leave.

They walked in silence to her front door. James carried her books.

"Do you want to come in?" Leslie asked finally. Unlike his house, hers was safe for visitors. She hoped it didn't offend him.

James frowned, his expression thoughtful.

"I'd better not," he said.

"You would be welcome to stay for dinner," Leslie pressed gently, detecting his hesitancy. He was considering it.

"No . . ."

"At least come see the way I have framed the picture you gave me."

That was a mistake. James stiffened and withdrew a step.

"I can't stay, Leslie."

"OK," she said lightly, reaching for her books, handing him his parka, all the while aching inside.

Leslie clutched her books against her breasts and looked

at the doorknob. All she had to do was touch it, and he would leave. She couldn't move.

"Hey," James said, touching her cheek with his finger, "Leslie."

"Yes?" Her eyes met his.

"Thank you for coming with me. I had a nice time," he said.

He kissed her, lightly, beside her mouth.

Then he left.

At the swim meet the next day, Leslie set personal and meet records in the one hundred meter individual medley and the fifty meter free-style.

"I guess you're feeling better," Alan said after the meet.

"What? Oh. I feel fine."

"Good. I'll pick you up at seven-thirty tonight."

The party at Larry's—nominally a Valentine's Day party—was a typical gathering of Leslie's friends. It provided a Saturday night social function for everyone. Those without dates visited with friends, gossiped about school, speculated about the college acceptances that would be sent in two months and discussed movies and albums and, in occasional philosophical moments, life itself. The couples usually retreated to the darkest room of the house to dance, to kiss or to be alone.

New relationships formed and old ones dissolved at such a rate that the profile of each party was unique. For the past three months, Alan and Leslie alone emerged as the enduring, constant couple. They were so comfortable with their relationship that they usually spent as much time visiting with their unattached friends in the brightly lit living rooms as they did closeted with the new couples in the darkened dancing areas.

But that night, troubled by Leslie's mysterious behavior the day before, Alan pulled her away from the others early in the evening.

"Let's dance, Les."

James arrived at ten. At least Leslie first noticed him

then, leaning against a wall in the dance room, smoking a cigarette and drinking beer from a can. He stared at her, his face eerily illuminated each time he inhaled.

Leslie stared back at James, her face resting against Alan's shoulder, her arms wrapped around him, swaying gently to the Beatles' "Hey Jude." Leslie's blue eyes didn't blink. They watched James with wide-eyed curiosity.

Do you want me, James?

James returned her stare, unblinking, unflinching, his eyes hidden in shadows between puffs of his cigarette.

Dance with me, James.

Halfway through the dance, Alan raised Leslie's chin with his hand and guided her mouth to his. They kissed, moving slowly to the music, for the rest of the song.

By the time they stopped dancing, James was gone.

Chapter Seventeen

April fifteenth was the date on which all colleges notified applicants of their acceptance—or rejection—by the school. That year—their senior year—April fifteenth was a Saturday. A victory party was planned. The party would be held at Alan's parents' summer cabin at Sparrow Lake thirty miles north of Seattle. It was scheduled to begin after the day's mail had arrived in Seattle and continue until midnight. The girls had to be back in their homes in Seattle by one. The boys would spend the night at the cabin.

Alan and James arrived at the cabin at ten Saturday morning to set up. They put food and beer in the refrigerator, gas in the water ski boat, wood in the fireplace and coals in the barbeque. Alan and James didn't need to wait for the day's mail. They already knew their college plans. James had been accepted at the University of Washington and had decided to attend. Alan had been offered numerous athletic scholarships. He decided to go to the University of California at Los Angeles because of UCLA's recent record in NCAA swimming championships.

But Alan was anxious about the news that the mail would bring to Leslie. She had applied to two schools in California: Pomona, in the Los Angeles area, and Stanford, three hundred miles away. The distance between Los Angeles and Stanford was substantial, but it was still closer than Leslie's first choice: Radcliffe was a continent away. Alan assumed that Leslie would be accepted at all three schools. He desperately wanted her to choose one of the California schools. He wanted to be near her.

In the past few weeks, Leslie and Alan had frequently discussed the decision Leslie would make. Sometimes their discussions were careful and gentle. Too often they were bitter.

It was Leslie's decision. Still, if by some chance she wasn't accepted at Radcliffe . . .

Betty, Joanne and Robin arrived at Leslie's house one minute ahead of the mail truck. Betty's mail had arrived mid-morning bearing news of her acceptance to Smith, her first choice. She had picked up Joanne, who already knew she was staying in Seattle at the University, and Robin, who was rejected by Vassar but still had the luxury of choosing between Bryn Mawr and Swarthmore.

Susan and Leslie were already at the curb watching the mail truck's painfully slow trek up the street.

Finally the mail was in Leslie's hand. She extracted the envelopes from Stanford University, Pomona College, Radcliffe College, Antioch, University of Michigan and Cornell University. She selected the one postmarked Cambridge, Massachusetts.

It was thin. Too thin, Leslie thought, her hands trembling. She took a deep breath and opened it as Susan, Robin, Betty and Joanne watched.

Welcome to Radcliffe College . . .

"I'm in," she whispered. "I got into Radcliffe."

"Hurray!"

"Of course you did. Whoever doubted it?"

"Congratulations, darling."

"Leslie, are you ready to go?"

"Now I am," Leslie said, lifting the bag that contained her swim suit, towel and extra clothes and handing the six envelopes, unopened except for the acceptance from Radcliffe, to Susan. "Here, Mom."

"Don't you—" Susan began, thinking abut Alan.

"I guess I'd better take these two," Leslie said, selecting the envelopes from Stanford and Pomona. "I'll open them on the way to the lake."

Leslie didn't want to open them yet. She didn't want to think about anything but how happy she was to have gotten

202

into Radcliffe. To be going to Radcliffe. She had made her decision as soon as she read the first word of the letter. *Welcome.*

The letters from Stanford and Pomona didn't matter. Except that she had to tell Alan. Maybe, if she was lucky, the letters from both would begin with *We are sorry to inform you . . .* or, *Unfortunately. . .*

Unfortunately, as Leslie discovered when she finally opened the letters five minutes before they reached the cabin, she was accepted by both.

Leslie, Betty, Joanne and Robin were among the last to arrive. Everyone else had shared their news, some jubilant, some disappointed, all adjusting as the afternoon wore on and they shared the joy and the disappointment with their friends.

Everyone knew how much Leslie wanted to go to Radcliffe.

"So, Leslie, are you going to be a Cliffie?" someone asked as soon as she entered the cabin.

"Yes," she said firmly, looking at Alan across the room. "Yes, I am."

For the next five minutes, Leslie learned about the fates, bad and good, of her friends. Eventually she worked her way over to Alan who had retreated to a far corner of the cabin and was staring at the lake.

"I'm going to Radcliffe, Alan," she said quietly.

"I heard."

"It's what I want. What I've been working for."

"I know," he said bitterly. It was what you were working for before you met me, he thought. And I haven't made a difference. He looked at her. "Did you get in to—"

"Yes. To both. Alan, you're being unfair. I didn't try to talk you out of going to UCLA, to get you to look at East Coast schools."

"I know. I wish you had. I wish you had cared enough to try."

"I'm not going to let you spoil this for me, Alan," Leslie said.

She grabbed her bag, crossed the living room and went

outside to the shed across from the main cabin. They used the shed for the girls' dressing area during parties. Leslie bolted the door and changed into her old blue tank suit. She hadn't worn it for years but decided it would be fine to wear under a wet suit if she did any water skiing. The water was too cold in April to swim or water ski without a wet suit.

Leslie was going for a swim anyway, despite the cold. She pulled on the tank suit she had purchased in eighth grade. It still fit perfectly in the hips and waist, but it was tight, *too* tight, over her breasts.

It didn't matter. No one would see her, and she had to swim. She had to swim, as fast as she could, until she was exhausted. She had to burn off some of her energy — her *ecstasy* — from being accepted at Radcliffe. And some of her anger with Alan. Then, when she was calm again, she would rejoin the party.

Leslie threw her towel over her shoulders, unbolted the shed door and walked, barefooted, across the lawn and down the four cement stairs that led to the sandy beach. She left her towel at the water's edge and walked without hesitation into the lake.

As soon as the water was deep enough, Leslie flopped onto her stomach and began to swim. She did the stroke that required the most energy and concentration: the butterfly. The water was barely tolerable.

After twenty minutes of swimming as fast as she could in the frigid water, concentrating on nothing but the style and pace and rhythm of her stroke, Leslie was exhausted. She swam back toward shore. When the level was waist-deep, she stood and trudged, head down, through the cold heavy water toward the beach. She thought about the reason for her icy swim — her acceptance to Radcliffe — and smiled. It still felt so good.

"A little cold, isn't it?"

Leslie looked up, startled. James sat on a piece of driftwood smoking a cigarette, staring at her. At all of her.

Her wet shivering body was covered with goose bumps as she hastily pushed her dripping wet chestnut hair off her face. James stared at the startled sapphire blue eyes and the full lips with the half smile that faded when she saw him. Her boyish hips and legs and her round firm breasts that pressed for freedom against the sheer fabric of the too small blue tank suit were subject to his gaze.

Leslie felt naked. She *was* naked except for the flimsy suit that became almost transparent when she was wet and her body was rigid from the cold.

James was staring at her, smiling, holding her towel.

"James," she breathed unable to move.

James stood up and walked toward her. He draped the towel around her like a cape. Leslie gratefully pulled the edges of the towel together. She was clothed again. Modest. Hidden from his inquisitive, penetrating eyes.

"Did you work it all off?" he asked.

"What?"

"Your fight with Alan."

"We didn't have a fight."

"Oh."

"He's annoyed because I'm going to Radcliffe instead of somewhere close to him."

"He's hurt."

"Hurt?"

"You'd rather go to a city where you know no one and take the chance of making new friends than be with him. It speaks for itself. Of course he's hurt."

"You think I should follow Alan to Los Angeles?"

"I think you should do what you want to do."

"I think I'm a little young to give up my life and my dreams for someone else, don't you?"

James shrugged. He stared at the water and avoided her eyes.

"If Alan were the right person for you, you could make the commitment," he said distantly.

I could stay at the University of Washington, James, if you wanted me to. I *would* stay, she thought, amazed at the realization. Or if you wanted to spend your life working at the logging camp . . . maybe I could be the cook. For the right person I could make the commitment.

205

"Leslie! James! We're going to water ski now. Leslie, you've already been in?"

Leslie and James were joined on the beach by the others. Alan continued to keep a cool distance from Leslie despite her attempts to approach him.

They water skied, played volleyball, barbequed hamburgers and roasted marshmallows. When the sun set, they turned down the lights and turned on the music. Leslie watched Alan dance with Betty, Joanne and Robin. He was showing her that he could have a good time without her.

It won't work, Alan, Leslie thought. I won't feel jealous or sorry. I won't apologize, and I won't change my mind.

Leslie glanced at her watch. Eleven. They had to leave by midnight. Maybe someone would like to leave now, but it didn't look like it. From her vantage point in the corner of an overstuffed sofa, no one was ready for the party to end.

"Let's go," he whispered in her ear.

James. She hadn't seen him for a while. She assumed he had left.

Without saying anything, Leslie followed him. James went to the kitchen for a can of beer, then he led the way outside toward the woods that surrounded the cabin. After five minutes, James found a fallen tree. He leaned against the stump and lit a cigarette.

"Leslie?" he asked offering her a cigarette.

"No, thank you. I've quit."

"That's good. Terrible habit. Would you like some beer?" he asked, raising the can of beer toward her. She could have some of his.

"No, I—"

"Don't drink. That's right. Too young. Against the law."

"It is," Leslie protested weakly.

"What's going to happen to you next year at Radcliffe? Everyone will drink or at least know how to drink. You may even be old enough to drink legally in Massachusetts."

"Nothing's going to happen to me."

"And what about dope?"

Leslie looked at him blankly.

"Marijuana," James said.

"I don't need it."

"Natural high?" James asked, his eyes mocking her.

Why was James acting this way? Did he resent the fact that she was going to Radcliffe, too? If he did, why didn't he tell her?

Leslie sighed and sat down on the log six feet away from James.

"I think you should at least know what it tastes like," he said quietly after a few silent moments.

"What what tastes like?"

"Beer."

"Oh."

"I have a way for you to taste beer without drinking it," he said.

James took a large swallow of his beer and walked toward her.

"Leslie," James said gently, carefully lacing his strong fingers through her fine chestnut hair. "Come here."

He pulled her mouth to his and kissed her, a deep warm passionate kiss that tasted, at first, like beer. Then, as the kiss became longer and deeper, it tasted like James.

The moment James's soft persuasive lips touched hers, Leslie knew what had been tormenting her, confusing her, exciting her for almost three years. It was desire for James. The need to have his lips on hers. The need to touch him and feel *him* touch *her.*

James, she thought as she curled her fingers through his black hair and felt her body pressing closer to his. Naturally. Instinctively. *James.*

His hands held her face as he kissed her. Leslie lost herself in the feel of him, the taste of him, the warmth and strength and touch of him. She heard—*felt*—a soft deep moan. It was a moan of pleasure and desire and need. Did the moan come from James? Or did it come from deep within *her?*

They kissed with mouths joined and bodies straining through layers of shirts and sweaters and coats until, breathless, James pulled away. He still held her face in his rough but gentle hands.

"You like it," he said staring at her, his intense serious eyes glazed with desire. Desire and a trace of worry.

Can I stop? he wondered. I have to.

"I like—" Leslie began, confused by his words and the power of his eyes and the feelings that pulsed through her body. *I like you, James, I like it when you kiss me.*

"Beer," he said. His voice was husky. It would be impossible to stop now. Impossible to lighten the mood. It wasn't what either of them wanted.

Leslie traced his lips with her fingers and felt her body sway toward his as if James's body were a powerful seductive magnet.

"I want to be closer to you," he whispered. He unzipped her ski jacket, then his. As he kissed her again, James removed her jacket and her navy blue V-neck sweater until all she had against the cold, April night air was a cotton blouse, a pair of blue jeans and the warmth of James's body. He murmured against her hair as he pulled her tight against him, "Too cold?"

"No," she whispered, cuddling against him, feeling her body fit into his.

He kissed her mouth, her hair and her long ivory neck. His hands felt the soft fullness of her breasts under the light cotton blouse. Leslie moved closer, her breasts welcoming his hands, wanting their touch, her hips pressing rhythmically against his. James unbuttoned her blouse and found the velvety warmth of her breasts and the strong pounding of her young athletic heart.

Without thinking, without urging from James, because it felt right, and she wanted to, Leslie took her hand from the cool damp skin of his back to his belt buckle. Then, confidently, she loosened his belt and unbuttoned the top button of his jeans.

"Leslie! Where are you?"

James and Leslie froze.

It was midnight. Betty, Joanne and Robin were ready to leave. The party was over.

"I have to go," Leslie whispered, pulling away from him, buttoning her blouse.

"I'll give you a ride home," James said calmly.

"Now?"

"In a while. I'll get you home on time," he said staring at her. *Don't leave, Leslie, not yet.*

"Leslie! Come on!" The voices were getting closer.

The spell was broken. The privacy invaded. Leslie couldn't hold James's gaze. She couldn't look in his eyes and tell him that she didn't want to stay.

"I have to go, James," she said, bending down to pick up her sweater and her jacket.

James shrugged. Then he casually rebuttoned his jeans and rebuckled his belt. He swung his jacket over his shoulder and took a swallow of beer.

"OK, Leslie, let's go," he said and began walking toward the cabin.

"There you are," Joanne said as she spotted James and Leslie emerging from the shadows of the woods.

"Time to go?" Leslie asked. What was she doing? She wanted to go back in the woods with James. Was he angry with her? He acted like it didn't matter, but he *had* asked her to stay.

Leslie noticed Alan leaning, sulkily, against the cabin door. She stared at him for a moment. *I don't owe you an apology, Alan. Not for anything,* her blue eyes blazed defiantly.

Leslie knew that they were all watching her, wondering what she had been doing with James in the woods and what was happening with Alan.

Leave me alone, Leslie wanted to scream. Leave me alone with James.

She turned, expecting to find James still beside her, but he had withdrawn. He leaned against his motorcycle, slowly dragging on a cigarette, watching her.

Without a word, Leslie got into the back seat of Betty's station wagon.

Two weeks later James telephoned Leslie. Susan answered.

"Dr. Adams, this is James. May I speak to Leslie, please?"

Susan found her daughter.

"Leslie, it's James. Did you tell him I got my Ph.D?"

"James! What? No. You just got it a week ago. I may have told him you would get it this spring," Leslie said as she rushed past Susan to the phone.

"James?"

"Hi, Leslie."

She had never spoken to him over the telephone. Leslie sat down, then stood up, then twisted the cord in her hands.

"Hi."

"Do you want to go to the Senior Prom with me?"

"Yes," she breathed. *Yes! Yes!* Then she said quietly, "But I can't."

"Oh. Oh?"

"Alan already asked me."

"Alan," James said flatly. Then he asked, "Are you still going to Radcliffe?"

"Yes. Of course," Leslie answered distractedly as she tried to decide if she could cancel her date with Alan and go with James. She knew that she couldn't. It would be too rude. She explained, "Alan realizes that he and I don't have a future, but he thought we should go to the Prom together anyway. For old times' sake."

"Great."

"I already said yes," Leslie said brusquely, angry with Alan for asking her so soon and angry with James for not asking her sooner.

"Well, have a nice time," James said.

"James," Leslie began.

"What?"

"Thank you for asking me." Ask me to do something else. *Anything* else, she thought.

"Sure," he said. Then, just before he hung up, he added, "See ya, Leslie."

*　*　*

210

James *didn't* see Leslie except from a distance. Six weeks later they graduated from George Washington High School. Leslie graduated first in the class. She was given the Rosemaiden award for the third time and received a special award for service and a scholarship from a local society. Leslie was voted the girl Most Likely to Succeed.

James graduated in the middle of the class. Despite his ability, his overall performance had been erratic. James received no awards. He had been nominated Most Likely To Get Arrested, Most Likely To Get Someone Pregnant and Most Likely To Die Of Lung Cancer. Leslie assumed the nominations had been submitted by some of her friends. Since she was on the Senior Class Graduating Committee, Leslie was able to intercept — and discard — the nominations for James before they were placed on the ballot.

In August, two months after graduation, Leslie saw James for the last time.

Leslie, Joanne, Robin and Betty were at the Seattle Center. It was a beautiful balmy summer evening, a perfect evening to go to the center and watch the fabulous light show at the water fountain. It was one of the few evenings they had left before disbanding for college, one last chance to celebrate their friendship, reminisce about high school and forecast the unknown, exciting future that lay ahead.

The serious conversations between Leslie and her girlfriends usually degenerated into irrepressible giggling. Or singing. Or dancing. They were happy; their lives were good and full of promise.

Usually their exuberant behavior was unwitnessed, except by each other, and confined to the privacy of a slumber party or a remote stretch of sandy beach, but that August night they were too happy, too eager, too full of anticipation. They sang and danced unselfconsciously around the colorfully illuminated water fountain.

Leslie did a pirouette without watching where the spin was taking her and pulled up abruptly just before colliding with James.

James. James had his arms around a girl, no, a woman.

She was a pretty woman, dressed up, who clung to James and eyed Leslie and the others with curious non-threatened amusement.

"James!" Leslie gasped, breathlessly.

"Leslie," he said, pulling away slightly from the woman. Enough, at least, to take a deep breath.

"Leslie, this is Cheryl. Cheryl, this is Leslie. And Joanne. And Betty. And Robin."

Leslie's friends viewed James with new curiosity. He wore slacks and a sport coat. He almost looked presentable. And Cheryl, older and sophisticated, was clearly intrigued with James.

Leslie could not speak. Her face was already flushed from exercise and exuberance. Now the warmth became hot and the color deepened for other reasons: embarrassment and mortification.

And something else. An emotion washed through Leslie that she didn't recognize. It was new to her and *strong*, whatever it was.

"You're not logging this summer?" Leslie blurted out. Why did I ask that, she wondered. Because I want *her* to know that I know James. That I know about James. That he is mine . . . The emotion was slowly, painfully, coming into focus.

"Yes, I am. I just came into town for the weekend."

To spend the weekend with Cheryl.

"Oh, well. Nice to see you, James. Nice to meet you, Cheryl," Leslie said with finality. She was suddenly desperate to get away.

"Good-bye, Leslie."

The feeling—the new emotion—stayed with Leslie, demanding definition, for two days. It was a gnawing, uneasy feeling. When she finally realized what it was and that she could only purge it by admitting it to *him*, Leslie wrote the letter:

Dear James,
    It is jealousy, I realize, after fighting with it ever since I saw you with Cheryl. I am so jealous of her

for being with you! For having you. For being your girlfriend.

I always wanted to be your girlfriend. I even thought I would be, when and if you decided to have a girlfriend. Silly, huh? Well, I'll survive, but it feels better to admit it. Even though you may be laughing.

As long as I've gone this far, since I'll probably never see you again, I might as well tell all. I think you're wonderful (I know you know this). So sensitive and talented. I enjoyed being with you so much (I am so jealous of Cheryl!).

I wish . . . I wish a lot of things . . . a lot of what ifs. . .

But, mostly, I wish you happiness.

> *Always,*
> *Leslie*

Leslie mailed the letter to James at the logging company in Snoqualmie, Washington. Leslie didn't reread it. She might not have mailed it if she had.

She wanted James to know her feelings for him had been real. Not silly. Not whimsical. It was important for her to tell him.

She decided that it didn't matter if James never acknowledged the letter. It didn't require an answer. But in the two weeks between the time she mailed it and the time she boarded the plane for Boston, a part of Leslie waited. Her heart pounded when the phone rang or the mail arrived or the doorbell rang.

But she didn't hear from James.

Not then. Not at all for nine years.

Not until that day in August when she was paged by the Department of Medicine secretary with a message to call Mr. James Stevenson.

Chapter Eighteen

Ross MacMillan watched Janet out of the corner of his eye, eager to see her reaction to mid-week, mid-morning Manhattan. Their limousine moved stealthily along the narrow, crowded side streets, smoothly dodging cars and pedestrians.

She has to think this is fabulous, Ross thought. His own heart pumped more swiftly, energized and stimulated by the activity that surrounded him: the fast, purposeful pace of the streets of Manhattan. Ross loved New York City. Even in mid-August, even in the midst of the worst heat wave in recent memory, he loved it.

Usually Ross took August off. It was the only natural break between the theater seasons. *Usually* he spent August in Carmel, leading a slow-paced, *no*-paced existence. *Usually* that month of enforced rest was a necessary break.

But this was not a usual year. This was the year of *Joanna*. This year there was too much to do. There was no time to take a break.

Just a week ago they closed *Joanna* in San Francisco. The show had already been held over twelve weeks. Every performance had been sold out. There were still many theatergoers on the West Coast who wanted to see *Joanna*, but they had to end the run. They were taking the show to Broadway.

Ross and Janet had arrived in New York City the night before. *Joanna* was scheduled to open on Broadway in

November. Ross was co-producing the New York production with Arthur Watts. Ross's maximum involvement would be in the preproduction phases, in the next three weeks, since he had to return to San Francisco by mid-September to give his undivided attention to the fall season at his own theater.

With two minor exceptions, all members of the original San Francisco company agreed to move to New York. No arm twisting was required. It was the chance of a lifetime to play on Broadway in an already critically acclaimed and box-office proven musical. The two company members that could not leave San Francisco "indefinitely" agonized for weeks over their decision.

It made life easier for Arthur and Ross that they would have the original company. It made it possible to close in San Francisco and open in New York in such a short period of time. The preproduction activity would focus on logistic, not artistic considerations.

They also both knew that the only cast member who was truly critical to the success of the smooth transcontinental move was Janet. It was her show. It was Janet's talent and energy and her unflagging professionalism that inspired tireless excellence from the rest of the cast. Janet was the unassuming and masterful leader. She quietly set a standard which they all, out of love or respect or pure role modeling, followed.

Janet was critical to the successful move, and Janet had not yet signed the contract. She had not yet agreed to star in the Broadway production of her show. She told Ross that she had never been to New York and that she was happy in San Francisco. She would have to see New York before deciding.

So Janet and Ross flew to New York in mid-August to see New York.

Ross watched her wide gray eyes calmly surveying the Manhattan scene through the tinted glass of the limousine.

Despite the fact that he had spent the past eight months working with Janet, Ross could not tell what thoughts lurked behind the gray. He was the director, and she was the star; *together* they had created a masterpiece. Their professional relationship was intense, intimate and creative, but he knew nothing—except the brief bits Kathleen had told him because of Mark—about her personal life. About who she *was*.

And the clear gray eyes provided no clue.

Until yesterday, on the flight from San Francisco to New York, Ross had never been alone with Janet outside the theater. Ross looked forward to the five-hour flight, sitting next to her in the first-class cabin. It would give him a chance to talk to her, to get to know her. But Janet started to read as soon as the plane took off from San Francisco International Airport.

Ross watched Janet read. She was completely absorbed in the book.

"Is that good?" he asked finally, gesturing to her book, Ken Follett's *Eye of the Needle*.

"Very good," she said.

"I wouldn't think spy novels would be your thing."

"It's not just a spy novel. In fact, it's more about relationships between men and women. Desires, needs—" Janet stopped abruptly and looked back at her book.

"Are you looking forward to seeing New York?" Ross pushed, pressing his advantage. She was a little off guard.

"I'm mostly nervous."

"Nervous?" he asked with amazement. He didn't think Janet had nerves. Just cool, steely calm and limitless energy.

"Of course."

"Why?"

"Because I'm afraid that I won't like it. That I won't be able to do the show there. And that will make you and Arthur angry with me."

Ross stared at her. He realized that she was being honest, and he realized for the first time that her decision about New York was not simply a matter of choice. Janet was not simply a star being stubborn. It *had* seemed out of character for her to behave like a prima donna. It wasn't her style. Her resistance to moving with the company to New York seemed inexplicable. As far as Ross could tell, Janet had no ties in San Francisco. Her injured but recovering ex-husband was in love with Kathleen.

Ross realized that Janet's reluctance about committing herself to the move to New York, sight unseen, was not a matter of whimsy. It was a matter of ability. Janet would move to New York if she *could*. If she could stand it. But why wouldn't she?

Now as he watched Janet watch Manhattan, Ross wondered what she was thinking. Did she like it? How *couldn't* she like it?

As they rode toward the theater where *Joanna* would play, Janet said nothing, and her expression didn't change.

They were met at the theater by Arthur, the director, the choreographer, the stage manager and the costume designer.

Arthur kissed Janet on the cheek.

"Hello, darling," he said brushing her cheeks lightly with his lips. "You look lovely."

"Hello, Arthur. Thank you," she said, smiling.

She likes Arthur, Ross observed. Maybe that will help. Ross wasn't convinced that Janet liked *him*, but of course he couldn't tell. There were no clues.

Janet walked around the theater and paced slowly on the stage.

"It's deeper than the one in San Francisco," she said, finally. "And not as wide. You'll have to restage at least two numbers."

"That's no problem."

She nodded.

"Janet, I want to hear the acoustics," Ross said. "Arthur claims they're the best in New York."

"OK. Do you want—"

"Sing *Dreaming*, OK? While I walk all around."

Without answering Janet began to sing. *Dreaming* was the song that had made her famous in San Francisco. It was a haunting love song. Ross had heard her sing it hundreds of times, but still, even now, even as he paced from one extreme of the theater to the other, it moved him, sending a tingling shiver through him.

"God, she's good," Arthur whispered to Ross.

"The best."

"Is she going to come?"

"I have no idea."

"What can we do to convince her?"

"Probably nothing we do will make a difference. She'll just decide. But what have you planned?" Ross asked, half listening to Janet sing, knowing that she would turn them down, wondering why.

"After an elegant lunch, I thought we could look at places to live. The theater has options on several penthouses earmarked precisely for imported talent like Janet. They are all spectacular. The best in New York. I don't think she'll be able to resist."

Ross shrugged. He had heard rumors that Janet lived in a small cottage in the country. Maybe they should drive to Connecticut.

"Then we could take a look at Fifth Avenue. That's pretty dazzling."

Ross didn't know what, if anything, dazzled Janet. Certainly not her own fame. It seemed to please her, but it didn't seem to *matter* to her. Janet didn't wear expensive clothes or jewelry, even though, because of *Joanna,* she could easily afford them. And the salary she was being offered to star in the New York production could make her a regular buyer at any boutique in the world.

They visited the penthouses, shopped on Fifth Avenue, went to the top of the World Trade Center and saw the Statue of Liberty. Janet wasn't dazzled, but she was wide-eyed and smiling and polite.

"Magnificent," she murmured appreciatively at the sight of the Statue of Liberty.

They dined at Manhattan's trendiest restaurant. They were seated immediately because Arthur was recognized and Arthur was powerful. They were seated ahead of other less prominent, but substantial, clients, many of whom had reservation times before Arthur's. That was the way the restaurant operated. Clients were seated, or not, at the discretion of the maitre d'. Reservations, even ones made months in advance, were a minor consideration. Arthur usually appeared without reservations and was always seated promptly.

Arthur, Ross and Janet were joined by three other theater principals — two women and a man — all of whom were committed to wooing the reluctant Janet to New York. If they expected a woman who simply needed an extra dose of flattery or the unending reassurances that many superstars required, they were surprised. Janet had none of the usual airs. She wasn't playing games. In fact, had they not known who she was, they would barely have recognized the quiet young woman studying the menu, artfully concealing her horror at the prices, as the romantic captivating star of *Joanna*.

The subject of Janet's decision was not discussed, but they eagerly discussed the upcoming production as if Janet would be in it. Ross watched her gray eyes carefully. He couldn't tell.

Early in the evening Janet seemed intrigued with observing the people around her, New York's wealthiest, in designer dresses, perfectly coiffed, bejewelled and elegant on this Wednesday evening in August. Janet did not recognize many faces. She didn't recognize their faces; but she instantly appreciated their wealth and power, and she would have recognized the names of the companies they owned and the people they controlled.

As the evening wore on and the conversation fortified by fine wine and gourmet food became more animated, Janet withdrew. Fifteen people had stopped by the table to speak with Arthur and to meet Janet. She smiled graciously, nodded pleasantly at their compliments — many had flown to San Francisco expressly to see her in *Joanna* — and then grew progressively quiet as each successive wellwisher left.

By the time the cream of asparagus soup was served, Ross's attention had been commandeered away from Janet by Stacy, one of the two women who had joined them for dinner. Stacy decided early on that she would have little impact on Janet's decision — *of course* Janet would decide to move anyway — and turned her full attention to Ross.

By the time the china plates, empty except for Janet's, were being expertly and unobtrusively removed from the table, Stacy's hand equally expertly massaged Ross's inner thigh.

It was only when Arthur suggested that they go to his club for dessert and dancing that Ross forced his attention away from Stacy to Janet. They would go to Arthur's club if Janet wanted to.

Ross looked across the table, expecting to see Janet's placid smile, and did a double take. Janet wasn't smiling, although she seemed to be trying to. Her full lips were quivering, and her always calm and serene eyes were turbulent. Stormy. Troubled.

Ross stood up abruptly, dislodging Stacy's hand, and walked around the table to Janet's chair. He casually rested his hand on her shoulder.

"I think Janet and I will pass on the rest of the festivities. It's been a long day. We both have a little jet lag," he said, gently lifting Janet up as he spoke. She came willingly.

Ross guided her quickly to the coat room and into a waiting cab that took them speedily to the Plaza.

It was midnight. The streets of Manhattan were still crowded, full of activity, full of the life and energy that Ross loved — the life and energy that, somehow, were too much for Janet. If that was the problem. Ross waited for her to tell him, watching her cower, trembling in the far corner of the cab, her head bent down, her eyes staring at her hands.

Janet said nothing.

They rode in silence on the elevator to the floor of suites at the Plaza. They had adjacent suites. Janet's hand trembled as she aimed her key at the keyhole. Ross took the key and opened her door for her. Then he followed her inside her suite.

"So?" he asked finally.

"So I can't do it, Ross. I'm sorry," she said, tears spilling from her opaque gray eyes like raindrops from a thunder cloud. Her eyes were dark, ominous.

"Why?" he asked helplessly, not expecting an answer.

"I can't live here. I am so out of place."

"You aren't at all out of place. You are special."

"I can't breathe here. I can't rest or relax. Everything, everyone moves so fast. Expects so much."

I know, Ross thought, that's what I love about New York: being part of that activity, feeling the pace, keeping up with the pace.

"People expect a lot in San Francisco."

"It's different," she said. "And you know it."

"I know. It's a difference that I love."

"And I don't. I would suffocate here, Ross. I would be afraid to leave my glamorous penthouse apartment, and I would feel like a trapped bird if I didn't leave. I could never call a taxi or order a dinner at a restaurant."

"Everything would be provided for you, Janet. You wouldn't have to do anything," he said, watching the fear in her face. He had never seen fear before. Only calm and confidence and serenity.

I don't want you to be afraid, Janet, he thought.

"That's not living, Ross. I would hate it. I don't want to be a fragile creature shuttled from one gilded cage to the other. Of course it could be done, but I would hate it. I would suffocate."

"Janet, you are a strong successful woman," Ross said, trying a new tactic. He didn't want her to be afraid, but he wanted her to move to New York.

"I can't live here," Janet repeated firmly.

"Is it because of Mark?" Ross asked, knowing that he had no right to.

"*Mark?* No," Janet said softly. "I told you. You just can't transplant a Nebraska country girl to New York City. At least not this one."

"Janet, you will win the Tony if you do this show on Broadway. Don't you want that?"

Janet shrugged.

"Don't you want everyone to know that you're the best?" he asked.

"The best . . ." she said almost to herself. "No. Being the

best has never mattered to me. I sing because I love to sing. I want you and Arthur to win the Tony, but you can do that without me."

"I don't understand you. You knock yourself out for each performance. You work like a maniac. You're a perfectionist whether you admit it or not, and now you say you don't want to be the best. After all that hard work, you throw away a career opportunity that most other women would kill for?"

Ross was almost shouting. It was so frustrating. He didn't understand her, and he wanted to. Needed to. She was making such a critical decision—a *wrong* decision—and he didn't know why.

Janet retreated to a blue silk chair in the corner of the suite. She said nothing, but the tears began anew, and the look of fear returned.

Ross stared at her helplessly, realizing again how little he knew about Janet. He knew her better as Joanna. Strong, beautiful, fearless Joanna. Ross was enchanted by Joanna, by the way Janet played Joanna. Ross was a little in love with Joanna.

But Joanna didn't exist. Only Janet. A woman he didn't know. She had the most beautiful voice he had ever heard and remarkable eyes that told him nothing. Her sensuous mouth smiled easily. She could own New York but wouldn't even give it a chance.

Janet, a woman who had been in love once. Ross had seen it in her eyes when she saw Mark after the performance on opening night. Ross had seen the love and sadness in her eyes. And in Mark's. Ross hadn't told Kathleen about *that*. There was no point. Ross had seen something else in their eyes: It was over—for both of them—but there were memories.

Who are you? Ross wondered. Joanna. Janet. Mark's ex-love. No one's lover.

"You're staring at me," Janet whispered finally.

"I'm trying to figure you out. What makes you tick."

"Music," Janet answered quickly, preferring conversation to Ross's probing stare.

"Not enough to stay here."

"If New York was the only place in the world that I could sing, I would stay," she said slowly.

"What if Arthur and I put the word out? Blackball you."

Janet frowned briefly then smiled.

"You wouldn't do that," she said simply.

"I wouldn't?" he asked.

"No. You are a fair man."

How do you know? he wondered, pleased. Of course he would do nothing to hurt her, whoever she was.

"What are you going to do?"

"I can see what community theaters are doing in the Bay Area. I don't even need to be paid for a while. You gave me so much money. . . ." she said quietly.

Gave is right, Ross thought. She refused to get an agent, to negotiate. She told him to pay her whatever seemed fair. He paid her a lot. It was fair.

"I don't suppose you'd want to hire me?" she asked carefully.

"For what?"

"For whatever you're doing this season. What *are* you doing?" she asked. She had been so involved with *Joanna* and so worried about the move to New York that she hadn't even asked.

"*Peter Pan*. The world is ready for a revival."

"With a female lead?"

"No. I *might* have considered you, but I've already cast Peter." Ross had cast the lead before he left for New York. Auditions for the other parts would take place during his absence. He would return to select, from the pre-auditioned finalists, in September. "He's a little older than the traditional Peter. He'll play Peter as a young adult. Beautiful tenor."

Janet nodded.

"Have you cast the entire company?"

"Janet. You are a major star. There are no major female roles in *Peter Pan*. I can't really see you performing in the company, can you?"

"*Yes*. Ross, I don't have to be the star."

"Do you want a drink?" he asked, walking to the fully stocked bar in the suite, stalling for time, his imaginative, innovative mind beginning to whir. How could he use Janet in *Peter Pan?* It would have to be a whole new production. Probably contemporary. He had already cast a slightly older Peter. Maybe a real love story? A romance?

"No, thank you. Ross, have you already cast—"

"Wendy," Ross said. Janet could play Wendy. Wendy and Peter could *really* fall in love. They could write a few new songs for Wendy. Love duets for Wendy and Peter. It could work. It would be risky, but it could be done. He had taken chances with *Joanna*, and it had paid off.

Largely because of Janet. And she had been the biggest risk.

Janet could play Wendy. Janet could create a lovely, romantic Wendy.

"Ross?"

"No, Janet, I haven't cast Wendy yet."

"Do you mind if I audition?"

Ross stared at her.

"Audition?" he repeated blankly. He was already thinking of ideas for the production.

"For Wendy. May I audition for Wendy?"

"Do you want Wendy? Even if she's a new modern Wendy who falls in love with Peter?"

"Yes!"

"OK."

"OK? I can audition?"

"OK. You're Wendy. I'll call Jack in San Francisco right now. We'll meet there a week from today," Ross said, almost talking to himself. He was mentally planning major productions in two cities. Because of Janet, the one in New York had just become more complicated, and because of her, the one in San Francisco had just become more exciting. "I have to stay here and start the search for a new Joanna. Janet, let's have lunch together tomorrow. To discuss Wendy."

"Oh. All right," she said hesitantly.

"Something wrong?"

"No. *No.* I . . . it's just that—"

"What?"

"I was going to leave first thing in the morning to visit my family in Lincoln."

"Don't you want to stay in New York as a tourist now that pressure is off?"

"No."

"Will you have breakfast with me? Before you go? I just need to make sure this all makes sense in the morning? OK? Eight o'clock? You can catch a noon flight."

"Yes, fine," Janet said, standing up as she noticed that Ross was moving toward the door. "I'll see you then. And Ross . . ."

"Yes?"

"Thank you," she said softly.

"Don't mention it," he said as he left. He had to make some phone calls. He had to let Arthur know the bad news and to let Jack know what, the more Ross thought about it, might just be the best news of the season.

Chapter Nineteen

Leslie didn't reach James until the day after he called. The first night she called too late. She left a message on the answering machine. The next evening he was still in his office when she called. He answered the phone.

"Hello."

"James?"

"Leslie."

"I was afraid I'd get your answering machine again."

"I'm expecting some calls. I haven't switched it over."

"What's O'Keefe, Tucker and Stevenson?"

"Architectural firm."

"You're an architect?"

"Uh-huh. And you're a doctor. And a television . . . uh . . . star."

"Oh, that's—"

"How I knew where you were."

"Oh," Leslie said and then fell silent. The memories of James flooded back at the sound of his voice. Why was he calling her after all these years?

"How is he?" James asked.

"Who?"

"The other resident. The one who was shot."

"Fine. He's fine," she said. After a moment of silence she asked, "How are you?"

"I'm fine. You?"

"Fine."

"Leslie, I'd like to see you. Explain to you about the letter—"

"The letter?"

"The one you wrote to me a million years ago. I didn't read it right away. I didn't even realize that you had sent it until ten months later. It's a little late to thank you for it but—"

"You're welcome."

"Can you have lunch with me? Or dinner? Or . . . ?"

"Lunch is hard. I can't get away. Dinner would be nice," Leslie said. Nice? A *nice* dinner with James? Dinner with *nice* James? Leslie's mind whirled.

"When?"

"It would be safest to plan for September, after I leave San Francisco General Hospital and go to University Hospital. Anything can happen here. Sometimes I don't get away until late. It's a little more predictable at University."

"Do you have your schedule?"

"Yes," Leslie said, looking at the pocket calendar provided by a pharmaceutical company. She had circled the on call days in red.

"Better make it after Labor Day," James said.

Leslie got the impression James was consulting his own calendar.

"OK. Let's see. I'm on call on the tenth so that's out. On the eleventh I'll be recovering from the tenth. How about the twelfth?" Leslie asked idly, trying to think why she had written the number twenty-seven on the twelfth.

"That's your birthday," he said quietly, wondering what he was doing. Leslie didn't have plans for her birthday. She must be uninvolved. But he wasn't.

"You're right," she said laughing. That's what the twenty-seven meant.

"So, are you free?"

"Yes," she said. There was something in his voice that made her ask, "Are you?"

"That night, yes," he said, hesitant. "My wife is working that night. She's a flight attendant."

"Cheryl?" Leslie asked quickly.

"Who? *No*," he said remembering. "No. No one you know. You aren't married?"

"No."

"So, I'll pick you up at seven," James said quickly before he changed his mind.

Leslie gave him her address and telephone number.

"You know the shot of you with your hair damp wearing that blue, V-necked scrub dress . . . ?"

"I never saw the pictures."

"Well, you looked exactly the way you looked at the lake that day. After you'd gone swimming in the ice-cold water. Remember?"

"I remember," Leslie said. How could I ever forget that day? Or that night?

"I don't think either of us should go," Kathleen said, gently touching his pale white temples with her barely tan fingers.

Usually by this time in August, her skin was golden brown, but not this year. She had spent every daylight minute of the past three weeks at the hospital with Mark, and now, finally, he was home. His hematocrit was twenty-seven, just over half of its normal value, and he was pale and weak; but he was home. She could take care of him all day and all night.

He caught her hand with his and pulled it to his lips.

"You're the maid of honor," he said as he kissed her hand and smiled at her. "And I want to go."

Mark didn't care about going to Betsey's and Jeff's wedding. In fact, he worried about his ability to do it. He was so *weak*. Just walking around his tiny apartment—it was so much bigger than his hospital room—left him breathless and damp and wobbly.

He didn't care about the wedding, but he wanted to be with Kathleen.

"You—we both—can change our minds anytime," she said firmly. Betsey could get married perfectly well without her. She wouldn't leave Mark home alone.

"Anytime in the next few hours?" he teased.

"It *is* only four hours from now, isn't it?" Kathleen gasped, glancing at her watch. "I wonder how Betsey is doing. . . ."

"She's probably worried that you won't be there. So, call her and tell her that we're coming."

"You're sure?"

"I'm positive," Mark said confidently. It would be good for him to get out. He could — *would* — make it. Besides, weddings were happy, joyous occasions. . . .

"Dearly beloved . . ."

The congregation remained seated during the vows. Mark was relieved. He wouldn't have to worry so much about his weakness. He could concentrate on the ceremony and watch Kathleen and listen to the vows.

"Do you, Jeff, take Betsey . . ."

Do you, Mark, take Janet . . .

Janet. Emotion swept through him as he remembered her gray eyes, brimming with love and joy and happiness, on their wedding day. She — *they* — had been so sure, so confident, as they had made those promises of forever.

"For better or worse . . ."

Or worse. He and Janet hadn't made it through that, and it was his fault. He hadn't let her help him. He hadn't shared the worst with her, even though he had made the pledge. He hadn't *known*. She had known. She had seen his torment. She had tried to tell him, to help him, to love him. But he hadn't believed her.

He had broken the pledge. And now — somehow, miraculously — it was *he* who had been given the second chance.

Kathleen. She stood a few feet away from Betsey and Jeff, smiling thoughtfully as she watched her dear friends exchange the vows. Mark gazed at her lovely profile, his mind spinning. Could he avoid the mistakes he had made with Janet? Could he, *would* he, share everything with her? Could they live and love through the best and the worst?

As Mark stared at her, lost in thought, wondering, hop-

229

ing, remembering, Kathleen turned her head to find him. Her glistening violet eyes—emotional, full of love—met his. Her lips curled into a soft smile for him.

As if giving him an answer.

Yes. We can do it. For better or worse.

"And forsaking all others as long as you both shall live . . ."

I do.

I do.

Janet called Leslie three days before her birthday.

"Do you have plans for your birthday, Leslie?"

"I'm having dinner with a, uh, friend from high school."

"Oh."

"How's *Peter Pan*?" Leslie asked, quickly changing the subject. She did not want to dwell on her date with James. More than once in the past few weeks, she had picked up the phone to cancel it, but she hadn't been able to dial.

"Fantastic. The man who plays Peter, whose name *is* Peter by the way, is terrific. The new Wendy is going to be a wonderful part for me. We're still in the brainstorming phase. Ross keeps coming up with something even better, more innovative. He is so talented."

"You like him," Leslie observed. Since her return from New York and Lincoln, Janet spoke of Ross often. Her voice softened a little when she did.

"I respect him, Leslie. He's very talented. He was so generous about my decision not to go to New York," she said thoughtfully. "I made such a fool of myself—in front of him—when we were there."

"Without missing a beat he hired you to play Wendy," Leslie observed.

"I'm good box office, Les. In addition to being a creative talent, Ross is also a very shrewd businessman. Our relationship is strictly business," Janet said emphatically. Because it was true.

"As you like it!" Leslie teased.

"Cute. Listen, do you want to do a late birthday celebration next week? Dinner somewhere?

"Sure. Let's."

James arrived promptly at seven.

"Hi," Leslie whispered, barely able to breathe.

James looked different. Older. *More* handsome. His green eyes seemed wiser, and his dark black hair was laced with a few strands of white. Older. Wiser. Even better than her memories.

"Leslie. You haven't changed," he said. Beautiful, sensual, naive Leslie.

Leslie smiled a soft confident smile.

But she *has* changed, James thought. Inside. She has become a woman with womanly desires and knowledge and confidence.

Leslie was older and wiser, too.

"You look good, James," Leslie said. Very, very good.

"So do you."

James took her to a popular Italian restaurant in North Beach with notoriously excellent food and slow service. They both ordered iced tea instead of cocktails.

"Happy Birthday," James said as he raised his glass of iced tea.

"This is a nice way to spend it. It's nice to see you," Leslie said. *Nice. Except that you are married.* She needed to hear about it. She needed to put an end to the fantasies once and for all. "Tell me everything. From that mortifying night — for me anyway — at the Seattle Center to O'Keefe, Tucker and Stevenson, architects."

"How about you telling me? From frolicking teenager to doctor and heroine. You go first."

"OK. It's quick and easy. I did just what everyone expected me to do: four years at Radcliffe; then back to Seattle to the University of Washington School of Medicine for four years; then to San Francisco as an intern and now a resident." Leslie paused. Then she smiled and said, "Your turn."

"Never married?"

"Very close once. But fortunately we realized the impending mistake in time. We were in medical school together. Classmates. We thought we loved each other until it came time to apply for our residencies. He wanted to do surgery at Harvard, and I wanted to come here. Neither of us cared enough to compromise. Scary, huh?"

"An old theme," James said. She had chosen what she wanted to do over someone to be with once before. "*Then* you said it was because you were too young."

"And you said that if it was the right person I would make the commitment no matter how young I was."

"I said that?"

"Something wise like that. And . . ." Leslie paused. Why not tell him? "When you said it, I knew that I could have made the commitment for you. I could have given up Radcliffe." *For you.*

James looked at his iced tea and frowned. Then he looked at her.

"Really?"

Leslie nodded.

"It wouldn't have worked," he said flatly.

Leslie smiled and shrugged her shoulders. "I'm just telling you how I felt. *Then.*"

James reached in his pocket for a cigarette and lit it. Leslie watched the smoke swirl in his eyes as the cigarette hung casually from his lips.

Sometimes when she was particularly tired or annoyed, Leslie would actually level her glacial blue eyes at a smoker and send a clear message of righteous indignation and censure.

Now she looked at James and thought, He is so handsome, so sexy when he smokes.

She shook her head, smiling. James noticed.

"What?"

"Oh, just a little internal paradox I'm trying to resolve."

"About my smoking?"

"Yup."

"I won't," he said, starting to stamp out his cigarette. "No. That's OK. Here's the paradox. I spend a lot of my life taking care of people who have irreversibly damaged—not to mention *killed*—themselves with cigarettes. Occasionally I even rant and rave about it. I've seen autopsies, specimens of blackened lungs and lung cancer—"

"I'm putting out my cigarette," James said pleasantly as he pressed it into the ashtray.

"But here's the rub. You look so good when you smoke. Most people don't, but you do. You always have. I like to watch you smoke."

"You want me to light up?"

"No," she said softly, seriously. "Because it's *my* indulgence and *your* lungs. And your life. The non-selfish part of me, the part that cares about you and not the thrill of watching you smoke, wishes you'd never smoke another cigarette."

James looked at her for a long moment. Finally the intensity of his gaze was too great. Leslie looked away.

"So, tell me about you. Starting with Cheryl."

"Cheryl," James mused. "Cheryl was the wife of my older brother's best friend. They were both in 'Nam, and Cheryl was lonely. It wasn't a meaningful relationship, Leslie."

"But a lively one?"

"It kept me busy that summer. Her husband and my brother returned from 'Nam in September. Physically whole but emotionally scathed," James said bitterly. "Anyway, Cheryl went back to him. Which is what we had planned."

"It looked like you liked her," Leslie said, remembering that balmy August night.

"Of course I liked her, but it didn't mean anything to either of us. It was just a hedge against loneliness."

Leslie shook her head.

"Leslie, what I had with Cheryl was no different than what you had with Alan. You knew it wasn't true love, but it felt good."

"But neither of us was married," Leslie said. Then she added thoughtfully, "And we never slept together."

"I didn't know that. I just assumed," James said, frowning, remembering. He had wanted to make love to Leslie that night at the lake. And a hundred other times. He had no idea it would have been her first time. No wonder she left.

"I was very naive in high school, James. You knew that. I grew up at Radcliffe."

James nodded. He wondered what other assumptions he had made that were wrong.

"So, I wrote you that silly letter," Leslie said.

"Not silly. A letter that saved my life."

"What?"

"It must have arrived at the logging camp with some letters from Cheryl. We only got mail twice a week, and Cheryl wrote every day. So it must have arrived with the other letters, and I didn't notice it. I usually only glanced at Cheryl's letters; they were all pretty similar. But I kept them all, including the unopened one from you.

"That fall I started school at the University of Washington as planned. The draft issue was still unresolved, and I had decided to give college a shot anyway. My enthusiasm for college lasted about two weeks," James said. He sighed and added heavily, "It was replaced by enthusiasm for drugs."

"Drugs?"

"Anything. Any form of escape," James said harshly, the memories bitter. "I'd been drinking alcohol for years of course. And a little dope . . . marijuana. But suddenly I had access to acid and amphetamines and mescaline. You name it."

"Why?" Leslie asked.

"Curiosity at first. Drugs were so available. They must have been available in Boston. You must have at least tried marijuana?"

"No," Leslie said remembering her own scorn for the students who used drugs, who *needed* to use drugs. Leslie's curiosity was satisfied by other things: the interesting people she met, her pre-med classes, campus activities, lectures. Her only experimentation had been sexual, and that hadn't come until her junior year and then only with someone she thought she loved.

"No? Well, I found they provided a perfect escape; I could make it through the day with pills. I saw lights and colors that weren't there, and I didn't see the things that were there, the real things, the things I would rather forget. I felt good about myself for once."

"Escape? Forget? Feel good about yourself? I don't understand."

"In high school," James explained slowly, "you always thought I was in control, knew what I wanted, was able to make choices. Right?"

"Right. You seemed so calm. Yes, controlled. And you were the only person in history who could choose to be with our group one day and your own gang the next. You bridged the gap effortlessly. Nothing seemed to bother you," Leslie said.

"It was all an illusion. I was a frightened little boy struggling to find a place where I could fit. I had no confidence that I could ever find such a place. Or that I would be accepted."

"But you were so talented, so capable!"

"I had no self-esteem. I didn't believe in myself. I only believed that ultimately I would fail."

"Why would you believe that?" Leslie asked, amazed.

"Because that was what I had been told," James said somberly. "Over and over by my alcoholic father."

"Oh!" Leslie gasped. Then she said softly, "The child of an alcoholic parent."

"Parents," James interjected. "Did they teach you about them—*us*—in medical school?"

Leslie nodded slowly, remembering.

"The alcoholic parent has no self-esteem and transfers his own self-hate to his children. The children are often over-achievers because they try to get parental love and approval; but the parent isn't capable of giving them that reassurance, so the child, externally successful, always feels like a failure. Doomed to fail no matter what," Leslie said, summarizing what she had learned about the recently recognized syndrome.

"That's right. Of course, as a child I didn't understand that it was his problem, not mine. I only knew that I kept letting him down. So, then, it became my problem. I kept letting myself down. People with self-esteem don't have affairs with the wife of their brother's best friend, and they don't take drugs all day every day. People with self-esteem don't try to destroy themselves."

"Children of alcoholic parents become alcoholics," Leslie said. She saw the pain in James's eyes. She knew that, somehow, he had survived, but she wondered about the torment he had endured and the damage that might have been done.

"I was well on the way. I drank to escape. Then I turned to drugs. I was, *literally*, continually stoned for the first three quarters of college. For a solid nine months I had some drug, often more than one, in my system at all times."

"How did you afford them?"

James smiled weakly.

"Leslie, even though you were there on a college campus in the early seventies, you seem to have missed the flavor. It was the era of free love, free drugs, brotherhood, escape. Turn on. Tune in. Drop out. Remember?"

"Vaguely," Leslie said, a little embarrassed.

"Anyway, the expensive drugs, like cocaine, weren't popular then. Most of the acid—LSD—was made after hours in the organic chemistry labs on campus. I got drugs from my friends. I had a series of girlfriends. I slept in fifty different beds, living a day or a week in one place, then moving on. For nine months my life was a hazy dream, a fog that never cleared. It wasn't all that unpleasant."

"It *wasn't?*"

"No, Leslie. In many ways it was very pleasant. I couldn't fail because I wasn't trying to succeed. I forgot about the ugly fights with my father. I was protected by a warm mist of drugs and sex and music. A lot of the time I felt good."

Leslie knew it was the alcoholic—the potential alcoholic—in him that was talking. A part of him environmentally, or genetically, yearned for escape from the painful

236

reality of life. James had been badly bruised as a child. Sometimes the pain was still too great.

"Did you go to class?" Leslie asked. She did not want to hear more about the decadent drug life James had lived. And *enjoyed*.

"No." He smiled. "But I took the exams. I studied just enough to pass the courses. Just enough to stay in college and out of the draft."

"You could study while taking the drugs?"

"Sure," he said.

Just like the successful alcoholics, Leslie thought. The doctors and lawyers and other professionals who were alcoholic but still performed. *Excelled*.

"What happened?" Leslie whispered. She knew something had happened. She knew from the iced tea that James ordered without hesitation that he didn't drink. She knew from looking at him — at the clear green eyes that smiled at her — that somehow he had escaped the lifelong ravages. Somehow James had found a place where he fit.

"One night toward the end of the first year of college, I went to my parents' home. I still had a room in the house. I even stayed there sometimes during the year. That night my father threw one of his rages, berating me, calling me a worthless drug addict." James paused then smiled wryly. "It was true. For once my father was right. I had taken the second hit of LSD an hour before going home. I needed the extra fortification."

Leslie cringed at his words. *Oh, James, how difficult this must have been*. It was difficult to even hear about, to watch him as he told her. I was so sheltered, Leslie thought. Maybe I still am.

"Anyway, he told me to clear out of his house for good. He gave me until morning to take my belongings or he would throw them away. He was drunk and I was stoned. It was very ugly. I locked myself in my room and began going through my worldly possessions such as they were. I found the shoebox with the letters from Cheryl and tossed it angrily across the room."

James stopped. His eyes softened and he smiled affec-

237

tionately at her. He was remembering naive, innocent eighteen-year-old Leslie.

"You don't know this, but when you're stoned colors can appear more vivid. Cheryl's stationery was cream colored. Your letter was written on pale yellow paper. When the envelopes scattered, yours caught my eye. It didn't look pale yellow. It looked bright yellow, and it *glowed*."

"James," Leslie said.

"Drugs and mysticism, Leslie, go hand in hand. The experience was mystical. *Something* caused me to notice that letter."

Leslie shook her head.

"Well, I read it, and I spent all night thinking about you and about the faith you had in me. You were the only one. You did, didn't you?" James asked gently. The painful memories were replaced by happy ones. By memories of Leslie.

"I thought you were wonderful," she said quietly. "I didn't know anything about you. I didn't need to. It wouldn't have mattered anyway. I knew how you made me feel."

"The only time I felt peaceful was with you."

"So why—" Leslie began.

"Weren't we together? I told you that once. That I had to find out about myself first. About who and what I could be. My father really had a stranglehold on my sanity. I was pretty convinced that I could never do or be anything. Except when I was with you."

"You were restless then. I sensed it but I didn't know why. Now you don't seem restless."

"I was lucky. My luck changed with your letter. That night, as stoned as I was, I made a resolve to become the James that you believed in. To stop the self-destruction. At least to try. The next morning I took all my clothes and your letter and left my parents' home, my home, for good. I spent the summer at the logging camp, detoxifying myself, strengthening my resolve and planning to see you. Those were the hardest three months of my life. The drugs didn't want to let go. Most of me didn't want to face the harsh realities of life."

"But you made it."

"I did. I returned to Seattle one day after you had flown back to Boston for your sophomore year. I telephoned your house. I don't think your father recognized my voice. I didn't leave a message."

"Why didn't you write?"

"It was still too soon. I had just made it through the summer. The real test was about to begin: returning to college, making choices and decisions. By Christmas break, I was ready to see you, but I heard from Robin that you were bringing a boyfriend from Harvard home for the holidays."

Leslie shook her head and grimaced. "It would take me a few minutes even to remember his name."

Oh, James, how different it could have been for us!

"Anyway, I decided that you had your life. And thanks to you, I was beginning to have mine. I wanted to let you know. I always hoped that someday I would have the chance."

This is the someday. On my twenty-seventh birthday, Leslie thought. Happy Birthday, Leslie.

"You became an architect."

"I got my degree in Seattle. Then I worked in New York City for a while. I joined the firm here eighteen months ago."

"And already have your name on the letterhead."

"I've done well. The luck has continued."

It's not luck, James. It's *you*, Leslie thought. Talent and hard work and the decision to make it. Not *luck*. Leslie realized that he still had doubts about his own worth. There were still vestiges — deep scars — of the damage done by his father.

"And you like it?"

"I love it," James said enthusiastically.

"Do you do houses?"

"For the past six months I've been working with an international land development company. The company has both residential and commercial holdings so, yes, I do

239

houses. And buildings. And shopping malls. And resorts. You name it."

"Sounds exciting and creative."

"It's both. I couldn't ask for a better job."

Leslie looked at her plate of barely touched veal parmigiana. As they talked, the waiters had—at carefully spaced leisurely intervals—served and cleared antipasto and bread, then salad, then pasta, then the entree. Leslie paid little attention to the food. She nibbled idly and focused on James. Leslie looked at James's plate of barely touched food and smiled.

"This is supposed to be one of San Francisco's best restaurants. We're not really giving it our undivided attention," she said.

"Do you want to?"

"No," she said. Then, pushing her food around her plate, she forced herself to say what she had been dreading. "Tell me about your wife."

"Lynne," James said quickly. "We met two years ago. I was flying from New York to San Francisco to interview for the job with O'Keefe and Tucker. She was—is—a flight attendant. She noticed that I was drawing a picture and came over to look at it. It was like the picture I drew for you of the meadow. Drawing is relaxing for me. Anyway, Lynne asked me if I would draw her a picture of a calico cat named Monica. I thought she was kidding; but she carefully described Monica's personality to me, and I spent the rest of the flight drawing the picture. I handed it to her as I was leaving the plane. She ran after me and asked if I would consider doing the illustrations for her book." James paused as he remembered how excited Lynne had been about the drawing.

"Was there really a book?" Leslie asked after a few moments.

"Oh, yes. Lynne writes children's books in her spare time. She had just completed the first book, *Where's Monica?* She was looking for an illustrator. *Not* a husband."

"And she got both."

"Uh-huh. We've done two books since *Where's Monica?* They also feature Monica the cat and are actually pretty successful."

"How long have you been married?"

"We got married the day I moved here. Eighteen months ago."

"Tell me about Lynne."

"Lynne. Well," James's voice softened as he thought about how to describe the woman who was so much a part of his life and of the happiness he had found. "Lynne has been through a lot. She's strong and independent. She's three years older than I am. She's still a flight attendant because she enjoys it although eventually she may quit to write full time. She's . . . I'm not really describing her, am I?"

"It's hard," Leslie said. The words don't matter, Leslie thought. I can tell from the tone of your voice how much you love her.

"It is."

"Do you have children?"

"No," James said slowly. "And we won't. Lynne can't."

"Oh."

"It's OK. She can't and I shouldn't anyway. Neither of us should. We both had dismal childhoods, hated our fathers and barely survived the early seventies. Lynne was at Berkeley at the height of the "flower child" era. She did her share of drugs and sex. The doctors have said that because of damage to her tubes from infections it would be almost impossible for her to get pregnant. Besides, while I was poaching my brains with drugs, I was probably damaging my chromosomes, too," James added seriously.

"I think there are enough normal offspring from hippies and flower children that the chromosome damage theory is out. So you aren't even going to try?" Leslie asked. A man as sensitive as James and a woman who writes children's books would make wonderful parents, she thought.

"Lynne has never used birth control, and she's never gotten pregnant. I think the doctors are right. Anyway, we're quite happy with Monica and all my buildings as our surrogate children."

"I can tell that you are happy, James. I'm glad," Leslie said honestly. But part of her wished that things had worked out differently. That *she* had had a chance to make him happy.

"A lot of it is because of you, Leslie," James said seriously.

"No."

"Yes. Believe me. I know what a difference it made to me that you were my friend."

"My pleasure." Leslie smiled, blushing. *It made a difference to me, too. I haven't been able to find anyone to replace you.*

James walked her to the door of her apartment. It was almost midnight.

"Thank you, James," Leslie said.

"It was wonderful to see you again."

"It was wonderful to see you," she whispered and retreated quickly inside the door. "Good-bye, James."

As she heard his car drive away, Leslie began to cry.

Why was she crying? Because James had struggled against all odds and made it? Because James was happy? She was glad he was happy, but he could have been happy with her. It could have happened. It *should* have happened.

I expected it to happen, Leslie finally admitted to herself.

During all those years she had fantasized about seeing James again. It didn't consume her. She went for long periods of time without thinking about him at all. Then she would look at the picture he had drawn—the picture that had hung in her dormitory at Radcliffe and in her room in Seattle and in her apartment in San Francisco—and start to think about him again.

She had known that someday she would see him again. And now she had.

Leslie thought about the facts of their reunion. If someone had submitted it as a script for a Hollywood movie, it would have been rejected outright.

Forget it, Joe. The audience would never buy it. He sees her on television, blood dripping down her face because she's just saved some guy whom she also loves, who doesn't know it, by putting her finger inside his chest on his artery? He sees her and remembers the letter that changed his life, that got misplaced until he discovers it one night between acid-induced hallucinations? Then he tells her now he over-came incipient alcoholism and drug abuse to become a successful architect? And illustrator of children's books? No way, Joe. The public has to have a little reality sprin-kled in. This is pure fantasy.

Besides, Leslie mused. It doesn't have a happy ending. The heros, Leslie and James, don't end up together. They don't fall breathlessly into each other's arms.

Leslie sighed. How often had she wondered where he was and what he was doing? Now she knew. He was very near. With Lynne. Happy. And the fantasy was over.

As he drove away from her apartment, James reached into his pocket for a cigarette. He pulled it out of the package with his lips and reached for a match.

Then he paused. His hand rested for a long moment on the matchbook in his pocket. Finally he took the unlit cigarette from his mouth and returned it to the package. Then he crushed the entire package in his hand and threw it across the front seat of his car.

Chapter Twenty

"How about dinner tomorrow night?" Ross asked Janet toward the end of September. They had just finished a long day of script rewrites for *Peter Pan*. "I'm leaving for New York the day after tomorrow."

"Oh? Sure," Janet answered absently. She assumed that Ross wanted to discuss some aspect of *Peter Pan* or *Joanna* with her before he left.

"What time would be good?"

"Why don't we just go somewhere nearby after we're done here tomorrow," she suggested.

Ross nodded. Janet didn't notice the look of surprise on his face.

At six-thirty the next evening, they walked two blocks to a French restaurant on Stuart Street.

"What did you want to discuss?" Janet asked after they had ordered dinner and been served drinks.

"Nothing."

"Nothing?"

"No, I just wanted to have dinner with you."

"This isn't business?" Janet asked weakly.

"No. It's a date."

"I thought you wanted to talk about the shows. If I'd known it was a date, I would have—" Janet stopped abruptly.

Gotten dressed up, Ross mused. Taken the day off to get ready?

"Would have what?" he asked, curious.

"I would have said no," she said flatly.

Ross's eyes narrowed. "What?"

"I'm not dating," she said carefully. His eyes were angry. Ross took a swallow of his scotch.

"I hope you're not waiting for your ex-husband to come back to you, Janet," he said acidly. "Because I happen to know that he is very much in love with someone else."

Janet looked at him, her gray eyes foggy.

"I know that," she said quietly.

They finished their drinks in silence and forced themselves to exchange pleasantries with the ebullient waiter who served the elegantly prepared salad of butter lettuce and shrimp and finely sliced egg whites.

"I had no right to say that to you," Ross said flatly. "I'm sorry."

Janet shrugged, blinking back tears.

"Why didn't you throw your drink at me? Or just leave? Why did you stay?" he asked.

Ross had invited Janet to dinner because he genuinely wanted to know *her*. To know Janet Wells. Whoever she was. Janet had captivated him as Joanna. Vital, courageous, energetic and beautiful. Now Joanna was gone, replaced by Wendy, and the enchantment was starting anew. Wendy—Janet's Wendy—was a wholesome, naive and charming seductress, and she was seducing Ross.

But who was *Janet*? Were there parts of Joanna and Wendy in Janet? Or was Janet Wells different still? All Ross knew was the shell. All he knew was the quiet professional with the limitless energy and unbounded talent.

"I stayed because we work together. If I had left, angry, we would have had to discuss it later. You're leaving tomorrow. It might have meant weeks of tension."

"So this is pragmatic? In the best interest of the show?"

"Ross, I know that Mark is in love with another woman. Let's be specific—he's in love with Kathleen. My relationship with Mark ended a long time ago, but I learned something from our failed marriage. I learned that letting anger fester, not talking about things when they happen, is terribly destructive."

"So you sat here, through the insult and the silence that followed, waiting for me to apologize."

"No. Waiting to see if we could talk about it. Trying to decide if I should apologize. You asked me out for dinner. I accepted thinking it was business. When I found out differently . . . well, I insulted you, too."

"You are really amazing," Ross said, not understanding her, but wanting to. Liking her. Smiling at her. "Why don't you date?"

"Something else I learned from the marriage that didn't work," Janet said calmly, tilting her head slightly. "I gave up my career for the marriage. Now I am discovering how much all this means to me. I enjoy it. I'm *consumed* by it. It's my whole life right now."

"No time for anyone else?"

"No energy. And no courage. It's much too soon for me. Even a casual dinner date. It disrupts the balance."

"A delicate balance?" he asked gently. She exuded such confidence and strength. And such tranquillity. But Ross remembered the fear in her eyes in New York. He had to believe her. He had seen her fear.

"I guess so. Getting stronger," she said.

"I am so sorry I said that to you about Mark. I was angry."

"It's OK."

It's *not* OK, he thought. It's not me. I can't believe I said that to her.

"How's the production going in New York?" Janet asked.

Ross smiled. They could make it a business dinner. Then they would both be comfortable.

"I can't tell. Arthur sounds funny. That's why I'm going back tomorrow."

"How long will you be gone?"

"Depends on the situation. I hate to be away from here. I'm so excited about the show here, but . . ."

"We'll call you if we make any substantive changes," Janet said.

"Please do."

"Will you be staying at the Plaza?"

"Uh, no. I'll be staying with Stacy. You met her that night. . . ."

"The one with her hand on your thigh," Janet murmured.

Ross raised an eyebrow. Janet shrugged.

"Stacy's father is a major backer for the New York production," Ross said, wondering why he was explaining about Stacy. "Stacy's a model."

"A cover girl, isn't she? At least I thought I saw her picture on *Vogue* a few weeks ago."

"You're very observant," Ross said. Starting with the hand on the thigh observation. "Anyway, I gave Jack the number. No surprises all right?"

"No surprises."

On September thirtieth James called the Department of Medicine office and asked the secretary to have Leslie call him.

Leslie was in the radiology department, waiting for an angiogram to be completed on her patient. It would be at least fifteen minutes. She returned James's call from the radiology department office.

"This is Dr. Adams returning Mr. Stevenson's call."

"Yes, Doctor. He is expecting your call."

"Leslie?"

"Hi," she whispered, her heart pounding. She had been thinking about him, *constantly,* for the past two weeks, from the moment he had left her apartment. She knew it was over. The story—their story—had ended. She knew it rationally, but she didn't feel it.

She simply felt restless.

"Can I see you?" he asked quietly.

"Yes," she breathed.

"Tonight? We'll go for a walk?"

"Yes. I'll see you at seven-thirty," she said, silencing the voice in her mind, in her conscience, that thundered No,

No, *No.*
Yes. I will see you. I will be with you.

Leslie dressed carefully. *For a walk* James had said. Leslie remembered the last time she had gone for a walk with James. It was that April night at Sparrow Lake, nine and a half years before. Then she had worn blue jeans, a light cotton blouse and a blue V-neck sweater.

She would wear the same outfit tonight. The blouse and sweater were new. The jeans, her favorite pair, now faded and soft and threadbare, were the same. They had gone with her from high school to college to medical school to residency.

Comfortable old friends, she thought as she pulled them over her hips, noticing that they were looser now than they had been in high school. Leslie tucked the pale yellow, cotton blouse into her jeans and pulled the V-neck sweater over her just-washed hair.

What am I doing? she wondered as she looked at herself in the mirror. Trying to turn the clock back nine and a half years?

It was folly to think that they could start where they had left off. James's life had changed too much. James had responsibilities and commitments.

But James had called. James was on his way over to her apartment.

Leslie opened the door and stepped back, allowing him to enter, unable to look in his eyes.

James had dressed, as she had, in commemoration of the night at the lake. He wore jeans, an oxford shirt with sleeves rolled casually to mid-forearm and a khaki Windbreaker.

James pulled the door behind him.

"Hi," he whispered, covering her mouth with his before she was able to answer.

Leslie answered with her mouth and her arms and her

248

body. The years vanished. They were back at the lake, controlled by passion and allowing the passion to control them.

"James," Leslie whispered, pulling away to breathe for a moment. And to whisper his name.

"Leslie."

James kissed her as he had that night at the lake. Gentle kisses on her face, her lips, her neck. He began to undress her, not the way a sexually experienced man undresses a woman, but the way a teenage boy discovers the wonderful forbidden secrets of a teenage girl.

James reached under her sweater and unbuttoned her blouse. He touched the soft fullness of her breasts under her clothes. Leslie slid her hands beneath his shirt and felt the strength of his back, strong and cool. She reached for his belt buckle just as she had years before. A remote corner of her mind expected to hear the voices of her friends calling to her because it was time to leave.

But not tonight. Tonight there were no curfews, no interruptions, no uncertainties.

They made love on the coarse rug, partially clothed, like teenagers desperate to be together but afraid of being caught. A stolen moment of teenage passion. It could have happened in a car or in the living room at her parents' home or on a bed of pine needles in the woods by the lake.

They made love eagerly, like curious teenagers full of wonder and passion. Afterward they lay on the floor exhausted, tangled in each other's clothes, holding each other.

Leslie closed her eyes and pressed against him, against his strong warm body, the body that had wanted her so much. She could lie here forever. With James.

Her mind spun. What had she done? Gone back to high school? No, the responsible adult in her chided. You *pretended* to go back to high school to justify making love with another woman's husband.

But she hadn't made love with James, Lynne's husband. Or with James the talented, successful architect. Leslie had made love with James the teenager, the loner, the deer hunter. He was the sensitive boy whom she loved and wanted. The only James she knew. James the boy.

Leslie felt James's face close to hers and the force of his eyes willing hers to open. When she opened them, who would *she* be? Leslie the doctor? Leslie the woman? Or Leslie the girl who had just been accepted at Radcliffe? She didn't know.

"Leslie," he whispered, his voice husky. A man's voice.

Leslie opened her eyes, afraid to look into his, but unable to resist. James's eyes told her of his passion, a man's passion for her. For Leslie the woman.

"You are so beautiful," he said, as he began to remove her clothes. This time there wasn't the awkward eagerness of a teenage boy. This time there was only the graceful ease of a sexually experienced man.

James removed all of Leslie's clothes and his, slowly, almost effortlessly as he kissed her. When they were both naked, he pulled her to her feet and led her into her bedroom.

They made love again, slowly, purposefully, carefully exploring each other and learning what gave pleasure, learning the rhythm and desire of the other. They had made love, with others, before. They were experienced, knowledgeable . . .

But still not in control. As James kissed her, as he explored her with his sensitive hands, his warm tongue and his soft lips, Leslie's body responded as it never had before, willing her to move, to touch him, to become part of him. As James felt Leslie's velvety skin, her round soft breasts, the rhythm of her body and the demands of her passion, his own control vanished and was replaced by a need to possess her. All of her. The need was urgent and powerful. It was a need to make their bodies one.

Leslie. His Leslie. At last.

Afterward, James held her, pressed against him, until her heart no longer pounded against his chest and her hands released their grip and rested softly on his back stroking him gently.

"What are you thinking?" he asked, finally, gently caressing the damp tendrils of her chestnut hair.

That earlier I made love with James the boy, she thought. *My* James. And now I have made love with James the man. Whose James? Mine? No. *Lynne's.*

Leslie shrugged. She didn't want to talk about it. Or even think about it. How could she make herself not think about it?

"Leslie?" he pushed, concerned, gentle, caring.

"That was wonderful, James," she said honestly. "Both ways were wonderful."

"You are wonderful."

"I wish . . ."

"You wish?"

"I wish we had done this a long time ago—that night at the lake—so we could have known how we felt."

"It would never have worked then," he said, kissing her forehead.

It won't work now, Leslie thought. In high school it was too soon. Now it is too late. Leslie remembered the love in James's voice when he told her about Lynne. She would never forget it.

But James was here, now, with her. He wasn't talking about Lynne; he was talking about her, holding her, loving her. Leslie wouldn't let herself think about Lynne. She wouldn't think about tomorrow. She wouldn't think about all the tomorrows without James. Not until she had to.

Leslie touched his temples with her fingertips, then moved her mouth against his, into his, seducing his body back into hers, needing him again, already, quickly. She needed James to make love to her, and she felt, as he responded to her touch, that his need was as great as hers. His desire was as strong and his passion as insatiable.

"Leslie!" he laughed softly, surprised, elated by her passion and by her willingness to show him.

"Is something wrong?" she asked, suddenly shy.

"No, my darling Leslie. Everything is perfect."

They lay in each other's arms, exhausted, unwilling to pull away.

"It's ten-thirty," James said, noticing the bedside clock.

Leslie stiffened, waiting for him to say, It's late. I'd better go. Good-bye, Leslie.

"We didn't go for our walk," he continued, kissing her ear, reassuring her.

"Disappointed?"

"No. Are you?"

"No. But I've always enjoyed our walks: evergreen-lined meadows, decks of ferry boats, woods by lakes. Very romantic."

James smiled and murmured gently, "Unlike this?"

Leslie smiled, turning to look into his eyes. "*Not* unlike this."

"We'll go for a walk next time."

Next time. Leslie's heart raced at the words. Next time. Nine years from now? Next life? When, she wondered.

"Next time," she repeated quietly.

"Will you see me again?" he asked in a tone heavy with meaning. It said, I have made a decision to see you, to be unfaithful to my wife, but you have to decide, too.

Leslie, the Rosemaiden, the most inspirational, the girl voted Most Likely To Succeed, would have answered with a resounding, indignant, self-righteous *No!* But that Leslie no longer existed. She had disappeared over the years, slowly, gracefully recognizing that life wasn't so simple and the answers weren't so clear, after all. The distinction between right and wrong was sometimes hazy, blurred by love and emotion and passion. Extenuating circumstances.

Leslie the Rosemaiden, the girl, had grown into the woman who lay in bed with James. Leslie had already made her decision. All that was wrong—knowing that James was married, sensing with absolute certainty that he loved Lynne, fearing that this would ultimately be painful for all of them—was offset, in Leslie's mind and heart, by what she knew was right. She loved James. She had always loved him.

Lying in his arms, making love to him and talking quietly to him *felt* right. Doing what felt right, that was what she had always done. She would do it now. For however

252

long. Whatever the consequences.

"Yes, James, I will see you again," she said seriously in a voice that matched his. They both understood the significance of what they were doing.

"When again?" he asked. He held her even closer in silent acknowledgment of what she said. Of what it meant.

"Well, this month I'm on call every third night. I'm on call tomorrow, the first. So the first, the fourth, the seventh—"

"Then," James said slowly, obviously visualizing another schedule, Lynne's schedule, "how about this Saturday, the third? Are you free?"

Free, Leslie mused. Yes, James, I am free. You're the one who is not free.

"In the evening?" she asked, trying to learn the ground rules.

"For any part of the day or night that you can spend with me."

"I have to make rounds in the morning. If the patients are stable, I should be home by noon. If not—"

"I'll be working in my office. Just call whenever."

"OK," Leslie said, sitting up, assuming that James was about to leave. They had made plans to see each other again. That usually signaled the end of a date.

"Do you want me to leave?"

"Oh! I thought—" she stopped, embarrassed.

"If you don't want me to stay, to spend the night—"

"I want you to stay," Leslie said. Then she added lightly, "But as long as I'm up, can I get you anything? A cigarette?"

"I don't smoke anymore."

"Really?" Leslie whispered.

"Really. I quit smoking as soon as I knew that I had to see you again."

"When was that?"

"The minute I left you that night. On your birthday," he said, pulling her back into bed beside him.

He knew it then, but he waited two weeks before calling

her. He spent those weeks thinking about it. He had to be certain of his decision, to be sure that it was more right than wrong. He realized, finally, after careful logical thought, that he really had no choice anyway.

He had to be with her.

Janet watched the red-orange autumn sun as it fell slowly over the rolling green hills and into the shimmering blue ocean. Her late afternoon walk had taken her, as it often did, beyond the vineyard, through the eucalyptus grove and up the gently sloping grass hills. From the top of the hills, she had a commanding view of the Pacific.

Her private hills, her private view, her private ocean!

How lucky I am to have found this place, Janet thought as she sat cross-legged on the grass watching the magnificent fiery sunset.

It had been a fluke. Or fate. Almost as if she were meant to find it.

It had been during one of her long drives last winter. Mark was gone, and all that was left of their marriage was the legal paperwork. Janet needed to escape the dreariness of the house that had been hers and Mark's. She bought an inexpensive used car and began to take drives, driving until she found an isolated beach or woods, or a meadow — where she could sing.

Janet's drives took her south to Carmel and Big Sur and north to the wine country, to Napa and Sonoma valleys. One afternoon in late January as she was driving back to San Francisco from the northern border of the wine country, she impulsively decided to return along Highway One, the Pacific Coast Highway, instead of the inland route.

Near Sonoma Coast Beach she saw a small cottage, barely visible from the road. She turned into the gravel drive that led to the cottage, wondering how she would explain herself to its inhabitants, but the cottage was uninhabited. She tiptoed up the red brick stairs to the wooden porch with a white railing. The door was padlocked. Janet peered in the windows.

She saw beautifully finished hardwood floors, a brick fireplace and a fresh yellow and white kitchen with lace curtains. And no furniture.

A beautiful, uninhabited cottage.

The next house Janet saw was a mile south of the cottage. Surrounded by a perfectly manicured lawn with boxwood hedges, the house itself was red brick with a cedar shake roof and white shutters. A car was parked in the circular brick driveway.

Janet drove in, parked, walked briskly to the front door and pressed the doorbell without allowing herself to reconsider.

A pleasant white-haired man, her grandfather's age, opened the door. Janet introduced herself and bravely began to ask questions.

Yes, it was his cottage.

"Would you be interested in renting it to me?" Janet asked, her heart thumping, her mouth dry.

"Renting?" he asked.

"Who is it, dear?" They were joined by his wife.

"This young woman would like to rent the cottage," he explained.

"I would take good care of it," Janet said quickly.

They smiled at her. She looked like a wonderful young woman, but every day they read or heard about horrible things being done by nice-looking people and about strangers taking advantage of the elderly.

"Well," the man began.

Janet sensed their reluctance and its reason.

"Why don't I give you my name, the telephone number where I work and some references? If you decide you would like to rent it, you could check up on me and call me with your decision."

Three days later they called her. Two weeks after that, Janet moved into the cottage that had been inhabited over the years by housekeepers, gardeners, grandchildren, and most recently a divorced but now remarried daughter.

The Browns had lived there for fifty years, raising their family and working the land. In the past ten years, they had begun to lease portions of the huge estate. The soil and gently sloping hills were ideal for growing grapes. Two of the largest vineyards substantially supplemented their yearly production by leasing from the Browns.

The revenue from the leased land was more than adequate. The value of the land itself was immense. The Browns had always lived modestly, and they loved their country home; but someday soon they would decide to live closer to their grown children and their growing grandchildren. The sale of the estate would make them very wealthy.

After Janet moved in, the Browns showed her a map of the property. It extended several miles north and south. And west, to the ocean.

"Of course, dear, you are welcome to go for walks on the property. Nothing is off limits."

Janet sighed, glancing at her watch in the autumn twilight. She had to start back soon, before it was too dark. Janet noticed the date on the face of her watch.

October second. It had been almost a year since she told Mark that they needed to separate. For a while. Forever.

As she walked back to the cottage, Janet's mind measured the sadness and the happiness of the past year. Was the great sadness of losing Mark and of their failed marriage balanced at all by the joy of singing and performing again? By her triumph as Joanna? And now by the challenge of the avant garde production of *Peter Pan?*

Her new life was satisfying and peaceful. The torment of the last year of her marriage was a vague, uneasy memory. She had handled small threats on her new-found peace and privacy—the threat of the move to New York and the date with Ross—honestly and directly. Little by little Janet was finding that she had control over her life. And over her own happiness.

Happiness? The word clawed at her. Was she happy? No. Not compared with the only happiness she had ever known, the happiness of falling in love with Mark, of being in love with Mark. Happiness was a word reserved for distant memories. A life lived years ago.

But she was content. Peaceful. Alone but not lonely.

She felt so much better than she had felt one year ago, or even six months ago. Every day she got a little stronger.

Janet heard the telephone in her cottage ringing as she walked up the brick steps. She rushed through the unlocked front door into the dark room, instinctively weaving around furniture toward the phone.

"Hello?" she answered breathlessly, simultaneously switching on the lamp.

"Janet, it's Ross."

"Hi. Are you in New York?" It was a good connection. He sounded close.

"Yes. Still here."

"Everything's fine here. I haven't called because there haven't been any problems," Janet explained.

"I know," he said. He didn't add that he spoke with Jack at least once a day. "This isn't a *Peter Pan* call. It's a call about *Joanna*."

"Oh," she said tentatively.

"I need your help, Janet."

"I can't move to New York," she said instantly. So much for artfully handling small threats, she thought.

"Don't worry. I don't want you to. You're Wendy this season. Not Joanna."

"Good."

"So," he said carefully, "you know the it's-a-nice-place-to-visit-but-I-wouldn't-want-to-live-there idea?"

Janet didn't answer. She wished she could trust Ross. She didn't know if she could. He wanted too much from her. He expected her to be stronger than she was.

"Janet, the show's in trouble. I have spent the past few days trying to figure out what's wrong, but I can't put my finger on it."

"It's the same company except me," Janet said acidly. *He is trying to get me to do the show no matter what he says.*

"I don't want you here as Joanna. I want you here, just for a day or two, as a critic. You have such a good eye, Janet. You can find the weak spots. I would like — I need — your opinion," Ross said with an edge. *Why doesn't she trust me? Why is she so cold?*

257

"One or two days?" Janet asked, skeptically.

"That's all."

"When?"

"If you could come Sunday evening. The same flight we took in August—"

"OK."

"Great. The tickets will be at the airport. Do you want to stay at the Plaza?"

"That would be fine. Ross, I'm not even sure about the nice place to visit part," Janet said, underscoring the fact that she had no intention of staying very long in New York.

"I get the message," he said coolly.

Chapter Twenty-one

Janet dialed Leslie's number as soon as Ross had hung up.

"Hi, Les. How about dinner tomorrow night?"

"Love to but I can't." *I have to be with James,* Leslie thought, her heart beating swiftly, remembering. Anticipating.

"OK."

Janet didn't pry. It wasn't her style. Privacy was important to her. Her privacy and everyone else's. It didn't mean that she wasn't interested or didn't care.

Even though Janet was her best friend, Leslie couldn't tell her about James, but that was nothing new. Leslie had never been able to tell her friends about James. Her friends in high school hadn't understood about James.

And Leslie wasn't sure that Janet would understand, either. Not if she knew everything.

"I'm going to New York on Sunday."

"Really? Why?"

"Ross wants me to look at the show. Tell him what's wrong."

"Do you think it's a ruse to get you there?"

"I hope not, Les." *I hope Ross wouldn't do that.*

"You don't have to do anything you don't want to."

"I know. Speaking of that," Janet said soberly, "have you seen Mark? Is he back at work?"

"He is back. On consults at the VA. I saw him at Grand Rounds last week. He looks all right," Leslie said. All right, she thought, but not fully recovered. Still a little weak and a little pale.

"Do you know if he's leaving in July? Did he get the fellowship in Boston?"

"He said he wouldn't hear until mid-October. I'm sure he'll get it. And I think he'll go," Leslie said, lost for a moment in her own thoughts. A month ago, even knowing how Mark felt about Kathleen, Leslie would have been saddened at the thought of him leaving. Now, because of James, because her heart and body and mind were consumed by him, the thought of Mark leaving didn't affect her. *That*—the whimsy and the strength of her own emotions—troubled her.

Except there was nothing whimsical about her relationship with James.

"Oh," Janet said thoughtfully.

"Does it matter, Janet?" Leslie asked carefully.

"No. Well, yes. It would be better if Mark left," she said firmly. As long as Mark and Kathleen were together, as long as Kathleen was involved with Union Square Theater and as long as Ross and Kathleen and Mark all saw each other socially, it would be awkward. It meant that Janet might see Mark.

It would be best if Mark—and Kathleen—moved to Boston.

"You're probably right," Leslie said, speaking of them all.

Leslie dialed James's office number as soon as she returned to her apartment at two-thirty Saturday afternoon.

The phone rang ten times. Then twenty.

What if he had changed his mind? What if he had decided, as she had decided a hundred times in the past two days, that it was wrong, that they should stop now? Leslie had made the decision a hundred times and reversed it a hundred and one.

Leslie hung up and re-dialed. Maybe Lynne was home. Maybe a flight had been cancelled. But James would have called her at the hospital. Except he always called the Department of Medicine office, and it was closed on Saturday.

What if he had been in a car accident?

What if—"

"Hello?"

"James?"

"Hi," he said softly, happy to hear her voice.

"The phone rang so many times." She breathed with relief as she pulled her mind away from the horrors of the what ifs and into the gentle promise of his voice.

"I didn't realize that the ring was disconnected. I caught the blinking light out of the corner of my eye. Have you been trying to reach me for a while?" he asked, hoping not to hear that she had been home for hours, that they had wasted precious time.

"No, just for the past few minutes."

"When will you be home?"

"I'm home."

"Oh," he said. More precious moments. He could have been there when she arrived. He added gently, "I need a key."

"You have a key," Leslie said quietly. The night before as she was having the key made for him, she chided herself. Silly. Presumptuous. But James wanted a key. Not so silly after all.

"Thank you. You have a calendar."

"A calendar?"

"Of October only. I didn't know if your schedule for November was the same."

"No, it changes to every fourth night." Leslie's mind spun. James wanted to know when she would be free in November. "In November I'll be at the Veterans' Hospital. Tell me about the calendar."

"It's just all the times that we can—could—be together. Red circles around the days. The odd drawing."

Nice, James.

"Are we going for a walk today?" Leslie asked.

"Sure."

"Where?"

"The beach. The wharf. Golden Gate Park."

"Then what?"

"Dinner. Wherever you want."

"Then what?"

"You know what."

"Good."

"Why are we talking on the phone instead of in person?"

"Because you have to hang up in order to come over," Leslie began then stopped. Silly. She didn't want to let go of him, even for a few minutes, even for the minutes it took for him to come to her. Just hearing his voice, talking to him, was such a luxury.

How could she explain that to him?

"I need a car phone, don't I?" he asked. He understood completely. He didn't want to hang up either.

"Yes," she whispered.

"I'll get one. But right now I just want to see you. Leslie?"

"James?"

"Do you care about the beach?"

"No."

"The wharf or the park?"

"Not at all."

"Dinner?"

"I have food here. If we get hungry."

"Janet!"

Janet stopped, confused. Had she heard her name above the hubbub of the Sunday evening crowd of travelers at LaGuardia Airport?

"Janet," Ross repeated, reaching her side, touching her arm.

"Ross!"

"You sound surprised."

"I didn't know you were going to meet me," Janet said. She wished she had known. She had spent the last two hours of the flight worrying about the logistics of getting her luggage and finding a taxi. Then she worried further about how much to tip and what to do if the driver over-charged her or took her the long way because she looked so gullible.

"What did you think I would do?" Ross asked as mildly as he could. Did she really expect he would have let her find her own way to a hotel?

"I don't know. I was planning to take a cab," Janet said confidently, now that she didn't *have* to.

I should have let you, Ross thought, like millions of businesswomen do every day in this city and others. Janet asked to be left alone. Demanded it. So why had he both-ered to meet her? Was he just being polite?

No, Ross decided, remembering the look of fear on her face the last time she was in New York. I met her because behind that cool independent façade is a fragile, vulnerable woman.

Janet's gratitude for his thoughtfulness was so deeply hidden behind those calm gray eyes that Ross was almost tempted to tell her to take the damned taxi cab.

It might be good for her.

They didn't speak during the twenty-five minute limou-sine ride from LaGuardia to the Plaza. Ross had planned to suggest that they have dinner. He could think of enough business to discuss to legitimize it as a non-date. In fact, he had told Stacy not to join them because they would be discussing business.

But he abandoned the idea. It wasn't essential that they discuss the show before she saw it herself. Maybe it was better if they didn't. He didn't want to influence her. He was counting on her honest, professional opinion.

Ross went inside the Plaza with her and stayed long enough to make certain that her room was ready.

"The limo will be here tomorrow at noon to take you to the theater."

"OK."

"Oh, Janet. I haven't told any of the company that you're coming. I don't want them to know until after you've seen the rehearsal."

Janet nodded. The only way she could see the production that Ross saw, the production that worried him so much, was if they didn't know she was there.

"I won't make any phone calls," she said before he left. It hadn't occurred to her to call members of the company.

It *should* have occurred to me, she thought, later, as she soaked in a bubble bath in her suite. They were my friends, my colleagues. I should have wanted to talk to them.

Why hadn't she wanted to? Because she knew that some of them resented her for not moving to New York to do the show? No. They understood her reasons. Because she didn't really like them? No. She liked them very much. The bond had been close and genuine.

Because it is easier not to get involved, Janet admitted to herself as she wrapped a large, pale pink bath towel around her, knotting it over her breasts. Easier. Safer. More peaceful to be alone. Caring was too painful. It was too painful to care about anyone else. It was hard enough to care about yourself.

Janet awakened early the next morning. By eight she had dressed, breakfasted on croissants and coffee in her room and read *The New York Times*. As she drank the last cup of coffee from the china coffee pot, she allowed her gaze to drift away from her safe, elegant suite through the bay window framed in pink silk curtains to the outside world. To New York.

New York. The city she had met once, briefly, and hated.

This morning the city didn't look so menacing. A soft wind breathed gently through the brilliant red, orange and yellow leaves of the maples in Central Park. Carriages drawn by horses moved slowly, leisurely, through the park. Joggers, in colorful outfits of green, turquoise, burgundy and crimson, trotted through the cool autumn air.

The realization came to Janet slowly, not fully formed until she finished buttoning her coat: I want to be out there. I am going out there. By myself. For a walk in New

Instead of walking across the street from the lobby of the Plaza to Central Park, Janet turned right, swept by the flow of people walking toward the business and shopping sections of Manhattan. Janet found herself in a sea of vigorous men and women. A sea of tweed jackets, Burberry raincoats, three-piece suits and leather briefcases. A sea of purpose and direction and magnetic energy.

I'm not drowning, Janet realized with a surprising rush of joy. I'm swimming, keeping pace, *enjoying* the activity and vitality of Monday morning Manhattan.

Janet felt like laughing. Or singing. Instead, she just smiled and kept walking, feeling part of it.

After a while, as her confidence grew, she realized that she could set her own pace. She could walk more slowly. She could stand at a corner and watch the crowd swirl past her. She could stand still, and she wouldn't sink. She could window shop at Tiffany and Gucci and Dior and Chanel.

By the time the stores opened, after she had walked for blocks and blocks, feeling the pulse, loving the feel, Janet was eager to do some shopping. Twice she had lingered in front of a designer boutique on Fifth Avenue, intrigued by a mauve, pale gray and cream colored silk dress in the window. The dress was feminine but not frilly. Elegant but soft. Womanly.

Janet had never owned a dress like that. She wore attractive, modestly priced clothes. Until recently, she never had money to spend on clothes, and even if she had, she would have selected conservative, neat, traditional clothing. Nothing with flair. Nothing that made a statement or would have so clearly been selected to draw attention to her stunning gray eyes and her sleek figure.

Janet had seen herself look dazzling, seductive and beautiful as Joanna, but that was make-believe. The clothes were costumes. Joanna was someone else—someone who didn't exist.

The mauve, gray and cream silk dress wasn't a costume, and the saleswoman was not acting when she told Janet how lovely it looked on her and that it was made for her.

Janet knew how it looked, and she knew how it made her feel: wonderful, full of energy and vitality. Like this city.

Janet bought the dress, a soft, cream-colored mohair coat, pale gray leather shoes and a matching purse.

Before returning to her suite to get ready to go to the theater, Janet stopped at the gift shop in the Plaza. She bought a coffee mug, bumper sticker and a key ring. All three were emblazoned with the logo: I love (a deep red heart) New York.

Why am I doing this? she wondered as she carefully applied eyeliner, mascara, eye shadow and pale pink lipstick. A little more than usual. A little stronger statement. A statement to whom? To what?

To New York. To vitality. To style. To feeling good.

Janet brushed her shoulder-length blond hair away from her face, teasing it slightly to add shape. As Joanna, she wore it swept softly off her face held by gold barrettes. Joanna had flair. That hairstyle suited Joanna; maybe, it would suit Janet.

Ross waited in the lobby. He smiled appreciatively at the striking blond woman with the gray shoes, the mohair coat and the dancing gray eyes. He noticed her from a distance, doing a double take because the look demanded it. And because there was something familiar . . .

"Janet," he whispered as she approached him. Joanna.

"Good morning," she said, her voice soft like his.

"You look . . ." Ross paused, searching for a word that wouldn't seem too personal, too private. Something that wouldn't offend her. He rejected wonderful, gorgeous, beautiful and sensational. He settled on a word that fit, an adjective he would never have used to describe her before. He said, "Happy."

"Happy," Janet repeated quietly. *Maybe I am. At least, I feel something. Something that feels good.* "Maybe that's it. I had a nice morning."

"In New York?" Ross teased.

"I'm hooked. At least, it's a nice place to visit."

Ross and Janet slipped into the theater unobserved. The company had already assembled and was just about to begin a full rehearsal. They met Arthur in the executive offices.

"You look fabulous, Janet," Arthur said without hesitation as he helped her with her coat. "What a dress."

"Thank you, Arthur," Janet said comfortably, obviously pleased.

Ross marveled at the effortlessness of Janet's and Arthur's exchange. If he had said the same words, Janet might have bristled, iced over. Arthur barely knew Janet. Maybe that was why he could be so relaxed with her. And she with him. Arthur treated Janet as if she were any other attractive woman.

Maybe she was. Maybe it was Ross who was trying to read between lines that weren't there, to find nonexistent depth beneath the still waters. Maybe Janet's iciness toward him was, simply, that she didn't like him. At least not personally.

Professionally, Ross worked with Janet more harmoniously than he had ever worked with an actress, much less a star. He respected her carefully considered opinions and her limitless talent. He listened to her, and she listened to him. When they disagreed—artistic differences—they talked about it. Janet's serious gray eyes would consider their disagreement thoughtfully, and they would sparkle when it was resolved.

So why couldn't he tell her that she looked fabulous?

Because she wouldn't let him.

"Let's go into the theater. They should be starting soon," Ross said.

"Janet, do you need a note pad? Something to write on?" Arthur asked.

Ross knew how Janet would answer. She never took notes. It was all in her head: every word, every scene, every flaw noted and not forgotten.

Janet smiled and shook her head.

Ross knew her very well, professionally.

They sat in the balcony, unnoticed. Watching. Not speaking. Occasionally Arthur would glance at Ross and grimace, or Ross would shift his position slightly, uncomfortable with something he had seen on stage. Janet watched intently, motionlessly, oblivious to Ross and Arthur.

They returned to Arthur's office during intermission.

"So?" Arthur asked as soon as he shut the door, looking to Janet for the answer.

She laughed. "So what?"

"So what's wrong with the show?"

Janet didn't answer but looked inquisitively at Ross.

"You know, don't you? You're just seeing if we come up with the same conclusion." It was so obvious. Ross couldn't miss it.

"I don't know, Janet. I honestly don't. Tell us."

"Let me wait until it's over. To be sure."

"That's fair," Arthur said. "But, Janet, give us a clue. Is it fixable?"

"Very."

"Are you going to want to talk to the company?"

"Do you *want* me to?"

"It depends on what the problem is, doesn't it?" Ross asked, annoyed that she wouldn't tell them, knowing that she was right to wait until the end.

"I think," Janet said slowly, weighing the pros and cons in her mind, "it would be helpful for me to talk to them."

"Today?"

"Sure," Janet said. She glanced at her watch. "Arthur, may I use your phone? I want to reach Peter in San Francisco before he leaves for the theater."

"Help yourself. I'm going backstage to tell them we'll do an hour dinner break at the end of rehearsal followed by uh . . . er . . . lengthy scene-by-scene critique. Sound reasonable? I mean, I don't want to pry."

"It's only your show, right, Arthur?" Janet answered lightly. "Sounds reasonable."

"Why are you calling Peter?" Ross asked mildly. "Or is it personal? Should I leave?"

"No! I just need to let him know that I'm here. I couldn't reach either Peter or Jack before I left. This looks like a very state-of-the-art phone that Arthur has," Janet added as

268

she looked for the telephone receiver.

"It's a speaker phone," Ross said. "No hands required. That box on his desk is a receiver and an amplifier."

"Oh."

They both heard the telephone ringing, a familiar San Francisco city-proper ring. Peter answered.

"Hi," Janet said without identifying herself.

"Wendy, my beloved. How are you? I spent the weekend in Carmel brooding about our love scene in the second act. I think I've come up with a solution. It's pretty racy."

"Great. I'm with Ross now. I'm sure he'll be pleased."

"Ross is back? Wonderful."

"No, Peter. He's not back. I'm in New York."

"Terrific. Maybe we should just open *Peter Pan* in the Big Apple. As long as the company has moved there." The annoyance in Peter's voice broadcast flawlessly from the box on Arthur's desk. Peter was unaware that Ross could hear him.

"Peter," Janet said quickly. "I'll be back tomorrow. Or Wednesday at the latest. I'll call you as soon as I get in. I can't wait to hear about the second act. I actually had an idea today, too. I think Ross will be back soon . . ."

Janet glanced over at Ross. He was scowling.

"I hope so. OK, love. See you soon," Peter said and hung up.

"We haven't accomplished much in your absence," she explained, shrugging. "We're still at an impasse with that scene in the second act."

Arthur returned before Ross could answer.

"Let's go, kids. Show time."

Ross, Arthur and Janet ate Chinese food in Arthur's office during the dinner break. They didn't discuss Janet's analysis of the problems with *Joanna*. Arthur announced that he was quite content to hear it fresh when she told the company as a whole.

Janet, Ross and Arthur joined the company on stage. Janet's entrance was greeted with gasps, curiosity and anticipation. What was she doing here? Was she joining them in New York after all?

269

Only Beth, the new Joanna, shuddered.

"Janet! You look great!"

"What are you doing here?"

"What a dress!"

"How long will you be here?"

Janet was surrounded. Her gray eyes dampened for a moment at the reception. They were her friends. Friends she had made no effort to see.

"Janet is here," Arthur said finally, "because, as you all know, the show's not quite right. Ross and I wanted her opinion."

The stage fell quiet. Had Janet just arrived or had she been there all day? Had she seen the rehearsal? What did she think?

Beth closed her eyes and sat down, exhausted, defeated.

"Hi, everyone," Janet began, trying to lessen the tension, knowing what they all didn't know, that her news was good, that the show could be fixed.

Janet walked over to Beth and offered her hand. Beth stood up and shook Janet's hand with her own cold, clammy one. Beth knew that she was shaking hands with the enemy, the woman that the company expected her to be, who she couldn't be, no matter how hard she tried. She felt their resentment. It was all because she wasn't Janet.

"You're terrific," Janet said to Beth. Then Janet turned to the assembled company and repeated what she had said. "Beth is a terrific Joanna."

Janet saw the skepticism, then confusion, on their faces. They trusted Janet. Janet wouldn't whitewash. Janet didn't say things that she didn't believe.

"Beth is a terrific Joanna. She's a *different* Joanna than I was. She gives Joanna a different personality that I did, but it's a perfectly legitimate interpretation. It's a valid, creative way to play Joanna. You never saw me do the show did you, Beth?" Janet asked.

"No," she answered almost apologetically.

"I think that's good. The problem is that everyone else here . . ." Janet said, looking for the first time at Ross. He was smiling, nodding. Maybe he hadn't known, but he knew now. He agreed. He knew that Janet was right. Janet smiled back at him and continued, "Everyone else here *has* seen me play Joanna. The entire company is still performing as if I were playing Joanna. But Beth's Joanna is different. Everybody has to change accordingly. You all have to adapt to Beth, the way you all adapted to me."

"How?" someone breathed. The "why?" that many of them felt was left unasked.

"First you have to decide that what Beth is doing with Joanna is valid. As I watched her do the first scene, so differently than I did, I thought, what is she doing? How dare she? Then I made myself watch, as an audience would watch, to see if her Joanna had life and appeal. And Beth's Joanna does, despite . . ." Janet paused. This company knew her. They knew she could be tough and direct. They expected her to be. She continued sternly, "Despite the lack of support Beth has gotten from the rest of the cast."

No one spoke. Beth wiped tears from her eyes, hoping no one would see her.

You're absolutely right, Janet, Ross thought. But how do you fix this kind of polarity?

"I am not coming back. I may never play Joanna again. If you all do this show right, the way you can, then Beth's Joanna, not mine, will become the gold standard."

"How, Janet?" someone else repeated.

"If everyone's willing, we should start now. First, Beth needs to tell us who her Joanna is. I'm sure you've done this already, but no one was really listening because you all knew Joanna. Right?"

A few reluctant defiant nods. Janet was right of course. Not that they were *trying* to undermine the show . . .

"So Beth tells us about Joanna. Then I'd like to just tell you, scene by scene, where I saw the weaknesses, where you weren't supporting *her* way and how I think you can change. The changes are minor, subtle but necessary, adjustments. If you don't make them, the show will flop. If you do make them, you might as well move here permanently."

Nervous, relieved laughter.

Janet looked at the director. He was new to the company, too. He had no idea, until then, what the real problem was. He had probably said the same words to them, trying in vain to get them to support Beth. Janet had invaded his territory, but he didn't look angry. He looked relieved. For the first time he sensed that they all might try.

As the evening wore on, as they played and replayed the awkward scenes, as they listened to Janet and to Beth and as they talked instead of arguing, they began to realize that it *was* possible. Exciting even. They weren't merely copying the San Francisco production; they were creating a new production with its own character and power. Everything was possible.

They worked until two in the morning. No one noticed the time. No one wanted to leave. Only Stacy—who arrived at seven and sat next to Ross in the front row for four hours—left before they were through.

Ross and Janet rode together in a taxi to the Plaza. Ross paid the driver and walked into the hotel with Janet.

"You're not staying here," Janet said as they rode up the elevator. "I'd forgotten."

"No. I thought I would see you safely to your room. It's late."

"Thank you."

Janet hesitated at the door of her suite. He had been so quiet. He hadn't even told her what he thought.

"Did you think it went all right tonight?" she asked. She held the key in her hand, but had turned, facing him with her back to the door.

"All right? Janet, you're a genius. Everyone managed to save face. Everyone felt so good. We're going to have a solid gold production. Yeah, it went all right," he said. Didn't she know?

"Sometimes you're hard to read. You were so quiet."

"I didn't want to meddle. It was your show," he said. It wasn't entirely true. He was quiet because he was thinking about her. "It always will be your show. I agree Beth has a good, valid Joanna, but I prefer the way you played her."

"I do, too," Janet said, frowning a little.

272

"What was that frown for?" Ross asked, as if Janet was just like everyone else. Ross didn't usually let frowns pass without comment.

"That was an ego frown," Janet said, shaking her head. "It matters to me, a little, that my Joanna not be forgotten."

"A little?"

"A little. A tiny frown. But it shouldn't matter at all. That sort of thing usually doesn't matter to me." But today, tonight, it mattered. Because of today. Because of feeling alive, vital, beautiful and proud. And happy?

"I'll never forget the way you played Joanna."

Janet looked up at him. Her gray eyes smiled appreciatively.

Ross would have kissed any other woman in the world who looked at him like that. Especially one that he had been wanting to kiss all night.

But, he didn't and the moment passed.

"I'd better go," Janet said as she turned to put the key in the lock.

"Are you leaving today?"

"Yes."

"What time? I'll send a limo."

"I'm not sure when I'll leave. But don't worry about me. I can get myself to the airport," she said confidently.

"OK. I'll see you Friday in San Francisco. Or maybe Thursday. Thank you again for what you did tonight."

"It was good for me," she said softly to his back as he left.

Chapter Twenty-two

Kathleen looked at her Cartier watch and frowned.

"It's exactly five minutes later than the last time you looked, right?" Betsey asked.

"Right. But it's already three-thirty in Boston. They should have called him by now," Kathleen said, stabbing a piece of butter lettuce with a silver salad fork, then, uninterested in eating, laying the fork back down on her plate.

"Mark knows we're at the Club. He'll call. I don't understand why you are so anxious about this!"

"Because it may mean that Mark is moving to Boston in eight months."

"That you *both* are moving to Boston."

"I'm not sure of that, Betsey. I don't know if Mark will want me to go with him."

"Kathleen, he is so much in love with you. It's so obvious. We're all a little jealous," Betsey said, looking at her own two-month-old wedding band.

"Well I'm a little jealous of you. You and Jeff know each other so well. You know how much you love each other. You know that it's right to spend the rest of your lives together."

"Don't you know that about Mark?"

"I know it. I think I know it. It's just that our relationship is so new—"

"So exciting, so wonderfully romantic," Betsey added dreamily.

"But not real. Think about it, Betsey. I met him as his marriage was falling apart. We spent four months apart to give him time to get over it. The separation made us desperate to be together. Then, just as we were starting to see what it could be like, being together every day, Mark was shot — " Kathleen's voice broke. The memory was still too frightening.

"But each of these crises brought you closer together," Betsey said.

"But life isn't a series of crises. It's living every day. It's being able to renew your love from within, not because a crisis reminds you. Even now, this Boston thing is forcing the issue."

"So you're not sure?"

"I'm sure, but I don't think Mark is. And he is so cautious."

"What do you want?" Betsey asked.

"Six months. OK, that's greedy. *One* month," Kathleen said, her violet eyes seeing a happy image. "One month in which our only crisis is that we are getting low on milk."

"I just spent a month like that," Betsey said. "It was a little boring!"

Kathleen laughed, shaking her head slightly. She stopped abruptly as she saw the waiter coming toward their table with a telephone.

"A call for you, Ms. Jenkins," he said, connecting the phone to a plug near the table.

"Mark?"

"Hi."

"You got the fellowship!" Kathleen could tell by his voice, by the way he said the one syllable word.

"Yes," he breathed, excited.

"Congratulations. The guys at Peter Bent Brigham don't know how lucky they are."

"Maybe," Mark began.

"You accepted, didn't you?"

"I told them I'd let them know tomorrow."

"Why?"

"Because I want to discuss it with you."

275

"Oh," she said quietly. *Oh*.

Mark waited, expecting Kathleen to say something else. She didn't.

"So, lady, how about dinner tonight? At Gerard's?"

It was Kathleen's favorite restaurant because it was so romantic.

"Sure," she said slowly, wondering what it meant, what there was to discuss. "Shall I make reservations?"

"I've made reservations. For eight o'clock. I should be home by six-thirty."

"I'll see you then," Kathleen said softly, thoughtfully as she replaced the telephone receiver in its cradle.

He wanted to discuss *it*—something about his move to Boston—with her. Or maybe he just wanted to tell her what he had decided and why. Maybe he was just going to explain why it was best for him to go by himself.

He had chosen her favorite place, but it was a public place. Was that good or bad? He knew that she would not make a scene in public. He should have known that she wouldn't make a scene in private, either. She would accept what he told her because she knew that he would have thought about it carefully.

His voice was so eager, so excited, so loving and gentle, she reminded herself repeatedly throughout the long afternoon. She reminded herself, but still her stomach churned, and waves of apprehension washed through her.

Mark had reserved *their* table at Gerard's. It was the most romantic, situated in its own secluded corner. Kathleen wondered when Mark had made the reservation. They would not have gotten that table if he had only called today.

Kathleen watched the candlelight sparkling through the golden bubbles of champagne. She couldn't look at him, even though she felt his eyes on her.

"So . . ." he began quietly.

"So," she echoed, still gazing at the shimmering bubbles, her heart fluttering. Please don't tell me it's been a great few months, but . . . or that you want to move to Boston by yourself *at first*. . . Just tell me that you know it's too soon to be certain and why don't we see how we feel in spring. . .

"So, will you marry me, Kathleen?"

"*Marry* you?" she asked weakly, looking up then, needing to find his eyes.

"You seem so surprised."

"I am," she said softly. Her violet eyes were moist with joy. "Are you sure?"

"I'm sure. But you're not," he said, concerned.

"No. I am sure. Yes, Mark, I will marry you," she said, looking into his eyes, searching for doubt or hesitation and finding none. Mark's dark brown eyes were steady, full of love, happy. "Of course I will marry you."

"When?"

"Whenever. Whenever you want," Kathleen said, her mind spinning in a whirl of disbelief and joy. "How about mid-June? Just before we move to Boston."

"Kathleen, we don't have to move to Boston. Your family is here—"

"I want to. I love Boston. It's so charming and traditional, so steeped in history. Besides," Kathleen said, twinkling, "I can't wait to tell everyone that my husband—my *husband*—the cornhusk will be doing his cardiology fellowship at the Bent Peter!"

"Who told you . . . ?"

"Hal, of course. Leslie's cute little preppie intern. One day when you were still in the ICU, Hal regaled me with, as he called them, the academic sobriquets of Boston. Let's see, Massachusetts General Hospital is The General. Beth Israel is The House of God. And Peter Bent Brigham is The Bent Peter. I like the medical community in Boston already."

"You're terrific."

"So are you. You want to go to Boston, don't you?"

Mark nodded. Then he said seriously, "What I want most is to marry you. If we move to Boston that's icing on the cake."

"Oh, Mark. I love you."

"I love you, Kathleen."

They held hands across the table, fingers entwined, gazes locked in a look of love and confidence. After a few moments, Kathleen frowned slightly.

"What's wrong?" Mark asked instantly.

"I need to tell you about my financial situation," she said. He had to know before he married her.

"OK. Why, am I marrying into some debts?"

"No. Not debts, but responsibilities. Liabilities even."

"I'm intrigued. Tell me," Mark said lightly, unconcerned. He knew what Kathleen's father did. He knew that Kathleen was used to doing whatever she wanted, going wherever she wanted, buying anything she liked, but Mark believed that it wasn't essential to Kathleen's happiness to spend money.

They had been so happy in his tiny apartment, the apartment Kathleen had painted herself. One day Mark would be able to support a more affluent life style for her. Kathleen seemed to know it would be a while and she never pushed. In fact, until now, she had never discussed money with him at all.

As if it didn't matter to her.

Kathleen told Mark then, in their quiet secluded corner, at the table with the pale pink table cloth and white roses, about her money. About her trust funds and her income. About her virtually limitless wealth.

"Your trust funds earn more money than I will ever make. More money in one year than I could make in ten," Mark said quietly.

Kathleen nodded, her violet eyes narrowed, trying to read the thoughts behind his serious brown eyes.

"I really had no idea," he said.

"I know. And we—my family—don't advertise it. That's the liability part. My wealth could make us and our children targets. Which doesn't mean we shouldn't enjoy it. The interest alone is far more than we could spend in a year even if we tried, and of course you would never have to pick up another stethoscope in your life," Kathleen said flippantly, then stopped, startled by the expression on Mark's face. It looked like relief. Like peace. But why? Mark loved medicine. He would never give it up, would he?

The expression passed quickly, leaving Kathleen a little confused.

"I think your family, your family lawyers, will insist on a pre-nuptial agreement," Mark said calmly.

"No! Don't be silly," Kathleen said, knowing they would strongly advise it. But it was her choice. Her money. Her marriage.

"I wouldn't object to signing one. I'm not marrying you for your money. I plan to stay married to you forever anyway," Mark said, smiling as he reached across the table to touch her face. He added soberly, "If anything did happen, I wouldn't want your money. You have my verbal pre-nuptial agreement."

"I don't want it because nothing is going to happen. I want you to promise that you will use the money. To buy a house if we want one. To take wonderful trips. To set up your office with its own cath lab. We don't need to struggle to make ends meet just because we don't want to touch my money."

"Just because . . . ?"

"Well, we can struggle to make ends meet if we *want* to, if it makes us feel like true newlyweds, but not because of any chauvinism about who should be the breadwinner. OK?"

Mark laughed.

"Kathleen, I really don't feel threatened by your money," he said truthfully. "Only amazed."

"And tempted to spend it?"

"Sure. For *us*. For a house that you love. For a trip we want to take. For things that make you happy."

"You make me happy."

"You make *me* happy."

"James, it's Eric. I think we've successfully negotiated for the additional property." Eric Lansdale sounded pleased.

"Great."

"Charlie's still hammering out the details, but it all looks very good."

"Charlie?"

"Charlie Winter. She's the corporate attorney. I'm sure you've spoken with her."

"*Ms*. Charlotte D. Winter? Of course. We've spent hours on the phone discussing easements and utility accesses. I've never met her. Somehow Charlie doesn't fit."

"It will when you meet her. Which may be soon. The three of us should go to Maui in the next week assuming this is all wrapped up. Will you be able to get away?"

"Sure."

"Good. Will you be at home this weekend? I may need to reach you if there are any problems. There has been some rumbling about sub-platting and not selling us the whole property. I'd want your input on what plats we must have. You have a copy of the plats, don't you?"

"Yes. Do you have my home number?"

"Yes. Let me check that it is correct."

James half-listened as Eric read the number. He had to give Eric Leslie's number. He had no choice. It was where he would be.

"That's right. But let me give you another number."

Eric wrote the number James gave him on a slip of paper and put it in his briefcase.

Eric smiled. He didn't know James Stevenson well, but he liked him. James was a tremendous discovery for Eric's company, InterLand. He was the most creative architect Eric had ever known. Creative and non-tempermental. And nice. James was a nice man — hard-working, professional, talented — and apparently not married but involved. It was nice that James had someone.

"James," Eric said still thinking about James's personal life. "You are welcome to bring someone with you to Maui. It won't be all business. We'll take the company jet. Plenty of room."

"Oh. Thank you."

"If I don't speak with you this weekend, we'll talk Monday," Eric said with finality. Charlie had just walked into his office.

"Fine. Have a nice weekend, Eric."

Charlie spoke as soon as Eric replaced the receiver.

"Those guys were tough," she breathed flopping with a sigh onto the cream-colored couch in Eric's office.

"Were?"

"I think so. Hope so. They may come back with a face-saving counter offer. They may want to keep a little of the land, but I think we've got them."

"Good attorneys?"

"Good," Charlie said smiling. "But not *great*."

"You're not an attorney, Charlie. You're a shark. *Ms*. Charlotte D. Winter," Eric said, his light blue eyes smiling at her, appraising her.

Charlie did look menacing in her attorney-at-law outfit with her attorney-at-law hairdo. Charlie wore a perfectly tailored, tweed suit with a silk blouse and a sensible, but expensive, Longines wrist watch. Her long, golden hair was pulled tight off her face into a secure chignon. Her soft, seductive brown eyes were hidden beneath a studied look of no nonsense efficiency.

"*Ms?* Who said that? Why are you laughing?"

"James said that. You have him completely terrorized. And Charlie, he's on our side. He's a good guy. And I'm laughing because you really can look ominous."

"Effective."

"Effective and efficient," Eric agreed, extending his hands to her, urging her to come to him.

"James is so serious. He answers my questions so carefully, so cautiously," Charlie said, shaking her head, refusing to walk toward Eric until he stopped mocking her.

"I think it's nice that someone who works for me takes spending millions and millions of my dollars seriously. I like a little caution," Eric said, slightly sternly. He gave Charlie almost free reign in negotiations like the ones today. Charlie was shrewd, but she wasn't afraid to spend money. The money she spent always returned many times over. Charlie had uncanny instincts. Eric added, "You and James need to meet. Face to face. On the beach."

"I picture a boring, unattractive egghead."

"I think that's the same picture he has of you."

"Are you trying to set us up?"

"No! He's not your type. Not that I have any idea what your type is. Anyway he's involved with someone."

"I thought you were my type," Charlie said softly. It was a statement deep with meaning that spanned almost twenty years and a gamut of emotion and passion and pain. A statement that they both knew wasn't entirely true. Or entirely false.

"Parts of me are your type," Eric said, moving toward her.

Charlie stood up. In two quick motions, she removed the pins from her tightly knotted hair. The silky, blond strands fell down her back and into her face. Her brown eyes softened and beckoned.

"I know," she whispered as his lips met hers. "Those are the parts that I like the best."

"*Ms.* Charlotte D. Winter," Eric murmured as he gently kissed her long lovely neck.

Part Three

Chapter Twenty-three

Philadelphia, Pennsylvania
November, 1945

"Charlotte D. Winter," Mary repeated firmly to the nurse on that snowy morning in Philadelphia, November 11, 1945. Her daughter was five hours old.

"Named after you, then?"

"Yes."

"What does the 'D' stand for, ma'am?"

"Nothing."

The nurse arched an eyebrow but entered the mother's name and the baby's name as Charlotte D. Winter.

"Father's name?" she asked.

"Max D. Winter," Mary said softly, hoping that the nurse wouldn't recognize that name, wouldn't accuse her, accurately, of making up all three names.

The nurse didn't blink. The only thing that mattered was the horrible war that had killed so many people — so many fathers who would never see their infant daughters — was all but over. Nothing else mattered. Something tugged at the back of her mind. Maybe it was just the hope that Max D. Winter would return from Europe, or wherever he was, to see his daughter Charlotte.

Mary knew that her baby's father would never see his tiny daughter. He would never even know of her existence. There was no Max D. Winter. Only John, with no last name, a private in the Army that she had met on Valentine's Day nine months before.

It was on Wednesday, February 14, 1945 that John visited the North Philadelphia Library, Mary's library, one of the few libraries in the city that remained open during the war. It remained open because of Mary, because Mary refused to close the door on her books and because Mary was willing to work for almost no money. Mary's best friends, her only friends, were the characters in the books. She knew them so well. She lived their lives and their loves. Mary wasn't greedy. She wanted to share her friends with others.

So in spite of the war and because of Mary, the library remained open. It was a refuge for Mary and people like her, providing an escape to other worlds and to happier times.

Mary was sitting at her desk when John walked in. He wore an Army uniform with a single chevron on the jacket sleeve. Mary smiled at him, her large brown eyes conveying a message of sympathy and an offer of help. He looked so young, so bewildered and trapped, like they all were, in an inexplicable horror of hatred and murder.

He had come to her library to find an escape, a little peace, if only for a moment.

"May I help you?" Mary asked.

John shrugged. "I don't know. I had a few hours. Sail tomorrow for Europe. I was just walking around, and I saw the library. I used to like to read a lot."

"What do you like to read?"

"Anything," he said. Then he added hesitantly, "Except war stories."

"What's your favorite?"

"I don't know. When I was a kid, I used to read *The Wizard of Oz*. I read it a few times," he said, his voice distant, as if remembering those happy trouble-free days. Or, was he simply thinking about the land over the rainbow?

"Have you read the other Oz books? *The Scarecrow of Oz? Return to Oz?*"

"No ma'am."

Mary found *The Scarecrow of Oz* for him. John settled into a chair in the far corner of the library. He didn't move, except for the eager turning of pages, for four hours. By then it was dark and already an hour past closing time.

"John," Mary said gently, startling him out of the Emerald City and back to Philadelphia, the cold dark library and the war.

"Yes?" he asked, focusing slowly, reluctantly.

"I have to close the library now."

"Oh. OK," he said, handing the precious volume to her.

"John, I can lend it to you if you want," Mary said, as she had said to so many young soldiers over the past four years, knowing she would never see the books again. Most of the books she gave away were from her own collection. They were her closest friends. But Mary was willing to share.

"Really? I will return it. I promise," John said as they all did.

Mary smiled. She didn't make them promise. She didn't want their minds cluttered with guilt. She wanted every part of the book to bring them happiness. She knew that some of the young soldiers would never return. It mattered so little—in contrast to *that*—whether or not they returned her books.

John asked her to have dinner with him. They ate in a small diner near the library. Afterward John walked Mary to her house on Elm Street.

"Would you like some coffee?" Mary asked as they stood on the porch of her house.

"Coffee? Yes, ma'am!"

Mary served coffee and fruitcake.

"What's your favorite book, ma'am . . . er . . . Mary?"

"*Rebecca,*" Mary said without hesitation.

"I've never heard of it."

"It was published just before the war in Europe. The author is Daphne du Maurier."

"It's a love story, isn't it?" John asked, the gentleness of his voice surprising them both.

"A love story. And a mystery."

"Do you have a copy here?"

"No. I took my copy to the library. I lent it out and haven't gotten it back yet," Mary said, remembering that she had given it, over a year ago, to a young woman whose husband had just been killed in the South Pacific. Mary had given it to the woman because, to Mary, *Rebecca* was a story of hope. Mary didn't expect to get it back. It didn't matter. Mary knew that book, like all her books, by heart. She didn't need to read the words. She knew the words and the characters and the scenes. "I haven't been able to find another copy. After the war . . ."

"Tell me the story," John said.

Mary told him about Rebecca, and about Max de Winter, and the woman Max married after Rebecca's death, a shy unassuming woman capable of great love and deep passion. A woman without a first name, the second Mrs. de Winter, was a woman like Mary. Mary had given her a name: Charlotte. Charlotte de Winter. Mary had named her after Charlotte Bronte.

As Mary talked, her eyes softened with love, and she became Charlotte de Winter while John became Max, the intense, secretive, powerful husband. Max, the wonderful romantic lover.

That snowy Valentine's night in February, Max made love to his precious bride Charlotte. John—Max—held Mary in his strong young arms until dawn. Then he left. He never knew that she had been a virgin. Or that they had conceived a child. Or that Mary was forty-two years old, exactly twice his age.

John knew only that Mary was a wonderful woman. He would never forget her, and he would return her book to her.

Eight months later, a month before Charlotte was born, Mary received a package at the library. It had been postmarked in London two months before. It contained *The Scarecrow of Oz,* and a beautiful leather-bound copy of *Rebecca* with an inscription that read: To Charlotte, All my love, Max.

Two weeks later, Mary received a letter postmarked a month before in London.

Dear Mary,

I hope that the books arrived. I found the copy of Rebecca *in a bookshop in London that had been closed during the war but reopened a month after VE Day. I read it before sending it to you. I think Charlotte is a perfect name for the second Mrs. de Winter. You are very like her, and she is a wonderful person.*

I have met a girl here — in London — and we will be married next spring. I enjoy England and look forward to making my home here. Maybe someday I'll even find a Manderley.

Love,

John

By the time Charlotte was one month old, Mary realized that she wouldn't have the courage to tell her daughter the truth. Mary didn't even know John's last name. Neither the letter nor the package had a return address. The war was over. Morality was rapidly returning. There were lots of fatherless children, but their parents had been married. Those children could hold their heads high.

Charlotte couldn't. Not if the truth were known.

No one had noticed Mary's pregnancy because no one noticed Mary. She had no friends, at least not flesh and blood ones. She hid her pregnancy under smocks, and convinced the city to hire an assistant librarian who managed the library for the eight weeks of Mary's mysterious absence.

When Mary returned to work, carrying the infant with her, she told the few people who asked that the child was her niece and had been orphaned when Mary's sister and brother-in-law had been killed in an automobile accident two weeks after the child's birth.

By the time Charlotte was old enough to need an explanation about why she had an "Auntie Mary" instead of a mommy and daddy, Mary had modified the story so that it conformed more closely to *Rebecca*.

Her parents, Mary told Charlotte, were killed in a sailing accident when Charlotte was one year old. Shortly after that, true to the fate of Manderley, their beautiful home mysteriously burned down. That was why Mary had no pictures of Charlotte's parents. All she had was the leather-bound copy of the book, *Rebecca,* that Max had given to Charlotte shortly before the birth of their daughter.

It was a book, Mary knew, that Charlotte should never read.

Charlotte accepted the story dispassionately and without a sense of loss. She had never known her parents. Her interest was curiosity not emotion, and Charlotte loved her Auntie Mary very much.

Mary devoted herself to her precious golden-haired daughter. Eagerly, lovingly, Mary introduced the little girl to her friends, the wonderful books that were her world. Charlotte loved the stories because she loved sitting on Mary's lap and watching Mary's huge brown eyes—Charlotte's eyes—twinkle and soften and glisten as she read.

As Charlotte grew older, she had a need for real friends, not imagined ones. She made friends at school. Charlotte preferred spending time with them to rushing home to hear about Jane Eyre or Amy, Meg, Beth and Jo or Scarlett O'Hara. Charlotte grew impatient with Mary's imaginary world and imaginary friends.

But she didn't grow impatient with Mary. She loved her. She worried about her friendless frail aunt, the lonely, aging woman who, as the years passed, seemed to retreat even farther into a world of make-believe.

Three days after Charlotte's sixteenth birthday, Mary knocked on Charlotte's bedroom door.

"Charlotte?"

"Yes, Aunt Mary? Come in."

Mary sat on her daughter's bed wringing her hands.

"Charlotte, darling. I am not well. I'm fifty-nine years old. I'm not going to live forever," Mary said slowly, hesitantly, not telling Charlotte the complete truth: *I am going to die. Soon.*

"Auntie! Fifty-nine is young! Maybe you shouldn't work so hard," Charlotte said, rushing to her side, putting her strong healthy arms around Mary's boney shoulders.

"Nevertheless, you and I must decide what will happen to you if I die before you turn eighteen. While you are still a minor."

"But you won't!"

"You and I have no relatives," Mary continued. "Your parents were both only children. I really have no friends who could take care of you."

I have friends, Charlotte thought. Parents of my school friends could take care of me.

"I couldn't bear the thought of you going to a foster home. So," Mary said firmly, her eyes seeing something far away, a far away make-believe friend, "I have created an aunt for you. I have told my attorneys that she exists, that she is my sister and that she lives with us now. She will take care of you if anything happens to me. She is a kind, lovely woman."

"Auntie —" Charlotte began then stopped. Her aunt was out of touch with reality. Charlotte knew it. She had learned it in little bits over the years. The only reality for Mary was her love for Charlotte. Even now this fantasy aunt was invented to save Charlotte from what could happen to an orphaned, under-aged child.

So she has invented someone — a kind, lovely woman — to live with me, Charlotte thought, watching Mary's loving eyes. But there is no lovely woman, no kind aunt. There is no one. If anything did happen to Aunt Mary, I would *really* be all alone; but she doesn't know it, Charlotte thought sadly, and I can't tell her. She wouldn't understand.

"What is her name, Aunt Mary?" Charlotte asked gently.

"She is your Aunt Louise. Louise M. Alcott," Mary announced proudly.

So out of touch, Charlotte thought, tears filling her own eyes.

Two months later, Mary died in her sleep. Charlotte found her in the morning and held her small cold body for a long time before calling the police.

"Yes, Aunt Louise is living with me," Charlotte assured the appropriate authorities a week later. "She is a kind, lovely woman just like Aunt Mary. She'd be happy to meet with you. Of course Aunt Mary's attorneys know her very well."

Everyone accepted the fact of Louise Alcott's existence. Everyone assumed that someone had met her. Certainly someone must have witnessed the signatures granting Louise Alcott power of attorney until Charlotte's eighteenth birthday. Surely someone had witnessed the signing of the guardianship papers, but of course no one had. The legal documents had all been signed by Charlotte, in a script quite distinct from her own unfrilly style, and had been returned to the attorneys by Mary.

Charlotte had signed the papers and discussed the logistics of creating Aunt Louise simply to humor Mary. Over the years, Mary had involved Charlotte, a knowing, willing, loving accomplice, in other delusions. They had all passed without harm. This death delusion was morbid but, Charlotte decided, just as unreal even though Mary pursued it in a greater detail than any of the others. . . .

Mary carefully, patiently told Charlotte about her bank account—a checking account—and showed her how to write checks, repeatedly reminding her that these would need to be written in Louise Alcott's handwriting. Mary also showed her the shoeboxes full of money—Mary didn't really trust banks, but the checking account was convenient for paying bills—hidden beneath blankets in her bedroom closet. The money in the shoeboxes was Mary's life's savings, the accumulation of years of hard work and frugality. Charlotte was amazed that there was so much money—it looked like so much—because Mary had never hesitated to spend money on *her*.

Then Mary died, and it was not just a morbid delusion. Mary was really gone, and Charlotte was really alone, frightened and confused.

Why had she died? Charlotte's mind screamed. Sometimes in the quiet emptiness of the house she would scream aloud, "WHY? Why, Aunt Mary? *Why?*"

"Your aunt was very ill," the doctor had said. Charlotte didn't think to ask, Ill from what?

Despite Charlotte's anguish and grief, she was able to appear calm at the requisite meetings with the attorneys, the authorities and the doctor. She *had* to. She didn't want anyone to find out that she was alone. If they did, they would take her away from the house. It was all that she had left.

Charlotte arranged the funeral. It was a *real* detail that Mary had neglected entirely. Mary's funeral was surprisingly well attended. Charlotte's classmates and their parents came, as did Mary's co-workers from the library. Many other people who Charlotte did not recognize also attended. Mary had no friends. Who were they?

They were people who had visited Mary's library and found solace there. Most of them had visited during the war: grieving widows, lonely soldiers, restless wives and girlfriends. They remembered Mary's generosity and the gentle loving care she had given each of them as she helped them find a book that would be a comfort to them. They remembered Mary, even though many of them hadn't seen her for years, even though none of them was her friend. And they came to her funeral.

For three weeks, Charlotte grieved silently, fighting anger, loneliness, betrayal and loss.

She waited, Charlotte realized with horror on the twenty-first day after Mary's death, for Aunt Louise to come and comfort her.

"There is no Aunt Louise!" Charlotte yelled at the silent walls in the living room of Aunt Mary's house, *her* house. "No Aunt Louise. No Aunt Mary. No one."

The tears came then, at last. Charlotte cried and sobbed, the pain and grief and anger spilling in hot, wet drops down her young face. After several hours, exhausted, her emotions purged, the tears stopped.

I am by myself, she thought. I have my life to live. Aunt

Mary has given me so much love. Even in her death, knowing how much I would hate having to live somewhere else, she has allowed me to stay here, in her house, in the house that I love.

The following day Charlotte returned to school, to her friends and real life. She told them politely, sparing details, that she and her Aunt Louise were doing "as well as could be expected."

Three weeks later, Charlotte was contacted by her attorneys. Mary had left a letter for Charlotte, with instructions that it be delivered six weeks after her death.

The letter began, *My darling daughter* . . .

In it, Mary explained about that Valentine's Day in 1945, about John (Max), and about her fear that people wouldn't understand and that Charlotte might be ostracized. The theme of the letter, a letter laced with guilt and doubt, was love. The deep irrefutable love that Mary felt for her daughter.

"Oh, Mother," Charlotte whispered softly, tears streaming down her face as she held Mary's letter in her trembling hands, "I love you."

Chapter Twenty-four

James arrived at Leslie's apartment two hours after he spoke with Eric.

"Hi," Leslie said, opening the door before he put his key in the lock. She had been watching for him. "What have you got?"

"Work," James answered, raising the hand that held a large black portfolio.

The other hand held his briefcase and an overnight bag. James was spending the weekend with her. Leslie's on call schedule at the Veterans' Hospital was every fourth night. It meant that once a month she had an entire weekend without night call, although she still made rounds each weekend day.

"Work?" she asked, laughing.

"Yes. I work, too. Even on weekends like you. I thought I'd work while you're making morning rounds. Or all-day rounds," he added, smiling, knowing that rounds could take a while. "How's your service?"

Leslie smiled back. James had picked up the medical jargon instantly. He was interested in what Leslie did. She told him about her patients. The happy outcomes and the sad ones. Sometimes she cried when she told him, and he held her, stroking her soft chestnut hair.

"My service," she answered, telling him about her medical service, her group of patients in the hospital, "is pretty sick. We had four very sick patients admitted last night."

"So I may get a lot of work done?"

"Uh-huh."

"Actually, that's OK. Just before I left, I got a call about the project I'm working on. They've just doubled the amount of acreage, so I have a lot of work to do."

"What is it?"

"A resort. In Maui."

"Really? May I see?"

"Of course," James said, moving to the table in the kitchen. They had never really discussed his work in detail. He had never brought any work with him before. "Until today we thought it would just be the main hotel. Which will look like this."

Leslie stared at the sketch that he handed her. It wasn't just a hotel; it was a work of art that blended elegantly, gracefully, *naturally* into the beautiful tropical setting. Leslie had never seen anything like it.

"James! This is so beautiful. This is yours?"

"It's my design, my project. I have tremendous creative freedom because the president of the company who commissioned it believes in quality above all. He doesn't limit me by the usual constraints of cost."

"It's wonderful," Leslie mused, still gazing at the sketch. "I've never been to Hawaii."

"Neither had I until last summer. I made the initial sketches over there. I have to go back this week now that we have more land."

"You'll still build this hotel, won't you?"

"Sure. In fact, construction is scheduled to begin next month. But now we can make an entire resort community," James said eagerly. It was obvious how much he enjoyed his work. "Now we have room for condominiums. Houses even. I'll make sample sketches of units this weekend, but I can't really do more until I go back and see the additional property."

"When do you go?" Leslie asked casually, even though she knew it might mean they wouldn't see each other as scheduled.

"I'm not sure. Next week sometime. The deal wasn't

completely signed, sealed and delivered. In fact, they may need to reach me this weekend. I gave them your number. I hope you don't mind."

"Of course I don't," Leslie said, putting down the sketch and turning toward him, sensing what they both sensed, that something was missing.

As his lips found hers, kissing her hungrily, Leslie realized what had been missing: the kiss, the touching. Their minds had said hello, but their bodies hadn't, until then.

"Hi," he whispered, kissing her neck, wrapping his arms around her, molding her body against his. "I've missed you."

"I've missed you, too," Leslie whispered back. She led him into the bedroom.

Leslie closed her eyes, her head swirling with images, her body trembling with sensations as James touched her. The images were lovely: an alpine meadow, a red-orange sunset, sparking blue water, sailboats with colorful spinnakers, sandy beaches, snow-capped mountains, a muted autumn sun. The images — warm, colorful and sensual — formed a collage of all the wonderful moments with James. It was a collage that would, one day, include this moment: the wonder of James in her bed, making love to her.

As he touched her, as the warmth and rhythm of their bodies moving together became totally consuming, the images melted into a yellow-gold glow.

"James," she breathed from a voice deep in her soul.

"Leslie."

It was three o'clock Saturday afternoon by the time Leslie finished her rounds. As she drove along the Great Highway beside the Pacific Ocean, green-gray under the November clouds, Leslie thought about James. About James and Leslie. And James and Lynne.

The thoughts weren't new. They were with her whenever she had a moment to think, whenever she was away from the hospital *and* away from James. Leslie couldn't think, not rationally or analytically, when she was with him. His presence was too powerful, too demanding, too wonderful to tarnish with the thoughts that plagued her when they were apart.

It had been six weeks. In those six weeks they saw each other whenever it was possible.

It should never have started. That was a given. Once it had started, once they realized they had to, finally, acknowledge the unspoken feelings they had shared in high school, it should have ended quickly.

They should have made love once, like groping teenagers, finishing the scene that had been interrupted at the lake so many years before.

That would have been an appropriate ending. Almost understandable. Almost forgivable.

But they made love again and again. As adults. As a man and a woman full of passion and desire.

They should have ended it after they had replayed every moment they had shared in high school, after they had asked each other what they had been feeling then, all those years before.

"Why did you leave the party that night when Alan kissed me?"

"Why do you think? I couldn't stand it. I wanted you so much."

"Why didn't you tell me?"

"You know why."

"Why didn't you kiss me on the ferry boat?"

"I wanted to. My lips were too numb from the cold."

Oh. *No*. What if he had?

"Why would you just dance one dance with me? Or say something to me in the halls and then leave? Or come stand beside me for a quarter of a football game?"

"Because when you spoke to me, when I touched you, when I even just stood beside you, it reminded me that no matter how bad everything was in my life, you existed. You were real, and you seemed to like me."

"*Seemed* to? It must have been so obvious. I couldn't even be clever and coy. Not with you. But why just one dance? One monosyllabic phrase?"

298

"Those brief moments made me feel so good, but the feeling was almost too strong, too good. It reminded me of who I really was—how I had no right to be with you. I had no self-esteem, remember. Of course I didn't know why. I only made it through those years because I was driven by an instinct to survive and by feelings that drew me to you."

They should have ended it after they had relived those high school days, after they had shared all the distant feelings and memories.

But they didn't. They began to share the rest of their lives. By the middle of November, Leslie and James were living entirely in the present, as lovers, as friends, as a man and woman who had met, learned about each other and chosen to be together.

Leslie knew it, but she sensed that James didn't. Somehow James had rationalized his relationship with Leslie so that it didn't jeopardize his marriage. Somehow the relationship with Leslie was still a relationship in the past. *Of* the past. It was not really happening in the present.

James had created his own private time warp. His relationship with Leslie should have happened years ago. It might have except for a misplaced letter. And it was happening now because it was destined—it had always been destined—to happen.

Leslie knew that as soon as James realized the folly of his logic it would be over. Leslie was a girl he had loved in his past, and she was a woman he *could* have loved in the present; but James had already chosen to spend his life with someone else. Lynne was his present and his future.

Leslie and James never discussed Lynne, but Leslie had seen his eyes that night, at her birthday dinner, when he told her about Lynne. James's life was with Lynne. The rest of his life.

There was no point in even thinking about what would have happened if James had not been married. Would this wonderful, passionate relationship they had now continue forever? Or was it stoked by the knowledge that it was fleeting, a nostalgic moment kindled by the unfulfilled desires of youth?

There is no point in thinking about *that,* Leslie thought as she parked in front of her apartment building, pulling into a space in front of James's car. No point in thinking at all, she decided, as she felt her heart quicken in anticipation of seeing him.

James was on the telephone.

"Monday morning?"

"I know it's short notice, but since we've got every square inch of the land, I thought the sooner we—you—saw it, the better."

"Monday's fine."

"We'll take the corporate jet. Plan to leave at eight-thirty. That will get us into our hotel by early afternoon. We'll just settle in on Monday. Then we'll go to the site and meet with the local contractors on Tuesday and Wednesday and fly back Thursday morning. Will you be bringing anyone?"

James looked at his pocket calendar. Lynne's schedule was written on it, and the days he could see Leslie were marked by a small blue dot. Lynne would return late Monday afternoon and fly again on Thursday. Unless she could join him in Maui, which was unlikely, he wouldn't see her for over a week. He wouldn't miss any time with Leslie. They would be able to see each other Thursday night, as scheduled.

"I don't think I will be bringing anyone."

"You're welcome to. You don't even need to let me know."

Before hanging up, Eric gave James directions to the private jet terminal at San Francisco International Airport.

"You're going Monday?" Leslie asked after James replaced the receiver.

James nodded, frowning slightly.

"James?"

"Sorry. I . . . uh . . . need to let Lynne know. She's"—he continued glancing at his watch—"probably in her hotel in New York by now."

"I'll go take a shower. Give you a little privacy," Leslie said, leaving the room.

James caught her hand as she passed.

300

"Hey," he said gently, holding her hand. "I'm sorry."

"James," Leslie said carefully. Maybe today would be the day it was over. "I'm the intruder. Not Lynne."

After Leslie left, James dialed the number in New York that was provided on the computer-generated schedule he kept in his briefcase. It gave all the specifics of Lynne's itinerary, including flight times and hotel locations and telephone numbers. James carried the detailed itinerary with him, but he rarely referred to it. They had decided early on not to call each other, as a routine, when Lynne was traveling. They made the decision then because James was just getting started, they had substantial mortgage payments and they couldn't justify the expense. Now they could easily afford it, but the habit not to call was well established.

Lynne answered the phone on the second ring.

"Lynne?"

"James! Is something . . . ? Is it Mother . . . ?" Or, Lynne thought, remembering the manila folder she had handed to him as she left the day before, have you read it? Lynne's heart pounded as she waited.

"No, Lynne. It's nothing. Nothing has happened. I have to go to Maui on Monday. Eric was able to purchase the adjacent land, so we're going over to take a look."

"Oh."

"Do you want to come?"

"I don't get back until Monday afternoon."

"I know that's your schedule. Maybe you could change. We're taking the company jet. We'll be back Thursday."

"No, I can't change," Lynne said flatly, wondering if she was his first or second choice, wondering where he was calling from and hating herself for calling their empty house all last night. Why did she need to prove it to herself over and over again? She knew. Without ever having made a call, without ever checking to see if he was gone all night, she would have known. She had known from the very beginning, the moment she saw him on September thirteenth.

She knew. That was why she had written the "Monica" chapter for him to read. She had to do something to make him talk to her about it.

"Have you read the chapter?" she asked quietly, knowing the answer. He wouldn't have read it last night. He wasn't home. He was with whomever it was who had taken him away from her.

"No, not yet. I'll read it before I go."

"No," Lynne said quickly, suddenly tired, too tired to deal with it. Too tired. She had been that way for the past four weeks: tired and weak and nauseated. She was too tired to argue or fight, or even to deal with the fact that she had lost her husband.

Tired. Defeated.

"You sure?"

"Yes. It isn't very good. I need to think about it a little more."

"OK. Are you feeling any better?"

"Not really. Each morning I hope that I'll wake up feeling normal. But . . . it's just the flu. Everyone has had it. Mine's just lasting a little longer," she said. *Because I can't really sleep, and I lie awake at night hating my husband for being unfaithful to me. I don't have the strength to deal with it. I have to leave him, but I don't have the energy.*

"Maybe you should see a doctor this week. You'll be home Tuesday and Wednesday. It might be a good idea."

"I know what's wrong with me. I have a bad virus, and there's a lot going on," she added icily.

"What?" *What did she mean?*

"Anyway, I am going to take some time off the following week. I'm going to spend Thanksgiving in Denver with Mother. I'll be gone from Tuesday until Sunday."

James looked at his pocket calendar.

"That means that the only time we'll see each other in the next two and a half weeks is the Monday before Thanksgiving."

"I guess so."

Neither spoke for several moments.

"Why don't I join you in Denver? At least for a few days?" James asked finally.

"No. I want to spend the time with Mother by myself."

"Lynne, are you all right?"

"No. I'm not all right. I don't feel well."

"That's all? Nothing else is wrong?"

"No," Lynne said, exhausted, but encouraged by the concern in his voice. Maybe she was wrong. Maybe it was over. Maybe . . . "No James, nothing else."

"I'll leave the name and number of the hotel in Maui on the refrigerator. And Lynne, please see a doctor."

Leslie finished her shower just before James hung up. She heard him tell Lynne to see a doctor.

"Is Lynne ill?" Leslie asked. *Why am I doing this? Why am I talking about Lynne? Am I trying to end it?*

"Oh. She's had the flu for four weeks."

The flu, whatever that is, doesn't usually last for four weeks, Leslie thought.

"What are her symptoms?" Leslie asked.

"Leslie, I don't want to talk about Lynne."

"Maybe we should. About Lynne. Or about us. About what's wrong."

"What's wrong with Lynne is she's got the flu and she hasn't been able to shake it because, as usual, she pushes herself too hard," James said firmly. Then he added more gently, "There is nothing wrong with us."

"No?" Leslie asked, weakening under his gaze, staring into the intense green eyes that said so much and made her want to believe this folly was possible forever.

"No."

"Oh."

"One thing wrong. One thing we should have done."

"What?" Leslie breathed.

"We should have made love on that ferry boat. Remember? Under the stairs."

"I remember."

"So, let's go find a ferry boat and make love. If we don't find one, we'll come back here to make love. We'll do that anyway. I just need to get out, get blown around by the wind for a while, OK?"

"You want me to come?"

"You're the one I plan to make love with."

* * *

Lynne felt unusually tired and ill as she boarded the nine-thirty flight from LaGuardia to O'Hare Monday morning. She had slept fitfully the past two nights. On Saturday night, after speaking with James, she tossed and turned, wondering if she could be wrong, hoping desperately that she was.

Finally at six A.M., three A.M. in San Francisco, she dialed their home phone number. She let it ring. Twenty rings. Thirty. Each unanswered ring harshly reminded her that she was right.

Lynne thought about the "Monica" chapter that she had left for James to read. It was so foolish. It was a *gentle* way of telling James that she knew, how hurt she was and how they had to talk about it. It began, *Large tears splashed from Monica's cornflower-blue eyes onto her soft fur. Monica was desolate. She had lost her best friend, Thomas* . . .

Thomas was Monica's best friend, and he was her boyfriend. Thomas was a regular in the Monica books. The chapter, written just for James, described Monica's suspicion that Thomas had found someone else and her bewilderment that it had happened. She had been so sure of their friendship and their love!

Lynne was glad that James hadn't read it after all. It made her seem pathetic and hurt. As she listened to the phone ring, unanswered because her husband was in someone else's bed, Lynne's true feelings crystallized. *Anger.*

Her inevitable confrontation with James would not be through an imaginary calico cat. It would be direct. She was leaving him as soon as she regained her strength.

On Sunday, Lynne worked, flying from New York to Atlanta to Orlando and back to New York. Sunday night she didn't sleep well, either, but this time she didn't call to check on James. She knew.

It was a short flight from New York's LaGuardia Airport to O'Hare Field in Chicago, but it was breakfast time and a meal was scheduled. It meant that the flight attendants had to move quickly and efficiently.

As senior flight attendant, Lynne worked the first-class cabin. Despite the short flight, two entrees were offered: Belgian waffle with sausage links or cheese omelette and fruit. Lynne had taken drink and entree orders before take-off. Even before the seat belt sign was turned off, she was in the galley preparing the meal service.

As Lynne reached for the hot coffee pot, the feeling hit her. The galley swirled, her head swirled and her world swirled. She was vaguely aware that she was falling, but she couldn't prevent it. Something very hot touched her thigh, accompanied by grayness and swirling and nausea. A sickening thud echoed and re-echoed in her head.

The passenger in the first row witnessed the episode but couldn't unfasten his seat belt quickly enough to break her fall. He was at her side, calling for help, within seconds.

A crowd—the other first-class passengers, another flight attendant and the co-pilot—huddled in the small galley watching Lynne struggling with consciousness. Her face was white-green. Her blond hair was matted with blood over the right temple where she had struck her head as she fell.

A passenger who was a doctor arrived, instinctively reached for her radial pulse and asked for a damp cloth to put on her forehead.

Lynne could hear his voice. She understood that he was speaking to her, but she couldn't answer him right away. The nausea and the whirling still swept through her in overwhelming unexpected waves. She tried to focus, but the faces were blurred.

"Something hot on my leg," she said finally.

Lynne had spilled the pot of hot coffee when she fell. The doctor examined her legs, as much as was possible given constraints of the crowd and her privacy. He could see enough to tell that most of the burns were first degree, painful but not terribly serious. Fortunately the coffee had not been boiling.

"Please get some towels soaked in cold water for her legs. As soon as we can get her up, we'll need to remove her skirt

305

and nylons and bundle her up in a blanket," he said to the other flight attendant. "What's her first name?"

Lynne's badge said Mrs. L. Stevenson.

"Lynne."

"Lynne? Can you hear me?"

Lynne nodded slightly. The cold towel on her forehead and the cold towels on her legs helped. So did lying very still on the floor.

"How do you feel?"

"Sick. Whirling," Lynne whispered. "Better."

"She's been sick for weeks, Doctor. The flu. But she's kept working."

"Lynne, open your eyes. Good. Follow my finger."

Lynne's eyes moved from side to side.

"Does that make you feel worse?"

"No."

She doesn't have nystagmus, he thought. He said aloud, "I thought it might be an inner ear infection — labyrinthitis — that sometimes follows a viral syndrome, but there's no evidence of it. Has this ever happened before?"

"No."

"Do you remember your heart pounding or fluttering before you fell?" Her pulse had been steady, but a little weak, since he had been feeling it.

"No."

"Did you eat any food that seemed bad to you?"

"Airline food you mean?" Lynne answered, her strength returning. And with it, relief. And a little humor. "No, nothing that seemed bad."

"Are you pregnant?"

"No, not me," Lynne said a little wistfully.

"Ulcers? Stomach pain? Bleeding?"

"No."

"Have you been eating normally?"

"No. This flu has made me sick. I've lost weight."

"Maybe it's only a virus with dehydration, but, young lady, you need to be checked. For now, I see a little pink in your cheeks where the green used to be. Want to try sitting up?"

306

One of the other flight attendants, Carol, helped Lynne into the bathroom, out of her coffee-drenched clothes and into a dress that Lynne had packed in her overnight bag.

"How are you doing?" Carol called through the door.

"OK. Wobbly. I may need to lie down again."

There were empty seats in the first-class cabin. Lynne lay across two seats, curled up, until she had to sit up for the landing. By the time they landed at ten A.M. Chicago time, Lynne felt a little better.

"I'll take you to the crew lounge. We'll call James and then arrange to have you dead-headed back to San Francisco," Carol said as soon as all the passengers had deplaned. "They're bringing a wheelchair for you. Maybe you should go to a hospital here."

"No, I'd like to go home. I feel better. I can make it as long as I can just curl up. Oh, I forgot. James is going to Maui today. He's probably leaving about now. I have no idea how to reach him. He has to go on this trip anyway. Carol, can you see if I can get on something to Denver?"

I can really go home, Lynne thought. Home to Mother.

Chapter Twenty-five

James arrived at the private terminal at the San Francisco International Airport at seven-forty-five. His identification was carefully checked before he was permitted into the waiting lounge. Yes, his name *was* on the list, but would he mind providing proof of his identity?

As soon as James entered the private lounge, he understood the need for special precautions. People who flew on their own jets were a different breed. They expected excellence and quality. And they expected security. They were targets: targets for kidnapping and targets for terrorism. They expected protection.

Once in their secure private lounge, they could behave like anyone else, drinking coffee, reading *The San Francisco Chronicle* and *The Wall Street Journal* and watching the morning news shows. They behaved like anyone else, but they didn't *look* like anyone else. They looked powerful.

They looked, James realized, like Eric Lansdale. Eric was a nice, very powerful and extremely demanding man. Eric expected perfection, just like everyone else in this exclusive lounge.

James looked for Eric in the lounge, but he didn't see him. James only saw men who reminded him of Eric. Many men. And one woman.

She stood at the large window of the lounge, gazing out at the fleet of unmarked corporate jets. Their jets were unmarked for the same reason that the men in the lounge didn't advertise who they were. The jets were identified by numbers only. No names, no logos, no publicity.

The woman wore a yellow and white cotton print dress. Her dazzling golden hair fell to her waist, casually swept off her face by a pair of sunglasses that rested on top of her head. She turned toward James, aware of a new presence in the lounge, as if she were expecting someone.

Her huge brown eyes registered surprise. He was not who she was expecting, but he was interesting. Handsome. She smiled briefly, appreciatively, before returning her gaze to the airfield.

A minute later, Eric entered the lounge. Eric was with a man whose resemblance to Eric was so striking that James assumed he was Eric's older brother. As Eric and the other man approached James, James saw the beautiful blond woman begin to cross the lounge, smiling.

"Hello, James," Eric said. "This is my father, Robert. He has just arrived on the red-eye from Philadelphia."

"James, I am so pleased to meet you. Eric has sent me the sketches of course. Truly brilliant."

"Thank you, sir."

The blond woman joined them.

"Good morning, Robert," she said warmly. "You look rested even though you must be exhausted." Charlie meant that he looked wonderful. Robust, youthful. Too young to be Eric's father.

"Hello," Robert said, returning her warmth, kissing her briefly on the cheek. Then he sighed and added, "I am tired. I don't sleep on planes. At least not on other people's planes. I plan to sleep all the way to Maui if you won't consider me too antisocial."

"Not at all. Eric, who's this? Not the ever dour James?" Charlie asked, deducing that the handsome, sexy man with the green eyes, black hair and seductive smile must be James.

"You're not — " James began as amazed by her as she was by him.

"*Ms*. Charlotte D. Winter," Eric said.

"I'm Charlie," she said, extending a long, graceful hand

to James.

"I'm James."

The interior of the plane was like a home, beautifully decorated and impeccably maintained. It contained a large, comfortable living room, a formal conference room, a kitchen and dining area, two large bathrooms with showers and four bedrooms. As soon as the captain announced that it was safe to remove their seat belts, Robert withdrew to a bedroom.

"See you all in Maui. Eric, I plan to be so rested that I'll be ready for a game of tennis in the late afternoon."

"You're on."

During the five-hour flight, James and Charlie and Eric studied James's recent sketches, talked, read, drank coffee and ate the croissants and fruit that had been boarded moments before the plane left San Francisco.

"I didn't have them board a lunch. We'll be at the hotel in Maui by two. So—" Eric began.

"Basically, James, Eric didn't have them board a lunch because Eric never eats lunch," Charlie interjected, narrowing her brown eyes at Eric, taunting him.

"Who does?" James asked.

"Just me, I guess," Charlie said, reaching for another croissant.

"Charlie is actually capable of eating continuously without gaining a pound. She's always been that way," Eric observed.

Always, James thought. I wonder how long they have known each other. A long time, he decided. The three of them—Charlie, Eric and Robert—seemed like a family. Eric and Charlie seemed like a little more than a family. Something more than siblings.

Lynne can eat constantly, James thought, and she is thin. But her energy level is so high—at least until recently—that she needs the calories to keep up with the energy output.

"My wife—" James began, then stopped. Charlie and Eric were off on another topic. They didn't hear him.

* * *

310

After settling in his elegant suite with the panoramic ocean view, James took a nap. He had left Leslie's bed at five, returning home to pack and to leave the name of the hotel on the refrigerator for Lynne. He noticed the manila folder with the "Monica" chapter. He had time to read it, but Lynne had said no. She was sensitive about him reading her work if she wasn't happy with it. James left the manila folder, untouched, on the kitchen counter.

Rested and refreshed after his short nap, James decided to sit by the pool and read in the fading rays of the late afternoon sun. They had agreed to meet at six in Eric's suite. He had time.

"I hope you have sunscreen on."

James looked up at the sound of her voice behind him. She moved in front of him, blocking the sun. Her face was lost in shadows, but her hair shone brilliant gold as the sun's rays filtered through it.

"Number six."

"That's probably all right especially since it's almost sunset. You look like you've been under glass all your life," she observed uncritically.

James's skin was pale, but creamy, rich and smooth. He looks like a marble statue of a Greek god, Charlie thought. Even at rest, lying on the chaise longue, James's muscles were well-defined, delicately laced with blue-purple veins. Gorgeous, she thought.

"Not all my life. I used to spend summers working in a logging camp, sweating with the guys under the summer sun," James said.

"May I join you?" Charlie asked, still standing in front of him.

"Of course.'"

James watched her gracefully lower her lovely tan body onto the adjacent chaise longue. She wore a brown one-piece bathing suit. Modest but revealing.

"Eric and Robert are playing tennis."

"This is better."

"I think so," she said, smiling contentedly, stretching.

She tossed the mane of spun gold behind her.

"Eric says you have a girlfriend," Charlie said casually, looking at him.

Charlie watched as a cloud of worry flickered across his eyes.

"Boyfriend?" she asked.

"What? No. I'm married."

"Oh. Well, he did say he thought you were *involved*. I assumed girlfriend. I guess marriage also falls into the involved category."

"I guess," he said, sitting up, looking at her. "Why?"

"Why am I asking you about your personal life?" Charlie paused, considering her own question. Then she said, "Why not?"

James laughed. "That's fair. What about you? Boyfriend? Girlfriend? Husband?"

"Attorneys prefer to ask questions, not answer them," Charlie said amiably. "But, fair is fair. None of the above. Not involved."

"Never married?"

"No," she answered immediately. Then she said, laughing lightly, "Yes I was. I'd forgotten."

"No," James said, aghast.

"It was a very forgettable marriage. And it was a long time ago."

"Why did you get married?"

"Because I was angry," Charlie said slowly, her eyes closed, her body arched elegantly toward the tropical sun.

"Angry?"

"With someone else. Not the poor groom-to-be. I married him to get even with someone else."

"Someone you loved?"

Charlie nodded her head slowly. Then she turned to look at James and said firmly, "Let's talk about you."

"You're more interesting."

"We don't know that."

"I do."

"You're just a happily married guy with no problems?" she asked, her tone implying that she knew differently. She

312

had seen his eyes when she asked about his girlfriend.

"Boring," James said carefully.

They sat in silence for several moments.

"Tell me about your girlfriend, James," Charlie said, finally.

James sighed. It might be nice to tell someone about it. Maybe. It would at least be nice to have some time to think about it. He could do that on this trip. He could do it now if Charlie wasn't sitting next to him asking him.

Something about Charlie—something about her curiosity that was neither idle nor malicious—made him decide to tell her. Maybe it was because she reminded him of Lynne: blond, strong, independent, energetic; but also fragile, easily hurt. He could imagine Lynne marrying someone out of anger.

"Girlfriend isn't a good term," he began carefully.

"Lover?" Charlie offered.

"Let's just call her Leslie."

James told her about Leslie—and the relationship that never quite started—or ended—in high school. James didn't tell Charlie about his father, and he skipped the sordid details of his first year of college; but he told her that Leslie sent him a letter that changed his life, and that he saw her again, after nine years, on television in August.

"I saw her, too! I guess everyone did. The entire city," Charlie said. She vividly remembered the blood-stained face and the remarkable blue eyes that flashed with concern and astonishment and rage. "It made me want to meet her."

"It made me want to see her again," James said. "I wanted her to know, finally, how I felt about her. I—we—needed to finish what we began in high school."

"Finish? Is it finished?"

"No."

"What about your wife?"

"It doesn't have anything to do with Lynne."

"*What?*" Charlie sat bolt upright and stared at him. "What?"

"It started before I met Lynne. Leslie had already happened in my life. I wasn't carrying a torch. If I had been, I

313

would have tried harder to find her, wouldn't I? And I wouldn't have fallen in love with Lynne," James said seriously. "Leslie is my past. Lynne is present, my future."

"That's complete nonsense!" Charlie exclaimed. "Leslie *is* in the present. When did you last make love with Leslie?"

James stared at her, but he answered.

"Last night."

"And Lynne?"

James narrowed his eyes as he tried to remember. When? Before Lynne had gotten sick. How much before? Before Leslie? Since Leslie?

"Lynne has been ill."

"This gets worse and worse."

"Not that ill. A bad virus. Enough to make her not interested in making love."

"That's pretty bad. Unless of course, the whole illness is just that she knows about Leslie."

"She doesn't," James said swiftly, confidently.

"What if she did?"

"I would never forgive myself," James said honestly. It would destroy her. She would never understand. Understand what? Why somehow it was permissible for him to have an affair with Leslie? Why he wasn't really breaking any rules? Not violating any trust?

"She knows, James. She has to know."

"No."

"Who are you going to spend your life with?"

"*Lynne.* I told you that. I *am* spending my life with her."

"Does Leslie know that?"

"Yes."

"So it's really perfect, isn't it?" Charlie asked with more than a trace of sarcasm. "Except that your wife is ill and you can't remember when you last made love to her."

James was silent. Lynne can't know, he thought. I would know if she knew. She would tell me. She would get angry. Lynne would do what Charlie would do.

"What would you do if you were Lynne and you found out?" James asked.

"Is she like me?"

314

"I think so." It's probably why I feel comfortable talking to you, he thought.

"I would let you know what I thought of you and your silly rationalization. Then I would leave you. In my younger days, I might have married someone else as quickly as possible." Charlie watched James, the frown on his face, the concern in his eyes. "James, I believe that you love them both. But you've promised your life and your dreams to Lynne. I think you would be devastated if you lost her. You're playing with a hot, dangerous fire."

James looked into Charlie's soft brown eyes.

"You're a wise woman, Charlotte D. Winter," he said.

"No, James. I am experienced, and some of my most important experiences were painful ones."

"Do you think you'll get married again?" James asked. He was ready to shift the conversation away from himself. He had heard what Charlie said. They were words he should have said to himself. Everything she said was true. Still, Lynne didn't know. It would never hurt her because she would never know.

He and Leslie knew, although they didn't discuss it, that they couldn't—wouldn't—continue much longer.

It was wrong. But when he was with Leslie it was good and right because she was good and she would never harm anyone. She didn't want to hurt Lynne any more than he did.

"Maybe. Probably. But will I ever fall in love again? I don't know. I may be too old."

"Really! How old are you, Charlie?"

"I'm a year younger than Eric. To the day. We were both conceived on Valentine's Day, the result of a special Valentine from our mothers to their soldier lovers. Eric was born on November eleventh, 1944. I was born exactly a year later."

"Is Robert really Eric's father?"

"Yes. Robert was just eighteen on that Valentine's Day in 1944. Eric's mother was a quite attractive and very wealthy twenty-three-year-old debutante. Robert didn't know her very well, but they got together that night. The next morning Robert went to the war in Europe. Two months later when the families—both steeped in wealth and blue-bloodedness—discovered that she was pregnant, they orchestrated a retroactive marriage between the two. So Eric wouldn't be a bastard. But, of course," Charlie said smiling but with a slight sharpness in her voice, "Eric *is* a bastard. So am I."

"Not so you'd notice,"James said quickly. "Was Robert surprised when he returned?"

"I think the mail caught up with him before he returned two years later. He liked his wife well enough to have another child with her. They remained married for almost thirty years," Charlie said factually. Then her voice softened, and she said gently, "And, of course, Robert adored his little toddler son with the light brown hair and pale blue eyes just like his."

"They do look like brothers. And they seem so close," James said as he thought about his own father for the first time in years. James tried to remember a time when they were close. He couldn't. All he could remember was hatred and disappointment.

"The closest. They are best friends. They care so much about each other."

"And Eric's mother?"

"She and Robert were divorced six or seven years ago."

"That's too bad."

"Not really. Robert is much happier. He seems younger and freer."

"You've know them a long time, haven't you?"

"A long time," Charlie repeated distantly. So many memories. "I met Eric when I was sixteen."

Six months after the death of my mother, she thought but didn't say.

Chapter Twenty-six

Somehow Charlotte survived the months after her mother's death. She paid the bills—carefully writing the checks in Louise Alcott's elaborate script—and bought what food she ate with the money from the shoeboxes. She kept her clothes clean and ironed, went to school, maintained her excellent grades and pretended to her friends and teachers that she and her Aunt Louise were managing quite well.

Charlotte survived without help from anyone because she steadfastly refused to feel the pain. The pain of loneliness and loss and grief and even betrayal was replaced by numbness, an absence of feelings. Charlotte felt neither pain nor joy. She simply existed, plodding from day to day without thought or reflection.

For a week after receiving Mary's letter, Charlotte allowed herself a wonderful fantasy. She would find her father. He would be handsome and loving and oh so happy to see his daughter. Maybe she would even have a half brother or sister. She would move to England. She would have a family.

She would run an ad in the London papers. *Looking for John (Max), who made love to Mary (Charlotte) on Valentine's Day 1945 in Philadelphia. You have a daughter.*

Reality crashed down around her before Charlotte ran the ad. His name probably wasn't really John. He probably didn't live in London, or even England, anymore. Why would he read an ad in the personal section, anyway? He might not *want* to have an illegitimate daughter. He might be a horrible man. A rapist. A murderer. Mary had thought he was wonderful, but Mary lived in a dream world, a world of fantasy.

This is a fantasy, Charlotte realized one day with horror. I am creating a fantasy about my father. I am beginning to believe it, to believe in a world that doesn't exist.

Don't do it, her mind screamed. Don't become like your mother. Don't lose touch with what is real.

Charlotte forced herself to forget about John just as she forced herself to feel no pain.

That summer Charlotte got a job as a lifeguard at the Oak Brook Country Club. Located in Philadelphia's most elegant residential area, the club boasted an exclusive membership. All help, including lifeguards, was hired from outside the membership. Even though the teenage children of club members would have competed enthusiastically for the lifeguarding jobs, it simply wasn't done. Children of club members didn't work. At least, not at the club.

Charlotte Winter had a healthy wholesome look, the personnel manager at the club decided. Clearly not aristocratic—she wouldn't compete with the members' daughters—but quite acceptable. He hired her. He had hired the five lifeguards every summer for the past ten years. This was the first time he had hired a girl.

The Oak Brook Country Club was five miles from Charlotte's house on Elm Street. She rode her bicycle to and from work, pedaling fast in the coolness of the early summer morning and pedaling more slowly in the humid evening heat.

There were four of them. They arrived together during Charlotte's third week at the club. She watched them arrive, immediately struck by the casual, buoyant way they walked. Their nonchalant, self-assured, easy gaits sent clear messages of confidence and control. And why not? The world was theirs—a sumptuous buffet of experiences and pleasures. All they had to do was choose.

As they approached the pool area, the teenage girls who had been relaxed and giggly for the past weeks came to

318

attention.

This is who they've been waiting for, Charlotte thought. She watched the four young men — four healthy, handsome fashion plates in light cotton slacks and designer polo shirts — survey their territory, smiling appreciatively at the girls. The girls smiled back with coy, carefully studied smiles and perfectly posed bodies. It was a ritual, Charlotte realized. It marked the beginning of summer at the Oak Brook Country Club.

One of the young men grabbed one of the girls and threw her, squealing with delight, into the pool.

Charlotte immediately, reflexively, stood up and blew her whistle. At first no one heard it above the laughing, giggling, squealing and splashing that followed as all the girls were thrown, willingly, into the aquamarine water.

Charlotte blew her whistle again and again.

Finally the pool area fell silent. Then all eyes were on her. Startled, amused eyes. One pair of pale blue eyes approached her.

"Is something wrong, lifeguard?" he asked smiling.

"Pushing, shoving, throwing people into the pool. It's not allowed," Charlotte said looking down at him from her perch.

"Since when?" he asked mildly.

"Since always."

"It's never been enforced. Not here."

"It will be enforced this summer. It's too dangerous," Charlotte said firmly, her heart pounding, her face suddenly warm.

"How will it be enforced?"

"I have the authority to prohibit people who break the rules from coming into the pool area. It's all written down in the club's policy manual," Charlotte said, feeling the dampness of her palms and a cold wave of fear washing through her body.

He sensed her fear. And relented.

"OK. You're the boss. It looks like we have one tough cookie on the lifeguard tower this year," he said to the still-mute group. Then he looked up at Charlotte. "I guess we're

319

going to have to have our fun somewhere else."

Everyone laughed. Uneasy laughter. Then eager laughter. Maybe it would be *more* fun. Maybe they would have to save their touching for more private places. Maybe the sexual tension created at poolside would find a more intimate release.

The pale blue eyes looked back up at Charlotte, trying to learn a little about her. Charlotte's golden-blond hair was tucked, completely hidden, under the too large safari hat, and her enormous brown eyes were lost in the shadow of its brim. All he could see were her full lips and her flawless body in the emerald-green tank suit issued by the club.

"What's your name?" he asked.

"Charlotte. What's yours?"

"Eric. And this is . . ." Eric introduced the assembled group. Charlotte had been there three weeks. In that time, only the mothers with young children had introduced themselves. They asked if she would be giving swimming lessons and made certain that she would watch the wading-pool area carefully. No one Charlotte's age had made any attempt to speak to her.

Now Eric, even after their awkward initial exchange, was making introductions. Because, Charlotte realized gratefully, he is so well bred. His politeness is instinctive. He *could* treat her like a servant, like everyone else at the club did, but he didn't.

By the time the introductions were over, the chatter and laughter in the pool area had returned. When Eric spoke to her again, no one else heard.

"Charlotte, huh?" he asked, peering up at her, trying unsuccessfully to see her face.

"Charlotte," she repeated tentatively.

"I think I'm going to have to call you Charlie," he said finally. Without waiting for her reply, Eric headed toward the men's locker room to change into his swim trunks.

Over the next week, Eric and Charlie didn't speak, but he waved pleasantly from his chaise longue by the pool. Sometimes, grinning at her, he pretended that he was about to toss someone in the water. But he didn't.

Charlie learned a little about him that week. She learned that Eric and his three friends had just graduated from a prep school in New Hampshire and that Eric would be attending Harvard in the fall. Charlie decided that he didn't have a steady girlfriend, that he was immensely charming and that his life had been unencumbered by even a moment of sadness or denial. Eric had everything, and he was probably even kind.

Charlie ran into him in the parking lot one evening as she was leaving.

"Hi, Eric," she said smiling.

"Hi," he answered politely, a little confused by the beautiful girl with the flowing blond hair, and huge brown eyes and the vaguely familiar voice and lips. "Charlie?"

"Charlie. Without the safari hat."

"Wow," he said effortlessly. It was part of his charm. He made people feel wonderful.

"Well," Charlie said shrugging, suddenly uncomfortable. "See ya."

"Wait. Charlie. Do you want to go have a Coke or something?" he asked, gesturing toward the club.

"Oh. Thanks. It's getting dark and the light on my bicycle is broken. I should get going," she said truthfully. She had stayed late after work for a lifeguards' meeting. It was already dusk.

"Your bicycle? How far do you live?"

"About five miles," she answered, uneasy at the tone in his voice when she mentioned her bicycle. He probably didn't know anyone who didn't have a car. Mary had never owned a car. She had never learned to drive.

"Even if you leave now, it's going to be dark by the time you get home."

"I know. I'd better go."

"Wait. Why don't we put your bicycle in my car? I'll drive you home. We can have dinner if you haven't eaten."

Eric put Charlie's bicycle into the trunk of his car, a cream-colored Mercedes with blue leather interior.

As they ate pizza and drank Coke, Eric entertained her with stories about prep school, previous club lifeguards and

321

his friends. Charlie listened appreciatively, her huge brown eyes focused, intent, smiling. Her laugh flowed easily from deep within her, swept by a rush of joy she hadn't felt for months. If ever. With Eric, Charlie felt alive again, no longer numb or empty.

When Eric asked her about her life, her family, Charlie just encouraged him to tell her more about himself.

Eric had never known anyone like Charlie. She was so natural, so unpretentious. She didn't even know that with every gesture, every glance, every laugh, she was seducing him, making him fall in love with her.

It had never happened to Eric before.

It had never happened to either one of them.

At eleven-thirty, Eric suddenly became aware of the almost empty pizza parlor.

"Charlie, it's eleven-thirty. I hope you won't be in trouble."

"No. I won't be."

At midnight, Eric parked in front of the tiny pale-green house on Elm Street. He noticed immediately that the house was dark.

"I'm afraid they may be mad at you," Eric said. "They didn't even leave any lights on."

"There is no one there," Charlie said reluctantly.

"No one home? They leave you alone?" Eric asked incredulously as they walked up the walk toward the dark front porch.

Suddenly Charlie froze. She was unable to force herself to walk a step closer to the dark empty house. She had to be numb to do that, and tonight, with Eric, she no longer felt numb. She felt alive and happy.

Now, seeing the house and unprotected by the armor of numbness, the emotions that Charlie had denied since Mary died rushed into her, consuming her with dread and pain and loneliness. *They leave you alone?* Eric's words thundered in her brain.

"Charlie?" Eric turned toward her, wondering why she

had stopped.

The emotions erupted into a sob. Charlie couldn't control the sob or the trembling that accompanied it. She covered her face with her hands and shook her head, unable to move, unable to stop crying, unable to even understand what had happened.

"Charlie!" Eric's arms were around her. "What's wrong?"

"There is no one," she sobbed softly into his chest. "I live here by myself."

"No one? Charlie, I don't understand. Charlie. Tell me," he urged, holding her tighter, trying to move her toward the house.

"I'm afraid to go in there," she whispered almost frantically.

"OK. Let's go sit in the car. Charlie, you need to tell me what's wrong."

She did tell him. Slowly and painfully, over the next hour, she told him everything.

"Why don't you come home with me? We have plenty of room," Eric said finally, holding her against him, not wanting to let her go.

"No. I feel better. It helps to have talked about it. I haven't told this to anyone. I'm sorry. It's not fair to have done this to you."

"I'm glad you told me. It makes me feel closer to you, and I want to be as close to you as I can," Eric whispered, pressing his lips against her silky golden hair.

"I should go in now," Charlie said with bravado.

"I'll go with you," Eric said, half dreading seeing the inside of the house himself.

But with the lights on, the house was cheerful, not oppressive. It had once been a happy place to live, filled with Mary's love for her daughter.

"You should go," Charlie said.

"I can stay a little longer. I need to call my parents, though, anyway. Do you have a phone?" he asked.

Charlie nodded. She didn't need a phone. Her school friends didn't call often anymore. She never used it, but a phone was a lifeline to reality. She was afraid to sever it.

Robert answered the phone on the second ring. It was one in the morning. He was working, reviewing a brief, in his study.

"Father, I know it's late."

"Are you all right?" Robert had been worried.

"Yes. I'm fine. I'm with a friend who needs me. I still won't be home for a while."

"Is there something I can do?"

"No. Not now. But my friend may need your help. Will you be home for dinner tonight?"

"Sure."

"Great. Will you tell Mother that I'm bringing a friend home for dinner, then?"

"OK. Eric, does your friend have a name?"

"Charlie."

After Eric hung up, Charlie stared at him, her eyes full of doubt.

"Eric, I don't want your father to know."

"I won't tell him, but I want you to think about telling him yourself. He's a lawyer, and he's a wonderful man," Eric said proudly. "Charlie, I'm just afraid that this could all backfire legally. I just want to be sure that you're not in trouble."

"What if I don't want to tell him?"

"Then no one knows but you and me."

She watched him in silence for several moments, her eyes full of sorrow. She wanted to turn the clock back, back to dinner and to the wonderful feeling of laughter and joy.

Eric walked toward her, disturbed by the look, by the sadness.

"What are you thinking?"

"That I never wanted you to feel sorry for me," she said.

"I don't. I feel sorry about what has happened to you."

"But, going to dinner at your house—"

"I decided to ask you before any of this happened. I decided while we were eating pizza."

"Really?" Charlie asked, brightening a little.

"Really," Eric said, folding his arms around her.

"Who's Charlie?" June roared at the breakfast table the next morning. June was three years younger than Eric. She wrinkled her freckled nose. "Probably some yucky preppie friend of his."

"I don't know," Robert said.

"I've never heard him mention a Charlie," Florence, Eric's mother, said a little skeptically. "When did Eric get home last night?"

"Late," Robert said. "But he did call."

Florence Lansdale's skepticism increased the moment she saw Charlie. Charlie didn't look like one of *them*. Her skepticism was instantly confirmed when June gleefully recognized Charlie as Charlotte, the lifeguard at the club. Charlotte was teaching June and her friends water ballet.

Robert Lansdale quietly admired his son's taste, wondered about Charlie's problem and made a vow to help her in any way that he could.

As soon as she met him, Charlie decided that she could trust Robert. He was a slightly older—old enough to be Eric's *father?*—version of Eric. He had the same kind blue eyes. Unlike his son's, Robert's eyes had seen sadness and pain—they had been to war—but still they were unafraid, full of life and hope. And something else. Something that Charlie didn't recognize, something she had never seen before. Robert Lansdale's pale blue eyes had the calm confidence of power.

Someday Eric would look exactly like Robert. His youthful good looks would mature into the strong handsomeness of his father. It made Charlie tremble a little in the way she had trembled when Eric kissed her last night.

After dinner, much to June's and Florence's annoyance, Robert, Eric and Charlie retreated into Robert's study. Robert listened without obvious emotion as Charlie told him her story.

Inside, Robert's stomach was churning with anger. How could a loving mother have done this? How could *anyone* do such a thing to this lovely, innocent, sensitive child? Charlie was so vulnerable, and this crazy scheme only made her more vulnerable.

"What do you think, Father?" Eric asked after Charlie was done.

"Charlie, I need to see all the papers. Your . . . uh . . . mother's will, the trust agreement, the guardianship documents. Everything. Can you get those?"

"Yes."

"Bring them all to me. And any other documents you have. I'll need to see them before I can decide what's best to do," Robert said firmly, concealing his own anxiety. Many laws had been broken. Mary's attorneys were probably innocent victims just as Charlie herself was, but they *were* victims. It all had to be handled carefully and discreetly, with a minimum of damage.

It was lucky that Robert Lansdale was one of the best attorneys in Philadelphia. And one of the city's most powerful men.

Over the next few weeks, while Robert studied the documents, made phone calls, persuaded various officials to find unorthodox solutions for their unorthodox dilemma, Charlie and Eric fell in love.

By summer's end when it was time for Eric to leave for his freshman year at Harvard, a few momentous decisions had been made. Robert decided that, despite Florence's protests, he would become Charlie's legal guardian.

"She's a waif, Robert. Her mother—Well! There were stories about her when she kept the library open during the war," Florence hissed.

If pressed, Florence would have been forced to admit that the stories weren't bad. Mary was known as a strange, but kind and generous woman. But Robert didn't press her because during the past two months he had learned things about Mary that troubled him deeply. Things that Charlie didn't know, that she should never know.

Florence did not win the guardianship argument, but she successfully drew the line at allowing Charlie to move into *her* home. Robert only relented because Charlie herself insisted on staying in her tiny house on Elm Street.

"I am comfortable there, Mr. Lansdale. It's a safe neighborhood. I'm established at the high school. I would prefer to stay there," Charlie said, convincingly, sensing how Florence felt about her.

"We have to maintain close contact, Charlie," Robert said.

"We will, Father," Eric said. "I'll be home every weekend to see Charlie."

"Not every weekend," Robert said mildly. Weekly commuting would be too disruptive to Eric's studies.

"Maybe not. On the weekends that I'm not home, Charlie can meet you for lunch downtown. Something official like that."

Then there was another momentous decision: Eric would see Charlie as often as he could, and she would apply to Radcliffe so she could be with him next year, as soon as she graduated from high school.

Charlie made a decision of her own too. She decided to be a lawyer, like Robert. In the hours she spent with him that summer, carefully going over all the papers, listening to his explanations of the law, of how the law could be applied and interpreted, Charlie felt happy. Law was real, tangible. It required thought and reason. It was open to interpretation but free of fantasy. It was a game of intellect. It stimulated her, and it couldn't get her into trouble. As a lawyer she would be unlikely to lapse into a world of delusion.

Charlie was so *afraid* of becoming like Mary.

She told Robert about her decision at lunch on Saturday the following spring. Eric was in his dormitory room at Harvard, studying for mid-term examinations. Charlie had just received her acceptance from Radcliffe.

"I've decided what I'm going to be when I grow up, Mr. Lansdale."

"What, Charlie?"

"A lawyer. Like you."

"You think you'd like to do what I do?" Robert asked, obviously pleased.

"I think so."

"You'd make a wonderful attorney, Charlie. You have the right kind of mind," Robert said.

"Thank you, Mr. Lansdale."

"Can't you call me Robert?"

"No," Charlie said smiling shyly, "I can't."

"Maybe someday? Maybe when we're working on a case together?" he asked.

"Maybe then."

Eric's and Charlie's first year together in Boston was blissful. By the second year, they began to have arguments. The arguments were bitter and damaging. Eric and Charlie had only two issues on which they disagreed . . . but they were major ones. The first was sex. The second was Charlie's career.

Charlie would not make love. She had promised herself that she would be a virgin until her wedding night. It was a promise she made the day she read Mary's letter, a letter from an unwed mother who was too ashamed to admit the truth to her daughter until after her own death. Charlie would not make the mistakes her mother had made. She would not live in a world of make-believe.

And she would not make love before she was married.

"Charlie," Eric would say, sometimes gently, sometimes in a rage of frustration. "I want to marry you. I *plan* to marry you. We could get married now."

"And I could give up my virginity and my career in one simple step?"

"Charlie, we have been more intimate than most married couples ever are."

It was true. Charlie was sexually uninhibited, eager, curious, loving. They had a perfect sexual relationship except . . . they didn't do *It*.

"So? Isn't that enough for now?" Charlie asked.

"It's just that it's so silly. Saving your so-called *ultimate closeness* after all the other things we've done."

"It's just the way I feel, Eric. You know it. I don't see

328

why you can't respect it."

"I *am* respecting it, Charlie. But it is getting damned hard."

At the beginning of Eric's senior year—Charlie's junior year—the issue of Charlie's career became a source of friction. Eric told her that he planned to return to Philadelphia when he graduated from Harvard to get his Master's in Business Administration. That way he could spend his spare time at InterLand, Robert's company, while he was getting his degree. Robert decided that as soon as Eric completed graduate school he would assume the presidency of InterLand. That would permit Robert to devote more time to his true love, the practice of law.

"Why don't we get married in June right after I graduate from Harvard? We can spend the summer in Europe and get back to Philly in time to settle in before school starts."

"Eric, what about me?"

"What do you mean?"

"I want to go to law school."

"That's fine, Charlie."

"I want to graduate from Radcliffe and go to Harvard Law School. You're asking, no, you're *telling* me to transfer from Radcliffe at the end of my junior year, spend a year in school in Philadelphia and apply to law school there."

"Is there anything wrong with going to school in Philadelphia? I'm getting my MBA there, remember? Besides, InterLand, which happens to be the company that I am going to own and run, is in Philadelphia. Charlie, that's where we're going to live. That's where you're going to practice law. That is, if you plan to marry me."

Charlie did plan to marry him. She loved him deeply, passionately, and he loved her; but on these two issues they made each other very angry.

"InterLand could be headquartered in Boston," Charlie said sullenly.

Eric glowered at her. She was right of course.

"Is that what you want? You're right. I can have Father

move the whole company to Boston. I can get my MBA here. But what do we do if Charlie doesn't get into Harvard Law School after all?"

"I'll get into Harvard Law School."

"So, shall I tell Father that my first official act as president will be to move the company?"

"Yes!" she yelled. Then she said, "No. Eric, I don't know. It's just that you never even considered what I wanted in all this. Never even asked me."

"I thought you wanted to marry me. I thought you wanted to spend your life with me."

"I thought you wanted to marry *me,* spend your life with *me,* too."

By the middle of autumn quarter of Eric's senior year, the arguments became almost constant. Although she agreed to get married in June *and* to move to Philadelphia, Charlie still fought it. Fought *something.*

They would argue bitterly about her career. Then they would collapse, finally, in each other's arms, needing love and comfort. But Charlie's determination not to make love would propel them almost immediately into another bitter argument.

By November, they argued more than they laughed, glowered more than they smiled and pushed each other away more than they held each other.

"We've reached an impasse, Charlie," Eric said one night, exhausted, defeated. "I don't know what's really wrong, but I know that this is no good."

"I agree," Charlie answered hotly.

"Let's spend some time apart. A few weeks to cool off."

"Fine," she said, leaving his dormitory room, slamming the door behind her, tears flowing from her eyes.

I don't know what's really wrong either, she thought as she stumbled across Harvard Square in the darkness. Except that it's something wrong with me, not him.

Chapter Twenty-seven

Eric had known Victoria Hancock for years, from the pool at the Oak Brook Country Club, from dances and debutante balls, from dinners arranged by her mother and his. Victoria was the closest to a real girlfriend that Eric had had until he met Charlie.

That November when Eric returned to Philadelphia for a long weekend, to escape from Harvard and Charlie, he called Victoria. He needed someone to talk to; someone to laugh with; someone who knew him well enough that he didn't have to try; someone who would remind him of those carefree summer days at the pool — like those summer days when he met Charlie.

Eric had no intention of making love to Victoria when he called her. But it happened. It happened that weekend. And again at Thanksgiving. And again at Christmas.

Eric tried to reconcile with Charlie in early December. It worked for two weeks. Charlie was soft and loving. They talked about their wedding and their honeymoon. Eric didn't try to make love with her.

"Why aren't you pressing me to make love with you?" she asked, teasing, one night.

"I thought we were saving the *ultimate closeness* until June," he answered quickly. Too quickly.

"I am," Charlie said quietly, "but are you?"

Eric didn't answer her. His silence was answer enough.

"You made love to someone else?"

"Yes, Charlie. When we weren't together."

"I spent those weeks agonizing about what I had done wrong, how I could change to make our relationship better, and you were sleeping with someone else?"

"Charlie, it meant nothing. Besides, you're the one who has reservations about our relationship, not me. I agonized, hoping you would find out what was really wrong."

"You didn't agonize. You played. You had sex with someone else!"

"It meant nothing. I missed you."

"So you found a surrogate? Is that what's going to happen every time we have a fight for the next fifty years?"

"Christ, Charlie. Don't be irrational."

"I hate you, Eric," she yelled. Irrational. Mary was irrational. "Get away from me."

Eric spent Christmas in Philadelphia with his family. Charlie refused to speak to him, except to admit, angrily, that she was planning to spend Christmas in the mountains. Eric decided that there was no way he could force her to spend the holidays in Philadelphia with him, but it worried him to think about her being alone at Christmas. Whatever was wrong—whatever made her so afraid of getting married—wouldn't be solved by her spending Christmas alone in the mountains hating him.

Victoria called Eric on December twenty-seventh, chiding him gently for not calling *her*. She had heard that he was home alone. She convinced him to go skiing with her the next day.

Charlie did not spend the Christmas holidays in the mountains. She spent them in Philadelphia in the little green house on Elm Street. She had decided to sell the house. She spent the cold days of Christmas week filling boxes with the bittersweet memories of her childhood. Most of the boxes—most of the memories—would be thrown away. Charlie kept all of Mary's books, including the leather-bound copy of *Rebecca* and the photograph album of Charlie's childhood that Mary had carefully, lovingly, maintained. Charlie kept the album because it contained a few rare photographs of her mother.

Charlie met with real estate agents and put the house on the market at a below-market value. Charlie wanted to sell it quickly. She might need the money for tuition at Harvard Law School.

On December twenty-seventh, Charlie met with Mary's doctor. Maybe he could give her the answers she was looking for.

"Doctor, after she died, you told me that she was very ill. What did she have?"

"I don't have a name for what she had. She was very troubled. She lived in a world of make-believe. She was delusional, sometimes even paranoid. She had periods of profound depression. Medications didn't help. She didn't fit into any specific psychiatric diagnosis. She took wonderful care of you. She was dysfunctional in many ways, but she cared for you. And for her library," the doctor said, his voice gentle as he remembered troubled, loving, frightened Mary.

"But why did she die, Doctor? What killed her?"

"Nothing killed her," he said carefully, watching Mary's daughter. Everything killed her, he thought. Life killed her. "She killed herself."

"Oh *no*."

As Charlie spent the evening thinking about her mother, she was filled with a strange sense of peace. Finally she had her answer. Finally she knew what was wrong, what it was that made her fight her marriage to Eric, fight making love, fight anything that might cause her to have children or a family.

She had to let Eric know. She had to set him free, to let him know that she had found out in time.

She dialed Eric's home number early the next morning.

Florence and Robert were eating breakfast. Eric and Victoria had already left to go skiing.

"No, Charlie, Eric is away for the day," Florence said. At the mention of Charlie's name, Robert moved quickly beside Florence. He had watched Eric's suffering as he worried about Charlie. Robert worried about her, too.

"Let me speak with her," Robert said reaching for the

phone. Florence handed it to him. "Charlie, it's Robert. Where are you?"

"At the house," she said. Her voice was flat, lifeless. Its tone worried Robert very much.

"Charlie, I need to see you."

"Why?"

"Business. Minor details from the trust."

"Oh. All right. I'll tell you what I needed to tell Eric since he's away."

"Are you leaving?"

"Yes. This evening."

"I'm coming over to the house right now, Charlie," Robert said firmly and hung up.

"What's wrong?" Florence asked.

"I don't know. She sounds strange," Robert said as he rushed past Florence and out of the house. Maybe Charlie has found out, he thought, depressing the accelerator a little more.

As soon as he saw her, Robert knew. Her brown eyes were clouded with hopelessness and resignation.

"Hello, Mr. Lansdale," she said quickly.

Robert, he thought.

"Hello, Charlie. You look as if you've had some bad news."

"It's bad and good. It's good for Eric and you. And your wife."

"What is it?" Robert asked gently, already knowing all of it.

"I've been struggling—I'm sure you know this—about the marriage. I made my career, and even sex, seem like obstacles. Eric and I couldn't make sense of it, but it had nothing to do with Eric. It was all inside me, and now I know what it was."

"What do you know?"

"That something inside me knew that I shouldn't marry him."

"Why not?" he asked carefully.

"Because my mother was crazy. She killed herself," Charlie said simply, without emotion. Then she sighed and

334

added, "And I am my mother's daughter."

"NO!" Robert said with such energy that Charlie jumped. "No, Charlie. You aren't crazy. You can't inherit what your mother had."

"How do you know what my mother had?"

"I know, honey. Maybe I should have told you. I would have if I'd known how much it worried you. I spoke with her doctors. And I spoke with teachers, school counselors and doctors who knew you. They all agreed that you are fine. Healthy. Normal. You're not at all like her. You never will be."

What Robert said was mostly true. They all agreed that Charlie was a remarkably well-adjusted, mentally healthy child. But no one could *guarantee* that what Mary had wasn't hereditary. How could they? They didn't know what it was.

Still, they all believed that Charlie was—would always be—perfectly healthy.

"You knew she killed herself?" Charlie asked, amazed. "Does Eric know?"

"No."

"Sometimes I feel crazy," she said urgently. She wanted to believe what Robert had told her. But . . . "I've felt crazy these past few months."

"You can make yourself *feel* crazy. Anyone can. Everyone does at some time. But you're *not* crazy," Robert said emphatically. He continued gently, "You've just been troubled by some understandably troublesome questions. And now that you have the answers, you should feel relieved."

"I *was* relieved, in the opposite way. Because I could set Eric free."

"Don't you dare. It was *fair* for you to be angry about giving up your dream of Harvard Law School. That wasn't crazy. My son needs to be reminded of his egocentrism at times. He talked to me about moving InterLand to Boston. We can do it, Charlie. We *will* do it."

"You really think I'm not crazy?" she asked, still wanting to be sure, wanting to believe him, barely hearing anything else he said.

"I *know* you're not crazy."

"And you want me for a daughter-in-law?"

"Desperately. And a law partner. Even if it means I have to take the Massachusetts Bar," Robert said laughing, relieved to see the clarity and sparkle begin to return to her eyes.

"I don't mind moving here. Penn has turned out some pretty fine attorneys," she said, teasing him about his own alma mater.

"Are you really leaving tonight?" Robert asked, noticing the almost empty house for the first time. All his attention had been focused on her.

"No. I guess I should see Eric. When is he returning?"

"This evening. He's gone skiing for the day. Why don't you spend the day with me? See what being an attorney's really like," Robert suggested.

He didn't want her to be alone today. Not in this house after what she'd been through. A fine guardian he'd turned out to be. He should have insisted that she see a counselor, someone to help her after her mother's death. He should have anticipated her anxieties. Maybe he should have simply told her what he knew about Mary.

He had planned to, eventually, when she was older. But it was the fragile, sensitive little girl who had needed to know the truth and had suffered needlessly because she didn't know.

As Robert waited for her to finish packing, he hoped that Charlie's suffering was finally over and that she and Eric could have the happy life they deserved. And Robert hoped that his son wouldn't bring Victoria home with him that evening.

When Eric returned at nine, exhausted from a day spent in bed at Victoria's parents' ski cabin, he was alone. Charlie greeted him at the door with a smile that made him wish he had never seen Victoria in his life. Charlie told him what had happened, what she had learned and how Robert had helped her. She believed—as she thought about it more carefully, gently and patiently guided by Robert—that she really was fine. She had just been so scared. She had almost been a victim of a self-fulfilling prophecy.

"I inherited a lively imagination from my mother," she said sadly, "But maybe, hopefully, that is all."

Except I hope I inherited her boundless capacity to love and to give and to understand, Charlie thought as Eric held her. She knew he had spent the day with that girl, whoever she was. I have to try to understand it, she thought, succeeding a little, *enough*. She could see the regret and guilt in Eric's eyes.

"I love you so much, Charlie," he whispered.

"I love you, Eric. Make love to me."

"No."

"Yes. Tonight. Tomorrow night. Every night."

"No. On our wedding night. The reason I wanted to make love to you so desperately was because I was trying to get even closer to you, to find out what was really wrong. Now we know. Now I can wait. You really do want to wait, don't you?"

"Yes."

In the middle of February, Victoria telephoned Eric's room in Cambridge. Charlie was there with Eric. She saw the horror on his face and heard his words.

"How could you let this happen? . . . I thought you *were* protected . . . Why didn't you tell me? . . . Are you sure it's . . . What do you want me to do about it?"

Victoria told him that she was pregnant. Almost three months. It must have happened at Thanksgiving. The baby was definitely his.

For the next two weeks, Eric and Charlie talked about it, cried about it and tried to find a way to make it right.

There was only one way.

"The baby has to have its father," Charlie said from a belief rooted deep in her soul. She hadn't had a father. Babies needed their fathers.

"All I know, Eric, is that the joy of watching your child grow is the greatest joy in life," Robert said, aching for Eric and Charlie but remembering his own joy when he saw his

337

tiny son for the first time. Even now as his beloved son's life was altered—exactly as his own life had been altered—by a senseless moment of lust, Robert believed that the pain would give way to pleasure as soon as the baby was born.

Eric would be happy. Victoria would be happy. The baby would be happy.

Florence was *already* ecstatic. Eric and Victoria were meant to be together. Charlie had been all wrong for Eric.

Eventually they would all be happy.

Except Charlie. Charlie would suffer, as she had before, an innocent fragile victim. Charlie might never recover. Robert lay awake at night worrying about Charlie. He would call her often, he decided. He would see her when he could. He would try to help her through this great loss. This *other* loss.

As Eric and Victoria were exchanging wedding vows in front of their families in the middle of March, Charlie was experiencing the *ultimate closeness* with a first-year law student she had met three days before.

Two days later, she sat in the Dean's Office at the Harvard Law School. The dean had received her letter, and he had called her in.

"You want to start law school this fall? After only three years of college?"

"Yes."

"That's why you took your LSATs last fall?"

"Yes."

"Why did you wait until now to apply? The deadline for applications was months ago."

"I thought I would be moving to Philadelphia. I was planning to be married. But not anymore."

"And that won't change."

"No. He married someone else." Charlie had waited until after the wedding. Until the end, she had hoped that it wouldn't happen. Even though she knew it had to.

"Well, your grades are exceptional. As are your LSATs. As is your letter of recommendation."

"What letter?" she asked anxiously.

"From Robert Lansdale."

338

"I didn't ask him to write a letter. I wanted to do this on my own," Charlie said weakly.

"You did it on your own. I made up my mind before I asked you to come see me. Mr. Lansdale's letter just arrived today. He offers to pay for your entire education."

"It's not necessary."

"That's between you and Mr. Lansdale. Anyway, Charlotte, I am happy to offer you a position in next fall's entering class at Harvard Law School."

On the way back to her dormitory, Charlie met Eric. It wasn't an accident. He was waiting for her. She noticed his shiny gold wedding band immediately.

"Eric, I can't stand seeing you," she said, desperately trying to get past him, away from him. Eric stood his ground, blocking her path, forcing her to look at him. "I know you have to finish your classes up here this quarter, but let's try to avoid seeing each other. *Please*."

"Charlie, I just wanted to tell you—"

"What?" she asked helplessly. *Leave me alone*.

"That I love you."

"Well don't. Don't say it or think it or feel it. Another woman needs your love now, Eric. Give it to her," Charlie said. Tears streamed down her face as she ran away from the man she loved.

Charlie married the first-year law student a few months later. The marriage lasted six months.

During her three years of law school, Charlie spoke to Robert every few months. If he didn't call her, she called him.

"Listen to this torts problem, Mr. Lansdale," she said one day over the phone, her voice lilting, her love of law school obvious.

"Call me Robert."

"Maybe after I graduate."

They talked about Eric only once, two years after the baby, a son, was born.

"How's Eric?" Charlie asked softly. She didn't hate him

anymore. She was happy in law school. She hadn't found anyone to love, but she was happy. She missed him only when she allowed herself to think about him, but she didn't allow herself to often. *No fantasies.*

"He's good, Charlie. He's a much better president for InterLand than I ever was."

"You really wanted to practice law full time," she said.

"Yes. But Eric has a knack for business. He loves buying land and building beautiful buildings. Which is, after all, what InterLand is all about. He's opening corporate offices in Dallas, Chicago and San Francisco. He's already taken over some smaller development companies in those areas," Robert said proudly. InterLand was flourishing under Eric's able management.

"How's the baby?"

"Bobby? He's wonderful. Eric loves him very much. He's Eric's life, really. Eric's work keeps him busy, but Bobby is his life," Robert said gently as he thought about his son and his grandson, his namesake. Eric had the kind of relationship with Bobby that Robert had with Eric. It was what Robert had hoped for his son.

And Eric loved Victoria, the way he, Robert, loved Florence, as a friend, companion and the mother of his precious child.

Robert attended Charlie's graduation from law school. He visited her once at her office with one of Boston's most prestigious law firms. They didn't talk as often after her graduation. Robert knew that she was doing well. He could hear it in her voice. And as much as he liked talking to *her,* Robert worried that his voice only reminded her of Eric. And all that unhappiness.

Robert and Charlie hadn't spoken for almost six months when he called her. It was late on an autumn night, five and a half years after Eric married Victoria.

"Charlie, it's Robert."

"Robert!" Charlie exclaimed, calling him Robert for the first time, without even thinking about it or realizing it because there was something so personal, so emotional, in his voice.

"Eric needs you, Charlie. Please come to him," Robert said.

Chapter Twenty-eight

James let the phone ring twenty times. Then he hung up and re-dialed. After twenty more unanswered rings, he telephoned the airline. Lynne's flight had arrived, on schedule, six hours before. Then James phoned their neighbor. No, she hadn't seen Lynne's car. Only the living room light was on. James had turned it on before he left.

James looked at his watch. Ten minutes before six. He had to meet the others in Eric's suite in ten minutes.

Where *was* she?

James dialed Lynne's mother's number in Denver. He didn't want to alarm her, but he was alarmed, and she might know.

Lynne answered the phone. It was beside her bed.

"Lynne!"

"James? How did you know I was here?"

"I didn't. You weren't at home. I thought your mother might know where you were. Why are you there?"

Lynne told him about what had happened that morning on the flight from LaGuardia to O'Hare.

"Have you seen a doctor?"

"I have an appointment for nine tomorrow morning. I feel better now after resting all day."

"But you'll keep the appointment," James said emphatically.

"Do you think my mother would let me miss it?" she asked lightly, forgetting for a moment that she was talking to the new James, the James she hated, the James she had to leave. He sounded like the old James, her caring, loving James. "Why did you call home?"

"Because I wanted to see how you were feeling. And because I wanted to talk to you about Thanksgiving." And because he had spent the afternoon with a woman who reminded him of Lynne, who reminded him how much he loved Lynne. What he and Charlie talked about had scared him.

"The plans for Thanksgiving will have to change anyway. I'll probably take this week off instead. I guess I'll be working Thanksgiving week."

"If you're well."

"I will be. How's—" Lynne stopped. She started to ask him about his trip to Maui. It was a question she would have asked the old James.

"What?"

"Nothing."

"I'll call you tomorrow to see what the doctor said. It may be this late or later. We're spending the day at the construction site."

The family practitioner who Lynne saw at nine the next morning made the diagnosis almost immediately. He confirmed it by running a blood test that returned within an hour. He referred Lynne to a specialist in Denver. Lynne met with her that afternoon. She confirmed the diagnosis, performed several additional tests and provided Lynne with the name of a specialist in San Francisco.

When James called that night, Lynne told him, truthfully, that the doctors told her she had nothing serious. She would be fine.

She didn't tell him that she had to be checked again in a month. Then, if the diagnosis still held, she would have to leave him, quickly, before he found out. She only hoped that her strength would return in time.

The doctors said it would. But she had to eat. And rest.

Peter Pan opened on Thanksgiving Day. James and Leslie sat four rows away from Kathleen and Mark who sat next to Ross and Stacy. Eric and Charlie sat in the first patrons' box, theater left.

When the final curtain fell, the audience was silent, stunned, not wanting it to be over. Ever. *Not* wanting to leave. *Wanting* to hear the love duets again. Wanting it all to begin again.

Wanting to stay in Never Never Land with Peter and Wendy.

Finally, a single clap broke the silence. Then another. Then the sound, a faint rustling of the entire audience standing up almost in unison, was heard. Then, with the roar of clapping and shouts of "Bravo," the spell was broken. It had to be. Unlike Peter, they had to grow up. They had a real world to face.

After the final curtain call, the audience filed out, strangely silent. The theatergoers were lost in thought, knowing they had witnessed a most remarkable theater event. They had been part of it, and now it was part of them.

"Wouldn't it be wonderful to be so young and so talented?" Charlie asked Eric as they drove to his penthouse in Pacific Heights. "I can't believe she's the same person who played Joanna. Two unforgettable roles. I wonder what she's like."

"I want to go backstage for a minute, Stacy," Ross said begrudgingly, giving way to the reality that the show was over. He had seen it in rehearsal a hundred times, but tonight it moved him as it never had. Wendy moved him. He wanted to see her.

Ross forgot for a moment that he would be seeing Janet, not Wendy.

"To congratulate the Ice Maiden?" Stacy asked, a little annoyed.

344

Ross frowned at her, but it *did* make him remember that it would be Janet backstage.

"Does it bother you to see her, Mark?" Kathleen asked. It bothered *her*. Janet's—Wendy's—allure, her sensuality and her loveliness were irresistible. Even Kathleen felt it.

"No, Kathleen," Mark said firmly.

Leslie hadn't seen James for ten days, not since before he left for Maui. Lynne had been at home recuperating. She was better now, James said. She was flying again.

James held Leslie's hand as they left the theater and in the car on the way home. They didn't speak. Both were deep in thought. Because of *Peter Pan*.

I'm living in Never Never Land, James thought, squeezing Leslie's hand, not wanting to let go, knowing that, like Peter, he would have to. Someday. Someday soon.

Oh, James, Leslie thought. We are saying good-bye, aren't we?

Each time Leslie and James made love—that night and the other nights in the three weeks until it was over—it was as if they would never touch each other again. It seemed they were both trying to remember every part of it because soon they would only have the memory. In those weeks, Leslie and James gave each other the indelible memory of a love that had to stop but would never really end.

James was waiting in the apartment when Leslie arrived home on December fifteenth. He stood up when she came in, but he didn't move toward her. Leslie saw the key, the still-shiny key that she had given him ten weeks before, lying on the coffee table.

Leslie knew this day was coming. She was prepared for it. Still, the hot tears splashed down her cheeks. At the sight of her tears, James's eyes filled, and he broke the vow he had made.

He put his arms around her, holding her, rocking her. "Leslie. Don't cry. Please."

"I'm sorry, James. I will miss you so much."

"Leslie," he whispered, unable to speak.

345

They had both planned for this moment. They had rehearsed the mature, sensitive, brave things they would say. They both believed it had to be this way. It was best. They were lucky to have had the time together. They would always care. . . .

But neither could speak. The emotion was too strong. They just held each other tightly. Finally, moving at the same moment, they pulled away.

"Good-bye, darling Leslie," he whispered hoarsely.

"Good-bye, James," she whispered through her tears.

James returned to his empty house. Lynne was in Chicago. She would be back in the morning.

Lynne. Her energy had returned, but she seemed different. Preoccupied. Almost compulsively busy. She spent every evening, long after he had gone to bed, writing. She had created her own deadline—*soon*—for her next Monica book, but she hadn't asked him to start illustrating it.

Lynne was pleasant, efficient and energetic. *Impersonal.* They still hadn't made love.

James decided that Lynne was simply rebounding from her illness. Now that her energy had returned, she was making up for lost time.

Lynne's behavior was different, but it was not how she would behave if she knew about Leslie. She would confront him with it.

Still, they needed to talk. Now that *she* was well and *he* had said good-bye to Leslie.

James realized how little he and Lynne had said to each other in the past three months. He wanted to get close to her again. He wanted to fall in love with her again and to renew the promises—promises of love and friendship and trust—they had made to each other.

Lynne had the repeat test on December fourteenth. It confirmed the diagnosis. It meant she had to talk to James soon, as soon as she returned from Chicago. She called

346

him at his office when she returned on the sixteenth.

"Lynne? Is everything all right?" James asked. She never called him at work.

"Yes. Fine. I just got in. James, we need to talk," she said tentatively. *How can I confront him with this? I know I'm right, but I don't want to hear about it. I don't want to see his face.* She decided, then, impulsively, to tell him over the phone. "James, I know that you're having an affair. I know it started September twelfth. I haven't had the energy to deal with it until now. But now I do. I want a divorce, James. I can't live with you anymore. I *can't.*"

Lynne stopped abruptly, breathless, her heart pounding, her stomach aching.

"It's *over,* Lynne," James said quietly, shaken.

"Does it matter?" she asked sharply as her anger returned. He had admitted it. It was all true. A tiny part of her had held on to the hope that there was, that there could be, some other explanation.

"I love you."

"No," she said swiftly. "Not if you did this to me. To us."

"Lynne, we have all the time in the world to end our marriage. Let me talk to you. *Please.*"

"It's pointless. And painful. I just want out, James. Please don't make it hard for me. It's not fair. It's been hard enough."

He could hear the pain—pain from months of suffering—in her voice. She had known for a long time. For the entire time.

"I'm coming home now. Wait for me. Please."

On the way home, James's mind spun as he tried to remember why it happened, how he could have let it happen. How could he have believed she wouldn't know? How could he have done this to Lynne? To Lynne, of all people. . . .

It was what Lynne's father had done to Lynne's mother. Over and over. They stayed together because of their baby girl, because of Lynne, but it harmed Lynne much more than growing up without a father would have harmed her. She watched her mother suffer with each of his affairs. She learned to hate her father.

And she learned to distrust all men. When she grew up, Lynne played with men, toying with their feelings, hurting them the way her father had hurt her mother. And her.

Lynne hated men, distrusted them all. Until she met James.

Slowly, carefully, they had learned to trust each other.

How could I have done this to her? James's mind screamed at him as he drove home. It had all been so easy to rationalize because the proviso had always been, *Lynne will never know.*

Lynne was in the living room curled into the far corner of the overstuffed sofa. When she saw James, she pushed herself deeper into the cushions.

"Lynne, I am so sorry," he said moving toward her, seeing in her eyes that she didn't want him near her. He stood at the opposite end of the sofa.

"You know what's funny?" she asked, her voice bitter. "I really believed we had something. I believed that we had defied the odds. I didn't even have a clue that we were in trouble. Then—*overnight*—everything was different. How could you fall in love with someone else overnight?"

"I didn't, Lynne. She was someone I knew before I met you. I hadn't seen her for nine years. I saw her again by accident. I felt, I *convinced* myself, that I was doing something I should have done nine years ago. I even convinced myself, somehow, that it—our affair—was happening in the past."

James shrugged, realizing the emptiness of his words and how foolish they sounded.

Helplessly, he watched Lynne cry. He watched her pain and felt his own. Pain and regret.

"Talk to me, Lynne."

"Why? Do you want to hear about how much I hate you? About how much I hurt inside?"

"I want you to tell me how we can make it through this," James said firmly, evenly.

"We can't."

"You won't even try?"

348

"No. Why should I?"

"Because I love you."

"James. I've heard those words before. My father always told my mother that. For years she even believed him."

"Your father never felt this way about your mother. You know that."

"I do? From here it looks like, feels like, you're exactly the same kind of man."

James sighed. Why should she believe him? He hadn't given her any reason to.

"I stopped seeing her because I didn't want to take the risk that you would find out. I didn't want to risk losing you."

"That's why you ended it," Lynne said slowly. "But why did you start it?"

"It seemed different, Lynne. Something that was very important to me personally. It was a way to make sense of what had happened in high school. It had nothing to do with you and me. Really. I don't know how to make you understand that. It didn't have anything to do with us. I didn't look for her because I was unhappy with us. I wasn't. I'm not. I want to spend my life with you. I didn't look for her at all. It just happened. It could never have happened with anyone else. It could never happen again."

Lynne's tears stopped as she listened. Her brown eyes stared at him with curiosity. She knew James so well. She knew that James—the James she had loved and trusted—didn't lie.

"I almost believe you, James," she said softly. "*Somehow* you honestly thought this didn't break the rules, that it transcended the rules."

James waited, barely breathing. Lynne was talking to him now, not as the little girl hurt by the father she hated but as Lynne, the woman he loved, the woman with whom he had created a union of love and trust.

But Lynne didn't say any more. She just stared at him, loving him, hating him and wanting him. Wishing it all was different.

"Will you give it a chance, Lynne?"

"I don't know." *Yes.*

"We can't lose more than we've lost if you leave now."

"Oh yes we can," she said instantly, without thinking.

"What?"

"We can lose it again," Lynne explained, flustered for a moment. "We can get it back and lose it again. It's already happened once."

"It won't happen again, Lynne. It won't. It can't."

Lynne sighed. It was a great risk. Maybe too great. She could only give it a month. She couldn't let him find out. Not unless she was sure of him and of his love. How would she know?

She would know. *But* she had known before. She had known, confidently, that he loved her. Until one day he changed.

Now he was back.

"James, I am so afraid," she whispered.

He moved to her then, carefully holding her hands, gently touching her tear-damp cheeks.

"I'm afraid, too, Lynne. I'm afraid of losing you."

Shreve and Company, one of San Francisco's oldest jewelry stores, located two blocks off Union Square near Gump's and Abercrombie and Fitch, was cluttered with shoppers. It was Christmas Eve. Decisions *had* to be made. A gold necklace for a girlfriend, diamond and sapphire earrings for a lover, an eternity ring for a wife, gold cufflinks—they could be engraved later—for a husband or a boyfriend.

Mark was there to pick up Kathleen's engagement ring. The store manager had promised that, despite the Christmas rush, the flawless, two-and-a-half-carat brilliant cut diamond would be in the six-pronged Tiffany setting by Christmas Eve. The diamond wasn't a family heirloom. It was simply a perfect diamond that Kathleen's father had purchased years before as an investment.

It had already quadrupled in value and was now worth at least a quarter of a million dollars. But when William

Jenkins saw the look in Kathleen's eyes when he offered it to her — as long as Mark didn't object — it became priceless. And valueless. Because it would never be sold.

Mark didn't object. He was genuinely unthreatened by Kathleen's vast wealth.

Janet was in Shreve and Company on Christmas Eve to buy a pair of pearl earrings. It was a combination Christmas and birthday present to herself. Since her shopping spree in New York in October, Janet paid more attention to her appearance and to things that made her feel good. She had been thinking about buying a nice pair of pearl earrings for two weeks.

But not today, Janet decided after a few moments in the store, after gazing over the sea of anxious, indecisive shoppers. She shook her head slightly and turned to leave. Janet met Mark at the revolving door as he was leaving, the purple velvet box with Kathleen's ring tucked safely in an inside pocket.

"Janet!"

"Hello, Mark," she said, then almost immediately was swept out the door by the press of the crowd.

Mark was behind her, but he paused to let several women enter the revolving door ahead of him.

Janet stood outside, uncertain whether to leave, to lose herself in the crowded sidewalk, or to wait. Why wait for him? Why not?

Mark smiled when he saw her, obviously pleased that she had decided to wait.

"Hi. It's pretty crowded, isn't it?"

"Too crowded," she said, suddenly wanting to escape from the crowds. And from him? No. Seeing him didn't make her hurt. Not yet.

"Would you like to go for a cup of coffee? A hot buttered rum?"

In Omaha, at Christmas, they would drink hot buttered rum in front of a roaring fire. In Omaha, at Christmas, they had snow. In San Francisco, at Christmas, it was fifty degrees and the sun was shining.

"Sure," Janet said, glancing at her watch. She had time

before the evening show. "Coffee would be nice."

The Christmas Eve crowds were in the stores, at the cash registers and cluttering the sidewalks, but the restaurants were empty. It was the last minute. The frenzied shoppers could not stop to eat. No more procrastination.

Janet and Mark found an almost empty bakery with a small dining area decorated with white wrought iron chairs and tables with green and mauve linen. Homey. Quaint.

"This is nice," Janet said, referring to the bakery. Maybe referring to seeing him.

"It's nice to see you," Mark said, meaning it, aching a little. "How's the show?"

"We've added five matinees for this week alone!"

"It's an incredible show. You are incredible."

"Oh, you've seen it?"

"Opening night."

"What did Kathleen think?" Janet asked, amazed at how easily she said Kathleen's name. "I got the impression from Ross that she and some of the other board members opposed the changes we made. Too iconoclastic."

"Kathleen was raised on *Peter Pan* in all its innocence."

"We all were."

"Anyway, all her doubts were erased when she saw it. In fact, she's seen it about five times. It's what she does when I'm on call."

"Have you seen it again?"

"No," Mark said, looking down at his coffee, away from her wide gray eyes. He could see it once, see her once, but after that it would be too hard.

"Leslie says you're moving to Boston."

"Yes. To do a cardiology fellowship. And . . ." Mark paused. Leslie had probably told her the rest.

"You're getting married," Janet said.

He looked at her quizzically. He was talking to Janet about his marriage to Kathleen. It felt strange. Wrong.

"Mark," Janet said, suddenly smiling, suddenly feeling better than she had felt in a long time, "I'm happy for you. I honestly am. We had our chance. It didn't work. It doesn't mean we shouldn't have other chances."

Janet stopped, amazed by her own words, amazed by the hope in what she said. Hope for his happiness. And for her own.

"Are you involved with someone?" Mark asked carefully.

"No," she said tossing her blond hair, a little embarrassed. Then she said, seriously, honestly, "Not yet."

But someday. Maybe.

After she left Mark, kissing him lightly on the cheek, wishing him only happiness, Janet walked back to the theater. Her spirits soared. She had seen him and it hadn't hurt. Not *too* much. Seeing Mark made her remember the possibility of love, the hope of love. Not with him. But, maybe, sometime with someone else.

Janet felt free, happy, almost whole again as she turned into the front door of Union Square Theater and into Ross.

"Oh! Ross. Sorry!" Janet giggled.

"It's OK," he said surprised, intrigued. What was going on? Where was the famous off-stage reserve? "You seem a little up."

Janet shrugged amiably. The glow didn't fade.

"I guess I am," she said as she breezed through the foyer toward her dressing room.

After ten feet, she stopped and spun around.

"Ross?"

"Yes?"

She walked back toward him, her heart pounding.

"I wondered if you would like to come over for dinner."

"Sure," he said calmly, carefully. "When?"

"Umm," Janet hadn't thought it out. She hadn't thought at all. It was an impulse. "Some night when we don't have a show."

"That's almost never. At least in the near term."

They were running the show every night—except Christmas—throughout the holidays. Maybe longer. The demand was that great, and so far the cast was willing.

"Tomorrow night," she said suddenly.

Christmas. It was the only night they weren't performing.

"It's Christmas!" Ross said immediately, before the

meaning of her suggestion registered. It meant that Janet had no plans for Christmas.

Ross planned to meet Stacy's flight from New York at seven in the evening and take her to the Carlton Club Kids Christmas Celebration. Expendable plans, he thought, looking at Janet. Except that he couldn't really cancel his plans with Stacy at this late date.

"I know," Janet said, shrugging, suddenly feeling foolish, the glow a little dimmer. "It's just a night when we don't have a show."

"I have plans for the evening but none for the day. How about breakfast or brunch or lunch?"

"Brunch. At my cottage. It's a bit of a drive."

"That's OK. Now what's wrong?" he asked. Janet was giggling.

"I don't have any food! The stores are going to be closed tomorrow morning, aren't they? I don't really have time to go out now, not before the show," she said shaking her head, smiling.

"This is a great invitation," Ross teased.

"It seemed like a good idea at the time. Maybe we should do it some other time?"

"No," Ross said lightly but firmly. "Let's go into the office right now so you can make me a shopping list and draw me a map. I'll go to the store while you're in makeup. We can put the groceries in your car after the show."

Janet followed him into the theater administrative offices. She still felt good. *This* felt good.

"Let's see. Eggs. Milk. Cheese. Butter."

"Pretty low cholesterol so far."

"Oh! What do you want to eat?"

"No, I'm teasing. It's fine."

"All right. Chocolate cake mix. Double fudge frosting mix—"

"Whoa."

"It's my birthday."

"Christmas?"

Janet nodded.

"In that case," Ross said, "we'd better add champagne to

this list."

Long before Ross arrived at the cottage at eleven Christmas morning, Janet regretted her impulsive invitation.

I don't know him. I have nothing to say to him. Nothing personal. We can talk about the show. Then what? I wish I hadn't . . . what? Seen Mark? Felt so good?

Janet didn't know except that the good feelings were replaced by anxiety as she waited for Ross.

But Janet's worry about conversation was unnecessary. Ross had a lot to say and many questions to ask as he poked around her cozy cottage while she made omelettes.

"Who owns this?"

"The people in the big house down the road. They're away for the holidays."

"How did you find it?"

"I was on a drive."

"Way up here?"

"I used to go for a lot of long drives after Mark and I separated," she said, then blushed.

"Is there anything between you and the ocean except those hills?" Ross asked, swiftly changing the subject. He didn't want her to retreat.

"No." She smiled, relieved, appreciative that he didn't press her about Mark. Even though she felt better — good — she didn't want to talk about Mark. "Just very pretty land that all comes with the rent. We can take a walk, later, if you have time. It's so beautiful."

Ross studied the photographs of her from *South Pacific* and the productions she did at the University of Nebraska and in community theater in Omaha.

"This was really all you'd done before you showed up for the audition last year?"

"I guess it was enough. I think I learned a lot from those amateur groups. No one was a prima donna. No one was a star. Especially in the community theater in Omaha. We were a family."

"Plenty of prima donnas started in community theater.

355

You just don't have the prima donna personality."

He asked her about her childhood. She told him, briefly, pleasantly. Then she asked him about his. Ross told her, expansively, because his anecdotes made her laugh. He kept talking because of the soft interested look in her serious gray eyes as she listened. And because of the way her eyes sparkled when she laughed.

They walked all the way to the ocean. Janet showed him her favorite spots. She led him along her favorite path through the lane of eucalyptus trees.

"This is where I practice," she said, spreading her arms toward the green rolling hills and the blue ocean beyond. "And no one can hear me except the seagulls and the rabbits and the deer."

"Sing something for me," Ross said lightly.

Janet frowned, her eyes squeezed shut. The pain of a memory had hit her, unexpected, surprising, unsettling.

"I can't," she said finally, opening her eyes. She sang all day every day for Ross at the theater, but this was different. Private. Intimate. It was what she used to do for Mark. It wasn't something she could do again. Not yet.

Ross smiled, sorry he had said something to upset her, but relieved that it had passed quickly.

They walked along the beach, the cold wind blowing their hair and putting color in their cheeks. They didn't try to talk above the wind. Ross realized, as the afternoon wore on, that Janet didn't need to talk. She was comfortable with silences. She was comfortable to walk beside him, enjoying the beauty, without speaking.

Janet was peaceful. It made him feel peaceful to be with her.

She walked out to his car with him when he left at five. He had already stayed too long. He would have to drive directly to the airport.

"Thank you," he said. "Happy birthday."

Janet smiled at him, swaying almost imperceptibly closer to him.

His lips found hers, soft, warm and eager for his. He folded his arms around her and felt her softness press against him. Willing, sensual, passionate. They kissed for a long, soft, warm moment.

"I don't want to leave you," he whispered into her ear.

She looked up at him, her eyes glowing, her cheeks pink. She touched his lips lightly with her finger.

He didn't want to leave, and she didn't want him to. But he had to.

"I'll see you tomorrow," he whispered hoarsely as he got into his car. And the next day. And the next, he thought, forgetting for a moment that Stacy was arriving for the week.

Stacy. Everything had changed. Plans were expendable, after all.

Chapter Twenty-nine

Slowly, with painstaking care, James and Lynne fell in love again. Most days, because they were trying so hard, because they wanted it so much, they made some progress; but some days, they seemed to lose all that they had gained, and it seemed hopeless.

They spent the evenings they had together talking quietly, sitting together, holding hands. James called her from work when she was at home during the day, and he called her when she was away, every time she was away, talking for hours long distance.

James called her on Christmas night in her hotel room in Dallas.

"What's wrong, Lynne?"

Her voice was flat, defeated.

"You know what I thought about all day?" she asked weakly.

"No. Tell me," James urged, knowing that it had to be something—something painful—about Leslie. But knowing, too, that they had to talk about it.

"You quit smoking for *her*, didn't you?"

"Lynne," James began. It was something Lynne had tried gently, without nagging and without success, to get him to do. Now he had done it, quit for good, because of Leslie. But he had done it for Lynne, too. For the rest of their lives together.

"Well, I know you did. I've spent the whole day thinking about it, hating both of you, torn apart by anger. I can't get rid of the feeling. In the past nine days, I thought we made progress, but today, tonight, I'm back where I was," she said. Wanting to leave, she thought. Needing to get away from you.

"I tear myself apart with anger, too, Lynne. But the difference is that I know it will never happen again. I know what it meant. I know how I feel about you. *I* know that you can trust *me*, but I can only tell you that. I can't make you feel it or believe it."

"I want to believe it." I am just going to have to decide, she thought. By mid-January at the latest. So much depends on it: my life, James's life, and another life, an innocent life that could be damaged, either way, if I make the wrong decision. Lynne sighed heavily, weighted by the burden of the decision that was hers to make. "James, talk to me about something that has nothing to do with us. I'm wallowing and I'm getting nowhere."

They spent hours talking about the news, books, politics and the weather. Anything to keep communication open. Something drove them both to try to make it work, but they couldn't force it. It had to happen. They had to give it every chance.

By the end of the third week, they had begun working together on Lynne's new Monica book. They spent the evenings talking about the illustrations that Lynne wanted. Sometimes it felt almost normal. Almost good.

James called her at home one afternoon. He had an idea for an illustration. She sounded distracted. She had been writing.

"Hi, am I interrupting something?" he asked as soon as he heard her voice.

"No," she said. "Yes, you are, James. I'm having an affair with a guy I've known since kindergarten."

They were both silent, shocked for a moment. Then she laughed. And he laughed. And he told her he was on his way home to put an end to it.

They made love that afternoon and that night, for the first time since September eleventh, the night before James took Leslie out for her birthday dinner. The next day Lynne hated him again, remembering what he had done, but the anger only lasted for an hour. It disappeared before she had a chance to tell him about it.

A week later Lynne returned at seven in the evening. She had been gone for two days. She found James sitting in the living room. The curtains were drawn, blocking the view of the South Bay and preventing anyone from seeing in. They usually didn't need such privacy in the living room.

Lynne's heartbeat quickened and her entire body tingled with anticipation. When she saw his eyes, she knew.

"Take off your clothes, Lynne," he said softly, seductively, not moving.

She closed her eyes for a moment. James.

It was *her* fantasy. One of the sexual fantasies she had trusted him enough to tell him. She had told him all of them. They were similar. They allowed him to control her as she had never allowed any man to control her. She was excited by his sexual power and by his desire for her.

James would interrupt whatever she was doing, quietly taking the pen out of her hand if she was writing, firmly turning off the stove if she was preparing dinner. . . It didn't matter what she was doing. That was part of the fantasy: When he wanted her, nothing else mattered. She never said no.

James would tell her to undress, and he would watch, his eyes appreciative, passionate and full of desire for her. Then she would stand in front of him naked, proud of her perfect body, feeling him wanting her, feeling her body respond to his gaze.

Sometimes the pleasure would be only for her. James would kiss her, warm gentle kisses until she lay exhausted and satisfied, and he would still be dressed. Sometimes he would undress, too, and make love to her slowly, forcing her to wait, not allowing her to be impatient. Sometimes they would make love quickly because just the sight of each other from across the room made them ready, desperate to be together.

They did whatever James wanted. It was part of the fantasy—her fantasy. James was in control. Because she trusted him. She never said no.

"Take off your clothes," he repeated.

"James, no," she said weakly. She wasn't ready for this.

He was forcing her to prove that she trusted him again and that she would allow him to control her. No, her mind screamed. But her body trembled. *Yes, I want this. I want him. I need to be wanted this way again. By him.*

But what about . . . ? her mind screamed back.

He won't notice. It's barely noticeable, her body argued, pulsing with excitement.

"Yes, Lynne," he said. He commanded.

Lynne watched him as she removed her uniform: the tailored jacket, the checked blouse, the straight skirt. Their eyes locked, eloquently transmitting the feelings and desires of their bodies across the room. She moved closer until she stood almost in front of him. Then she took off the rest of her clothes.

When she was naked, he pulled his eyes away from hers, as he always did, to look at her. To caress her body with his eyes. She felt his eyes on her neck, her breasts, her stomach and between her thighs. She shuddered as waves of desire swept through her.

Then suddenly, he frowned and looked at her.

"Lynne?" he asked, his voice husky, but the mood suddenly, inexplicably shattered.

"What?" *What's wrong? Don't do this to me! I am trying to trust you.*

"Come here," he said tentatively.

"What, James?" *No, he can't tell. I can't even tell.*

He put his hand carefully on the lower part of her abdomen. The bulge was almost imperceptible, but it was there.

"Lynne?" he asked softly, looking up at her face.

Tears streamed out of her sad brown eyes. She cried silently.

"You're pregnant?"

Lynne nodded slowly, soberly. It was too soon. She still wasn't sure. And now it was too late. Now he knew.

James pulled her onto his lap, gently wrapping his arms around her trembling, naked body.

"Really?" he asked softly. She nodded again, looking at him. She had never seen such happiness in his eyes.

"Really," she said, wiping her tears.

"When?"

"When else? The last time we were together. September eleventh. The baby's just four months old."

"And it's OK?" he asked, the realization sweeping through him in waves of elation.

"So far. It's where it should be. In the uterus. Growing normally despite the scar tissue from the infections."

"This is what made you ill?"

"Yes. I wouldn't have felt so ill—so frustrated at being ill—if I'd had any idea. The G.P. I saw in Denver diagnosed it immediately even though I told him it wasn't possible. I guess even the whirlies, like I had on the plane, aren't uncommon."

James held her face with his hands, looking into her eyes, making her look at him.

"Were you going to tell me?"

"Not if we got divorced. No."

"I had a right to know," James said sharply.

"You gave up that right the night after the baby was conceived," Lynne answered with a sharpness matching his.

Lynne watched the effect of her words register as pain in his eyes. The eyes that had been so happy a few moments before. *Am I ever going to stop punishing him? Or myself?*

Lynne curled her arms around his head and kissed his forehead.

"I'm sorry, James. Since I've known, all I have thought about was how to give this baby the best possible chance. I want the baby so much. I want it to feel safe and happy. I don't want it to have the kind of childhood I had."

"Or I had," James murmured.

"We're not likely candidates for parents of the year, are we?"

"Maybe we are, Lynne. At least we know how not to do it. And we both want the baby so much."

"You do? I didn't know."

"Neither did I. I guess we had rationalized it all pretty well since we didn't think we could have children. But when you told me, I felt something I've never felt before. I want

362

our baby, Lynne. Just like I want our baby's mother."

James kissed her until she trembled against him and her body moved in a rhythm of love and desire.

"Is it all right to make love?" he asked, lowering her beneath him on the sofa, taking off his clothes.

"Yes, James. Mothers-to-be have their fantasies, too," she said, knotting her fingers in his black hair, breathlessly anticipating the feel of his naked flesh against hers.

"I love you so much, Lynne," James whispered. And as they moved together, he said over and over, "So much. So much."

The next day, James called her from work.

"I want you to stop flying. We don't need the money. You can write your books and be at home with me. I want you at home. I want both of you at home."

"All right, James," Lynne said laughing. "I'll quit."

"Really?"

"That easy."

The next week he arrived home with his black portfolio full of sketches.

"I want to show you something."

"Maui?" Lynne asked, interested. He had been working so hard on the resort project. Days, nights, weekends. He would make love to her, tuck her into bed and then return to the kitchen table to work into the night.

"No, you've seen all the Maui sketches."

"All the *sensational* Maui sketches."

"Thanks," he said. Eric and Charlie raved about the Maui project every time James saw them, but it was nice to hear it from Lynne. "No, this isn't Maui. It's Monica Manor."

"What?"

"It's a new addition for the house. A room for Monica. A study for you. A study for me. It's principally for Monica, but I threw in some rooms for us, too."

"James, we don't know that the baby is Monica. The baby *could* be James junior."

"The baby will *never* be James junior, but we both think she's a she, don't we?"

"Yes, we think that. But we don't care, do we?"

"No. Not a bit."

James called Lynne in the middle of the afternoon on Friday, two days before Valentine's Day. He knew she had spent the morning supervising the first day of construction of the new addition.

"Hi. How are you?"

"Good. Do you really think these guys are going to pay any attention to all those intricate little lines you drew?"

"I really think they'd better. How's Monica? And Monica?"

"Monica the cat has gotten herself in an almost insoluble dilemma. I'm having a cup of tea hoping she'll be better by the time I return. And," her voice softened a little, choked with emotion, "Monica, the baby, *moved*."

"She did? Really? Why didn't you call me?"

"I called the doctor. It was a funny fluttering feeling. I wanted to be sure everything was OK, but that's what it feels like, and this is when it's supposed to start, in the fifth month. I didn't call you because I didn't think I should bother you." She had almost called him. She had been so excited.

"Call me."

"I will."

"What do you want to do for Valentine's Day?"

"You know."

"So," Mark said, walking up behind Leslie in the tenth floor nursing station, "this is a pretty miserable way for two off call residents to be spending the evening."

"Mark! I just thought I'd check a few charts before I left."

"On your rock-steady patients?" Mark teased. "At eight o'clock on Friday night?"

Leslie smiled at Mark, noticing, as always, how handsome he was. But her heart didn't pound and she didn't tremble.

I've outgrown whatever it was I felt for him, she thought comfortably. Love? *In* love? Now he is a good friend. A dear, good friend.

"I can understand what a single, unattached woman such as myself is doing hiding in the hospital," Leslie said. "But I can't figure out what you're doing here."

"Kathleen's in Hawaii plotting the wedding. She and her friend Betsey did this last year when they planned Betsey's wedding. I'm on my own for a week. So, what about drinks at the Cliff House?"

"You're on."

Their arrival was perfectly timed. The pre-dinner cocktail crowd was just leaving; the after dinner crowd hadn't arrived. They were seated at a window table. The pale yellow moon cast a long shimmering beam across the Pacific Ocean. The waves glowed in the darkness as they crested before crashing onto the rocks and beach below.

"Did you get the invitation to our engagement party?"

"The *engraved* invitation? Yes. Thank you. I'm planning to be there," Leslie said. She had decided she should go. It would be interesting if nothing else. It was in three weeks. She already knew that she wouldn't be on call.

"You can bring a date of course."

"I would if I had one to bring," she said lightly.

"What about the man you were with at *Peter Pan*?"

"Oh. You noticed."

"Naturally," Mark said. Actually, Kathleen had noticed them first, initially simply admiring James and then realizing that he was with Leslie.

Leslie looked at Mark. She hadn't told anyone about any of it.

"He was married. He *is* married. It's a long complicated story, but, basically, that's the bottom line."

"Did you think he was going to leave her for you?"

"No, I never thought that. I never even wanted it," Leslie said truthfully. In the months since James left, she had

365

realized that. Even though she missed him all day—every day, every night—she would not have wanted him to leave Lynne because of her. "But it was nice while it lasted."

"I wonder who the right man for you will be," Mark said thoughtfully, considering his own question. "You're such a superwoman. Bright, strong, independent—"

"You make me sound awful!"

"No, Leslie, you're incredible."

Leslie shook her head and held up her hand, signaling him to stop.

"I'm serious, Les," Mark continued, calmly ignoring her protestations. "You're beautiful and gracious. You know exactly what you want to do, and you're doing it. You don't have obvious needs. You'll have to find a man who's as capable and secure as you are."

"I thought you were Mr. Right," Leslie interjected, fortified by the scotch she drank too quickly as she listened to Mark. It made her feel warm and courageous.

"Me?" he asked, genuinely surprised, obviously flattered.

"Yes. I had such a crush—not an intern on resident crush like you thought—on you."

"Why didn't I know that?" He could tell from the serious blue eyes that she meant it. That it—he—had been very important to her.

"Because you weren't interested. But it's polite of you to pretend that you might have been."

"I'm not being polite," Mark said seriously, frowning slightly. Why hadn't he known? Because that was his specialty: not knowing the important things that affected himself and the people he cared about.

"Anyway, I had a crush on you while you were falling deeply, irrevocably in love with Kathleen," Leslie said lightly.

"I am deeply, irrevocably in love with her," Mark said gently, his voice becoming tender at the thought of her. Still . . .

"When's the wedding?" Leslie asked suddenly, focusing on what was real, not fantasy.

"June eleventh. I think those invitations are still at the engraver. I hope you can come. It will be at the Carlton Club. It should be nice."

"I'm in University Hospital emergency room in June. If I'm lucky, I'll be off on the eleventh," she said politely, not knowing if she really meant it.

They sat in silence for a while, watching the glittering waves and the winter moon.

"I saw Janet a few months ago," Mark said finally.

"I know. She told me. I think it did her a lot of good to see you."

"Really?"

"Yes. She just seems a lot more relaxed. More comfortable."

"She needs to find someone."

"I think she will," Leslie said. I think she already has, she thought. But there was no point in telling Mark about Ross. Ross, Kathleen's friend.

Their world was already too small.

"I can't go to Mark's and Kathleen's engagement party, Ross."

"You can. It's on Sunday evening. There's no show that night. Only the matinee."

"I don't want to go."

"I thought you said you were over him."

"I *am*."

"So?"

"It doesn't mean that I want to go to his engagement party."

"Why not?"

Janet sighed. Why was he pushing her? Why couldn't he just put his arms around her and tell her that he understood?

"Why not?" he repeated.

"Ross, Mark and I did something very sad and painful to each other. We made promises that we couldn't keep. We turned our hope into anger and bitterness. We're not angry and bitter any longer, but what happened still makes us sad. I think it makes Mark a little sad, a little wistful to see me. I feel the same way about him. There's just no point."

"You think Mark would care if you came to the party?" Ross asked, incredulous. He had seen Kathleen and Mark together. Nothing, no one, could put even the tiniest dent in their obvious joy.

"Yes. I think he would." Janet looked at him, her gray eyes sorrowful. She didn't want to argue with him.

He scowled at her. He didn't want to fight with her. He just wanted to hold her, to walk beside her on the beach, to hear her laugh, to hear her sing and to talk quietly to her.

He wanted to make love with her, but he was waiting for her to let him know when it was time. He was waiting for her to make the next move. He wondered if she would. She was so passionate. And so shy.

He scowled at her, wanting her, angry with her for throwing up this ridiculous obstacle.

He stood up to leave.

"It hurts my feelings, you know, Janet. *I* care about *you,* but *you* won't go to a party with *me* because it might make your ex-husband a little sad. Where does that put me in the list of people that you care about?"

"I'm sorry," Janet whispered to his back as Ross left, slamming the door behind himself.

"Katie?"

"Ross! Hi."

"Katie, do you think Mark would care if Janet came to the engagement party?"

"With you?" Kathleen asked. Then she added coyly, "Ross, are you going out with Janet?"

"Would Mark care if Janet came with anyone," he repeated flatly, avoiding Kathleen's question.

"No, of course he wouldn't care."

"Will you ask him?"

"Why?"

"Just to humor me."

"Sure. *Are* you coming to the party?"

"I don't know. I'd like to. Let me know what Mark says beforehand, though. OK?"

"Sure. I'll call you in a couple of days."

Kathleen didn't call Ross back until the night before the party.

"Here's what he said: 'Of course she can come . . .' "

"Ah-ha," Ross said. It didn't really matter. He had already made up his mind.

"No, wait, that's not all. He said, 'Of course she can come, but it might make us both a little sad.' "

"Oh," Ross murmured. "Does that bother you?"

"No. He's just being honest. I'd be sad if I tried to make a life with someone like Mark, or Janet, and it didn't work out. You make a lot of promises when you get married," Kathleen said.

If Ross came to any of her performances in the five nights following their argument about the engagement party, Janet didn't know it. She didn't see him at the Sunday afternoon matinee, either. She didn't see him, and she didn't talk to him.

By the time she got to her cottage Sunday evening, it was almost dusk. She changed into jeans, found a flashlight and headed toward the ocean.

Ross arrived an hour later and found the cottage empty. He took the flashlight from his car and began to walk toward the eucalpytus lane that by now had become familiar to him.

At first, Ross thought the noise was wind, or a seagull, except that it was night. Finally, as he drew closer, he recognized the haunting, seductive notes of *Dreaming*, Joanna's love song.

Ross stopped. He was invading her very private territory. He had asked her to sing for him once, out here, in her lovely, natural theater, and she had refused.

369

He waited until the song was over. Then, in the silence and darkness of the moonless spring night, he called to her.

"Ross?" she answered, her voice distant. She was much farther away than he had imagined. Or maybe she was just speaking softly.

He saw a light in the distance.

"Hi," he called, waving his flashlight.

"Hi." Her voice was barely audible.

"May I join you?"

"I'll meet you."

They moved toward each other, guided by the beams of their flashlights and their knowledge of the terrain.

When they reached each other, Ross extended his arms to her, folding them around her as she fell, gratefully, against him.

"You drive me crazy, you know," he said.

"You didn't go to the party."

"I realized," he said kissing the top of her head, "that the only reason I wanted to go to the party with you was to be with you. And you're here. So I'm here."

Janet pulled her arms free from his grasp, put her hands gently on his cold cheeks and guided his lips to hers. They kissed until all they felt was the warmth of their mouths and their bodies and forgot the cold ocean wind.

"Janet, Janet," he whispered to her.

"What?"

"What am I going to do with you?" he asked gently. "You drive me crazy."

"Make love to me, Ross," she said so quietly that he wasn't certain he had heard her correctly.

But as they lay on the dew-covered grass, as he made love to her in her own private theater, as he felt her body respond, instinctively, to his, he knew it was what he had heard. He knew that she wanted him.

Chapter Thirty

The June dawn filtered through the powder blue curtains in Janet's bedroom, its pale yellow rays awakening her gently, with warmth and light. Janet got out of bed, careful not to disturb Ross.

As quietly as possible, she started a pot of coffee in the kitchen then tiptoed onto the back porch while the coffee brewed. She curled into a painted cedar chair, closed her eyes and sighed with pleasure. She felt the warmth of the new morning sun on her face and the gentle breath of the soft ocean breeze finding her flesh under her modest cotton nightgown. She heard the quiet whispers of the eucalyptus leaves and the early morning songs of the gulls.

It was a perfect day. It felt like she felt: fresh, clean, full of hope and promise.

Janet sighed. She was so lucky.

"Good morning," he said, carrying two mugs of hot coffee. He was naked except for a pair of khaki trousers. He smiled as he handed her a mug and sat down opposite her, leaning casually on the porch railing.

"Good morning. Thank you. I didn't mean to waken you."

"This is too beautiful a day to waste in bed. By myself, anyway. What shall we do with this glorious day?" Ross asked, gazing out at the emerald-green hills toward the sapphire-blue ocean and avoiding looking at her as he asked the question.

It was Saturday. June eleventh. They both knew that it had special significance. It was a perfect day for a wedding.

Janet didn't answer.

"How about a picnic at the beach with long walks on either side?" Ross asked.

"How about an early picnic lunch so that you'll have time to make it to Atherton for the wedding?" Janet asked lightly.

"I'm not going to the wedding," Ross said. He had told her that six weeks ago. They hadn't talked about it since.

"Kathleen is one of your closest friends."

Ross turned and looked at her, then reached tenderly for a golden strand of hair that covered her eyes. He wanted to see them.

"*You* are one of my closest friends."

"Ross, it won't bother me if you go. I think you should. It's just that I can't."

"I know. I don't even know why we're discussing it. So, may I change the topic?"

"Sure."

"Arthur called me yesterday."

"Oh? How's Arthur? Still in seventh heaven about his Tony for *Joanna?*"

"The eight Tonys. All of which should have been yours for saving the show. . . ."

"Ross," she began, shaking her head slightly.

He didn't know why it made her so uncomfortable to be complimented, to be told how good she was, how talented she was, how beautiful she was. She would have to get used to it. He wasn't going to stop telling her the truth.

"Anyway, guess *who* Arthur wants to have bring *what* show *where?*"

"You to take *Peter Pan* to Broadway. *When?*"

"To open in late September. Only he doesn't want me. He wants you. Although he's pretending that he wants both of us."

"Arthur has his own wonderful local talent. After all, Beth won the Tony for *Joanna.*"

"Another of your Tonys. So," Ross said slowly, "how about it? We get a beautiful penthouse overlooking Central Park and do a four-month run in the Big Apple?"

"No," she said simply, pressing herself deeper against the chair as if to say, I won't leave here, this spot, ever. "No New York."

"Janet, you are drinking coffee out of a mug that says 'I love New York'!"

"You brought it to me!"

"It's your favorite mug!"

"It is," Janet answered, nodding her head, giggling. "I admit it's my favorite mug, but I don't want to move to New York."

"OK," Ross agreed quickly.

"OK?" Janet asked, surprised. He wasn't going to push her?

"Yes. I told Arthur you wouldn't want to, but I promised to ask you anyway. Besides, I have a much better way for you to spend your fall."

"What?" she asked, a trace of uneasiness in her voice.

"Harper and Peterson, the ones who wrote *Joanna*, have written a new musical. I just got it this week. It's called *San Francisco*. I think they wrote it precisely for you to perform in this city. I'd like you to take a look at it. If you like it, we'll open it this fall. If not, we'll find something else."

"*San Francisco?* Is it gold rush or earthquake or—" Janet asked eagerly. Not that it mattered.

"Contemporary. Flower children and little cable cars. . . ."

"Where is it?" Janet asked, unable to breathe, unable to conceal her excitement.

Ross smiled. He loved to see the enthusiasm in her eyes just like he loved to see the desire in them when they made love.

"It's somewhere near."

"You tease!" Janet stood up. "Where?"

"In the trunk of my car. Sit back down. Let's take it with us for our picnic at the beach. We can spend this entire day reading the script and watching the waves. How does that sound?"

"Wonderful. Let's go."

"Janet." Ross's voice became serious. Janet sat down in

her chair and looked at him carefully.

"What?"

"What about the other part? You said no New York but . . ." he paused. He'd given this a lot of thought. It was what he wanted. He had no idea how she would react. "How about the we'll get a penthouse part?"

In the months since that moonless March evening when they had made love for the first time in the hills behind the cottage, they had spent almost every weekend together there, in Janet's tiny house. But they were apart during the week. Ross had to be at the theater early every weekday. *Peter Pan* was only one of his productions.

Janet worked late every night. By the time she left the theater, it was usually midnight. If she drove straight home, it was almost two by the time she got to the cottage, and she didn't always go straight home. Sometimes Ross saw her leave with Peter.

One Wednesday night, Ross took Janet home with him to his fabulous condominium located ten minutes from the theater. They watched the twinkling lights of the city below, drank champagne, made love and fell asleep in each other's arms, but in the morning, Janet was restless to leave, pacing like a trapped, displaced animal, uncertain of her role or what she was doing in *his* home at seven in the morning.

They had never discussed it, but a pattern evolved. They spent two nights together and five nights apart. It wasn't enough for him, but he had no idea how she felt. He needed to know.

Now, in response to his question, Janet wasn't saying anything. She just looked at him, a little confused, a little surprised, a little worried and a little excited.

"Do you think it's wrong for people to live together?" he asked. We could get married, he thought. But it was much too soon for that.

"No. I think it's a good idea," she said honestly.

"In general, or for us?"

"In general," she said, then smiled coyly. "Maybe for us."

"I thought we could spend weeknights in the city at my place. I think if you brought some of your things, made it your home, too, you would feel comfortable there. And we could spend weekends here. More time when we're between productions. All of August."

"The Browns are planning to put the entire estate on the market," she said suddenly, remembering the disquieting news she had learned the day before. She sighed, "So I may be looking for a new place anyway. I'm sure that this property will sell quickly, even at the huge asking price, because it's a natural for residential development. I'm going to hate to leave."

"We'll find you another place. One with lots of property and a house big enough for script rewriting sessions by the sea and a piano and your clothes and my clothes and your books and my books and your albums and my albums. This cottage is cozy but awfully small."

Ross's observations about the size of the cottage were intentionally long-winded. He was giving her time. He could see that her serious gray eyes were considering his question, weighing it carefully, cautiously.

Finally she reached for his face with her hand, softly parting his tousled white-blond hair, tracing the lines at the corners of his eyes and touching his lips.

"Sometimes," she said, "you get angry, annoyed with me. I'm not always sure why."

"Because sometimes you seem to withdraw, get quiet," he said seriously. It worried him. Less and less each day, but still . . .

"I don't get quiet, Ross. I *am* quiet."

"I know," he said, reaching for her hand, kissing it. "I'm learning that. But sometimes you do put up walls. Your gray eyes cloud over and you hide."

"Maybe sometimes I do."

He pulled her head against his warm bare chest, cradling her for a moment, gently untangling her uncombed silken hair.

"So what do you think?" he whispered, holding her tight.

"I think we could try," she said slowly. Then she pulled herself free, her eyes flashing, "But what about Stacy?"

"*Stacy?* I haven't seen her since Christmas."

"Oh. Good."

"What about Peter?"

"Peter?"

"You know. Your leading man. The guy you leave the theater with when you don't leave with me. The guy who calls you all sorts of terms of endearment off stage as well as on. That Peter."

"Are you jealous?" she asked, laughing.

"Maybe."

"Peter's my friend. Sometimes we go for dinner after the show because we're starving and we like to rehash the performance. Are you really jealous?"

"This isn't very much fun."

"Ross," she said, kissing him playfully on the lips. Then she said, "Ross. Peter's gay."

"Oh," he said, kissing her seriously. "Oh."

"I, Mark, take you Kathleen . . ."

They stood beneath an arch of white lilacs and soft pink roses, eyes locked, hands joined, as they made their promises of forever in the lovely fragrant south garden at the Carlton Club.

Her glistening violet eyes told him much more than the words ever could. His moist, brown loving eyes answered back, eloquently.

I love you, Mark, with all my heart.

"For better or worse . . ."

I promise, Kathleen. I want you so much.

". . . as long as we both shall live."

Afterward, as they stood in the reception line, greeting their many guests, Mark felt Kathleen's hand tighten around his forearm and heard the uncharacteristic strain in her gracious, lilting voice. He covered her hand with his, and she responded instantly, almost desperately, by intertwining her fingers with his.

As soon as the last guest had wished them well, Virginia Jenkins urged them toward the elaborate multi-tiered wedding cake.

"I need a private moment with my wife, Virginia," Mark said pleasantly but firmly. "Just a moment."

Mark led Kathleen across the perfectly manicured, emerald-green lawn to a private, secluded alcove behind a pink and lavender hedge of rhododendrons.

"Darling?" he asked when they were alone and away from view.

Tears spilled from the violet eyes. Kathleen couldn't stop the tears, and she couldn't speak.

"Second thoughts?" Mark asked easily. He knew that wasn't it, but it would draw her out.

"Oh, *no,* Mark, no," she answered quickly, touching his face with her trembling hands. She gazed into his eyes. "It's just . . . I just want to make your—our—life perfect. *Always.* I want it so much it scares me. . . ."

I'm afraid, too, Mark thought as he wrapped his arms around her and pulled her tight against him, but my fears are real. I've made mistakes before. What if . . .

"You do make my life perfect," he whispered, kissing her black silky hair. "You don't even have to try."

"Did you go to the wedding, Leslie?" the head nurse in University Hospital emergency room asked when Leslie arrived for work that evening.

"No. The ceremony was supposed to start at four. I couldn't have made it back here on time," she said, glancing at the large institutional clock that read five-thirty-five.

Leslie's shift started at six P.M. and lasted until eight A.M. They called it the Lindbergh shift: a long, lonely, solo flight into the night.

"It's too bad you missed it. You and Mark are such good friends."

"It's just the luck of the draw," Leslie said flatly. She was glad she was working. She didn't really want to go to the wedding after all. "So, where's Dave? I might as well begin now, send him home a little early."

* * *

377

Eric answered the phone on the fifth ring.

"Hi," Charlie said. "Did I interrupt something?"

"No. I cut my damned hand. I was just trying to put another bandage on it."

Charlie recoiled at the anger and frustration in his voice.

"Another bandage? When did you cut it?"

"What time is it now? Seven? I cut it about one. I was washing those Saint Louis crystal highball glasses we used last night."

"Six hours ago? It's still bleeding?"

Eric didn't answer. He was staring at the huge gash on the palm of his hand and at the blood that flowed freely from the gaping wound. He put a cloth over it as he had repeatedly for the past six hours and clenched his fist. He could make the bleeding slow but it wouldn't stop.

"Eric?"

"I'm here."

"It sounds like you need to go to the hospital."

"It will stop."

"I know you don't want to go," Charlie said. It made her sad to think of him having to walk into a hospital. "But you may have to. I'll come over. If the bleeding hasn't stopped, we'll go. I'll go with you."

"*That* isn't necessary."

"I want to."

They arrived at the triage area of University Hospital emergency room at eight. The triage nurse examined Eric's hand and took him immediately into one of the acute trauma rooms. Charlie sat in the waiting area. For a while she stared at the prototypic emergency room posters on the gray-yellow walls. One was a compelling call for blood from the American Red Cross, another, the A,B,C's of basic life support from the American Heart Association and a third, a message about smoking from the American Cancer Society.

Some enlightened soul, probably in defiance of hospital policy, had hung a poster of two puppies curled in a wicker basket with a small fluffy kitten.

Charlie studied the posters for a while. Then she thumbed through the women's and sports magazines that lay on the tables, idly turning page after page, absorbing nothing. Finally, she put down the magazines, closed her eyes and succumbed to the memories.

She needed to remember because she knew that Eric was remembering. They were *his* horrible, painful memories, but she had to be there, then, to help him. She was here to help him now. The memories flooded her with thoughts of that interminable, senseless nightmare. Memories that started with a late-night phone call from Robert ten years before.

"Charlie, it's Robert."

"Robert!"

"Eric needs you, Charlie. Please come to him."

"Robert, what is it?"

"Bobby—" he began, then was forced to stop because of the emotion in his throat. In a few moments he said the rest, hating the words, almost unable to speak them. "Bobby is dead."

"No, Robert. *No.*"

"Please come, Charlie."

It started as a simple case of chicken pox. Bobby wasn't even very ill, his charming pleasant personality only slightly dampened by the common childhood virus. He stayed in bed, coloring and playing games with Victoria and Eric, while he watched TV, drank Seven-Up and took the children's aspirin that Victoria gave him for his fever.

It all seemed like a very routine case of chicken pox. Then Bobby started vomiting, becoming a bit confused and irritable. Quickly, almost in front of their eyes, he became comatose.

"It's called Reye Syndrome," the pediatrician said, the graveness in his voice giving them their first clue to Bobby's prognosis.

They stood outside the pediatric intensive care unit. Inside, a team of specialists hovered over their precious five-year-old boy. The team had already learned from laboratory studies that Bobby had liver failure, a low serum glucose and cerebral edema. They learned from his parents that he had had chicken pox and that he had been given aspirin.

"Reye Syndrome?" Eric asked.

"It's a newly recognized syndrome. It usually follows influenza or chicken pox. We don't know what causes it. It affects the liver and the brain."

"What about the aspirin? Why did they ask us about aspirin?" Victoria interjected. The doctor was about to tell them Bobby's prognosis. She didn't want to hear it. She knew. They both knew.

"There has been an anecdotal association made between aspirin and chicken pox and Reye Syndrome. It's just an observation at this point. It needs to be looked at scientifically," he said.

Still, as Eric and Victoria tried to deal with the senseless but inevitable death of their child, they had to find blame. They blamed the aspirin. And Eric blamed Victoria for giving it to Bobby, for killing their son.

"Why did you give it to him, Victoria?" Eric asked angrily, emotionally.

"We always give him aspirin when he's sick," she pleaded.

"If you hadn't given it to him—He wasn't that sick."

"Eric, don't you remember? That night you were reading to him?" she asked desperately. "You felt his forehead and told me to give him some."

"You had already given it to him. The day before."

The marriage ended the day they buried Bobby. Eric and Victoria left the funeral in separate cars with their own parents. They couldn't grieve together. There was too much anger and blame. They didn't have enough love to help each other. All their love had been for their child. He was the only reason they were together.

Without Bobby they had nothing. Nothing but pain and anger and hatred.

Charlie arrived at Eric's family home three hours after

the funeral. She hadn't seen Eric since the day she was accepted to law school, two days after his marriage to Victoria five and a half years before. She hardly recognized the thin, sad man with the dark circles surrounding his lifeless, pale blue eyes, the light brown hair that should have been cut a month before and the hopelessness carved, deep, in his handsome face. Bobby had lived for five weeks. Eric had been with him every minute.

Without a word, Charlie walked past Robert and Florence and June. She put her arms around Eric and held him as he cried.

No one else had been able to touch him, to even begin to console him. Not even Robert.

In all those weeks, Eric hadn't cried, not until Charlie held him.

Charlie took a leave of absence from her law firm. Over the ensuing weeks, she listened to Eric's stories about his little boy. She learned to love the little boy that she had never known. She grieved for Eric, and she grieved with him.

They took long walks. They held each other. They spent entire days together without speaking and sometimes stayed up talking until dawn. They stayed in Robert's and Florence's home in separate bedrooms. Robert and Florence left them alone.

At the end of two months Eric said, "Charlie, you have a life to live."

"So do you," she observed gently. Then she asked, wondering if he knew, "What are you going to do?"

"Move InterLand to San Francisco," Eric said. He had just decided. "We have a corporate office there. I'm going to turn it into our headquarters. Want a job?"

"No, thank you," she said, hesitating a moment. Then she added firmly, "I have a job in Boston."

"Still?" he asked. He held her hand and gazed into her eyes. "I would never have made it through this without you. I haven't made it yet. But I'm healing. I will make it."

"I know you will, Eric." *I hope you will.*

Two years later, succumbing to pressure from Eric and

ready for a change in job and geography, Charlie moved to San Francisco. She became InterLand's principal attorney, indispensible to the company and to its president.

Charlie and Eric made love to each other for the first time six months after she moved to San Francisco. Charlie finally experienced the *ultimate closeness* with the man she had loved so desperately years before. Their lovemaking was sensitive and intense, pleasurable and emotional, careful and caring.

But it was not the eager limitless passion of a man and a woman in love and full of hope for their love. Eric and Charlie weren't in love anymore. Too much had happened.

They weren't *in love,* but they loved each other. Deeply. The love grew even stronger as the years passed, as she worked beside him every day, as they laughed and talked and argued and teased. They made love often and traveled together whenever they could. They knew each other so well. They cared about each other so much.

Sometimes, sparked by a smile or a touch or a kiss, the magic of their past love would reappear, suddenly, in a warm, surprising, breathtaking rush, and they would be reminded, for a moment, of the wonder of that love and of the great joy they had once shared. . . .

Charlie sighed, opening her eyes to the too bright lights of the emergency-room waiting area.

She hoped this wouldn't be too hard for him. Her best friend. Her wonderful lover. Her beloved Eric.

But she knew it would be.

Chapter Thirty-one

"The fellow in room One has a bad hand lac, Leslie," the triage nurse said, emerging from the room after obtaining Eric's vital signs. "I've got a tourniquet around his forearm. He's got an arterial pumper."

"Think it's an ortho case?"

"At least to stop the bleeding. He says the sensation in his fingers is fine."

"Good. I'll go take a look. Would you order an X-ray and page orthopedics? By the time they call back, I'll know if I need them. It sounds like I will. What's his name?"

"Lansdale, I think. His chart's still being made up. I just brought him right back."

Leslie walked into room One and looked at the man lying on the stretcher. He wasn't aware of her presence at first. He lay very still with his eyes closed.

In pain? Leslie wondered. In shock? No, his vital signs were fine. His cheeks looked pink, not white, under his tan.

"Mr. Lansdale?"

The eyes opened. Pale, pale blue, startled eyes.

"I'm sorry if I startled you. I'm Leslie Adams, the resident on call. What happened?"

"Crystal highball glass. I was washing it."

"Oh. Let me take a look," Leslie said as she sat on the

stool next to him and carefully removed the sterile saline-soaked gauze dressing that the nurse had placed over his palm.

The wound was long, straight and deep. It looked almost surgical, as if cut with a sharp precise blade. Glass could do that. He had probably grabbed the already broken glass, forcing the razor-sharp edge into his palm.

It wasn't bleeding now. The tourniquet on his forearm occluded the arterial flow. Watching the wound, Leslie reached for the tourniquet and slowly released it. The white hand turned pink. Blood oozed into the wound and spilled, overflowing onto his hand. At one end of the wound, Leslie saw a rhythmic movement beneath the blood, causing a turbulence in the surface, like water just about to boil. He had a small arterial pumper. It would have to be clamped and tied, after his hand was anesthetized and after the wound was cleaned.

Leslie tightened the tourniquet again. The bleeding stopped.

"How long ago did this happen?"

"At one."

"Seven and a half hours ago?" As she had been examining the wound, she had been observing him, too. Despite his reserve, he seemed very much in control. *In charge,* even though his hand was bleeding without control. He was impeccably dressed, polite, handsome.

He did not look like the kind of man who would allow his hand to bleed uncontrollably for seven and a half hours. He did not appear to be intoxicated or drugged. He just seemed a little remote and preoccupied.

"Has it been bleeding like this for seven and a half hours?" Leslie asked the question again.

"Off and on."

"We'd better check your blood count. You may have lost a lot of blood."

"Is that necessary?"

"Yes," she said firmly. She had to be in control. "Let me first test the sensation in your hand and fingers. If that's OK, I'll put in a nerve block at the wrist to anesthetize your

384

hand. Then we can clean it well—it needs extra cleaning because it's been open for so many hours—and sew it up."

"No anesthetic," Eric interjected. He wasn't specifically thinking, No one gave Bobby an anesthetic before they stuck needles and tubes in his small sick body. He wasn't thinking at all. He was just feeling. The aching, empty feeling from deep inside him made him say, again, more forcefully, "No anesthetic."

"Oh! Are you allergic?"

"No."

Leslie looked at his eyes and decided not to press the point. Patients with minor lacerations, patients who prided themselves on being impervious to pain and patients who dabbled in self-hypnosis occasionally opted for no anesthetic.

But this wound was not minor. It had to be extremely painful. The wound cleaning and repair that she had to do would cause even more pain. It would make her task more difficult, even if he didn't let her know how much it hurt, because she would know she was hurting him.

Leslie didn't argue. She knew, from his eyes, that she wouldn't win.

A woman dressed in surgical scrubs covered by a white coat entered the room.

"What have you got, Les?" she asked, nodding curtly, pleasantly at Eric.

"Sue, hi. I didn't realize I'd get the *chief*. Mr. Lansdale, this is Dr. Susan Miller, the chief resident in orthopedic surgery. I want her to look at the wound as well since it's such a deep cut to the hand."

Eric nodded silently. A specialist. He had met a lot of specialists. None of them had been able to help his son.

"It's a glass—crystal—cut. Seven and a half hours old. Sensory and motor are intact. He has an arterial pumper that needs to be ligated and a small tendon lac that's not through and through but may be suturable."

Together, Susan and Leslie cleaned and examined the wound. Susan had no idea that Eric's hand had not been anesthetized. She probed deep in the wound, looking for glass, for tendon lacerations, for foreign material. The careful exploration was necessary. Eric never flinched.

Susan tied off the small severed artery and put two sutures into the tendon. Then she left to join the rest of her team in the operating room to put a steel pin in the hip of a patient with an intertrochanteric hip fracture.

"I'd give him prophylactic antibiotics, Les. No data, of course, but a hand wound that deep and that old . . ." she said as she took off her mask and blood-covered gloves before she left.

"I agree. A cephalosporin?"

"Sounds good. Take care, Mr. Lansdale. Bye, Leslie."

"Thanks, Sue," Leslie said, settling onto the stool that Susan had vacated. Leslie put on a new pair of sterile gloves before suturing the wound closed. It would take a while to pull the edges of skin back together, stitch by stitch. As she selected the appropriate gauge suture material, a needle holder and a pair of smooth forceps, Leslie said to Eric, "She's a very good orthopedic surgeon."

Eric nodded.

"Would you like me to inject some local anesthetic before I close the wound?"

"No," Eric answered swiftly. Then he added, looking at the concerned blue eyes staring at him over the aquamarine surgical mask, "Thank you."

It took Leslie thirty minutes to close the wound. The skin came together well. If it healed without infection, the scar would, in time, be simply a thin white line.

During the thirty minutes, neither spoke. Leslie concentrated on her suturing, and he, she noticed when she looked away from the wound to get more suture or reach for a sterile saline-soaked cloth to clean the field, was concentrating, too. Not on her, or his wound, or the pain but on something else. Somewhere else.

Usually patients were garrulous while their lacerations were being sutured. Usually the fear that entered the emergency room with them abated once the anesthetic took hold. The fear subsided and the relief pulsed through them making them euphoric, ebullient, talkative.

The light banter that normally accompanied suturing a laceration made the experience enjoyable for Leslie and her patients. It eased the tension and distracted them both away from the intimacy of what was really happening. The intimacy of touching. The *invasive* intimacy of forcing needle and thread into another person's flesh.

With Mr. Lansdale there was no light banter. Leslie knew he felt every touch. She knew that he felt the touch of her warm hands and the sharpness of the needle as she pushed it through his skin and the pull of the thread as she brought the raw edges together.

I'm sorry, Leslie thought, with each thrust of the needle. I'm sorry that I'm hurting you.

Finally it was over. Gratefully Leslie replaced the instruments and removed her gloves and mask.

"All done," she said, startling him.

"Great," he said absently, not even looking at the wound. Not asking, as most patients asked so they could tell their friends, how many sutures she had placed. Not teasing her, as most did, about what a great seamstress she was.

He should look, Leslie thought. It's one of my best suturing jobs.

"The nurse will come in and bandage it while I go write your instructions and get your antibiotics," she said, leaving the room.

When Leslie returned five minutes later, Eric was sitting in a chair, calmly resting his bandaged hand on his lap. He smiled politely when Leslie entered.

It always amazed her how different people looked when they were sitting up than they looked lying down on stretchers. Leslie had decided, as she observed his profile on the stretcher, that he was a handsome man. Now she saw the full measure of his looks, the pale blue eyes in the aristocratic face and the controlled body that sent a message of strength and power.

"Here are the wound care instructions," she said, suddenly feeling uncomfortable, remembering that she had touched this man, put needles and thread in his skin, questioned him about his delay in coming to the hospital. She continued with effort, "Someone should look at the wound in four days — sooner if there is any problem — just to make certain it's healing well. Your own physician can do that."

"I don't have a physician."

"You're welcome to come back here. Just stop by at your convenience. Any of the doctors can look at it."

"Wouldn't it be best to come when you're here?" Eric asked.

Of course it would. Leslie always tried to schedule the patients she sutured to come back for wound checks while she was on duty. It was best for them. It gave her feedback. Why was she treating him differently? Why was she *encouraging* him to see another doctor?

"Yes," she breathed.

"So, what shift will you be doing in four days?"

"This shift. Six in the evening until eight in the morning."

"What would be the best time to come?"

"It's unpredictable. If we get busy . . . if someone comes in who's critically ill . . . it could be a wait," she said, looking at him, thinking he was not a man who was used to waiting.

He didn't look disturbed at the possibility of a wait, but Leslie had already learned something about his politeness and his control.

"Would five-forty-five Wednesday evening be convenient for you?" she asked.

"Sure. But you won't be here," Eric said pleasantly.

"I'll be here. I always get here early. I'll see you right before my shift starts." *So you won't have to wait. So I won't have to worry about you waiting.*

"That's very nice of you."

"No problem."

Leslie didn't watch him walk down the corridor toward the waiting room. She didn't see the beautiful woman with the long blond hair and the concerned brown eyes touch his face tenderly, thoughtfully. Leslie didn't see them hold each other, tightly, for a few moments before leaving the emergency room.

Leslie didn't see any of it because she was already in

another room talking to a young woman with a urinary tract infection.

Four hours later, at one-thirty Sunday morning, the emergency room was finally quiet. Leslie had seen all the patients. They had all gone home — their throats cultured, their fractures set, their infections treated, their corneal abrasions patched and their lacerations closed — or been admitted.

Leslie sat in the triage area at the entrance of the emergency room beside a stack of patient charts that awaited her record of the patient's visit to the emergency room.

Leslie sat at the triage desk so that she would know immediately if any new patients arrived.

The red trauma phone rang. It was a direct line used only by ambulances and medic units. The triage nurse answered the phone and listened a moment while Leslie watched, curious. Then she shook her head at Leslie and wrote on a pad of paper L and D.

Labor and Delivery. It wasn't for the emergency room. They received calls from all ambulances coming to the hospital even if the patient was being directly admitted to a specific patient care floor. The ambulances all came to the emergency room entrance no matter where the patient was going.

After the triage nurse forwarded the call to labor and delivery, she said, "A little Gemini about to be born."

"Gemini? Is that good or bad?" Leslie asked idly.

"Neither. It's just what he, or she, is. It may begin to matter when he or she begins to socialize."

"Do you really believe that?" she asked, a little curious.

"I don't live by it, but I think it's interesting. We talk about *chemistry* between people. That's about as mystical as astrology!"

Leslie laughed. "I'm a Virgo, what does that mean?"

"It means you're strong and perfectionistic. Critical of others to some extent, but, mostly, you place demands on yourself."

"Sounds awful," Leslie said seriously. *It sounds accurate. It sounds like what Mark said that night at the Cliff House.* "Who am I supposed to be compatible with? If anyone!"

"Someone even stronger. A Scorpio, for example. They are very strong. Powerful," she said. "You need someone like that."

Mark had said that, too, Leslie mused, returning to the stack of unfinished charts.

The ambulance arrived five minutes later. The drivers waved at Leslie and the triage nurse as they wheeled the stretcher carrying the pregnant woman toward the elevator.

Ten minutes later the automatic sliding glass doors to the emergency room opened again. Leslie looked up when she heard the noise.

"James!" she gasped.

"Leslie," he breathed.

"What—"

"Lynne is about to deliver. She should have just arrived."

"She did. She should be up in labor and delivery by now. I'll show you how to get there," Leslie said, looking at him, her heart racing, her physician's mind wondering what Lynne was doing at University Hospital. It was a referral hospital for complicated pregnancies.

Her worry increased as she looked carefully at James. There was fear in the fearless green eyes.

"What's wrong, James?" she asked as they walked toward the bank of elevators.

"They aren't sure. She was fine until tonight. She suddenly had severe, tearing pain and bleeding. They think part of the placenta has torn away. They're transferring her here so they can monitor the baby. They think they'll have to do a Caesarean section."

Leslie nodded. Lynne probably had had an abruption of the placenta. Perhaps it was related to the uterine scarring that James had said would prevent them from ever having children.

James. Lynne. Lynne pregnant with James's child. James almost frantic with worry.

Leslie walked with him to the elevator that would take

him to labor and delivery.

"I'll be here all night, James," she said. *If you need me.*

When James returned to the emergency room two hours later Leslie had just completed the meticulous notes she wrote on each patient's medical record. Another time, eight months ago, she might have shown him the picture she had drawn of the hand on the record of E. R. Lansdale, and James would have laughed at the sketch with its stubby fingers and poor proportions.

But tonight was a different time, Leslie thought, looking at his exhausted, worried face. At least the fear in his eyes was a little less.

"How is she?"

"Sleeping. They have her sedated and they've given her medications to stop labor. The baby is being monitored. They say she seems fine."

"She?"

"Or he. We just have assumed she will be a she," James said. Despite his fatigue and worry there was a trace of excitement and pride in his voice.

"What are the plans?" Leslie asked carefully. She knew that if Lynne had a partial abruption it was simply a matter of time before more placenta tore away. When it did, if they couldn't intervene quickly enough, the baby could die from lack of oxygenated blood, and Lynne could die from uncontrollable blood loss. What were they waiting for?

"To keep her stable overnight and do a Caesarean section first thing in the morning. If there's a problem, they'll do it sooner, as an emergency."

She's stable now, Leslie thought. Why wait until it becomes an emergency? She knew the obstetricians at University Hospital. They didn't wait to do necessary surgery for luxuries such as daylight or a newly rested team. They operated when it was necessary, *whenever* it was necessary. When they were tired, adrenaline and pure skill got them through.

A piece was missing. Something James didn't know.

"You should get some rest," Leslie said, almost reaching to touch his face, to move the black lock of hair that fell into his troubled eyes.

"I'm going to. I just wanted to tell you what was happening. There's a waiting room upstairs full of expectant fathers."

"There's an empty apartment five minutes from here," Leslie said removing her apartment key from her key chain. "Lynne's sleeping, gathering strength. You should do the same thing. Give the L and D nurses my number; they won't recognize it."

"When will you be home?" he asked, taking the key. He wondered what she had done with his key.

"Eight-fifteen. You'll have to let me in."

"I will," he said, smiling weakly, resisting the urge to touch her flushed cheek. "Thank you."

After James left, Leslie called the labor and delivery nursing station.

"Hi, this is Leslie Adams. What resident is taking care of Lynne Stevenson?" she asked. I shouldn't be doing this, she thought as she waited.

"Michael Leary."

Leslie hesitated. Michael Leary. One of the best residents in the Ob-Gyn program. And a fine man. He was the first man Leslie dated after James left, a man who might have meant a great deal to Leslie at another time. But then, in December and January, all that Leslie knew was that Michael Leary was not James. It had ended awkwardly with Michael. Leslie never really explained to him what happened.

"Is he around?" she asked finally.

"Right here. Michael. Leslie Adams is on line two."

"Leslie?" Michael answered.

"Hi."

"Hi."

"Michael, I don't want you to give me any specific information since I don't have her permission, but . . ." Leslie hesitated. She had no business knowing anything about Lynne's condition. James could tell her but Michael couldn't because Leslie wasn't medically involved with the case.

"What, Leslie?"

"Lynne Stevenson's husband is an old friend. He's pretty worried, but I don't know if he really understands how serious it could be. Maybe it isn't that serious. I'm just guessing based on what he's told me. Anyway, Michael, if anything happens to her, if James needs someone, will you call me?"

"Sure, Leslie. Thank you for letting me know," Michael said. He hesitated a moment, took a deep breath, and began, "Leslie, as long as I have you on the line, let me tell you about a patient we have up here. I want you to know about her, in case we get in trouble. I may need your help."

"OK," Leslie said.

As Michael spoke, as he told her about his patient, Leslie realized that he was telling her about Lynne, involving her medically so that she would know how serious it was. So that she could help James. Or Lynne.

"She's a time bomb, Leslie, but I can't operate on her until I have blood for her. She's already anemic. The blood bank is having trouble cross matching her. The bank is low on blood anyway. They haven't recovered from Memorial Day weekend. Nobody's donating because of the AIDS business—"

"Not *donating* because of it? That doesn't make sense."

"I know. But people are afraid they might get AIDS by giving blood as well as receiving it. I'm not transfusing anybody these days who doesn't need it. The patient I'm telling you about may not need it, but I can't begin the operation without blood available because if she starts to bleed we may not be able to stop her. On top of everything, she has a minor bleeding disorder. The hematologists are in now trying to figure out what it is."

So Leslie had her answer. They were waiting because they had to. They were waiting until they had blood in case they needed it and until they could figure out a way to make her stop bleeding if she started again.

"How's the baby?" Leslie asked.

"Baby's fine. But that could change quickly, too."

"Let me know if you need my help."

"Thanks, Leslie, I will."

By eight-fifteen, when Leslie arrived at her apartment, James had showered and dressed. Leslie could tell that he hadn't slept much.

"The hospital just called," he said. "They are going to operate at nine-thirty. Apparently they were waiting to get blood for her and to run some sophisticated coagulation tests."

Good, Leslie thought, Michael is telling him more. That was good. James could handle it. He needed to be a little prepared.

"They said I can be with her from nine to nine-thirty. But," James said, his voice heavy with worry, "they won't let me be in the operating room. We had planned that I would be there for the delivery. I thought they usually let fathers in the delivery room even if it was a Caesarean."

They probably do, James, Leslie thought grimly. But not in this case. Not when it may be a blood bath. They don't want you to watch your wife and baby die. Oh James!

"They said they may need to do a hysterectomy," he continued distractedly. "They said that the scar tissue may bleed so much that they may have to remove Lynne's uterus."

"That doesn't matter, does it?" Leslie asked gently. If the only casualty of the operation was Lynne's uterus, they would be very lucky.

"No. I guess not. I don't know. I just want it to be over. For Lynne and the baby to be safe," James said emotionally.

He knows, Leslie thought, wanting to hold him. He knows.

"I'd better go," James said.

"Do you—" Leslie began, then stopped. Want me to go with you? she had almost asked. "Will you call me? Let me know?"

"Yes."

After James left, Leslie took a shower and got into bed.

The bed where James had slept. The bed where she and James had slept. She fell asleep, thinking about him, praying for him and Lynne and their baby.

At first the loud noise was part of the dream, an ambulance's siren, an ambulance rushing the dying mother and her infant to the hospital. But gradually the noise pulled Leslie out of her nightmare, ringing relentlessly, rhythmically.

Not a siren at all. A telephone. Ringing.

Leslie glanced at her bedside clock. Twelve-thirty. It was light out. Half past noon. She had been asleep for three hours. In five and a half hours she had to be back to work. Who could be calling? Why hadn't she disconnected the phone as she usually did?

The fog of her deep, troubled sleep suddenly cleared as she remembered.

James.

"Hello?"

"Leslie?" It was James, his voice faint, full of emotion.

Oh no, James.

"Yes," she said softly.

A long silence.

"They're OK," he said finally. The emotion was joy not grief, but it still left him speechless.

"They're OK?" Leslie asked, her own voice weak with emotion.

"Yes," he repeated, his voice a little stronger. "They are both fine."

"Oh, James. Thank God," Leslie breathed, her eyes brimming with tears. "Lynne's fine?"

"Yes. They did remove her uterus to stop the bleeding. They didn't give her any blood, though," James said thoughtfully. He knew a little about AIDS. He and Leslie had talked about it, about Mark's refusal to accept blood transfusions. James was glad that they hadn't had to transfuse Lynne. "She'll be anemic for a while, but . . . I just saw her. She looks fine."

"And the baby?"

"It's a boy," James said proudly, incredulously.

"A boy? James, you have a son," Leslie said softly, curling under the covers of her bed. "What's his name?"

"I don't know. We never talked about boy names," James said slowly, Leslie's words still echoing in his mind. You have a son. A son. James thought of his father. James's son would have a different kind of father. "Do you want to see him, Leslie?"

"Yes," she said. *No. I don't know.* She wasn't part of their life. James and Lynne and their baby boy. "If you want me to."

Leslie met James outside the nursery at five. They stared through the glass at the tiny boy, James's son, wriggling energetically in his crib. Lynne was asleep — not that Leslie would have met Lynne — but it meant that she and James could go for a cup of coffee in the cafeteria before her shift began.

"He's beautiful, James," she said.

"Oh, we have a name. Michael."

"After Michael Leary?"

"Uh-huh."

"That's nice. He's a nice man. It's a nice name." *Nice James.*

They drank coffee in silence.

"She probably got pregnant the night before your birthday," he said.

"Oh." *That was why she was ill.*

"She knew about us from the very beginning."

"Oh, no," she said, looking at the pain in James's eyes.

"She had planned to leave me, never tell me about the baby."

"How did you find out?" *When did you find out? Is that why we stopped seeing each other?*

James hesitated. He couldn't tell Leslie how he found out, while he and Lynne were acting out one of Lynne's sexual fantasies.

396

"I just did."

"And now?"

"Now," James said slowly. "Now we have a perfect little boy. It was a struggle, Leslie, trying to put our marriage back together. But we did. We are very lucky."

"You just love each other very much," Leslie said quietly, looking at James, knowing it was true.

They looked at each other for a long moment.

Finally Leslie noticed the time.

"I have to go. Do you want to stay at the apartment tonight?"

"No. Thank you. I'll go home," he said gently.

Home. Where he belonged.

Chapter Thirty-two

Eric Lansdale was already in the emergency room when Leslie arrived at five-thirty Wednesday afternoon.

"Hi, Mr. Lansdale. You're early."

"So are you."

"I always am," Leslie said lightly. She had come in early to say good-bye to James. Lynne and Michael were scheduled to go home in the morning. It had been a quick good-bye. They had said good-bye before. There wasn't much left to say. "How is your hand?"

Leslie sat on a stool in front of him and carefully removed the bandage. Without speaking, she squeezed the tips of his fingers with her hand, testing their strength and warmth, traced the suture line with her finger and examined his forearm for signs of ascending infection.

"Any pain?" she asked, wondering if he would even tell her.

"None. No pain or fever or drainage. I think it's healing well."

"So do I," she said, still holding his large hand in both of hers, naturally, as she would do with any patient. Then she looked at him and released his hand, suddenly uneasy. Too intimate. Much too intimate.

"Good," he said, smiling slightly. "When do the stitches come out?"

"In six days."

"Will you be here?"

Leslie looked at her pocket calendar. "Yes. I'll be working the day shift that day. From eight in the morning until six at night."

"I'll be here at five-forty-five. If that's all right."

"That's fine."

After he left, one of the nurses said to Leslie, "Who was that?"

"Mr. E.R. Lansdale," Leslie answered quickly, concretely, still confused about her discomfort at examining his hand.

"He is gorgeous! I wonder what he does for a living. He looks rich."

He looks *something,* Leslie thought as she picked up the chart of her next patient, a third-year medical student with a sore throat.

It took less than five minutes for Leslie to remove the twenty-seven stitches she had so carefully sewn into Eric Lansdale's palm. The wound had healed beautifully.

"There," she said when she was done. "You're a free man."

"Are you free?" he asked casually.

"What?"

"Are you free for dinner? Tonight?"

He could tell by looking at her that she was and that she was reluctant and tempted at the same time.

"I made reservations at The Blue Fox, one of my favorites, for eight o'clock," Eric continued, calmly, insistently, sensing that she was considering it. "I'm already dressed. So why don't I just go with you to your place? I'll make myself a drink while you change. All right?"

Leslie did not remember agreeing, but ten minutes later they were on their way to her apartment.

"This certainly is a convenient location for you," he said as he parked his jade-green Jaguar in front of her apartment building two minutes after they left the emergency room patient parking area.

"A short walk to University Hospital. But I also work

at San Francisco General Hospital and the VA. I bet a Jaguar has never been parked on this street before," she added, suddenly giggling.

"What's so funny?" he asked, his own eyes laughing.

"Nothing. Everything. This is so strange. I don't even know you," she said. *But I feel like I've known you forever, and I can either giggle or become mute because you make me feel wonderful and terrified. I have never felt this giddy, anxious, euphoric feeling before. This is so easy and so hard.*

"You're not afraid of me, are you?"

"No!" Leslie said lightly. *Yes. A little. A lot. Afraid of the way you make me feel.*

While Leslie took a shower and got dressed Eric poured himself a bourbon on the rocks, idly admired the framed etching of a meadow signed *James 1971,* and finally sat on the sofa in the small living room. He glanced at the stack of medical journals that lay on the coffee table, but he didn't reach for any of them. Then he noticed the thick book that lay on the end table beside him.

When Leslie returned to the living room, she found Eric reading *Moby Dick.* She wore a pale pink cocktail dress and pearls. As soon as he saw her, Eric stood up.

"And I thought a white coat stuffed with a stethoscope, tongue blades and pens looked fabulous on you," he said, obviously admiring her surprising softness.

Leslie blushed. "I don't get a chance to wear civvies very often," she said, shrugging.

"Too bad," Eric said. "Can I make you a drink? We don't need to leave for half an hour."

"I don't—" Leslie began then stopped. She had started to say, I don't usually drink. It was true. Even before last fall, even before James, she drank very little. Alcohol made her sleepy, and since the beginning of her internship, she was always a little behind on sleep anyway. But she kept a supply of liquor so that she could offer drinks to her rare visitors. "Sure, thank you. I'll have whatever you're having."

"Bourbon on the rocks," he said, pouring her a drink, then

handing it to her.

"Thanks. Were you reading *Moby Dick?*"

"I was just looking at it, wondering if I had ever really read it."

"I know I hadn't. Not really. Not with any appreciation. It is so powerful, so beautifully written. Like poetry," Leslie said.

Last summer as she watched Mark's pleasure—despite the pain of the bullet hole in his chest, his broken ribs and his weakness due to anemia—as he read the classics, Leslie felt a pang of conscience. She had read them all once as required reading in high school and college, but she had read them quickly, dutifully, without enjoyment or appreciation.

Watching Mark, Leslie wondered what she had missed. In the long lonely nights after James left, after she realized that it was useless to date anyone else for a while, Leslie discovered why Mark and her parents jealously guarded the hours they set aside to read the books they loved so much.

"Sometimes I read aloud to myself. Melville writes with such rhythm. It feels like the ebb and flow of the sea," Leslie said, feeling warm from a too large swallow of bourbon.

"Call me Ishmael," Eric began, reading the first line of the leather-bound volume.

"Ishmael," Leslie said softly.

"Eric," he said, realizing that she had never called him anything but Mr. Lansdale.

"Eric. That's what the E stands for."

"You didn't know my first name?"

"No. All our records have you as E.R. Lansdale."

"I guess the friend I was with the first night did that," Eric said absently. Charlie protected Eric's anonymity. And her own. Not that Leslie had ever heard of Eric Robert Lansdale. Eric doubted that Leslie had the time or interest, between the stack of medical journals and *Moby Dick,* to read the social or financial pages of *The San Francisco Chronicle.*

Eric read aloud the first paragraph of the book. Then the second. Leslie curled into her favorite chair, across from him, listening to his voice, watching his eyes and his mouth, feeling warm and secure. And anxious. She wanted the moment never to end.

"This is wonderful," Eric said after he read the first two pages to her. He looked at her and made a vow to himself, I am going to read this entire book to you. This book and a hundred others.

I don't even know you, he thought. But I am so sure.

They learned a little about the facts of each other's lives that night. They discovered that Eric had graduated from Harvard six years before Leslie entered Radcliffe. Leslie told Eric that she loved being a doctor. Eric told Leslie that he loved building beautiful buildings.

They learned a little about each other, but they learned a lot about how it felt to be falling in love.

They only touched once that night. Eric noticed the scar on her palm and reached for her hand.

"What happened?" he asked, tracing the edges of the large, irregular puckered scar left by Mark's shattered bone piercing her skin.

Leslie told him, briefly, wondering if he would remember seeing her on the news. If he had seen her, he would remember. He didn't.

"Not the kind of sewing job I'm used to," he said, looking at his own, thin, even scar.

Leslie smiled.

"They didn't even try to close my wound," she said. "It would have gotten infected." If you had come in any later, we might not have been able to close yours either, she thought. Why did you wait so long? she wondered but didn't ask. Maybe someday she would ask. Maybe someday he would tell her what he was thinking about that night, why he refused the anesthetic. . . .

It was midnight when he walked her to the door of her apartment.

"When can I see you again?" he asked.

"Whenever," Leslie said effortlessly, meaning it.

"I have a business dinner tomorrow night. How about Thursday?"

"Thursday's fine."

"Good," he said. Then he drew a deep breath and frowned.

"Eric? What's the matter?"

"I forgot all about a trip I'm taking at the end of the week. I leave Friday morning for Tokyo and Hong Kong," he said soberly.

"That sounds wonderful," Leslie said enthusiastically, but wondering, anxiously, how long he would be gone. "Does that mean Thursday night is no good?"

"No. That means I definitely have to see you Thursday night. Do you think it sounds wonderful, really?"

"Yes. Aren't you looking forward to it?"

"It's business. I go to those cities at least twice a year," Eric said. How jaded am I? he wondered. Do I look forward to anything? The pleasures in his life — a successful business transaction, a spectacular new building, making love with Charlie — seemed insignificant now, compared to the importance of being with Leslie. He was looking forward to Thursday night, and he was looking forward to returning from his trip. Unless . . . "Could you come with me?"

"To Tokyo and Hong Kong?" Leslie asked, incredulous.

"Yes. It's a ten day trip. It *would* be wonderful if you could come."

"I can't. Even if I had vacation time left, which I don't, I couldn't leave on such short notice."

"Because they need you?" *I need you.*

"Because they need warm bodies in all the acute medical units."

"I'll be here at seven Thursday night, then," he said. "Good-night, Leslie."

They didn't kiss. They would kiss next time. Or the time after. All their lives.

"Good-night, Eric."

403

At ten the next morning, the chief medical resident notified Leslie that, because another resident had just been diagnosed with serum hepatitis, she would have to fill in on the inpatient medicine service at San Francisco General Hospital.

"Who's covering here?" she asked.

"The consult residents will take turns."

"The new interns start today!" Leslie exclaimed, the magnitude of her new assignment settling in: the toughest ward service, the sickest patients and brand new interns. "Do I get some special compensation for this?"

"Isn't it enough that you were hand-picked because you're the best?"

"*That* worked last June. Can't I just ease into being an R-3 like everybody else?"

"It's only for nine days."

Nine days. It would keep her very busy while Eric was away. The time would pass quickly.

"OK."

"OK?"

"You mean I had a choice?" she teased, laughing. "Really, it's fine."

It was fine until she discovered that her first on call night was Thursday. She wouldn't be able to see Eric before he left.

Leslie found no listing for Eric Lansdale, or E. Lansdale, in the directory, but she found a listing for InterLand. He had said something about a company named InterLand.

Leslie spoke with three secretaries before she was finally connected with Eric's personal secretary.

"Mr. Lansdale's office, may I help you?"

"This is Leslie Adams calling for Mr. Lansdale. Is he available?"

"I'm sorry Ms. Adams, he is in a meeting. May I take a message?"

"Let's see. Tell him that I've just been transferred to

San Francisco General Hospital and I'm on call Thursday night."

"All right. And that's Ms. Adams?"

"Well, it's Dr., but it doesn't matter. He'll know."

"I apologize Dr. Adams."

"It's fine, really."

"Thank you. Is there anything else I should tell him?"

"No. Yes. Tell him, *Sayonara.*"

Eric got Leslie's message at three in the afternoon. It helped him make a decision he had been toying with all day. At five minutes past three he called Robert in Philadelphia, and at four-fifteen he walked down the private corridor that connected his office with Charlie's.

There was room, in the innermost part of the executive suite, for a third person. Eric had been looking for someone with whom he and Charlie could work creatively and effectively and compatibly. Now Eric had found him. James Stevenson. By mid-July the private corridor would provide undisturbed access between his office and Charlie's and James's. After the month he was spending with his wife and infant son was over, James would not return to his office at O'Keefe, Tucker and Stevenson on California Street. Instead, he would move to the executive suite on the fortieth floor of the InterLand building in an office with a panoramic view of San Francisco Bay.

The door to Charlie's inner office was open. She didn't hear Eric's footsteps on the thick wool carpet, nor did she immediately sense his presence. She was absorbed with the work that lay in front of her on the carved oak desk.

Eric smiled, watching her. When Charlie was working, she was so serious! She always has been, he thought, remembering the strong-willed lifeguard with her spun-gold hair hidden inside an over-large safari hat. He looked at her hair now, its golden brilliance knotted severely on top of her head. Her attorney look. It was very much like her lifeguard at the Oak Brook Country Club look. So serious.

405

"Hi," he said finally.

"Eric! Hi," she said, pushing the papers she had been reading away from her. "I will be so glad to leave this all for ten days. It will be a nice change, don't you think?"

Eric was silent, steeling himself against her brown eyes, now soft, radiant and eager about their trip to the Orient. They were closest when they traveled together. It was the closest they came to recapturing the magic — *their magic* — of being young and in love.

"We have the Empress suite at the Akasaka Prince in Tokyo. It's a three-bedroom suite. One for each night, I guess. Then, in Hong Kong, we're staying at —"

"I'm not going," Eric said flatly.

"The trip's off?"

"No. *I* am not going. The trip's still on. The meetings we have scheduled are necessary, especially the negotiations in Tokyo."

"I know that. That's why you have to be there."

"You're my negotiator."

"We do it together. Besides, Eric, it's the Orient. They won't negotiate with an unescorted woman. It's just not done."

"True, even though you do it all, a male figurehead is necessary. So I've arranged for the best, the very best figurehead for InterLand, not to mention a rather skilled negotiator and attorney. Just in case you need help."

"Robert?" Charlie asked weakly.

"Yes. I just spoke with him. He'll fly out tomorrow so you can leave, as scheduled, on Friday. He sounded excited about doing this, Charlie. It's been a while since he's been on the front lines negotiating. He's looking forward to it."

"Robert," Charlie repeated almost to herself. She couldn't travel with Robert, be with him constantly for ten days. What would she say to him? How would she and Robert fill the hours that she and Eric would have filled with quiet conversation, holding hands and making love? What would she and Robert do during the hours between meetings? What would they find to say at breakfast, lunch and dinner every day? She added weakly, "I don't know Robert."

"Of course you know him."

"I won't feel comfortable traveling with him," she mused. "We have to change all the hotel accommodations."

"Not really. A three-bedroom suite should give you both enough privacy. Charlie, why are you acting nervous about this? You travel with other attorneys all the time. All over the world. And you've known Father for twenty years."

"I don't know," she said honestly. It just feels strange, she thought. Charlie looked at Eric then and asked the question that he had been waiting for, worrying about. "Why aren't you going?"

"Because," he said slowly, watching her eyes, "I have met someone. I just met her. I don't want to be away right now."

Charlie took a quick breath. Over the years, Eric had met many women. He had had relationships with them just as Charlie had had relationships with other men. But Eric had never met anyone who could make him cancel a business trip, even a trivial one, and certainly not one this important.

In all those years, Eric had never met a woman who would make him cancel his plans to travel with Charlie. No matter what else, who else, was happening in their lives, Eric and Charlie would always travel together, rediscovering each other and the bits of magic that still were theirs.

Now, thirty-six hours before they were scheduled to leave on a trip that they had planned for months, Eric was telling her he couldn't go because he had just met someone.

"Who is she?" Charlie whispered.

"Someone. No one you know," he said carefully. He saw the hurt in her eyes. And the love. They had talked about this. That one day they might, if they were lucky, fall in love with someone new. They wished it for each

407

other: to find a love untarnished by pain and hurt; a love they could protect and treasure; a love like theirs had been, once. Before all the pain.

Charlie doubted it would happen. Certainly not to her. And probably not to Eric. But now it *had* happened. . . .

"Tell me about her," Charlie said, her surprise giving way to curiosity. And to excitement for Eric. If I'm hurt by this, it's my own fault, she told herself sternly.

"There's nothing to tell," he answered, relaxing a little as he heard the teasing lilt in her voice. She would be happy for him in time. "I barely know her."

But I want to be with her, he thought. More than anything else. And I don't want to talk about her, share her, with anyone else. Not even the people I love. Not yet.

"Did you tell Robert?" Charlie asked.

"Yes! But he doesn't know any more about her than you do," Eric teased lightly. He remembered that Robert had been hesitant, at first, about making the trip, but when Eric told him the reason, Robert suddenly seemed eager to go.

"At least this will give Robert and me something to talk about," Charlie said slowly, her voice reflecting her uncertainty about traveling with Robert.

Eric telephoned Leslie's apartment hourly during his dinner business meeting. The prefix and the quality of the ring seemed vaguely familiar, but he had never dated anyone who lived near Parnassus Avenue. Throughout the evening, there was no answer at Leslie's apartment. At eleven, when he returned to his penthouse in Pacific Heights, he tried again.

"Hello?" she answered breathlessly.

"Leslie, it's Eric. Did I wake you?"

"No. I just got home. I heard the phone ringing as I was fumbling with my keys. I thought it might be one of my interns," she said. *I'm glad it's not. I'm glad it's you.*

"Are you expecting them to call?"

"Not really. I just left them fifteen minutes ago. But,

it's the first day of the internship. Total chaos," she said laughing, tired, falling into the overstuffed chair. "What a day!"

"Tell me," Eric said carefully. *Just don't tell me about sick little boys*.

"OK. Just the highlights. Let's see. One intern decided to quit because another resident yelled at her. She isn't used to being yelled at, only praised," Leslie said, a little sympathetically and a little annoyed.

"Did she do something that wrong?"

"No. I actually have a low tolerance for the resident who yelled at her — for residents that yell at other residents in general — so I dried her tears and convinced her that this is all part of the magnificent learning experience of being an intern."

"She bought that?"

"I think so. I'll find out at eight o'clock tomorrow morning. My *other* intern decided to quit because one of our endocarditis patients threatened him with a scalpel."

"*What?*" Eric asked, suddenly concerned.

"The patient is an intravenous drug user — heroin mostly — which is why he has endocarditis. My intern needed to draw some blood from him, to monitor for toxicity due to the antibiotics we're using. The patient did not want a novice intern quote messin' with my veins end quote. He had a scalpel, complete with a very sharp blade, hidden under his pillow. He underscored how little he wanted the intern touching him by waving the scalpel at him."

"So, you had the man arrested," Eric said flatly.

"No!" Leslie said lightly, smiling at Eric's concern. It made her feel warm. His voice made her feel warm. Warm and eager. "I had a talk with the patient."

"*You* saw the patient?"

"He's my patient, too. I've actually taken care of him a few times. Anyway, I told him that he would let the intern try to draw the blood — one try, then I'd do it — or he could sign out against medical advice, which would probably kill him. I also told him that I was considering calling the police about the scalpel. That was a bit of a bluff."

"What happened?"

"He gave me the scalpel—not that he can't get another—and let the intern try. Miraculously, the intern hit the vein immediately and got the blood. He, too, will hopefully be there at eight o'clock tomorrow morning."

"I don't think you should work there," Eric said firmly. "I don't like it."

"It's safe, really," she said, loving the sound of his voice and his gentle concern. Safe, she mused, thinking about Mark, thinking about another resident who had been held at knife-point three months before. She added, a bit uncertainly, "You just have to be careful, sensible."

"You must be tired," he said.

"A little," she said. Exhausted. Physically and emotionally drained. Of course, if he wanted to see her. . . No, she had to sleep. She was on call beginning in nine hours. She added begrudgingly, "A lot. Did you get my message?"

"I'm not going away after all."

"Really?" *Really?*

"So. How about dinner Friday night?"

"I doubt if I'll be able to leave by dinner time," she said tentatively. And I'll have been up all night Thursday night, she thought, frustrated that she had agreed to cover at San Francisco General.

"Do you want to call me when you get off?"

"It may be late."

"It doesn't matter."

Eric gave her the unlisted phone number at his penthouse and the number to the private direct line in his office. He told her to call him whenever she had the chance. She wouldn't be interrupting anything.

Leslie didn't call him until ten o'clock Friday night. She called him from the intensive care unit.

"Eric, it's Leslie. I'm sorry, this is the first chance I've

410

had to call."

"How are your interns?" he asked, relieved to hear from her. He had been thinking about scalpels hidden under pillows.

"The *kids?* They're fine. They've learned a lot in the past three days."

"Still not independent?"

"Aaah. No," she said wistfully. It was why she had to stay late: to double-check their orders, to discuss every aspect of their patients with them. It was what she was there for.

"On your way home?" he asked.

"In five minutes, I think."

"Do you have to go in tomorrow?" Saturday. Eric knew the answer.

"Oh, yes. Just to make rounds. But that may take all day," she said. *I want to see you.*

"Sunday?"

"I'm on call again Sunday."

"Are you too tired tonight? I could come over, read you a page or two of *Moby Dick,* watch you fall asleep . . ."

"That would be lovely."

What am I doing? Leslie thought as she towel dried her chestnut hair. She looked at herself in the bathroom mirror. She wore a long, modest cotton nightgown under a light-blue terry cloth robe. Very modest. Very decent. Except that she was getting ready for bed while a man she barely knew waited in her living room.

She parted and combed her dark hair that, wet, fell below her shoulders. She looked at the dark circles around her blue eyes and sighed. I look tired. I *am* tired. Too tired to speak, or think, or analyze what I am doing.

"You look like a freshly scrubbed little girl ready for a bedtime story," Eric said gently when she wandered, awkwardly, into the living room. "A little girl up way past her bedtime."

"I am tired," Leslie said, enervated by the hot bath, too tired to think of what else to say.

"Come on, little one," Eric said, taking her hand, leading her into her bedroom and pulling down the bedcovers. "Crawl in."

Leslie slid out of her robe and under the covers. She smiled sleepily at Eric.

"May I join you?" he asked.

Leslie nodded, closing her eyes, succumbing to the cool softness of the bed and the warmth of his voice.

By the time Eric locked the door, turned out the lights, undressed and joined Leslie in her bed, she was almost asleep. She curled against him, her slightly damp, clean hair falling across his chest. He circled his arms around her, pulling her body, modestly covered by her nightgown, against his.

"You're a warm, snuggly kitten," he whispered, brushing his lips lightly on her head.

"Mmmmm," she murmured.

"Mmmmm," he answered, pulling her even closer.

In a few moments, he felt her breathing pattern change to slow, deep, peaceful breaths. She was asleep, peaceful in his arms.

"Precious little kitten," he whispered.

Leslie awakened promptly at six-twenty-five, her internal alarm reliably signalling to her five minutes before her alarm clock did. His arms were around her, gentle but secure. Carefully, Leslie pulled away, watching him, amazed at the wonderful, handsome stranger who was in her bed. Whom she wanted in her bed. Who *belonged* in her bed.

Quietly, without waking him, Leslie made coffee, showered and dressed.

I won't wake him, she decided. I'll just leave him a note.

It wasn't easy to write a note. What should she say? What *could* she say?

Dear Eric, Sorry about last night. Maybe tonight? No.

Eric, There's coffee in the coffee maker. . . . Of course there is. He doesn't need to be told.

Eric, Here's a key to the apartment. . . . Too pushy.

Dear Eric, You are cordially invited for dinner tonight. . . . Assuming I get home on time.

"Good morning," he said. He was fully dressed, but unshaven, his hair hand combed. "What are you doing?"

Leslie looked at the crumpled sheets of paper on the table. And the still-shiny extra key. James's key.

"Good morning. I was writing you a note. Trying to," she said, smiling at him, so glad to see him, so happy about the way he looked at her.

"It's hard to write me a note?" he asked, moving beside her, resting his hand on her shoulder.

"It is. I don't really know you," she said.

"You know I want to see you tonight."

Leslie reached for his hand, their fingers interlocking instinctively.

"Why don't I drive you to work? I have to go to my place to clean up anyway."

"You'd have to pick me up," she said, her heart pounding. It would be nice to have him drive her to work. It meant they could be together a little longer.

"I don't have anything else to do all day. Except maybe make my famous chicken cacciatore," he said, amazed at what he heard himself say. Eric couldn't remember a weekend when he hadn't worked most of each day. At least, not since Bobby. . . . He hadn't *really* cooked for months . . . years, but today all he wanted to do was putter around her apartment, cooking for her, waiting for her to call.

Eric smiled. He was looking forward to the day. It made him feel full of hope.

Leslie gave him the extra key to her apartment. She giggled as they got into his Jaguar. She held his hand as they drove to the hospital.

"Just pull in here," she said, pointing to the emergency room entrance. It was the safest entrance. It was guarded

413

by police officers.

"I'll be back at your apartment in about three hours," Eric said.

"I'll be here for at least six."

Eric smiled, leaned toward her and kissed her on the lips. His lips were soft, smooth and warm, surrounded by the roughness of his early-morning beard. It was meant to be a brief, good-bye kiss. But it was their first kiss. It lingered, until, suddenly, Leslie remembered where they were.

She pulled away then, gently, reluctantly. She looked into his eyes and trembled as she saw his desire. She whispered softly, "I'd better go."

"Have a nice day," he said, like a husband to a wife. It was the comfortable good-bye of a long-standing relationship, a relationship that had a history and would last forever.

It felt wonderful.

"Is that your famous chicken cacciatore?" Leslie asked, inhaling deeply as they walked into her apartment at six that evening.

"It needs a little more time. Do you want a drink?"

Leslie smiled. He was so at home in her apartment.

"Sure. Thanks. I'm just going to change out of my work clothes."

Leslie returned in ten minutes.

"You made the bed!" she exclaimed.

"I've had a wonderfully domestic day," Eric said as he handed her a drink. I've never had a day like this, he thought. And it's even better now. Perfect now. Because you're here. "I know your apartment very well."

"A little uninspired, isn't it?" she asked, knowing that it didn't matter to him, that he understood how busy she was. He knew she spent most of her life at the hospital, not in the small, bland apartment.

"Who is James?" Eric asked.

"James?" she repeated, her heart stopping for a moment.

"*James 1971.* The drawing."

"Oh!" Relief pulsed through her. Eric had simply noticed the one *inspired* item in her apartment: James's drawing of the deer in the meadow. "Someone I knew in high school."

"It's very good."

"Yes," Leslie agreed. Then she added with finality, eager to leave the subject of James squarely in the past, "He was a talented boy."

"My place is uninspired," Eric said, realizing for the first time that although his penthouse was stylishly and expensively decorated it lacked personality. It was a sterile showcase not a home.

"Not really," Leslie began. It was hard to imagine.

"Really. You'll see. It's all on a grand scale. The top floor of a condominium building in Pacific Heights. State of the art *Architectural Digest.* But," he said slowly, "it's just a place to sleep."

"This is just a place to sleep, too," Leslie said. *Unless you're here. Then it transforms.*

"No. This is a place to make chicken cacciatore and read *Moby Dick* and laugh and—" Eric stopped, distracted by her bright blue eyes, wondering how much he should say.

"And?" she asked innocently. She had no idea what he had been about to say; but she wanted to hear it. She wanted to hear all his thoughts. She wanted to know everything about him.

"And," Eric continued, honestly, gazing at her, "fall in love."

"Oh!" she said, startled, unable for a moment to hold his gaze. Then she looked at him again and murmured meaningfully, quietly, "Oh."

"Oh?" he repeated gently.

The kiss began then, in the small kitchen in Leslie's apartment. It was a long, deep warm kiss that made her mind swirl and her whole being tremble. The kiss continued, in leisurely sensuous moments, as they ate dinner, becoming wine flavored as they drank the Robert Mondavi chablis. It continued after dinner, gaining intensity and urgency, as they washed the dishes, whispering, laughing softly, touching.

"Shall we go to bed?" Leslie asked finally, sighing softly.

"I don't want to push you, Leslie."

"You're not pushing me," she said seriously to his concerned, passionate, pale blue eyes.

"Without even asking I've just—" Eric began.

"Made yourself at home? It's OK. Wonderful. You belong here," Leslie whispered, knowing it was true. *Whoever you are.*

"Where have you been all my life, darling Leslie?"

They made love slowly, discovering each other, lingering over each new discovery. It was a slow, leisurely lovemaking that celebrated the beginning of forever, *their* forever. There was no need to rush—until the sensations became too demanding, too intense, too undeniable—no reason not to savor this, the first of an infinite number of moments of pleasure. A lifetime of pleasure and love lay ahead for them.

They both knew it as their lips, their eyes, their hands and their flesh affirmed the knowledge quietly, passionately.

Over and over.

Chapter Thirty-three

"What are you thinking about?" Robert asked.

Charlie stiffened a little at the sound of his voice and continued to gaze out the window at the Pacific Ocean five miles below. In an hour they would land in San Francisco. Tomorrow Robert would return to Philadelphia, and she would return to work and report the tremendous success of the trip to Eric.

These past ten days would be a memory, a dream that had seemed so real at the time but faded quickly under daylight's scrutiny. In an hour she would wake up and return to the bright, harsh lights of reality. It would be over.

She was thinking, when Robert asked, how easy it had been to be with him. They had had so much fun touring the palaces and shrines and museums, walking for hours through fabulous gardens, dining at the finest restaurants in the Orient, while laughing, talking and learning about the culture. Learning about each other. She was thinking how wonderful he had been during the negotiations. She was in charge, but he was there, watchful, supportive, communicating with her through his eyes.

Charlie was thinking, when he asked, how much she would miss him.

"What, Robert?" she asked, turning to him.

"You've been staring out the window for the past hour, *thinking*, I assume, since your mind is never idle. I wondered what you were thinking about."

"Everything," Charlie said.

"That's what I thought," he teased. Then he continued seriously, "Were you thinking about the mystery lady?"

Charlie smiled. She hadn't really been thinking about Eric or the woman that had caused him to cancel the trip. Charlie hadn't thought about either of them for days.

"I wasn't, really. But we will know more, soon, won't we?"

"Maybe. Although I expect Eric will be very cautious. This time," Robert added carefully.

"This time? As opposed to—"

"The only other time he fell in love. With you."

"He wasn't cautious then?" Charlie asked, knowing the answer. Neither of them had been cautious.

"No. He didn't know it. None of us did. You were so young, so much had happened to you, so many unresolved questions. You were grieving for your mother, trying, by yourself, to understand her inexplicable death. And her inexplicable life. We all underestimated the emotional toll that it was taking on you. You hid it so well. None of us had really experienced a tragedy . . ." Robert's voice faded.

Until Bobby, Charlie thought.

"So I wasn't emotionally equipped to fall in love?" she asked after a moment. She wanted to know what Robert meant.

"Equipped, of course. Probably better equipped than most sixteen-year-olds. You had learned a lot about love from your mother. Prepared, no. Ready, no. Not until you got the answers that you needed."

"Which I did, finally, four years later at Christmas. Do you think," Charlie asked slowly, "that Eric and I could have made it then?"

If Victoria hadn't gotten pregnant.

"I think so, don't you?" he asked, looking carefully into her thoughtful brown eyes.

"I think so, too. It felt different—I felt different—for the two months that we had after that Christmas." Until the call from Victoria that changed everything. Charlie stared out the window, her eyes unfocused, seeing something that wasn't there. Something that used to be there but was no longer. "But now, as close as we are, as much as we care about each other—"

"So much has happened. Too much."

"But we didn't intentionally hurt each other."

"But you were hurt. You both were," Robert said. He looked at Charlie then asked a question he had wanted to ask for the past ten days. "Will you be all right if Eric falls in love?"

"I think he already has. I seem all right, don't I?" she asked lightly, uneasily. I've been all right for the past ten days, she thought. How will I be tomorrow? How will I be when this dream is over?

"You are a survivor, Charlie. You always have been."

"What about Florence?" Charlie asked quickly, wanting to change the subject.

"*Florence?*" Robert repeated, surprised.

Victoria and Eric had not been the only Lansdale couple to get divorced following Bobby's death. Robert's and Florence's marriage, already having outlived its viability and held together in large part by their love for their grandson, crumbled quickly.

"Will it bother you if she falls in love with someone else?"

"No! It would make me happy, assuage a little of my guilt."

"Guilt?"

"I was never in love with Florence. We got married because of Eric. We stayed together because of Eric and June. It wasn't unpleasant. Florence was—is—a loving, protective mother."

"A mamma bear protecting her cubs!" Charlie interjected.

"She wasn't very nice to you," Robert began, his brow furrowed, wondering if Florence had done any damage to the confused, tormented sixteen-year-old orphan.

"Robert, Florence was never unkind to me," Charlie

said emphatically. "A little indifferent, but never unkind. I know I made her nervous."

"You did. Your effect on Eric did."

"Do you know my most vivid memory of Florence?" Charlie asked, nodding to the stewardess who was checking to be sure that seat belts were fastened for the imminent landing in San Francisco.

"No, what?"

"She threw pennies away," Charlie said seriously, still bewildered by the memory. "I watched her clean a kitchen drawer once. She just tossed the pennies in the garbage. So wasteful. So terribly wasteful."

"I used to be afraid of Orion," Janet said, looking up at the stars that glittered above the cottage. It was a balmy August night. The black, moonless sky sparkled with stars, brighter and more plentiful because there were no city lights to compete with their brilliance.

"Afraid of Orion?" Ross asked.

"I didn't know that *he* was a constellation. I just knew that he was out there, up in the sky, a huge, ominous hunter. I was afraid he would come after me. I used to hide under the covers when I knew he was out," she said thoughtfully. It was a silly memory, but it recalled the fright—her fright—of a four-year-old child.

"I keep forgetting how timid you are," he said gently, kissing her hand.

"Timid," she mused.

"Personally timid, professionally bold. It's a beguiling combination."

"Have I beguiled you?" she asked, holding his hand against her lips.

"You know you have."

"Timid, Nebraska country girl and sophisticated city playboy—"

"*Playboy?*"

"That's what they say."

420

"They don't say that anymore, do they?"

Ross and Janet had been living together for two months. *They* knew it.

"No."

"So, playboys grow up. At least," he said, pulling her gently, leading her off the porch toward the bedroom, "this one has. Come with me. I'll protect you from Orion."

They began to make love the way they had made love since that first night in March. The only way that Janet knew how to make love: traditional, exciting, timid.

That night Ross did something different. He moved down her body, kissing her breasts, then the hollow of her stomach beneath her ribcage, then her navel, then the firmness of her lower abdomen, then—

Janet's body stiffened. She curled her fingers in Ross's blond hair, stopping him.

"Ross, please."

Ross sat up slowly, heavily. He had found another obstacle. Another hidden secret that she hadn't, wouldn't, tell him. Something that pushed them apart just when he had been feeling so close to her.

It was something to do with Mark—an intimacy between Mark and Janet—not to be shared with him.

"What, Janet?"

"I don't—" I don't know what you're doing, she thought. I don't know what I'm supposed to do. She saw the anger in his eyes. Why was he angry?

"You don't want me to make love to you?" he asked bitterly.

"Yes! It's just—"

"That some things are off limits? Reserved for someone else? Like your feelings?"

"Ross, *no*. What are you saying?"

"I'm saying," he said with carefully controlled rage as he dressed, "that you can't just give little parts of yourself. We're in much too deep for that. I'm in much too deep. Maybe you aren't in this relationship at all."

"Ross, where are you going?" The fright in her voice almost stopped him. Maybe it was something else. Maybe it wasn't Mark, a memory of Mark.

"I'm leaving. I'm going to *my* place in the city," he said, emphasizing his use of my. In the past months he had called his condominium in the city *our* place, but tonight they weren't sharing. They were separate. Again.

"Ross," she whispered to his back, tears of confusion spilling from her eyes. "I'm sorry."

"This every-sixth-night call is almost livable," Eric said.

Leslie curled against him on the sofa. The past six weeks, since she had simultaneously left San Francisco General Hospital and become an R-3, had been wonderful. They spent five of every six nights together. Even when she got home late, after her on-call night, he was there to tuck her into bed, to crawl in with her and to make love with her when she awakened in the middle of the night or in the morning.

Even on the nights when Leslie was rested they stayed home. They preferred to cook dinner together, alone, than to share each other with the world. They read *Moby Dick* aloud and talked and went to bed early.

"Mmmmm. Livable. But not the real world," Leslie said.

"Aaah. The work issue," he said, kissing her hair. They had discussed this before.

"Now, if you would alternate reading chapters about our friend the great white whale with reading selections from my stack of the unread *New England Journal, Annals of Internal Medicine* and *American Journal,* I would be a happy and well-read resident," she said, frowning at the stack of ever accumulating literature that needed her attention.

"And what will you do while I'm studying contracts, financial reports, land surveys, blueprints . . . ?"

"I'll take a nap or a bubble bath. Or I'll just watch

you."

"Very helpful," he teased. Then he said seriously, "Do you think we can work effectively under the same roof? Or are we going to have to enforce time apart?"

Leslie knew that before he met her Eric often spent his nights and weekends working. He had to. He had that kind of job. And that kind of personality. So did she. They both had careers that came home with them, went to sleep with them and woke them up in the middle of the night. They always would.

"We have to be able to work under the same roof," she answered seriously. It had to become part of the life they were building together, part of making it livable, part of making a forever.

"I know, darling. And we can. Workaholics can conquer all obstacles, even passion. We start this weekend."

"Right. Let's discuss the ground rules. Can we touch while we're studying?"

"*Touch?*"

"Just feet, maybe?"

"Maybe."

"Good," she said, kissing him. "Why don't we start the weekend after next?"

The telephone interrupted what might have led them into the bedroom for the night.

"Who could that be?" Leslie asked, pulling away.

"Anybody. It's only seven-thirty for the rest of the world. Even though it's our bedtime."

"Hello?" she answered, laughing.

"Hi, Les, it's Janet. Am I interrupting?"

"Janet, you sound upset," Leslie said quickly. She hadn't heard such flatness in Janet's voice since the October night that Mark left. "What's wrong?"

"Ross and I had a fight. Two nights ago. He left. I haven't spoken to him since."

"A fight about what?"

"Oh, Leslie, I don't know. I think the specifics triggered some bigger issue. But I don't know."

"Well, what were the specifics?"

"Oh. Uh, I can't really even talk about it," Janet said. *I wish I could. I wish I could just ask Leslie.*

"Janet, why don't you come over? We'll talk," she said, looking at Eric, smiling at him, feeling warm and generous and so lucky.

"No. Leslie, I don't even know why I called. . . . . If I talk to anyone, it should be Ross."

"You've had misunderstandings before. Things that weren't even really conflicts once you discussed them. You two tend to get your signals crossed," Leslie said buoyantly, trying to encourage Janet, feeling on shaky ground since she didn't know the issue. Still, it was true Ross and Janet had a history of misinterpreting each other. They needed to talk.

"I do need to talk to him. I'm just trying to build up the courage." Timid Janet.

"Why don't you come over?"

"No. It's not over, anyway. I'm two hours away."

"I'll be here."

"Thanks. How are you? How's Eric, whoever he is?"

"I'm fine and he's fine. Let me know, OK? Keep in touch."

Leslie put down the receiver and sighed.

"That was Janet," Leslie explained to Eric.

"The one who got divorced and is—*was?*—involved with someone who you think is good for her." Eric smiled wryly. Leslie and Eric spent almost no time discussing each other's friends. He accurately summarized the brief description Leslie had given him of Janet a month ago. "Right? Is she a resident?"

"Janet? No," Leslie said, realizing that she hadn't even told him Janet's last name. He would know Janet. Leslie was certain that Eric would have seen *Joanna* and *Peter Pan*. He would be surprised. She smiled, "No, Janet's an actr—"

The telephone rang again.

"I guess you'll get to meet her," Leslie said, assuming it

was Janet having decided to come over after all. Leslie answered the phone on the second ring, "Hi. We'll see you in two hours!"

"Leslie?" the voice echoed a little. It was a familiar but distant voice.

"Mark?"

"Greetings from Boston."

"Hi! Is Kathleen on the line, too?"

"No, she's at a bridal shower for a classmate from Vassar. It turns out that she has about as many friends in Boston as she does in San Francisco. She didn't even know it until we got here."

"That's nice for her, since you're probably busy."

"We're both busy. Kathleen's already joined the major committees and boards, including the repertory theater and the history society!"

He's so proud of Kathleen, Leslie thought, detecting the love and pride in his voice. She is so good for him.

"How's your fellowship?"

"Great. The best. Very busy. Very stimulating. How are you?"

"I'm fine, Mark," she said looking at Eric, shrugging slightly. "Oh, a friend has been reading *Moby Dick* to me. Out loud. It's wonderful."

"A friend? Anyone I know?"

"No."

"Tell me about him. Or is he right there?"

"He's right here. Looking at me. Wondering who you are."

"This sounds serious."

"It is."

"Well, then, you are both invited to dinner at the Carlton Club in October. We're flying in for the weekend—the Jenkinses' anniversary—and Kathleen's planning a dinner party at the club."

"The Carlton Club. Maybe I'll see it yet. Of course, I'm in the intensive care unit at San Francisco General in October."

"I hope you can come. I'd like to see you. Kathleen will let you know the specifics. *Moby Dick,* huh? Sounds nice," he said a little wistfully.

What sounds nice, Leslie wondered. Having someone read it to you? Having time to read it? Anything but medicine?

No, she thought. Mark sounds happy.

"I hope we can come, too, Mark. Give my best to Kathleen," Leslie said before hanging up. As she slowly replaced the receiver she mused, I wonder why he called. . . .

"That," she explained to Eric, "was Janet's ex-husband. How strange for them both to call."

"Does he belong to the Carlton Club?"

"You've heard of the Carlton Club?"

"I am a member of the Carlton Club."

"I thought it was just very old, very wealthy Atherton with some San Francisco proper thrown in."

"*Very* proper. It is. But there's reciprocity with the very old, very wealthy Oak Brook Country Club in Philadelphia. I don't spend much time at the Carlton Club, but if your friend's a member, I may know him."

"His new wife is a member. Kathleen Jenkins was her maiden name."

"Kathleen. I know Kathleen. We were on the Union Square Theater Board together for about four years."

"She's beautiful," Leslie said, her heart sinking. Has Eric been with Kathleen? Did Kathleen have *Mark* and *Eric?*

"Yes, she is. Bright, too," he said idly, holding his arms out to Leslie, wondering why she wasn't coming to him. "Leslie?"

"Did you date Kathleen?"

"What? Would you come to me?" Eric waited until he held her in his arms. "I never dated Kathleen Jenkins. I never even considered it."

"Really?"

"Really."

426

"I don't ever want to meet anyone that you dated," Leslie said thoughtfully.

"No?" he asked gently, realizing that he felt the same way.

"No."

Eric was silent. He couldn't agree to it. Someday, Leslie would meet Charlie.

"Oh," Leslie continued, wondering. "were you on the board when they auditioned for *Joanna*?"

"That was my last year. I was just too busy, even though I enjoyed it. I go to all the productions. I even invest in a few."

"I hope your investing in *San Francisco*, the new one."

"I am, but how do you know about it? They're playing it pretty close to the chest, planning a big surprise."

"Janet is—"

"Janet Wells," Eric said, searching his memory. He had heard some rumors. Charlie kept him informed, even though he had very little interest in the lives and loves of people he barely knew. *Charlie*, he mused, frowning slightly. Then he said, "Let's see, I even head a rumor that she was dating Ross MacMillan."

"Was. Is. That's the question. Do you know him?"

"Sure . . . I think he cares a lot about Janet," Eric added, surprising himself, realizing that was not information from Charlie. It was his own observation. He remembered the way Ross talked about Janet—the tone of his voice—when he and Eric discussed Eric's investment in *San Francisco*.

"I hope he does," Leslie said. She pressed close to Eric. "This is nice. You already know my friends. Or at least my friends' friends."

"So, I don't have to meet them? Good. That's one less venture into the real world that we have to make."

"Do you think we'll always be this antisocial?"

"We're very social. We're just limiting our socializing to each other. We'll make the requisite forays, just like we'll start working at home, together. Besides, you don't know my friends. They are already bursting with curiosity."

"Are there lots of them?"

"Only three. My father and the two people that I work with most closely." Charlie, he thought, whom I loved and almost married. Would have married. And James, who has become my friend.

"When do I meet them?" Leslie asked, curious but not eager. They had so little time together.

"In November if not before. We're planning a trip to Maui. It's at the same time as my birthday, but it's not a birthday celebration. It's just a celebration. Can you get away?"

"I think so. I'll be ready for a celebration in early November. I spend October in the intensive care unit at San Francisco General. For part of the month I'll be on call every other night."

"Every *other* night?"

"It won't be a good month for us," she said apologetically.

"We'll manage. We'll just keep thinking about Maui."

"Maybe I should meet your friends before November. Will they be annoyed?"

"One will." *Charlie. The one you don't want to meet.* "But I'm not going to share you until I have to. And I have to in November."

"They're your friends."

"They'll be your friends, too," he said, knowing how much Robert and James would like her, how they would understand why he had just wanted to be alone with her.

And Charlie? How could he ask Charlie to hide *their* past to protect Leslie? Did he have any right to ask that of Charlie?

He would have to think about it. He would have to think about all the things that he should tell Leslie, all the things he *needed* to tell her.

He had until November. At least.

* * *

Janet arrived at Ross's security condominium building on Sacramento Street at eleven P.M. She used her coded card to activate the locked garage entrance.

I should park on the street, she thought. I should go in the front door and have the doorman announce me.

But then the doorman would know that she and Ross were having problems. For all of July she had lived there with Ross. In July she had belonged there.

And now? What if she asked the doorman to announce her and Ross refused to let her come up?

Janet parked her car in the space—her space—next to Ross's car. At least he was home. She took a second coded card and activated the elevator.

Her hands trembled.

What am I doing here? she wondered as waves of panic swept through her.

Three and a half hours before, she had left the cottage with a vague plan to visit Leslie after all. She had driven down the coast highway, across the Golden Gate Bridge and into the city. But instead of driving toward Leslie's apartment on Parnassus Avenue, Janet had driven, without apparent aim, around the city. Without apparent aim except that the drive had ended in Ross's garage. Was that her subconscious plan all along?

"Hello," she said when he opened the door. She looked at him briefly, noticing immediately how tired he looked. Then, she looked away, avoiding his eyes, afraid of seeing the anger.

"Hello. Come in," he said seriously.

The living room was cluttered with pages of script and musical score for *San Francisco*. Ross had been working on the staging for her show.

"You've been working."

"Trying to."

"August is your vacation month."

"I didn't feel like playing," he said flatly, wondering if she was going to talk to him, if they were going to talk to each other.

Wondering if they were even going to look at each other.

"Ross . . . I—" Janet began.

"You what?"

"I'm sorry. I don't know what happened."

"What do you *think* happened?" he asked hotly.

"I think," she said carefully, looking at her hands, "that I was, uh, uncomfortable about what you were doing, and it suddenly became a big issue. A bigger issue."

"What's the bigger issue?" he asked, moving closer to her, trying to make her look at him.

Janet shook her head then whispered, "I don't know."

"Sure you do."

"I *don't*," she said, her eyes, turbulent gray thunder clouds, meeting his, finally. "I don't know."

"OK," he said, barely controlling his anger and frustration. "Try this. I am tired of coming in second behind Mark. I'm tired of losing to Mark, to the *memory* of Mark. I can't do it. I won't do it anymore."

"*Mark?* What do you mean?"

"Remember Mark's and Kathleen's engagement party? Remember their wedding? No, of course you don't," he said bitterly. "You didn't go. We didn't go."

"I thought you understood. You said that you didn't resent it at the time," she pleaded. *You said, then, that you just wanted to be with me.*

"I've reconsidered it in light of the present situation."

"That's not fair."

"All's fair, isn't it?" Ross asked casually, knowing that it wasn't fair. He *had* understood why she couldn't see Mark and Kathleen. He hadn't resented it once he understood, but there were other examples. "You wouldn't sing to me, remember? That was because of Mark, wasn't it?"

"It was partly because of Mark, I guess, but it was mostly because I didn't really know you," she said thoughtfully. She added quietly, "I sing for you now."

"And now this," Ross said quickly. Janet did sing for him now. Privately. Whenever he asked.

"This?"

"I can only make love to you in a certain way. Part of you still belongs to Mark," he said bitterly.

"No," she said, tears spilling from her stormy eyes as relief began to sweep through her. Had he simply misinterpreted? Could they find a way out of this after all? Maybe. Maybe.

"No?" he asked, confused, encouraged by the half smile on her lips despite the tears.

"*No,* Ross. Mark never touched me there. No one has," she said, embarrassed, almost apologetic until she saw the look in his eyes as the meaning of her words settled. Ross looked happy. Happy. And amazed. And concerned.

"Then why? Why did you stop me?" he asked gently.

"I didn't know what you were doing. What I was supposed to do," she said quietly, shrugging slightly.

Ross held her then, kissing her tears, blinking away his own. He had almost lost her because of a foolish misunderstanding that was rooted in his own ill-founded jealousy of Mark. Ross had never been jealous of anyone in his life. And, maybe, he needn't be jealous of Mark.

It was just that he wanted her so much.

"Oh, Janet," he whispered. Lovely, timid, naive Janet.

Part Four

Chapter Thirty-four

San Francisco, California
September 1982

James glanced idly at the leather appointment calendar on his desk, then paused, staring at the date written in script at the top of the page: September Twelfth.

September twelfth. Leslie's birthday. One year ago today he had taken her to dinner.

James smiled. He could smile now, again, when he thought about Leslie. He hoped that she was happy, as he was. He hoped that she would find someone to love as much as he loved Lynne. And that, someday, she would have a child.

A child. James thought about Michael, his beloved son. He felt so lucky. He had Michael, and he had Lynne. His life was full—*overflowing*—with love and joy.

It would be safe to call Leslie, to wish her Happy Birthday and happiness.

A knock at his door interrupted James's reverie.

"Yes?"

"May I come in?" It was Charlie, looking like a corporate attorney but smiling a soft, womanly smile for James.

"Of course. What's up?"

"Nothing. Not true. *Everything*. But nothing that involves you. I'm just seeking refuge in your office."

"Be my guest," James said, smiling, gesturing to the burgundy leather couch that got no use by him but looked so comfortable.

"Thanks," she said, slipping off her heels and sinking into the couch. "I am so glad you're here. I used to be able to escape into Eric's office—"

"But?"

"He's no fun anymore. All business."

"You're all business, too. Except you're more efficient than me or Eric so you can indulge in these little breaks."

"Eric used to like the breaks."

"He's preoccupied," James said, defending Eric. James had never had a friend like Eric. James had never met a man he liked, respected or trusted as much.

"Yes," Charlie agreed.

"He's in love. He wants to get as much work done here as possible, so he'll be able to be with her. Is that so bad?" James asked. It was what James did, too, so that he would have as much time as possible to be with Michael and Lynne. Still, he usually had to work in the evenings, after they put Michael to bed. He knew that Eric *and* Charlie worked at home in the evenings and on weekends. They all did. They all had to.

"No," Charlie said wistfully. "It's not bad at all."

"Charlie, what's really bothering you?" he asked suddenly.

"I miss him, James. Not just the little breaks," she said wryly. "I miss the evenings and the nights and the weekends and the trips."

"Oh," James said slowly. "I didn't know. I knew you were close . . ."

So Eric hasn't told him about us, Charlie thought. How could he? The story of Eric and Charlie wasn't complete without the part about the little boy who had died. And neither Eric nor Charlie would tell James, whose life had been made perfect by the birth of his son, about Bobby.

"We've known each other, cared about each other, for a long time," Charlie said thoughtfully. Then she added something she had never told Eric. Something she had admitted to herself only recently because she had to. "I thought we might even get married someday, after all, if neither of us found someone else. Sort of by default."

"Default?" James gasped. He couldn't imagine either Eric or Charlie doing anything by default. They were both so confident, so competent, so controlled. Controlled and in control. They didn't make mistakes. They didn't run their lives by default. But Charlie was serious.

"Long story," she said shrugging, smiling slightly. "Anyway, it's a moot point now. I think he's really in love, don't you?"

"I think so," James said gently, wondering how much the fact of Eric being in love hurt her. He couldn't tell.

"Do you know anything about her?"

"Not even her name. He told me that she is coming to the opening of the resort on Maui in November."

"I didn't know that," Charlie said softly, her stomach aching slightly. She would meet Eric's love, get to know her and probably like her. It would be nice to have it behind her. In two months it would be behind her. "Are Lynne and Michael coming?"

"Sure."

"I'm looking forward to meeting Lynne. And Michael," Charlie said truthfully. "I guess everything worked out just like you said it would."

"It worked out, Charlie, but not the way I thought it would. You were right. Lynne knew about it. She knew from the beginning."

"She knew about Leslie?"

"I can't believe you remember her name!" James exclaimed. "She knew there was someone. She didn't — she still doesn't — know who it was, except that she was someone I knew from high school. Anyway, it's a long story, too. But, fortunately, we survived it."

"More than survived. You seem very happy."

"I am. Listen, Charlie, I'd really like you to meet Lynne—and Michael—before November. Why don't you come over for dinner?"

"James, you are so nice. I'm OK, really."

"I know you're OK, but I *really* want you to meet my family. This Friday, how's that?"

"That's fine, James, thank you. I'm looking forward to it," she said. She put on her shoes and got ready to leave, the break over. She paused at the door. "I really am looking forward to meeting them."

After Charlie left, James reached for the phone to call Lynne, to let her know that he had invited Charlie for dinner. As he dialed the phone, he thought again about calling Leslie.

He wouldn't do it. It was safe—like their affair was safe—unless Lynne found out. It wasn't worth it. James wouldn't do anything that could jeopardize his life with Lynne and Michael.

"This is déjà vu," he said.

Leslie spun around. She was in the small lab near the intensive care unit at the San Francisco General Hospital running a blood gas. It was three o'clock in the afternoon on Saturday, October sixteenth.

"Mark!"

"Hi."

"Hi. Please withhold your déjà vu comments until after I've done the gas and we can get out of here," Leslie said, shivering involuntarily as she remembered the last time she and Mark were here together. The day he was shot. "How are you? You look good."

Mark looked handsome, his dark handsomeness enhanced by the fatigue in his eyes and the strain on his face, but he did not, really, look *good*.

438

Something is wrong, Leslie thought. Something that would make him spend part of his brief visit to Atherton for Kathleen's parents' anniversary at the hospital on Saturday afternoon with her.

"I'm fine. We're sorry that you can't come to the party tonight."

"But this is really the mountain coming to Mohammed."

"I wanted to see you," he said.

"That's really nice," Leslie said. Why? she wondered. She looked at his serious brown eyes and knew that he was going to tell her.

"You really love this, don't you?" he asked. It was more of a statement than a question. An uncomprehending, wistful statement of fact.

"And you really don't," she said, looking at him. That was what he wanted to talk about. *Finally.*

"I like parts of it," he said swiftly.

He's still trying to convince himself, Leslie thought, still not allowing himself to quit.

"What parts don't you like?"

Mark hesitated. Then he said carefully, "I don't like the sadness. I don't like to see people who are sick, who are dying."

Who does? Leslie thought. I'm not a doctor because I *like* to see sickness and death. I'm a doctor because I want to help. But this isn't about why I'm a doctor. It's about helping Mark decide not to be one.

"What bothers you about it?" she asked, curious.

"It makes me feel sad. It makes me feel like I'm dying. It affects my whole life," he said. *It makes my life seem hopeless.*

"Then let it go, Mark. Get out of it," Leslie said emphatically. *Get out before it destroys you and Kathleen. Or before you destroy yourself.* She had wondered once before, in this tiny lab, if Mark had a death wish. Now she worried that he might see no way out but by his own death. What if he joined forces with the death and sadness that consumed him? What if, instead of fighting it, like she did, he gave in to it?

What if . . .

"I'm worried about you," she said seriously.

"Don't be, Leslie. I'm all right," he said unconvincingly. "I go for weeks at a time really enjoying my fellowship—"

"And then?"

"And then I go through periods of doubt. Don't you?" he asked hopefully.

That's why he's here, Leslie thought. To have me tell him that it's normal to feel the way he feels. To have me convince him not to quit.

"I feel the sadness. You know that. And sometimes I think it would be easier, emotionally easier, to be doing something else. But," she said firmly, "I don't feel consumed by the sadness or the death. Mark, what about your interest in English? In writing?"

"I think about it a lot."

"*Do* it," Leslie said urgently. "What does Kathleen think?"

"I haven't discussed it with her. I don't know what she'd think."

"Well, you know for a fact that she didn't marry you because you're a doctor," Leslie said, remembering the conversation that she and Kathleen had had the night Mark was shot. She married him in *spite* of the fact.

"I do know that?" Mark asked, surprised.

"You should know that. If I know it, and I do, you should. Mark, you really should involve Kathleen in this," Leslie said carefully. She didn't want to offend him. Was he making the same mistakes with Kathleen that he had made with Janet? Was he shutting her out? "Kathleen must notice that you are worrying about something."

"Oh, I don't know. I don't think so. I just wanted to discuss it with you, as long as I was in town," Mark said lightly. "So, tell me about Eric. Kathleen thinks he's terrific . . ."

Kathleen's fingers trembled as she dialed the number. This was a desperate idea, but she was desperate.

Ross answered on the fourth ring.

"Ross, it's Kathleen."

"Hi, welcome home. Sorry I won't see you this trip, but—"

"I know, I understand. Maybe I'll come back for opening night of *San Francisco* next month. In fact, that's sort of what I called about. Is Janet there?" she asked.

"She's gone for a walk on the beach. Why?"

There was a long silence. When Kathleen spoke again, Ross heard the emotion in her voice.

"I just wanted to talk to her," Kathleen said shakily.

"To Janet? Katie, honey, what's wrong?"

"I don't know what's wrong. Something's wrong with Mark."

"What's wrong with him?"

"He's moody. Sometimes he's fine, sometimes he withdraws from me. I thought he might be depressed. I read his textbooks. He doesn't have the classic symptoms of depression. He was like this a little before we got married. I thought he was just getting over his divorce. I don't know, Ross. Sometimes I think he regrets that he married me—" Kathleen was crying.

"Katie. No one would ever regret marrying you."

"Thanks," she sniffed. "But Ross, Mark is unhappy and he's married to me. Those are the facts."

"Why do you want to talk to Janet?" he asked uneasily.

"I just wanted to know if he was like this with her. Do you know?"

"I don't know. We don't really talk about her marriage to Mark," he said. *And I don't want to.*

"Will you ask her if she'll talk to *me* about it?"

"Katie . . ."

441

"Ross, please. If she won't, she won't."

"If you want me to I will," he said hesitantly. Who was he protecting? Janet? Their relationship? Everything had been so perfect since August. "Where is Mark now, anyway? Isn't he with you?"

"He's in the city visiting Leslie at the hospital."

Leslie, Ross thought. Mark's friend. Janet's friend. Eric Lansdale's love.

"Why don't you talk to Leslie? Maybe she knows what's wrong with Mark," he suggested.

"I can't talk to Leslie about this. Really, Ross. She thought I was wrong for Mark from the beginning."

"What?" Ross asked, amazed. "How could you be wrong for Mark? For anyone?"

"I don't know. I just got the feeling Leslie thought I was a gold digger."

"You're the *gold.*"

"Well, an emotional gold digger, then: too trivial for Mark, not sincere enough. I don't know. I just know that Leslie doesn't approve of me. I can't talk to her," Kathleen said then paused. What am I doing? she wondered. She added slowly, "And I can't talk to Janet, either. It was a dumb, impulsive idea."

"Katie, I will ask her if you want me to. If it might help," Ross said.

"It won't help. Not really. This is my problem. I guess I just wanted to tell someone. *You.*" Kathleen tried to sound positive.

"I'm sorry about this, honey."

"I know you are, Ross. Thank you. I've got to go," Kathleen said suddenly, fighting back tears.

"Keep in touch, Katie."

Ross hung up the phone just as Janet walked in the door, smiling, her cheeks rosy from her brisk walk and the cool October ocean breeze.

"Who was that?" she asked, smiling, kissing him on the lips.

442

"It was Kathleen."

"Oh! How's she?"

"All right, I guess," Ross said unconvincingly, obviously concerned. He was not sure that he wanted to tell Janet, but he was unable to forget the pain in Kathleen's voice.

"What's wrong?"

"Something about Mark being moody and withdrawn," Ross said with a sigh.

"Oh," Janet said sympathetically. "That's too bad. I know how she feels."

"Do you know why he acts that way?" Ross asked. Maybe Janet would tell him something that would help Kathleen. Something *he* could tell Kathleen.

"I have a theory," Janet said slowly, thoughtfully, remembering. "I think Mark doesn't really want to be a doctor. And I think it torments him."

"If he doesn't want to be a doctor, why doesn't he just quit?" Ross asked, a little impatiently. Ross didn't do things that he didn't want to do. Not without a very good reason. He didn't really want to live in Janet's too tiny, country cottage, but he did because Janet was a very good reason.

"It's not that easy."

"Sure it is," Ross interjected firmly.

Janet smiled thoughtfully at him. "You see things so clearly," she said, teasing him gently.

"I just don't have much tolerance for indecisive adults."

"I know. I don't think it's a question of indecision, because there weren't any choices. From the moment Mark was born, he was destined to be the *best*," Janet said, smiling sadly.

"The best," Ross mused quietly, wondering if this had anything to do with Janet's insistence that being the best—even though she was—didn't matter to her.

"Mark was—is—the best at everything he does. He was raised to be and now it is part of him. The compulsion

443

and the drive and the expectations are within him."

"I have no argument with people wanting to be the best," Ross said irritably, his impatience surfacing again. "But why doesn't he quit medicine and become the best at something he likes?"

"I think Mark actually believes that being a doctor *is* the best. He has spent all of his life—*all of it!*—preparing to be a doctor, the best doctor. Now he's there and he hates it. It's a tremendous failure, and Mark doesn't fail," Janet said, frowning.

He failed you, Ross thought without venom. Ross had met Mark a few times. He liked him, respected him. Ross cared deeply about both the women who had fallen in love with Mark. As he listened to Janet, Ross became more sympathetic.

A failed marriage. A career—the *only* career—that had failed somehow. It quickly added up to a failed life. Mark *had* to start making choices.

"He's not a good doctor?" Ross asked.

"Leslie says he's a wonderful doctor. The best. He just hates it and it torments him."

"He has to get out," Ross said emphatically, surprised by his own sudden concern. *He has to get out for Kathleen's sake. And for his own.*

"I know. It's so easy for us to see that. It seems so obvious. I don't think we have any idea how difficult it would be for Mark to quit. Maybe impossible. It's hard to give up something you've believed in all your life," Janet said thoughtfully, carefully. "Something that *is* your life, part of who you are. It's like giving up on yourself."

I know how hard I tried to convince myself that my marriage could work, she thought. Even long after I knew it was over. I know how much I was willing to suffer before, finally, giving up on us. Giving up on Mark . . .

Ross and Janet sat in silence for a few moments.

"Does Leslie know?" Ross asked finally.

"Ross, when I left Mark, *he* didn't know. It was just my

444

theory. But," she added, "I think that Leslie does know. Now."

Janet sighed and reached for Ross's hand.

"We are so lucky," Janet said.

Ross pulled her close to him and stroked her silky hair.

"So lucky," she repeated as she curled against him. "Until the new owner decides to stop renting the cottage!"

"He'll probably never decide that," Ross said. "This place is too small anyway."

"Do you think so?" she teased, feigning surprise. Ross complained almost daily about the tiny cottage. He needed floor space to spread his scripts; he needed his piano; he needed his stereo system. "Maybe someday we could buy a bigger place in the country."

"Buy a place together?" he asked.

"Yes," she said softly, realizing what she had just told him.

"Would you do that with someone if you weren't married to him?"

"No," she whispered, her cheeks flushed, her eyes glistening. It was what she wanted. It didn't scare her. It made her happy. If only he wanted it, too.

"Janet?" he asked carefully.

"What?" she asked, smiling, radiant.

"Will you marry me?"

"Yes," she breathed. "Yes, of course."

"Really?"

"Really."

"I love you."

"I love you."

Then Ross began to laugh.

"Ross!" she exclaimed, then started giggling. "Why are we laughing?"

"Because, in your—*our*—musicals at this point you sing a lovely song and wander off to bed with whomever."

"That sounds wonderful, as long as whomever is *you*."

"But we have something much more important to do,"

445

he said very seriously.

"We do? What?"

"We have to move. Into a bigger house with a bigger bedroom. Right now. Come on," he said, pushing her gently off his lap.

"Where?" she asked. Was it possible?

"Just a mile down the road."

"Ross. Really? *You* bought—" she stopped, unable to speak, tears filling her eyes.

"I did. It cost a pretty penny, too. And since the prettiest of my pennies are paying the salary of one beautiful, talented—"

"Are you marrying me for my money?" Janet asked with innocent, glistening, gray eyes.

"You bet. For your half of the mortgage."

" 'For your half of the mortgage.' What a wonderful title for a love song," she said dreamily as she followed him toward the door. "The house is furnished?"

Ross stopped, spun around and shook his head, smiling sheepishly.

"Maybe we should move in tomorrow, then," Janet teased gently, lovingly.

"Promise?"

"I promise."

"Let's go back to the traditional wandering off to bed with whomever, then," he said, taking her with him.

"To the tiniest bedroom in the world? With the man I love?" she asked seriously, kissing his lips hungrily.

"I love you, Janet."

Two hours after Mark left San Francisco General Hospital to return to Atherton, Leslie was paged to the pediatric intensive care unit.

"Hi, Leslie, this is Bruce Franklin. We just had a seven-year-old boy admitted with profound hypoglycemia and coma. It will probably turn out to be Reye Syndrome, but

446

there are some atypical features. Do you have time to stop by? We could use your input."

"Sure. I'm a long way away from my last pediatrics rotation—"

"I know, but this may be an adult illness appearing in a child. We could really use your opinion."

"I'll be right there."

The boy lay motionless in the bed. He could have been asleep. His eyes were closed, but his long dark lashes didn't flutter. He wasn't asleep. He was in a coma, his breathing supported by a mechanical ventilator, his blood pressure maintained by medications that dripped in carefully measured, carefully timed drops into his tiny blue veins.

"It could be Reye Syndrome, Les, except that he was apparently completely well until today. No antecedent illness at all. And his liver enzymes are normal. His mother tried to wake him from a nap this afternoon, but he didn't wake up. His serum glucose was twelve. His spinal tap, except for the low sugar, is normal."

Leslie approached the boy, closely examining his face. Then, lifting the covers, she examined his small body. The pediatricians watched in silence, witnessing her blue eyes change from professional, thoughtful concern to horror.

"He wasn't well yesterday, Bruce," she said flatly. "He's cachectic. He has no fat and very little muscle mass. He's severely malnourished, don't you think? He *must* have a chronic illness."

"We agree, Leslie," Bruce said carefully. "He doesn't look like a healthy little boy, but his mother says he was outside playing, as usual, yesterday."

"Is she reliable?"

"Seems very concerned. Anything else?"

"Well, he has abrasions on his wrists and ankles," she said. As she spoke, Leslie lifted his frail, thin arms to look at the abrasions on both wrists. Without realizing the implication of what she was doing, she crossed the

447

wrists, laying one on top of the other. The abrasions, abrasions that could have been caused by rubbing, met at the point where the bones of the forearms crossed each other. Leslie put the arms down quickly and looked at the ankles. The pattern of the abrasions was the same, caused by rubbing at the point where the bones crossed.

"Oh my God, Bruce," she whispered.

Bruce nodded.

"He was tied up, wasn't he?" Leslie asked in horror, realizing that Bruce and the others suspected it, too. She was their independent observer, their second opinion. "And starved—"

"And murdered," one of the residents said.

"Can't you save him?" Leslie asked.

"We're trying, Leslie. He's on maximal pressors and his pressure is still low. He has renal failure. He probably has hepatic failure, even though his enzymes are normal. He just doesn't have any viable hepatocytes left. We're giving him everything we've got," Bruce said, the emotion now evident in his voice.

"Do you think it's the mother?" Leslie asked, incredulous. Child abuse was a disease the pediatricians saw. Internists saw the ravages of self-abuse—drugs, tobacco, alcohol, obesity—but they rarely saw innocent victims. How could it be this little boy's mother?

"It almost has to be. When the medics arrived, he was in a bed looking like a child taking a nap, and she's the one who insists that he was outside playing yesterday. We know that can't be true."

"The father?"

"Apparently they're divorced. She has custody and a boyfriend who also seems very concerned."

"So what do you do?"

"We try to save his life. And we call the police. They may want to talk to you, Leslie."

"That's fine. Bruce, have you ever seen anything like this before?"

"We see it a lot, Leslie."

As Leslie drove to Eric's penthouse in Pacific Heights at four-thirty the next afternoon, she thought about what had happened. She was interviewed by the police. She saw the mother and her boyfriend, well-dressed, well-groomed, in tears as the police interviewed them. She watched the little boy die despite heroic resuscitative efforts. She thought about what Mark had said, about spending your life dealing with sadness and death and tragedy, about being consumed by it.

She was consumed by the horror of what she had witnessed last night. She had spent the night trying to understand how a human being could do that to another human being, how a *mother* could do that to her child. It was impossible for her to imagine, but it was real. The memory, the feeling in her stomach and her heart, would never leave her.

"You look exhausted, darling," Eric said, holding his arms out to her as she entered the penthouse.

Usually, despite her fatigue, Leslie was able to smile for Eric, to feel the rush of excitement at being with him again, but today there was no joy as she fell into his arms. Today she felt relief to be with him, to feel his warmth, his love, but she felt no joy.

The abused little boy was still with her. Her heart was full of him.

Leslie began to cry, silently, burying her head against Eric's chest.

"Leslie? What's wrong?"

She shook her head.

"Tell me, darling," he said warily, kissing the top of her head, catching strands of chestnut hair in his mouth.

Leslie hesitated. She knew that Eric didn't like to hear about her patients. They never discussed it, but he always seemed a little distant when she told him specific details

449

about a patient. It didn't matter if the story was sad or happy. He was always polite; but he didn't ask questions, and he didn't seem interested. He always changed the subject as soon as possible.

It was something they needed to discuss sometime when they were both rested. In Hawaii, Leslie had already decided. She needed to know why Eric didn't want to hear about her work. It wasn't a small issue. Medicine was a part of her life, part of her. What if someday something so horrible happened that she needed to talk to him? Needed his support?

And now it had happened. She needed to tell him—to tell *someone*—and he was the man she loved. She was too tired and too upset to discuss the *issue* first.

"I have to tell you, Eric," she said, almost apologetically. She heard the apprehension in his voice. And the love.

"Tell me."

"Last night they admitted a little boy to the pediatric intensive care unit. At first they thought he had what's called Reye Syndrome—" Leslie stopped abruptly. Eric's body stiffened, and he lifted his lips away from her head. "Eric?"

"I'm listening," he said hoarsely, pulling away from her. "I made some coffee, shall I get you some?"

"No, I just need to go to sleep," she said, following him into the gourmet kitchen with the view of the Presidio. "Anyway, they thought he had what's called Reye Syndrome. It usually follows chicken pox or—"

"I know what it is," he said flatly.

"You do?"

"Yes. But that isn't what he had, right?" he added quickly. "He was a victim of child abuse. It was in this morning's newspaper."

"The media doesn't miss a trick," she said idly, remembering that there had been reporters. Fortunately, she hadn't been who they wanted this time.

450

"No. It must have been awful, Leslie," Eric said. His voice sounded stilted, uneasy. "Why don't you take a shower and a nap?"

Why won't you talk to me, Eric? I don't want to tell you the facts. I want to tell you how I feel. Why can't you let me? she wondered.

It would have made her angry, except that she saw a look of pain, almost of fear, in his eyes.

He wants to help me, but he can't, she thought. For some reason he can't.

Tears spilled out her blue eyes. Eric came to her quickly, put his arms around her and kissed her wet eyes.

"Leslie, I'm sorry. Don't be sad. I love you so much."

"I love you, too, Eric." *I do love you. But we need to talk about this. Sometime. Some other time.*

Chapter Thirty-five

Eric met her at eight-thirty in the morning at the main entrance of the Veteran's Administration Hospital. Their non-stop flight to Maui was scheduled to leave at ten. Eric had decided against taking the corporate jet since they were all traveling at different times. Charlie and James were already there. Leslie couldn't leave until now, thirty minutes after her on-call night had ended.

"Good morning," she said, smiling, kissing him lightly on the lips.

"You look ravishing," he said.

Leslie had showered and changed into her travel clothes at the hospital. Her white coat and skirt and last night's colorful blouse were folded neatly in her overnight bag.

"I just look different than every other time you pick me up. No stethoscope, no rumpled white coat, no iodine stains. I also probably look happy. All last night I kept thinking, at the end of this tunnel is five days in Hawaii with Eric."

"All last night?" he asked as they drove out of the circular drive toward the coast highway and San Francisco International Airport.

"I'm afraid so," she said. In little bits, since meeting Eric, Leslie had abandoned her practice of staying up all night. If it wasn't busy she would try to sleep. "We were very busy. I was up all night, but I'm not the least bit tired. I'm not going to waste a second of the next five days sleeping!"

"Part of the next five days is for you to rest. You still haven't recovered from your month in the ICU."

"You need to rest, too."

"I plan to be right beside you the whole time."

"That makes it a lot more palatable."

They drove in silence for a while, holding hands.

"Oh, Janet called last night. I'm supposed to be sure that you don't think that she's upset that we're missing her wedding," he grimaced. "I think that was the message."

"Her wedding *and* the opening of *San Francisco*. These are five of the most eventful days of Janet's life," Leslie said thoughtfully, remembering how excited Janet had been when she called to tell Leslie that they had three weeks to plan her wedding. Her parents were coming out from Lincoln for opening night of *San Francisco*. Janet wanted to get married during their visit.

The guest list was small but important: loving friends and family; Janet's parents and Ross's parents; and a few friends like Leslie and Eric. After the ceremony they would all have dinner at the Carlton Club. The next night they would go to opening night of *San Francisco* starring Janet *MacMillan*.

Leslie remembered Janet's excitement. And she remembered her disappointment when Leslie told her that she and Eric would be in Maui.

"You're upset," Eric said.

"No. It's just too bad. I would like to have been there. She's a dear friend. But," Leslie said smiling, "she knows how happy we are for them. I have squandered yet another chance to see the Carlton Club, however."

"Is that a burning desire of yours?"

"No. Just a burning curiosity. My friends keep choosing it as the place to celebrate their weddings."

"Maybe we—" he began, then stopped. Maybe we should get married, he almost said. It would have been so

453

easy to say. It was what he wanted to say. But first, they had to talk. He had to tell her about Bobby. And Charlie. She must learn why it was so hard for him to hear about her patients and how he wasn't sure that he could have another child, that he could risk the pain, again.

They had to rest in Maui. And they had to talk.

"Maybe we?" she asked, curious, her blue eyes sparkling. She knew what he had almost said. And that he was saving that question for another time.

"Maybe we should have dinner there sometime," he said, smiling, not looking at her.

She would marry him now. And he would marry her. Even if they didn't talk about the obstacles they both knew were there, they would go into it blindly because they believed their love could overcome anything.

"Maybe we should!" she answered, laughing. *Take your time, Eric.*

Leslie had one glass of champagne and orange juice—a mimosa—once the plane reached a cruising altitude and slept, curled against Eric, for the remainder of the flight. She awakened, refreshed, as the wheels touched the landing strip of Kahalui Airport on Maui.

"What a warm, lovely fragrance!" she exclaimed as they walked, outside, from the plane to the baggage claim area.

"Welcome to the tropics, darling," he said, squeezing her. "It's a blend of plumeria and coconut and sugar cane."

"I love it."

They drove across the island along the Mokulele Highway toward Wailea. They drove through green fields of sugar cane blown by the warm tropical wind toward the bright blue Pacific, white-capped and sparkling in the distance.

"Who else will be here?" Leslie asked. It was time to learn about Eric's friends. They hadn't even discussed them.

"My two right hands. My attorney, Charlie, and my

architect, James."

My architect, James. The words thundered in Leslie's head.

James. How many architects named James were there in San Francisco? Hundreds. *Hundreds.* Still she didn't have the courage to ask his last name. It *couldn't* be.

"Do they work for you or do they have their own firms?" she asked carefully, her heart pounding.

"Charlie and James are both corporate officers with the company. They don't work for anyone else."

Good. That ruled out James Stevenson of O'Keefe, Tucker and Stevenson. Leslie's heart calmed slightly. Still, James had been working on a project in Hawaii. In *Maui*.

"This isn't a birthday celebration, but it's your birthday. . . ." Leslie began slowly, remembering what Eric had said in August. She needed more information. Even though she might not want it.

"Mine *and* Charlie's. No, we're celebrating the opening of a resort we built. It actually opened last week. We thought it would be good to see if it's really as sensational as advertised, as *we* advertise it."

"It's your resort?" Leslie asked, her uneasiness crescendoing.

"Yes." *Mine. And yours.* "We're almost there."

Three minutes later they reached the entrance. A large sign read: Ocean Palms — An InterLand Resort.

InterLand. Eric's company. James had never mentioned that name. Or Eric's. It couldn't be. It *can't* be.

But as soon as Leslie saw the hotel, the beautiful, real-life creation of the wonderful sketches James had proudly shown her, she knew. She realized vaguely, as her mind reeled, that Eric was watching her.

"Well?"

"Oh, Eric, it's spectacular," she said truthfully, her heart pounding.

It *was* spectacular. A lush, lovely tropical paradise. The elegant white marble hotel harmonized perfectly, naturally, with the magnificent tropical setting. But that was

455

James's special talent: his ability to translate his love of nature, his reverence for its grace and beauty, into the buildings he created.

Leslie stood in the breathtaking lobby of the hotel, waiting for Eric to register, eager to retreat to their room, wondering how—if—she could tell him. The lobby itself was a colorful fragrant garden of white, yellow and mauve plumeria trees, red and pink antherium and jade-green palms. Priceless oriental rugs lay on the white marble floors. A turquoise-blue waterway filled with red and gold and white koi flowed peacefully through the lobby. Beyond the tall, slender white pillars that supported the huge but seemingly weightless structure, Leslie could see the sapphire-blue ocean.

Leslie noticed the woman because even in the midst of the awesome splendor of James's creation *she* was striking. Her golden blond hair fell, free, to her waist, swaying rhythmically as she walked. She wore a white sun dress, cool, elegant against her golden tan. Her huge brown eyes softened as she saw Eric, then widened as Eric moved toward Leslie.

"Eric," she said smoothly, stretching a beautifully manicured hand toward him, smiling awkwardly at Leslie. It *can't* be her, Charlie thought. But those eyes. Those startled blue eyes. Charlie had seen those eyes before.

"Charlie. Hi. Charlie, I'd like you to meet Leslie Adams. Leslie, this is Charlie Winter."

Charlie and Leslie smiled at each other, both uncomfortable, both trying to appear unruffled.

"Hi, Charlie. I guess it's fair to say I had a different image," Leslie said lightly. Too many surprises, she thought, her heart racing.

You're not who, or what, I expected either, Charlie thought. She had been pacing back and forth in the lobby for an hour, waiting for them, preparing herself to meet the woman Eric loved, forming images of what that woman would be like. She had settled on someone young and dependent and naive. Someone, Charlie realized, like

456

she had been once, before she had been forced to become tough and independent.

But that wasn't Leslie Adams. Charlie knew Leslie Adams. She knew *about* Leslie Adams. She knew that Leslie could save the life of a colleague and be outraged that the media wanted to hear about her heroism. Charlie knew that Leslie could make a man like James put his belief in traditional morality on hold because he couldn't resist her.

Charlie knew that she would never like the woman that Eric had chosen to love; but now that woman was Leslie Adams, and Charlie already liked Leslie Adams. She had liked her the instant she saw her blood-stained face on television sixteen months before.

Charlie looked at Leslie. "I had a different image of you, too," she said pleasantly. Then she looked at Eric, frowned and asked, "Where's Robert?"

"He's not coming. It was a last minute decision. He couldn't get away."

"Oh," Charlie said, surprised by her own disappointment. She had been looking forward to seeing him. She hadn't seen him since their trip to the Orient in June. It would have been easier with Robert here. He made everything easier. He would know what to do about Leslie and James.

But Robert wasn't here. It was up to her.

"Eric, may I borrow Leslie for about twenty minutes?" Charlie asked suddenly.

"Now? Charlie, we haven't even gone to the room," Eric said, surprised but pleased that Charlie wasn't planning to ignore Leslie. Eric hadn't been sure how Charlie would react.

"I know. The owner of the pearl shop wants to give each of us, me, Leslie and Lynne . . ." Charlie paused as she watched Leslie drop her eyelids at the mention of Lynne's name. She knows, Charlie thought, but she just found out, too. She continued, "A special black pearl. It's a little mystical. She has to meet each of us, then she'll select the right black pearl. It's really very nice. The pearls are beautiful."

"This is an emergency?" Eric asked amiably.

"A true emergency," Charlie said, nodding solemnly but smiling. I have to talk to her, Charlie thought. A true emergency.

"Do you mind, Leslie?" he asked.

"Of course not!" *It will give me time to find James.*

"Good. I'll bring her to your room when we're through. It may be more than twenty minutes, if we get carried away."

"OK. What are the plans for this evening?" Eric asked. Then he explained to Leslie, "I'm sure that Charlie has something arranged."

"Cocktails and dinners here—at Jacques—at seven. *Birthday* dinner tomorrow at James's and Lynne's condo. Lynne's making a chocolate fudge and macadamia nut birthday cake," Charlie added without joy. When she and Lynne had planned it the day before, it had seemed like such a good idea. It would be a chance for them all to get to know Eric's love. An informal dinner among friends.

Oh my God, Charlie thought.

"It sounds very nice," Eric said, unable to interpret the look in Charlie's eyes. Or the look in Leslie's eyes. Maybe the next twenty minutes would help. Eric squeezed Leslie's hand before letting go and said, "See you soon."

Charlie waited until Eric was out of earshot.

"I assume you'd like to talk to James," she said flatly.

"Yes," Leslie breathed. How do you know? she wondered. "Does he know I'm coming?"

"No. James doesn't know it's you. Eric doesn't know about you and James, does he?"

"No, of course not." *How do you know?*

"Let's go to my suite."

Leslie watched as Charlie dialed the number to James's condo and heard her tell him lightly that she needed to see him about a business matter. Could he come to her suite? Yes. Now.

458

While they waited, Leslie noticed the suite, silently admiring the understated expensive decor: top-quality wicker furniture with pastel cushions, plush mauve, blue and cream area rugs on the white marble floor, silk curtains, eighteenth century French impressionist paintings and crystal vases overflowing with fragrant tropical flowers. The suite was like the entire hotel, a spectacular celebration of the natural beauty of the Hawaiian Islands.

Charlie's suite was cluttered with sundresses, belts and sandals strewn haphazardly in the living room. It looked as if Charlie had been trying to select the perfect outfit and had been wracked with indecision.

But who had Charlie been dressing for? Leslie wondered. For *her*, to make an impression on Eric's new friend? Charlie didn't have to try to make an impression. Her natural radiant beauty was irrepressible and unconcealable.

Or was Charlie trying to impress Eric? Or Robert? Leslie wondered, remembering the flicker of disappointment in Charlie's eyes at the news that Robert hadn't come.

Charlie offered no explanation or apology for the clutter. But, while they waited for James, Charlie wordlessly picked up the dresses and shoes and returned them neatly to the spacious closet in the bedroom.

"A business matter?" James asked, laughing softly as Charlie opened the door.

"No, James," Charlie said, standing aside so that he could see Leslie. "Something much more important."

"Leslie!"

"Hello, James."

"She's here with Eric," Charlie said.

"Oh," James said softly, smiling at her, trying to erase the worry from her troubled blue eyes. Good for you, Leslie, he thought. Good for you and Eric. "That's very nice, for both of you."

"Thank you," Leslie said gratefully.

"I think the three of us think it's wonderful," Charlie said impatiently, "but—"

"Lynne doesn't know your name, or that you're a doctor. She only knows that we knew each other in high school."

"Eric doesn't know that you even existed," she said, quickly explaining. "We haven't talked to each other about who we were involved with before we met."

James resisted looking at Charlie. This must be difficult for her, he thought. Difficult for everyone.

"Then, they don't need to know, right?" Charlie asked. "Lynne doesn't need to know, and Eric doesn't need to know. You can just pretend that you're meeting for the first time this evening."

Charlie only cares about protecting Eric, James thought. As difficult as this is for her, she doesn't want him to be hurt.

Leslie nodded slowly. She didn't want Lynne to know. There was no point, but she wasn't certain that she should hide it from Eric. She would have to think about it. It was her decision. Hers alone.

Three hours later Leslie heard herself being introduced to James. It was as if she were watching someone else.

"Nice to meet you, James," she heard a voice, her voice, say.

"Hello, Lynne."

Lynne. Leslie watched her with interest. She was softer, prettier than Leslie had expected. The hardness of Lynne's life—her troubled childhood, the toughness she was forced to develop in self-defense, the ravages of her years as a flower child, her husband's *affair*—was concealed deeply behind her soft brown eyes and easy smile. Lynne was happy. Just as James was happy.

Lynne raved about the resort, about Maui, about the tropical climate that, magically, made Michael sleep all night in the spite of his afternoon nap.

"I love it here. I'm coming back," Lynne said, smiling at James.

"She's already plotting an adventure for Monica in Maui," James added proudly. "And *insisting* on on-location writing."

"Lynne writes children's books," Charlie explained quickly to Leslie, remembering that Leslie *shouldn't* know about the Monica books. "And James illustrates them."

"How wonderful," Leslie said, looking at Lynne, wondering how deep beneath the surface the toughness lay. How would Lynne behave if she knew who Leslie really was?

During dinner Leslie sat very close to Eric. They touched only occasionally and then only briefly: a gentle squeeze of hands, a finger on a cheek. But they looked at each other often—loving, intimate glances—and smiled.

The topics of dinner conversation were neutral, orchestrated by Charlie. They talked about the resort, the wonderful gourmet food they were eating, books, movies and theater. They talked about Union Square Theater's production of *Peter Pan*. They had all seen it, which meant that James had seen it twice. Once, on opening night, with Leslie. And once again with his pregnant wife.

They talked about everything but Leslie for almost the entire meal, but just as dessert was being served, Lynne eyed Leslie for a long moment and said, "There is something so familiar about you, Leslie. Your name and what you look like. I know I've seen you before."

Leslie shook her head slowly. *No Lynne, you don't know me. You just know about me. I'm the one who almost ruined your marriage.*

"You were on television once, weren't you, Leslie?" Charlie asked, as if she had just realized it herself. "You saved another doctor's life."

Leslie smiled gratefully at Charlie.

"That's right," Lynne said, nodding. "When was that?"

Charlie cast a meaningful glance at Leslie. *You have to*

answer that, Leslie. Before James does.

"A year ago August," Leslie said quietly.

"I think I saw it after that," Lynne said. "As part of a documentary on photojournalism. It *was* dramatic. Did you see it, James?"

"Yes," James said, looking at Leslie. "I guess I did. Did you, Eric?"

"No," Eric said with finality. He gently touched Leslie's hand—the hand with the ugly puckered scar—sensing that the discussion made her uncomfortable. He asked lightly, rescuing her, "So, how is the caramel custard?"

Their words forced Leslie to remember that horrible night in August sixteen months before. How it—those few moments of terror and its aftermath—had changed her life!

That night she had reached into the bleeding, dying chest of the man she believed she loved. *Dear* Mark.

Then the vivid photographs of her blood-stained face had reunited her with a boy she had loved, and he became the man that she loved as much, more, than the boy. *Dearer* James.

Now Leslie wished that none of it had happened. Now she was—because she hadn't yet had time to think about it—concealing the significance of that night from the man who mattered the very most. *Dearest* Eric.

She hadn't had time to think about it.

But it didn't feel right.

Later that night, Lynne said to James, "Eric and Leslie seem very much in love, don't they?"

"We're very much in love."

"I know. And so are they. But," Lynne said, narrowing her eyes, "something was wrong. Everyone seemed a little tense. When I'm the most vivacious person at a dinner party, something's wrong."

"You were great."

"I really dredged up my best coffee-tea-or-milk flight

462

attendant manners, didn't I? I felt foolish, but I kept thinking there might be awkward silences. I wonder why."

"I told you about Eric and Charlie," James offered quickly.

"Maybe that's it. Maybe Leslie knows about Eric and Charlie. It was *Leslie* who seemed the most tense. Like she was hiding something."

You don't miss a trick, James thought. Please don't figure this out, Lynne.

"I'd better set the alarm," James said.

"You three are unbelievable. Is it really necessary to look at the property at seven in the morning?"

"Eric promised no business this trip," James said mildly, thinking about his friend. "Which means, business early in the morning only, so the rest of the day is free."

Eric kissed her as soon as they returned to their suite.

"That's too many hours to go without kissing you," he said.

"The price of socializing," Leslie said, kissing him eagerly, grateful to have his arms around her. "I guess we're not the public display of affection types."

"I never have been."

"No," Leslie said thoughtfully. Or was it because of James? Because he was sitting beside her, too? No, she decided. Then she added, truthfully, "Neither have I."

"Are you all right? You were awfully quiet," Eric said, frowning slightly, remembering the evening, troubled by it.

"I'm fine. Overwhelmed. Tired," she said. Then she added, almost as an afterthought, "I like your friends."

"Do you?"

"Yes. Very much." *One of them I have liked too much.*

Leslie lay awake long after Eric fell asleep, thinking, agonizing, weighing the impact of the truth against the discomfort she felt at the subterfuge and Eric's eventual reaction when, if, he ever found out.

463

I have to tell him, Leslie decided finally. I cannot hide this from Eric. Our relationship — our trust — is too important. I will tell him in the morning. As soon as he returns.

"Happy Birthday, darling," Leslie whispered to Eric's back. He was dressing quietly, trying not to wake her. It was six-thirty.

"Good morning," he said, sitting on the bed beside her, kissing her.

"I can't believe you're doing this."

"That comment brought to me by the lady who is on call as often as every other night?"

"You're right. It's your job," she said smiling sleepily. "I guess. But you *are* the boss."

"Tomorrow we sleep until noon."

"I may do that today. Or, at least, until you get back."

"It shouldn't be too long. We just need to decide if we want to purchase more land down the road for additional condos."

"Maybe you'll come back to bed?"

"Count on it."

"So what the hell is going on?" Eric demanded as soon as Charlie and James were in the car.

"What do you mean?"

"For months you've been teasing me for information about Leslie, counting the days until the unveiling, and now, nothing. Even if you didn't like her, you would have pretended to. You would have told me how much you like her. But neither of you has said a word about her."

"We like her very much, Eric. She's beautiful and smart. She's wonderful," Charlie said unconvincingly, looking anxiously at James. *Don't tell him.*

"At dinner last night," Eric continued, his anger beginning to surface, "no one asked her any of the usual questions. Where are you from, Leslie? How do you like being

464

a doctor, Leslie? How did you meet Eric, Leslie?"

"I have to tell him, Charlie," James said with a sigh.

"Tell me what?"

James took a deep breath. "Leslie and I have known each other for a long time. Since high school."

"James 1971," Eric said with sudden comprehension. "So you were lovers in high school?"

"No. More recently than that," James said, then stopped.

Eric frowned, then said slowly, "It was her number you gave me a year ago, wasn't it?" That's why the prefix seemed vaguely familiar.

James nodded.

"When did it end?" Eric asked.

"Last December."

"Because Lynne was pregnant," Eric said flatly.

"I didn't know Lynne was pregnant. It ended because it had to end."

James waited. Charlie waited.

"Christ," Eric whispered finally.

They drove in silence for fifteen minutes, finally reaching the land that Eric was considering purchasing. Eric parked the car.

"OK, if we buy this, we can put the resort condo design in this area. But, James, what can you come up with to put over there?" Eric asked as he pointed to the green sloping hillside in the distance.

Eric's voice was unstrained, natural, as if he had never learned that the woman he loved had had an affair with his close, trusted friend.

Chapter Thirty-six

Eric returned to the suite at ten. Leslie held her arms out to him, inviting him to join her in bed. Eric stood across the bedroom. He didn't move toward her. Leslie let her arms fall to her sides and sat upright in bed.

"Eric?"

"I know about you and James."

"It was over long before we met."

"I know. It still—" Eric stopped. Still what? he wondered. He needed time to think about it. He needed to understand why it bothered him so much. "I'm going to go for a swim."

Leslie watched silently, helplessly, as he changed into his swim suit and left the suite.

She watched him from the balcony. She had no idea he was such a strong swimmer. Eric swam out into the ocean, against the waves, against the current. He swam as fast as he could, as hard as he could.

Leslie had done that once, years before, the day she had been accepted to Radcliffe. She had swum as hard and as fast as she could, hoping to clear her mind as she forced her way through the cold waters of Sparrow Lake. And that day, when she returned to the shore, exhausted, he was waiting for her with a bemused look in his green cougar eyes.

James.

Eric. Come back to me, Eric. Don't let this hurt us. It isn't about us.

Leslie watched him swim for a while, as he tried to purge himself of the secret—her secret—that troubled him so much. Finally it was too painful to watch.

Leslie decided to shower and dress. She would wear the sundress she had bought especially because she knew how much Eric would like it. The dress was blue and white and feminine. The blue matched her eyes.

Maybe she would be on the beach, waiting for him, when he returned to shore. Like James had been waiting on the beach for her once.

Eric swam with his eyes open, even though the salt water burned. When he closed his eyes, he saw images: Leslie laughing with James, Leslie kissing James, Leslie in bed with James, Leslie loving James, Leslie *wanting* James.

With his eyes open, he could force himself to think.

You have been with many women, Eric, he told himself. You have laughed with them, kissed them, made love to them and wanted them. They all came before you knew Leslie, before you knew there would, could, be a Leslie for you in your life.

How would Leslie feel if she met any one of them?

How would Leslie feel if she knew about the one that mattered most? How would she feel if she knew about Charlie?

She would feel awful, he decided. Just as he felt awful knowing about James. Even though James was his friend. *Especially* because James was his friend. Because he could imagine Leslie and James together, knowing each other, caring about each other, loving each other.

I will never tell her about Charlie, he resolved. I won't do this to her. Somehow I will tell her what she needs to know—about Bobby—without telling her about Charlie.

Eric swam until he was exhausted, too tired to think anymore. Then he just wanted to be with Leslie. He wanted to make the images of Leslie with James go away.

Eric looked toward the shore, amazed and worried by the distance. He had swum straight out to sea, hard and fast. He was already exhausted. Already chilled. The tropical waters lost their warmth as they deepened, as the turquoise-blue water that caressed the white sand beach became blue-black. Deep. Ominous. Cold. All he wanted was to be with Leslie.

James closed the heavy bedroom curtains. Lynne looked at him with surprise.

"I thought we could take a nap while Michael is napping," he said.

"A nap?"

"No," he said, sliding his hand under the halter top that she wore, pulling her against him.

"No," she repeated, reaching for the button of his shorts, finding his lips with hers.

"Tell me about the fantasies of a new mother," he whispered as he kissed her. He removed her top, revealing her breasts, still large from her recent pregnancy and full because she was nursing Michael. James began to kiss her breasts, slowly circling her nipples with his tongue.

He kissed her nipples. Then gently, carefully he began to suck.

"James," she whispered, breathlessly. *I don't need to tell you my fantasies. You already know them.*

"Leslie?"

"Hi," she breathed, startled, her heart pounding. She was still in the shower. She waited.

"May I join you? I'm cold and salty," he said.

"Yes. I'm warm and clean."

Leslie opened the shower door and extended her arms

to him. They held each other tight for a long moment, immersed in the warmth and steam of the shower. Then they kissed, a deep, tender, needful kiss.

"You are salty," Leslie whispered softly, her lips touching his.

"And you are squeaky clean."

"Not really," she said. She could always defend, at least to herself, a relationship with a man she cared about. It was harder to defend an affair with a married man, even to herself, even with James. She had wondered, as she waited for Eric to return, how much that bothered him. What if it made him think less of her?

"Oh, Leslie," he said, holding her close. "I thought I was a rational man. I *was* until I met you."

"It doesn't have anything to do with us."

"I know that, rationally. But—"

"But what?"

"When I think of the two of you, together, I don't feel rational. I just *feel*."

"I've never been with anyone the way I've been with you. I've never felt the way I feel with you. I torment myself with images, too."

"Of?"

"Of you and all the unknown women. I wouldn't want to know any of them."

You won't, Eric thought. Not if I can help it.

"You know what I want to do today?" he asked.

"What?" she asked. Go back to San Francisco? Maybe they could go to Janet and Ross's wedding after all.

"Pull the curtains, get room service to bring us some supplies—"

"And hide out in our room?"

"Preferably under the covers."

"All day and all night?" Leslie asked enthusiastically.

"Well, no. We are committed for cocktails and dinner at, uh, James's and Lynne's at six."

"That's right, I'd forgotten. Your birthday dinner," Leslie said slowly. Happy Birthday, Eric. Then she added

469

brightly, trying to cheer them both, "And to see Michael."

As she spoke Leslie watched Eric's eyes. At the mention of Michael's name, they clouded for a moment. Why? she wondered. It was on the list of whys that she had planned to talk to him about during their five carefree days in Hawaii. But not now. Not this trip.

"So we spend from now until then making memories that will erase all other images once and for all?" she asked, kissing his lips hungrily.

"That's exactly what we do," Eric said as he returned her kiss, deeply, passionately.

Charlie pulled the curtains in the bedroom of her suite, darkening the room against the midday Maui sun. It would be easier to talk to him in the dark. Besides, it was already evening where he was, in Philadelphia.

Why am I calling him? she wondered as she dialed the number that was written in her address book, his home phone number, a number she had never used. I just am, she decided. For no reason.

"Robert? It's Charlie."

"Charlie! Is everything all right?"

"Everyone's all right, Robert. Every*thing* is a mess."

"It is hard for you, seeing them together?"

"Why didn't you come?" she asked, not answering his question.

Because I don't want to be your father, or your guardian, anymore. You have to get over my son on your own. Then . . .

"Did you want me to come?"

"Of course, Robert," Charlie said. "I thought you wanted to meet her."

"Meet Leslie?"

"Oh! *Have* you met her?"

"No. But I'm joining Eric and Leslie in Seattle — where her parents live — for Christmas."

"Oh," Charlie said. Christmas. Without Eric or Robert.

For the past ten years she had spent every Christmas with Eric. Sometimes she spent it with both of them. Time to grow up, Charlotte D. Winter. The fantasy is over. "Did you know she's a doctor, Robert? Eric met her when he cut his hand last June."

"I didn't know that," he said, the concern in his voice obvious despite the six thousand miles that separated them. "Has he told her?"

"About Bobby? I don't think so. He hasn't told her about me. And I don't think he will."

Charlie told Robert about James and Leslie, and how Eric's reaction—a reaction she sensed despite his outward control—made her wonder if Eric would tell Leslie about her. Or Victoria. Or Bobby.

"He has to tell her about Bobby," Robert said. Then he added softly, "And he should tell her about you."

"I don't think he will ever tell her about either of us."

"He *has* to tell her about Bobby," Robert repeated.

Robert and Charlie talked for three hours. After a few initial moments of awkwardness, their conversation assumed the easy, free-form style of their ten days in the Orient.

"What are you doing for Christmas?" Robert asked, just before he hung up.

"I haven't made any plans yet," she said.

"We'll only be in Seattle for a few days. Leslie has to get back to work, er, the hospital, I guess. I thought about going home by way of San Francisco."

"Oh," Charlie said. She waited, her stomach fluttering.

"Actually, I thought about spending the week between Christmas and New Year's at the Pebble Beach Lodge in Carmel. Going for brisk blustery walks on the beach, warming up with cappucino in front of the fire, reading a few good books."

"Sounds wonderful," she said carefully.

"So, will you join me? I've reserved a two bedroom suite. I thought Eric and Leslie might be coming down, but they won't be. I can probably get the management to

471

find a room for you."

"The suite is fine, Robert."

They walked at sunset from the hotel to James's condominium. The white rock path that ran beside the ocean was lined on one side with fragrant colorful hedges of plumeria, hibiscus and bougainvillea and on the other by white sand and azure sea. The sky glowed pink and gold. The huge, white fleecy clouds turned pink then red then black as the tropical sun fell below the horizon. A warm breeze caressed them gently as they strolled, hands together, fingers entwined.

They were whole again, one again. They had spent the afternoon cloistered, talking, understanding, loving. Nothing, no one could separate them. Nothing could threaten the security and confidence of their love.

Still, as they approached James's condominium, Leslie's heart began to pound, a restless, anxious, uneasy presence in her chest. Don't let this evening upset Eric, she thought. It would be so senseless. I love him with all my heart. Him alone. More than anyone. Ever.

"If we could just hold hands like this—" she began.

"All evening?" he asked.

Leslie nodded. "Is that too much of a public display?"

"I don't think so, do you?"

"No."

"Then I won't let go of you for anything." *Ever.*

But Eric did let go, once, early in the evening.

"Let's go see Michael. He's in the kitchen with Lynne," Leslie said, pulling his hand gently, meeting unexpected resistance, then release.

"You go. I want to talk to . . ." Eric began lamely.

Talk to who, Eric? *James?* No, of course not, Leslie thought. He just doesn't want to see Michael. Or is it Lynne? Why not, Eric?

Michael was a beautiful, smiling, happy baby with rosy cheeks and white blond hair and clear green eyes.

"He has James's eyes," Leslie said softly.

Lynne looked at her with surprise.

"Doesn't he? Doesn't James have green eyes?" Leslie added quickly, innocently, her heart racing, uncomfortable with the deception. . . .

But *this* deception—with Lynne—is necessary, she told herself firmly. If we are all going to be friends for the rest of our lives.

"Would you mind taking him to his daddy, Leslie?" Lynne asked, smiling lovingly at her lively, animated son. "He's not a big help in the kitchen."

"I'd love to. Then I'll be back to help you."

"Oh. Thanks, but don't bother. Without the distraction of Michael I'll be through here in no time."

Leslie carried Michael into the living room, his velvet-smooth, white dimpled arms clinging to her chest, his green eyes sparkling, curious.

"Look who I have," Leslie said as she joined Eric with James. They were discussing the condominium and the changes that James wanted to make in the new ones.

Michael began to wriggle with delight when he saw James. Leslie started to hand Michael to Eric to give him the wonderful pleasure of holding the happy, lovely child, but then she saw Eric's eyes. The pale blue had become dark, opaque and troubled.

He doesn't want to hold Michael, she realized. Why not?

As Leslie handed Michael to his daddy, she saw the limitless joy and pride in James's eyes. And the inexplicable pain in Eric's.

Leslie took Eric's hand. She would not let go again.

Chapter Thirty-seven

"Shall we go for a walk?"

"During half-time?" Charlie teased lightly.

"Charlie, my dear," Robert said soberly. "We're late in the fourth quarter. Even a miracle won't save them now. I'm afraid the national championship has already been decided."

"And the bad guys won?"

"The bad guys won."

"Then, let's go for a walk."

Charlie loved their walks along the cliff-edges of the Pebble Beach golf course, down the steep trails — when he held her hand to guide her — to the white sand dunes, blown by the crisp, invigorating, salty sea breeze.

Charlie loved their long walks on the beautiful beach, but, then, Charlie loved everything about the past six days with Robert. They talked, they laughed and they drank cappucino and hot chocolate and scotch in front of the pine-scented fire in their suite. They browsed in the quaint shops in Carmel and watched the sea otters frolic off Point Lobos. They had the famous Ramos Fizz brunch at the Highlands Inn and dined on abalone steak near Cannery Row. They drove along the Seventeen Mile Drive and south, along winding roads that hugged the rugged coastline, toward Big Sur. They watched the low, pale winter sun set from the porch at Nepenthe. And they watched it rise from Monterey Bay.

Six perfect days.

Tomorrow it would be over.

"It's pretty windy," Robert observed as he opened the door.

"In that case let me do something with my hair," Charlie said. "I've spent too much time untangling it this week. I'm going to braid it. It will only take a minute."

"Braid it?" Robert asked. "I haven't braided anything since—"

"Your boy scout days?"

"The war," Robert said calmly, remembering. It had been something to do during the long hours in camp or in the bunkers. They braided grass or string or strips of leather. It kept their hands busy, a welcome, if small, release for their anxious energy. Something to do other than simply wait. Or think.

"So?" she asked, turning her back to him, showing him the golden mane of pure silk that fell to her waist.

Robert's strong hands became gentle as he carefully divided the silk into three strands, his fingers brushing lightly against her temples and her neck. Unsummoned, surprising sensations—pleasurable and frightening— pulsed through her body again and again as his fingers touched her as he gently wove the gold into a long, thick rope down her back.

"How do I fasten it?" he asked, holding the loose end.

"Here," she said weakly, willing her hands not to tremble as she handed him a barrette.

"OK," he said as he closed the barrette over her hair. Then he touched her shoulders, turning her to face him. He studied the new hair style and said, "I like it this way."

I like it all ways, he thought.

Why did I feel that way when you touched me, Robert? she wondered.

That evening they sat in front of the marble fireplace in

475

the suite warmed by the roaring red-orange flames.

"Did you make a New Year's wish, Charlie?" Robert asked.

"A wish? Not a resolution?"

"Resolutions are just stepping stones to wishes. Just ways to make things the way you wish they would be. I prefer pure, undisguised wishes."

Charlie smiled. How like Robert. Robert believed that all things were possible. He made things possible. Robert was the most shrewd, powerful and sophisticated man that Charlie had ever known.

And, still, Robert made wishes.

"What do you wish, Charlie?" he pressed.

"I wish," she began slowly. I don't make wishes, she thought. Wishes are too close to fantasies. My mother believed in wishes and fantasies. I don't.

"You wish," Robert urged.

Charlie sighed. *If* I allowed myself a wish, what would it be? For a long moment she was silent. When she spoke, finally, the slow, careful words came from her heart, not her mind.

"I wish," she said simply, "that I knew where I belong."

"What does that mean?" he asked gently, knowing what it meant.

"It means," she began slowly. "It means that I didn't know I was where I belonged—with my mother—until after she died. And I didn't believe that I belonged with Eric until it was too late. Then he belonged with Victoria. And now—"

"Now he belongs with Leslie," Robert said firmly, watching the brown eyes under the golden hair.

"He does, doesn't he?" Charlie asked, realizing then that she hadn't even asked Robert about Christmas in Seattle with Eric and Leslie and Leslie's parents.

"Yes." Robert said. "He does. Does it bother you?"

"No," Charlie answered truthfully. "It did at first. I felt adrift. Again. Maybe I still do, given my wish, but I'm doing all right."

"I know you are. You always do," he said, gazing thoughtfully at the beautiful woman who was forced to be her own island, forced to be strong, forced to take care of herself. Even as a little girl she was alone, independent. No one had ever taken care of her. Not even the people who loved her. Not Mary. Or Eric. Or . . .

None of them had underestimated her strength, but they had all underestimated her needs.

"I'm just a survivor, I guess," Charlie admitted a little wistfully.

Just, Robert mused. Your life should be more than just survival.

They left Carmel early the following morning. Robert's direct flight to Philadelphia was scheduled to leave from San Francisco International Airport at ten.

"Are you all right?" Robert asked, breaking a silence that had lasted for twenty miles, from Santa Cruz to Santa Clara.

"Yes," she answered quickly, startled. "Why?"

"You're driving about twenty miles an hour below the speed limit."

"Am I?" Charlie asked, glancing at the speedometer. Robert was right. Charlie depressed the accelerator, shrugged and added sheepishly, "I guess it's the vehicular equivalent of dragging my heels."

"Why?"

"This has been so nice."

"It's been wonderful," Robert said and paused, watching her reaction to his words. He couldn't tell. Then he asked, "You don't mind going back to work, do you?"

"No. Not really. No." *I just don't want you to leave.*

"Sounds a little unconvincing, counselor. I thought you liked your job." Was it just because of Eric? Or was there more to Charlie's uncertainty? *Talk to me, Charlie.*

"It's a good job." *But it's not where I belong. Not anymore. Where do I belong?*

They drove in silence for five minutes. Charlie needed to constantly remind herself to maintain the car's speed. Her inclination was to let it slow down. She had to fight it.

"I wonder if you could pass the Pennsylvania Bar," Robert said mildly. A comment, not a question. Charlie didn't have to answer.

"The Pennsylvania Bar? Of course I could!" she exclaimed confidently. *"Why?"*

"Because any time you get disenchanted with this job, you're welcome to join me," Robert said, taking care to sound casual. Casual but sincere. He added, "Any time."

Charlie didn't answer. She just gnawed thoughtfully at her lower lip as they approached the airport.

The departing passenger area was tangled with cars and buses and taxis filled with holiday travelers returning home. Charlie stopped the car in front of the United terminal. Without warning, her eyes filled with tears.

"Charlie?" Robert asked, gazing at her sad, wet brown eyes, touching her chin gently with his finger.

"I don't want you to go."

"You don't?" he murmured softly, moving beside her, kissing her damp eyes, her flushed cheeks and, finally, her warm full lips.

It wasn't the kiss of a father. Or a guardian. Or even a dear friend.

It was the deep, probing, passionate kiss of a man who wanted her. A man who had wanted her for a very long time.

"I don't have to leave now, Charlie. Not this minute. Why don't we go somewhere?" Robert whispered, suddenly aware of the crush of cars and humanity that surrounded them. They had no privacy, and they needed privacy.

Trembling, her heart racing, Charlie shifted the car into gear. She wove through the traffic with difficulty, trying to concentrate on driving but wholly distracted by Robert's presence and the memory of his kiss. And by her reaction, by how much she wanted him.

Miraculously, Charlie negotiated the airport traffic in the departure area. As she drove away from the main terminal, she began to shake deep inside. What was she doing? What were *they* doing? Where was she taking them? She knew with certainty that she couldn't drive all the way into the city to her apartment. It was much too far.

Without making a conscious decision, Charlie turned into the driveway of a motel. They were still on the airport grounds. She parked the car near the motel lobby.

She smiled weakly at Robert, her eyes obscured by a curtain of gold that fell across her face as she bent her head. She would wait in the car while he registered.

Robert returned five minutes later with a room key. He opened the car door for Charlie and held her hand as they walked to the room. Once inside the room he held her, feeling her tremble at his touch. He held her tighter.

Then he kissed her. Charlie returned his kiss eagerly, hungrily.

Desperately, Robert thought. Sensing her tension, he pulled away and looked into her eyes: beautiful brown eyes, fawn eyes, passionate, sensual eyes, worried eyes.

"Do you want to do this?" he asked quietly. He didn't want to push her. It was too important.

"Yes," she breathed, finding his lips with hers. She began to unbutton her blouse as she kissed him.

"Charlie," he said, placing his strong hands over her trembling fingers, stopping them. "There's no hurry."

"Yes . . ."

"Why?"

"I'm afraid."

"Afraid?" he asked, suddenly concerned. Maybe it was too soon.

"I want this so much. I want it to be all right."

"I want it, too. I've wanted it for a long time. It will be all right. I would never do anything to hurt you. Don't you know that?"

"Robert?"

"Let me love you," he said, pulling her hands to his lips, kissing their ivory softness.

"Love me, Robert," she whispered.

At first, Robert controlled the pace of their lovemaking—a leisurely, sensual exploration—as he controlled her body, discovering desires and feelings that had been suppressed for so long. She responded to his touch instinctively, without thought or inhibition. Her natural sensuality escaped, freed by his careful sensitive fingers and his warm soft mouth. As her desire blossomed and she needed him urgently, he joined her, moving to her rhythm, her pace, meeting her passion with his own.

This is the ultimate closeness, she thought as they lay together, their bodies one. What I always knew—*believed*—it could be. Not a fantasy.

Just a wish come true.

"You wanted this for a long time?" she asked, remembering his words.

"A very long time. I remember a sixteen-year-old girl—"

"No," she whispered.

"No," he said, stroking her spun-gold hair. "But I was enchanted by you even then."

"I was enchanted by you," she said, realizing that it was true, that it had always been true. There had always been something so special about being with Robert, even in the beginning. "You wanted me to be with Eric, didn't you?"

"Of course. I wanted it because it was what you, both of you, wanted. Because it made you both so happy." *In the beginning.*

"And then?" Charlie asked, knowing the answer. And then Eric fell in love with Leslie.

"And then our trip to the Orient."

"You thought about us . . . *this* . . . last June?"

"You're not paying attention," he said gently, kissing her.

"How can I?" she whispered into his mouth, lost for a

moment in the warmth. She wanted to stay there forever, but she wanted to hear what Robert had to say even more. "Tell me."

"I thought about us long before last June, but you and Eric were still trying to make it work."

"Sometimes. If I had known—"

"A father doesn't compete with his son. I wouldn't do anything that could threaten Eric's happiness. And you would not have been receptive. You would never have left Eric."

Maybe not, Charlie thought, wondering what bound her so tenaciously to Eric for all those years. Of course she loved him. She always would. But they would never be in love again. Being with Eric seemed to be where she belonged. Or where she had once belonged. But maybe that was just because she didn't belong anywhere else.

"Why didn't you come to Maui in November?" she asked suddenly. Robert must have chosen to stay away for a reason. Something to do with her . . . *them.*

"You had to make peace with the reality of Eric and Leslie."

"And you didn't want to help me? To be there?" *You didn't want to be my father or my guardian. . . .*

"No," Robert said simply.

"Oh," she said, hungrily kissing his lips because she couldn't resist, because of what he had told her. He wanted to be her lover. Nothing else. Nothing less.

Robert answered Charlie's kiss by making love to her again. It was what she wanted, what her body demanded, what her heart needed. It was what they both wanted and needed, and as they made love again, they told each other of that need, that passion, that consuming desire. . . .

Afterward she lay with her head on his chest. After several silent moments Robert felt the dampness.

"Charlie?" he asked, lifting her head so that he could see her face. And her tears.

"I never cry," she sniffed.

"Until today. These don't look like tears of joy."

"I miss you already. *Again.* I missed you after our trip in June. Last time we said good-bye we didn't see each other for six months."

"You needed those six months," Robert said firmly.

To get over Eric, Charlie thought. To be ready for this. For Robert. Yes, I needed the time. But not anymore.

"It won't be another six months. I thought maybe just six days."

"Six days," Charlie repeated happily.

"There aren't any good transcontinental flights after about mid-afternoon. So, if we plan to work all day Friday, we should meet at some point midway: Dallas, Kansas City, Chicago."

"Chicago," Charlie said. "Or anywhere."

"We'll do Chicago this weekend. We can stay at the Drake and watch the snow fall on Lake Michigan. And, if we leave our room, we can see the Impressionist Exhibit at the Art Institute. OK?"

"Sounds wonderful," she purred. It all sounded wonderful, but the two words that sounded the best, the words that echoed in her brain, were *this weekend*. It meant there would be another weekend. Next weekend. And the next.

Four hours after Charlie's initial attempt to drop Robert off at the airport, they sat again in front of the United terminal.

"I'll call you when I get to Philadelphia," he said.

"It will be two in the morning your time."

"Is eleven too late to call you here?"

"No." *No time is too late. Or too early.*

"I'll call you, then." Robert leaned over to kiss her before he left the car.

"Don't make the mistake of kissing me like you did last time," she whispered, kissing him back. "Or you'll never get home."

"Was that a mistake?"

"You know it wasn't." *It was the best thing that ever happened to me.*

After Robert disappeared through the automatic doors, Charlie drove to her apartment. She was filled with a wonderful sense of peace.

Maybe it's because I finally know where I belong, she thought as warm tears splashed onto her cheeks for the third time that day.

Chapter Thirty-eight

Wednesday, January ninteenth marked the end of a week of unseasonably warm San Francisco weather. Leslie awakened to the sound of rain pounding against her window. The large, wet drops were hurled against the pane by a bitter winter wind. Leslie smiled as she gazed at the gray-black clouds and the rivulets of rain water swirling down the street below.

It reminded Leslie of Seattle. Gray, enveloping, cozy.

Besides, her spirits that rainy morning were pure sun. Eric was returning from New York after a three day — three *night* — business trip. It was their longest separation. And it was too long despite the phone calls. Work permitting, she would be at his penthouse to welcome him home when he arrived at seven.

The cold, mercilessly soggy day resulted in cancellations of the late afternoon appointments in Leslie's internal medicine clinic. Could they possibly reschedule with Dr. Adams next week? her patients wondered. It was so cold, and the roads were so slick. . . .

It meant that Leslie was at Eric's penthouse by dusk. She made herself a mug of hot chocolate and watched the gray mistiness of the day yield to the black emptiness of the winter night. The transition was breathtaking, somber but serene. By five-thirty the ominous darkness of night was dotted with the bright city lights, a galaxy of yellow-white stars in the blackness.

Cozy.

It took Leslie a minute to identify the harsh noise that intruded her silent night. An alarm? No. It was the buzzer for the intercom that connected the penthouse with the security guard in the building's lobby. Leslie had seen Eric use it once when Charlie dropped by with some contracts.

Leslie depressed the black button.

"Yes?" she asked.

"Mrs. Lansdale is here. She says that Mr. Lansdale is expecting her," the guard said.

"Oh. Yes, of course. Please send her up," Leslie said.

Eric's mother was expected *next* month. Was this a surprise visit? From everything that Eric had told Leslie about Florence Lansdale it would be very unlike her to make a surprise visit.

Slightly flustered, her peace suddenly disrupted, Leslie hastily turned on the lights in the dark living room. The room was immaculate as usual. Leslie glanced at the Tiffany clock on the mantel. Five-forty.

I guess I can entertain Eric's mother for an hour and twenty minutes, she thought uneasily. Unless she has already decided not to like me.

Leslie stood by the door and opened it promptly as the doorbell chimed.

"Hello," said the young woman with dark-red hair and inquisitive eyes who extended a ringless hand to Leslie.

"I'm Victoria Lansdale. You must be Leslie."

"Yes," Leslie breathed. *Who is Victoria Lansdale? How does she know about me?* "Come in."

"Eric isn't expecting me until tomorrow. You probably know that. Anyway, when the rains hit Palm Springs this morning, I decided to come a day early. Where is Eric?"

"On his way back from New York. He should be here about seven."

"Oh. Well, this way I get to meet you," Victoria said cheerfully. "Eric said you would be working, uh, on call tomorrow night."

"Yes, Leslie said. *That's right. Who are you?* "Let me take your coat. Would you like something to drink?"

"Thank you. Sure. Are you having something?"

"Hot chocolate," Leslie admitted.

"That sounds perfect. And just about strong enough. I need my wits about me when I see Eric."

Leslie frowned.

"Because I haven't seen him for almost eleven years," Victoria explained, responding to Leslie's perplexed expression.

"Oh, I see," Leslie said slowly as if Victoria's explanation helped. But of course it didn't. Nothing was clarified.

"Not," Victoria continued, her airy voice suddenly somber. "Not since Bobby—"

Victoria stopped abruptly and covered her mouth with her hand. Her eyes widened, then narrowed.

"Oh, my God," she whispered. Her voice was barely audible through her hand. "You don't have any idea who I am, do?"

Leslie shook her head apologetically as she handed Victoria a mug of hot chocolate.

"I'm afraid I don't."

Victoria's calm friendliness vanished, replaced suddenly by agitation and worry. She put the mug on the coffee table and started to move toward the closet to retrieve her coat.

"I'd better leave."

"Victoria, wait! I don't understand."

"Of course you don't. Eric hasn't told you a damned thing."

"Why don't *you* tell me?" Leslie urged uneasily. There was something she need to know. Some hidden knowledge. Would she *want* the knowledge after she had it?

"Oh, no. If Eric hasn't told you yet, it's for a reason. I don't want to make him angry. You know Eric's temper."

Eric's temper? No, I don't know Eric's temper, Leslie

thought. Just like I don't know about you. Or Bobby.

"Victoria. Please. You're here now. He knew you were coming."

"Tomorrow. When you would be working."

"Victoria," Leslie persisted firmly. "Who is Bobby?"

Victoria stared at her, *beyond* her to a distant memory, her eyes sad and thoughtful as she remembered her beloved son. Eric couldn't deny Bobby's memory. He shouldn't deny that Bobby existed.

"You have a right to know," Victoria said finally, shuddering inside. Eric would be furious, but it was her story, too. She had every right to tell Leslie.

Victoria returned slowly to the living room. She sat down on the cream-colored couch, wrapped her fingers around the warm mug of hot chocolate and sighed heavily.

Then, with great effort and emotion, she told Leslie the whole story. Beginning with Charlie and Eric. Victoria knew the details of Charlie's background and of her sometimes joyous, sometimes troubled relationship with Eric. Victoria told Leslie that it was during one of those troubled times that she, Victoria, became pregnant with Eric's child. With tears in her eyes Victoria told Leslie about their wonderful son. And about how they lost him.

As Leslie listened, waves of emotion swept through her: bewilderment, grief, anger. Some of Victoria's words echoed and re-echoed in her head.

Charlie was Eric's fiancée. Charlie loved Eric. Eric loved Charlie. Did they still love each other?

Bobby had Reye Syndrome. Now she knew why Eric had resisted coming to the hospital with his hand laceration. Why he had refused an anesthetic. Why he was reluctant to hear about the details of her work and his eyes filled with pain when she told him about the abused little boy. Why he couldn't hold Michael.

Charlie. Victoria. Bobby. Beloved by Eric. Part of Eric then and part of Eric now. Part of Eric's relationship with Leslie. It explained so much.

And he had never told her.

"I always wondered if Eric and Charlie would get together eventually," Victoria said quietly. "But—"

"Victoria!"

At the sound of his voice, Victoria stopped abruptly and looked up. He stood at the far side of the room.

"Eric," Victoria whispered, recoiling slightly. How long had he been there? Certainly long enough.

Leslie stood up to face Eric. She saw the anger—rage—in his eyes as he glowered at his ex-wife. It was the temper that Victoria knew and that Leslie had never seen.

After a moment, Eric shifted his gaze from Victoria to Leslie. His expression changed. The anger dissolved and was replaced by anxious concern.

"Leslie," he began helplessly. The ice-cold stare in her eyes—a look *he* had never seen—deepened his concern. How much damage had been done?

"I have to go," Leslie said urgently, suddenly feeling claustrophobic. *I have to get out of here. I have to think about what I have learned. I have to try to make sense of it.*

"Leslie, let me explain." Eric followed her to the foyer.

"Victoria already explained. I *appreciate* that she told me. I needed to know, Eric," Leslie said flatly, her voice as cold and lifeless as her eyes.

"Leslie, *we* need to talk about this."

"We *needed* to talk about it a long time ago."

"We need to talk now."

"I can't," Leslie whispered, her voice breaking slightly. *I love you. I hate you. Why did you do this to us? Why didn't you trust us?*

"I'll come over later," Eric suggested hopefully.

"No, Eric. Just leave me alone for a while. *Please.*"

After Leslie left, Eric returned to the living room. He sat heavily on the couch with his head in his hands. He was lost in his own thoughts, his own turmoil. He had forgotten about Victoria. After several minutes, he became aware of her, standing across the room, stiff and erect. She was steeling herself for his fury.

Eric looked at her with surprise, his eyes defeated not enraged.

"Don't blame me for this, Eric," Victoria warned, the strength of her warning undermined by the shakiness of her voice.

"Victoria," he sighed. It was an effort to speak. Impossible to be polite. And he didn't want to argue.

"I have finally, after all these years, convinced myself that I am not to blame for Bobby's death. You blamed me for his birth. And for his death. I believed you when you told me it was my fault. I always believed what you told me," Victoria said, her voice gaining strength. I believed you because you had such power over me, she thought. "But you were wrong to make me feel guilty, to accuse me of killing my own son."

Victoria paused. Her heart pounded with emotion. This was the reason she had decided to see Eric again after all these years. She wanted him to admit that he was wrong. Or did she only want him to forgive her?

As she watched his eyes, the surprise, the pain, the self-recrimination, her own anger subsided. Eric had suffered, too. He was still suffering.

"I never believed that Bobby's death was your fault. Not really," Eric said quietly, remembering the bitter accusations he had hurled at a time when he needed to blame someone. He hadn't meant them. He had no idea that Victoria had suffered even more because of what he had said in a moment of emotion and grief. If he had known, he would have told her. "I had no idea. I'm so sorry."

Victoria frowned. It wasn't what she had expected. There had been no battle. Eric had changed. Sometime in the past eleven years, his rage at the death of his son had abated. She saw sadness in his eyes. And pain. And wisdom. And love. Who had helped him make the transition? Charlie? Leslie?

Leslie, Victoria thought as she saw the sadness in his pale blue eyes.

"And I don't blame you for what happened with Leslie, either," Eric continued with great effort. He sighed heavily. "I have no one to blame but myself."

He stared at the half empty mugs of hot chocolate. How typically Leslie! What he would give to be sitting with her now, drinking hot chocolate, telling her how much he had missed her, holding her. Loving her.

Apparently Mark hadn't heard the telephone ring. He usually heard it, even when he was in his study with the door shut. Kathleen waited a few moments. When he didn't emerge from his study she went to the closed door and tapped lightly. No response. Finally, her heart fluttering inexplicably, she turned the knob and looked in.

"Mark?"

Mark spun around in his swivel desk chair.

"Kathleen! I didn't hear you," he said breathlessly.

"Absorbed in your work as usual," Kathleen said brightly. But she wondered, Why does he act so alarmed? What are those papers on his desk? Is he really trying to prevent me from seeing them? "You didn't hear the phone, either. It's for you. It's the hospital."

"Oh. Could you tell them to hold for another minute? I'll take it in the bedroom," he said.

"Sure." As Kathleen retreated her heart ached. He was obviously waiting for her to leave the room. *Why?*

Ten minutes later Mark appeared in the kitchen.

"It's an angioplasty," he said. "I'll be back in four hours."

The grandfather clock in the living room struck nine as Mark kissed her briefly on the cheek.

"Drive carefully, Mark. It's beginning to snow."

After Mark left, Kathleen sat by the kitchen window of their Beacon Hill home and watched the flakes of snow. They fell silently, gracefully, illuminated briefly by the archaic street lamps before disappearing into the blackness. A fleeting moment of brilliance. Then darkness.

490

Death.

I have to do something, she thought. It was the same thought she had every day. Over and over. But what could she do? She didn't know what was wrong.

She could hope that everything would—miraculously—be better again. That was what had happened after their trip to Atherton in October. It had been so unexpected. So welcome. In those few blissfully happy weeks, they had fallen in love again.

Ross called her during that time, only a week after her desperate phone call to him in October.

"How are you, Katie?" His voice conveyed his concern for his friend.

"I'm fine," Kathleen said buoyantly. "I'm sorry about last week. I was such a goose."

"A *goose?* That's cute British phraseology. Massachusetts is no longer a colony, you know," he teased, already relieved by the lilt in her voice.

"I'm just a little giddy. That's all."

"Things are better with Mark?"

"Wonderful. Starting about five minutes after I spoke with you." As soon as Mark returned from his visit with Leslie, Kathleen thought, pushing the thought away as soon as it surfaced. *Leslie.* "A little touch of hysteria, I guess."

Ross had never known Kathleen to be hysterical. Her despair had been genuine and deep-seated. He was glad that the storm had passed but decided to tell Kathleen what Janet had said anyway.

"Mark doesn't like medicine?" Kathleen's voice registered amazement and disbelief. How could Janet think that? "No Ross, I am sure that Janet is wrong. Mark loves medicine. It's his life."

"If he was torn—ambivalent—it would explain his moodiness, wouldn't it?" Ross pushed. Janet had convinced *him*.

"It could. Except that he's not moody anymore. And he loves medicine!" Kathleen exclaimed. But even as she

491

spoke, a trace of doubt flickered across her mind. What was it? A distant memory ... the look of peace in Mark's eyes when she had told him about her wealth and had teased him about never having to pick up another stethoscope.

"Well. I just thought I would pass it along. Janet thinks that Leslie believes it, too."

Leslie, Kathleen thought. Leslie knows something. Leslie made Mark feel better.

By the end of four weeks, Mark had lapsed back into moodiness. He retreated to his study every evening, closed the door and came to bed long after Kathleen had fallen asleep. Long after Kathleen had cried herself to sleep.

There were brief respites in the moods. Mark would unexpectedly emerge from his preoccupation and discover her again, almost surprised by her presence and her loveliness. His passion would leave her breathless and confused. She wanted to tell him, but in the moments when they *could* talk, when they held each other and loved each other, the words she planned to say sounded foolish. Because, then, there was nothing wrong.

When the bad periods came, as they did more and more often as the weeks passed, she couldn't talk to him because then he didn't hear her.

I have to do something, she thought again as she watched the snowflakes glitter and die. That cold snowy January night Kathleen made a decision.

It was wrong. It was an invasion of his privacy, but she had to know. Maybe it would give her the answer. Quickly, before she lost her courage, Kathleen went to Mark's study.

She looked at the desk in dismay. Mark had straightened it before leaving for the hospital. The top of the carved oak desk was bare. The mysterious papers had vanished. Mark had carefully put them away—hidden them—before he left, so that she wouldn't see them.

I have to do this, she told herself, fighting her own guilt. She closed her eyes and tried to visualize what had been on the desk.

A book. Large. Blue. Kathleen searched the bookshelves. It was on the lower shelf. A textbook of cardiology. Kathleen's fingers trembled as she flipped through the pages of scientific text interspersed with electrocardiographic tracings.

It has to be here, she thought. Whatever it is that Mark is hiding from me.

The twenty sheets of lined paper filled with Mark's meticulous, distinctly non-medical handwriting fell to the floor from the middle of the textbook. The top sheet was a list. The heading at the top of the page was *To Do*. Kathleen scanned the list briefly. The items seemed routine. Some were crossed out.

Kathleen drew a breath when she saw the last item on the list. Not routine. Not an item. A name.

Leslie.

Kathleen quickly turned to the other pages. It was a story.

Kathleen fell weakly into the overstuffed chair in Mark's study and began to read.

Leslie didn't drive straight home. Her apartment wasn't home anyway. Not without Eric. It was only a place to sleep, and she was exhausted but not sleepy. Instead, she drove west toward the ocean, finding her way through the blur of the blinding rain and her own tears. It was a route she knew by heart, the same route she took from Eric's penthouse to the Veterans' Hospital in Lincoln Park. She drove from Broadway to Divisadero to California to Park Presidio to Geary Boulevard and to Point Lobos Avenue. Her winding path brought her finally to the Great Highway and the beach.

Leslie parked her car and walked through the heavy, wet sand to the water's edge. The storm-tossed waves crashed violently at her feet splashing her face with wet salty drops. Huge cold rain drops, propelled by the brisk icy wind, pelted against her. Amidst the chilling dampness of the ocean and the rain. Leslie felt a surprising warmth on her numb cheeks. Tears, she realized. Her own hot tears.

At another time, in a different climate, she would have trudged into the ocean. She would have swum until the turmoil inside her had been purged, thrashed out of her heart and her mind as she thrashed through the pounding waves.

But this was no night for a swim. It was too dangerous, too cold, too sinister. And this problem would not be solved by one swim or a thousand. It could not be so easily purged. It would thrash back at her heart and her mind.

Why didn't he tell me? her mind thundered loudly as if competing with the roar of the waves and the hiss of the wind. Why didn't he make me part of his life? Why did he hide it from me? Why? Why? Why?

The answers didn't come. Just the questions, as cold and relentless and punishing as the winter storm. Finally the numbness of her cheeks and the trembling of her body forced her back to her car. The route to her apartment was familiar: Lincoln to Seventh to Parnassus. But tonight the rain-slick streets were hostile, treacherous. Leslie drove carefully and slowly. There was no hurry. No one was waiting for her.

Two minutes after Leslie entered her pitch-black apartment, the phone rang.

Eric, she thought as she subconsciously counted the rings. If I don't answer it, he will just call back.

Ten rings.

If I never answer he will come over.

Fifteen.

He will worry if I don't answer.

Twenty.

I don't want him to worry.

"Hello?"

"Leslie! It's Kathleen."

"Kathleen." Leslie shifted quickly into a different frame of reference, a different anxiety. Kathleen sounded frightened. It was midnight in Boston. *Mark.* "Kathleen, what's wrong?"

"It's—"

"Has something happened to Mark?" No, please, *no.* Without summoning the memory, Leslie recalled the night she told Kathleen about Mark being shot.

"No. He's all right," Kathleen began. Not really, she thought. I don't know.

It had taken Kathleen an hour to decide to call Leslie. After she read and re-read Mark's story. After she studied the *To Do* list with Leslie's name on it. In the end it wasn't a decision. She had no choice. She needed Leslie's help. She was desperate.

"Oh. Good," Leslie said, relieved only a little. Something was wrong. Something to do with Mark.

Slowly, disjointedly, Kathleen told Leslie about the story and the list. It was clear that if Kathleen knew their meaning she wasn't going to say it out loud. One of the possibilities was unspeakable.

From what Kathleen told her, Leslie concluded that Mark had decided to quit medicine. But what else had he decided to quit? All of it? His life? From what Kathleen told her, Leslie couldn't tell. And Kathleen couldn't tell. Maybe Mark didn't even know.

"Kathleen," Leslie interrupted a long silence. "Let me call you back in five or ten minutes, OK?"

"OK. Mark won't be home for at least half an hour."

Leslie made three phone calls—one to another R-3, one to the chief resident and the third to an airline—and called Kathleen back.

"Kathleen, I'm going to fly to Boston early tomorrow morning," Leslie said definitively.

"Thank you," Kathleen whispered gratefully. She hadn't expected it, but she wouldn't protest. She needed help.

They didn't say the words, but the emotion and tension in their voices articulated fear. Leslie wondered what Kathleen feared. Was it simply fear of losing Mark? Or was it the bone-chilling fear that Leslie felt? The fear that Mark was planning something more than quitting medicine.

She feared that he was carefully, meticulously planning to kill himself. The *best* planned suicide ever. Planned to look like an accident.

"What shall I tell Mark?" Kathleen asked helplessly. She couldn't think of a plausible reason to explain Leslie's sudden visit.

Leslie thought for a moment. Then she sighed.

"Tell him that I need to get out of San Francisco for a few days because I just broke up with Eric," Leslie said slowly, with great effort. Her words made her ache deep inside, but her words were, simply, the truth.

Chapter Thirty-nine

"Thank you for coming to meet me," Leslie said to a gaunt, strained Kathleen. Her healthy vivaciousness was gone. She looked sallow and weary. It wasn't a change that had taken place overnight. It represented weeks and weeks of constant worry and sleeplessness.

Mark must have noticed, Leslie thought. If he hadn't, it was a grim barometer of his own internal turmoil.

"Thank you for coming, Leslie. I'm sorry about Eric."

"So am I," Leslie said with finality. She didn't want to talk about it. She needed time, private, uncluttered time, to think about it. Since Kathleen's call last night, her thoughts and her restless, tormented dreams had darted at random between Eric and Mark.

She had to focus on one at a time, and she had come to Boston because of Mark.

"We have a cab waiting. We had a lot of snow last night. I'm not comfortable driving in it," Kathleen explained apologetically.

She is really defeated, Leslie thought. The Kathleen that Leslie had known was the Kathleen who had confidently found her way through the maze of tubes and lines and cords and amazed ICU nurses to be with Mark. The only Kathleen Leslie had ever seen was unafraid. She would have been unafraid of driving in the snow.

"I could have taken the subway," Leslie said. "I know

Boston. I went to college here."

"To Radcliffe?"

"Yes."

"I didn't know that. Well. I wanted to meet you."

Kathleen had almost brought the list and the short story with her. She wanted Leslie to read them as soon as possible. She wanted to be reassured that nothing was wrong.

As she watched Leslie's face as she studied the list and read the short story an hour later, Kathleen knew that Leslie couldn't reassure her.

First Leslie looked at the list labeled *To Do*. It was, generically, like the scut list that she and Mark and every other resident made every day. At work the list included lab results to check, social workers to contact, consults to call, X rays to order and articles to read. One by one each item on the scut list was crossed off. When every item had been crossed off, it was time to go home. One didn't let scut spill over to the next day because each day had its own long list. It couldn't be allowed to accumulate.

Leslie studied Mark's list. It was a personal scut list. *Journal subscriptions* (crossed out). Had he cancelled them or renewed them? Cancelled, Leslie decided as she read the other items on the list. *Grant application* (crossed out). *Textbooks — to medical school library? Instruments. Summary of Patients* (crossed out). He wants his patients to be well taken care of, Leslie thought sadly. Only the best.

At the bottom of the list, Leslie saw her name. Underlined but not crossed out. He was going to talk to her, or write to her or leave something for her.

What does Mark get to do when all the items on his scut list are crossed out? Leslie wondered grimly. Does he get to go home?

Then Leslie read the story.

It's so beautifully written, Leslie thought as she began

to read. He is so talented.

After a few pages, Leslie could no longer be objective about the writing style. She focused only on the words carved from the soul of a man about whom she cared very much.

It was written in the third person, but it was Mark's story. It was a story about a man driven by himself and others to be something he didn't want to be. A man driven to be the best. A man who was not allowed to fail. A man who was deeply in love with a woman.

It was a story of triumph. Toward the end, the man makes the courageous tormented decision to quit the life he hates and to find, *make,* something better. He has the support and love of the woman. Together they can find happiness. No matter what.

But the story didn't end there. There was a brief epilogue. The man and the woman went for a boat ride.

He held her hand. It made him strong. They stood by the railing, gazing at each other, lost in their love and oblivious to the roughness of the sea. The boat lurched suddenly. The jolt tore them apart and hurled him over the side into the dark emptiness.

Where all is forgiven.

Leslie said nothing for several moments after she finished the story. She couldn't be sure. He had made the decision to quit medicine. He was systematically cancelling journals and compulsively leaving no loose ends. He even finished a grant application for research he would never do. It all seemed logical and rational. Typical, compulsive Mark.

The story was a thoughtful, insightful look at himself. It was almost a celebration of the difficult decision that he made.

Almost.

"I don't understand the ending," Leslie said. Kathleen had told her about the story last night and its ambiguous ending, but Kathleen hadn't been able to interpret it. Now, even after reading it herself, neither could Leslie.

"The rest of the story is clearly about Mark."

"That's about Mark, too," Kathleen said. "He likes to go on the harbor cruises. He had mentioned how easy it would be to be tossed over the railing."

"So you swim to shore," Leslie said simply. "Or wait until someone tosses a lifebuoy."

"Leslie, Mark doesn't know how to swim," Kathleen whispered, her voice laced with fear. "Not even how to tread water."

"Oh," Leslie said quietly. She realized then that Kathleen *did* know. She just couldn't, wouldn't, say it.

The *best*-planned suicide.

But it was a story, not a plan. Fact-based but fictional. A fantasy. One of many possible outcomes.

Mark's intention to quit medicine was real. The list proved it. The rest was . . .

"He loves you very much," Leslie said suddenly.

"Do you think that's me?" Kathleen asked weakly. It had been the only part that had given her hope.

"Of course it's you. He describes you—your energy, your vitality, your loveliness—perfectly," Leslie said. She saw the hope and the doubt in Kathleen's violet eyes, the eyes that used to sparkle. Suddenly Leslie realized that she had something to do with the doubt. Leslie smiled and said gently, compassionately, truthfully, "It's you, Kathleen. It's not Janet. *And* it's not me."

"Your name is on the list."

"He loves *you*." *He held her hand. It made him strong.* Leslie remembered the words from Mark's story. And she remembered Mark's remarkable recovery from the gunshot wound. Against all odds. With Kathleen by his side.

Kathleen was what he lived for.

"Yes, she's here, Mark. She's OK," Kathleen said when Mark called at five-thirty that evening. "I'll be leaving in ten minutes to go to dinner and a movie with Sally. I'll be back at about eleven. There's food here if you don't go

500

out."

It was what Kathleen and Leslie had decided. Leslie would talk to Mark alone. She would try to find out what he was planning *without* telling him that they had read his story. But if it was necessary to tell him that they had invaded his privacy, she would.

Kathleen and Leslie were both willing to accept the consequences of his anger at their betrayal.

He looks fine, Leslie thought when he walked in the front door twenty minutes after Kathleen left. Handsome, focused, smiling.

But Mark looked different, too. The change was subtle. What was it?

He looks calm, Leslie decided. At peace. At peace with his plan. Whatever it is . . .

"Leslie, I'm so sorry," Mark said walking toward her.

Sorry? Leslie wondered. Then she remembered. Mark thought she had come because of Eric. *Eric.* All day she had shoved him away from her thoughts, but she had felt a terrible emptiness in her heart. Because of him. A constant, subliminal, mournful presence.

Now as Mark approached her, his brown eyes full of compassion and concern for her, Leslie began to cry.

Mark wrapped his arms around her as he had done the night Jean Watson died. For a moment, Leslie succumbed to the comforting warmth and strength of him. She pressed her face against his chest as he gently stroked her hair. She felt so safe, so secure. But it was an illusion.

After a few moments, Leslie pulled away.

"Tell me what happened," Mark said gently.

"I didn't really come here because of Eric," Leslie said softly. "I came here because of you."

"Me?"

"Kathleen called me last night. She's very worried about you. She thinks you are planning something."

Leslie watched his reaction carefully. He looked surprised and a little embarrassed that they were so worried about him. But he was not angry or defensive. Not as if he had anything to hide.

"I am planning something," he said calmly. "I am planning to quit medicine."

"When?"

"*Tomorrow,* actually. I have an appointment with the cardiology fellowship director at ten. I was planning to call you tonight to tell you."

"What about Kathleen? When were you going to tell her?"

Mark looked confused for a moment, as if he had already told her. He *had* told her in the story, but not in real life.

"Tomorrow night. After it was over. I had no idea she was so worried," he said quietly, frowning, concerned.

"When was the last time you really looked at her, Mark?" Leslie asked forcefully, remembering how Kathleen had looked as she left for the movie. Remembering how Janet had looked in the months before her marriage to Mark ended.

Mark's frown deepened.

"I know that these past few months have been hard for her. They've been hard for both of us. I'm not as oblivious as you think. I needed time and privacy. I had to work it out myself. Maybe that was too selfish. I thought I was protecting her."

"You were excluding her," Leslie said gently, relieved that at least he knew.

"Not from my plans," Mark said quickly. *Not from my life.*

"What *are* your plans, Mark?" Leslie asked. It was the key question. So far his explanation had seemed honest and logical. He wasn't hiding anything.

"English grad school," he answered. He seemed a little surprised that she asked. That was what he—they—had always talked about. "What's going on, Leslie? I thought you would be happy about this."

"I am happy, Mark. I know it's right. It's just—"

"Just what?"

"Kathleen was so worried. Imagine what it took for her to call me," Leslie said gently.

"And she obviously transmitted the worry to you. That's why you came," he said sheepishly. "That was really nice of you, Leslie. I'm a little embarrassed. There's nothing to worry about."

Isn't there? Leslie wondered. What about the ending of the story, Mark? In your story the prince and the princess don't live happily ever after.

Leslie retreated to the guest bedroom long before Kathleen was due to return. She was emotionally and physically exhausted, too tired to think. Even about Eric. But the ache was with her, and the ache didn't fall asleep even though she did. The ache surfaced in her dreams. She dreamed—horrible vivid dreams—about Eric and Mark and Bobby and Michael. She dreamed about little boys who fell over boat railings into black cold water. She tried in vain to save them. Eric and Mark tried to save the little boys, too, but they couldn't. Instead, they were consumed by the terrible depthless sea.

In all the dreams, as desperately as she tried, Leslie couldn't save any of them.

Mark stood by the window waiting for Kathleen. When he saw her he went outside into the snowy, cold January night without coat or gloves. He put his arm around her and guided her through the slippery packed snow into the house.

He held her for a moment before speaking. Then he gazed at her, at her dark circles, frightened eyes and pale skin. Leslie was right. He *hadn't* looked at her for a while. Not really. He had been so preoccupied with his decision, *his* plan. It was for both of them, but he had *shut her out*.

"Oh, Kathleen," he whispered, pulling her close to him.

"I am so sorry. I didn't want you to worry."

"Mark—" she began then stopped.

"There is nothing to worry about, darling. I had to make a very tough decision, a decision about which I had to be absolutely certain. That's all."

"Why couldn't I help you with it?" she asked weakly.

"Maybe I should have asked you to," Mark murmured uneasily. *For better or worse.* The words, the promises, echoed in his brain. He should have shared it with her. He continued, a little shaken, "I believed that you would support my decision—"

"Of course I would support it. Will support it. What have you decided?"

"I'm going to quit medicine, Kathleen," Mark said slowly, carefully, watching her reaction.

"Good," she said instantly.

"Good? You're not surprised, are you? I guess Leslie probably told you."

Leslie. And Janet through Ross. And your private papers . . .

Kathleen shrugged.

"It's good because it's what you want, and because you'll be safe and happy," she said as she touched his cheek gently. *I love you so much, Mark. Please don't leave me. Please be safe and happy.*

"I want to show you something," Mark said impulsively. He led her by the hand into his study. He took the heavy blue textbook off the shelf where Kathleen had carefully returned it with the papers inside.

Mark removed the top and bottom sheets—the *To Do* list and the epilogue—and handed the rest to her.

"I want you to read this," he said. *I want to share this with you.*

"I've read it, Mark," she whispered, her violet eyes full of apprehension. She gestured to the two sheets of paper that remained in his hand, the sheets he hadn't given to her. "I've read all of it."

She must have read it last night, Mark realized. After

he had written the epilogue. No *wonder* she was so worried.

"And Leslie read it?" he asked. Now he understood Leslie's guarded enthusiasm about his decision.

Kathleen nodded slowly, watching him.

"Mark, I'm sorry," she said. "I was desperate. I didn't know what was happening. I know it was wrong."

"No. It's all right," he said unconvincingly. He wished Leslie hadn't read it, but it was his fault that he had isolated Kathleen to the point of desperation. He had to accept the consequences of his decisions. Beginning with his meeting with the fellowship director tomorrow, there would be many consequences.

"I'm sorry, Mark," she said, shivering involuntarily.

"It's OK," he repeated. This time his voice was convincing.

Mark set down the sheets of paper and took both of her hands, holding them, cupped, between his.

"What does it mean, Mark?" she asked.

"What?"

"The ending. The epilogue," Kathleen said as tears moistened her violet eyes. *The part you didn't want me to read.*

"It means," he said slowly, his voice breaking slightly, "that I am afraid."

"I love you so much, Mark." *Don't be afraid.*

"I love you, too." *More than anything.*

None of them slept well. Leslie awakened frequently, driven into gasping consciousness by the horror of her dreams. Mark and Kathleen lay awake holding each other. They knew they needed to rest. The hard part was just about to begin. But they couldn't sleep. They were both worried about what lay ahead.

They all tried to be cheerful at breakfast, but it was useless. The tension was palpable. Kathleen and Leslie knew how difficult the day would be for Mark. He had made the decision, he had put it on paper, but now he had to say the words out loud to people who didn't love him the way Kathleen and Leslie did. He had to say them to people who wouldn't understand. To people who might make him feel guilty. To people who might tell him—yell at him—that he had failed.

Today was just the beginning.

"Maybe I should go with you this morning," Leslie said.

"I'm not a little boy, Leslie. This isn't the first day of school," Mark snapped.

Leslie recoiled. *It's not the first day; it's the last. Where is the celebration?*

"I really didn't mean to be *with* you. I would like to see the hospital."

"Sorry," he said with an edge. Then he asked more gently, "Why?"

"Well. I happen to know that there is going to be an *unexpected opening* in the cardiology fellowship program . . ."

"I thought you were going to Stanford."

"Maybe I need to get out of the Bay Area after all," Leslie said thoughtfully. *Maybe I need to get away from Eric and the memories.*

"You're serious, aren't you?" Mark asked.

"I just thought as long as I'm here—"

"OK, Dr. Adams. We leave in twenty minutes."

Leslie left to get ready.

"When do you think you'll be home?" Kathleen asked.

"By noon," Mark said decisively, but uneasily. *They couldn't force him to stay no matter what they said. Could they?*

"Is there anything I can do?" she asked hopefully. *Anything other than pace and worry.* She wished she had a reason like Leslie had to go with Mark, but she didn't. Except that she loved him.

"Just be here when I get home," he said, kissing her gently on the mouth.

"Give me a project, Mark. Anything."

"OK. You can put all my medical books in boxes. I'll

take them to the medical school library next week."

"I wonder if the public library could use them," she mused. *I don't want you to have to go back next week.*

"Maybe. That would be fine if they could."

"You don't want any of them?"

"No."

All right, she thought, her tired violet eyes sparkling a little. At least he was letting her help.

Mark gave Leslie a quick tour of the Peter Bent Brigham Hospital. The tour ended at the cardiology research lab. Mark introduced her to two other fellows who were working in the lab.

"Leslie might want to apply for a position here," Mark explained.

"Great," they said in unison, smiling warmly at Mark's pretty blue-eyed friend.

"I have to go see Dr. Peters," Mark said when it was almost time for his appointment. "I'll leave Leslie here."

"We'll take care of her," one of the fellows said.

Leslie asked questions about the cardiology fellowship program, but after a while the conversation shifted to Mark.

"He was my resident when I was an intern," Leslie explained a little nostalgically.

"I bet he was a terrific resident."

"He was."

"He's about the best fellow anyone's ever known," one of them said without a trace of envy in his voice. They all respected Mark. Everyone always had.

The best. Of course, Leslie thought. Mark had been in with the director for thirty minutes. What if he convinces Mark to stay? Or what if he tells him he is making the biggest mistake of his life?

"Mark's a wonderful man," Leslie said. *Whether or not he's a doctor.*

Mark returned fifteen minutes later. He looked strained

and pale, but he smiled at her. Then he retrieved several sheets of paper from his coat and handed them to one of the other fellows.

"This is a list of patients that I have seen in cardiology clinic or in consultation who need follow up."

Both fellows looked at the list. It was written in Mark's neat handwriting and described the patients' problems, medications and Mark's long-term plan for their care.

"Are you going somewhere, Mark?"

"I'm leaving," he said firmly, looking at Leslie. Her eyes glistened with support.

"Where are you going?"

"I'm, uh, quitting medicine. Right now I'm going home." Mark tried to sound pleasant. They were his friends, his colleagues, but they wouldn't understand.

He shook their hands quickly, warmly, capitalizing on their stunned silence to make his escape.

"It's been nice working with you," he said. "Good-bye."

Mark and Leslie walked briskly, without speaking, along the shiny corridors and down the concrete stairs until they reached the main entrance. The main *exit*. Leslie touched his arm lightly.

"How about your pager, Mark?"

"I gave it to the director's secretary. She said she'd take care of all the paperwork." Mark didn't slow his pace. He wanted to get out. To escape. Freedom was only a few feet away.

Then, only two paces from the front door, from escape, he stopped.

"I have to call Kathleen," he said firmly.

Mark retreated into a wood-framed phone booth in the hospital lobby. He emerged a few minutes later. There was life in his brown eyes again.

"We can't go home yet," he said smiling.

"No?"

"No," he said. His voice was soft, loving. "Kathleen is up to something. Besides, she's given us a shopping list that will keep us busy for at least an hour. She wants to cook a magnificent dinner."

Good for Kathleen, Leslie thought, admiring her. She is going to fight to make this work for Mark.

Between the liquor store and the fish market, Leslie finally asked Mark about his meeting with the director.

"In the end, he was very gracious. I don't know if he ever understood. He spent a lot of time talking about the brilliant career I was throwing away. Wasted potential—"

"You expected that," Leslie interjected.

"Yes. But it was hard to hear it from someone I respect so much," Mark said soberly. He sighed. "Anyway, in the end he shook my hand and wished me luck."

"That's nice," Leslie said. *I wonder if your father will be so gracious.*

Chapter Forty

Kathleen greeted them at the door. Her cheeks were flushed with excitement, and her violet eyes sparkled.

She is so resilient, Leslie thought, admiring Kathleen again. And so courageous.

Somehow, despite her worry and fatigue, Kathleen managed to look fresh and eager. The apprehension, the knowledge that this was just the beginning, that they weren't home free, flickered in her eyes, but it was almost vanquished by the confidence and determination and vitality that, until recently, had been her trademark.

It must have taken great effort, Leslie thought, wondering where Kathleen found the energy and the strength. In her love for Mark, Leslie realized as she watched Kathleen look at him. Because she loves him so much.

"What are you up to?" Mark teased lightly, lovingly.

"Nothing. I just redecorated your study. Come and look," Kathleen said, pulling at his wrist.

"We have a car full of groceries. I guess nothing will melt, but some things could freeze."

"OK. The study can wait."

It became obvious to Leslie as they unloaded the groceries and put them away in the kitchen that Mark and

510

Kathleen needed to be alone.

She needed to be alone, too.

"I'm going to take a walk," she said.

"It's zero degrees."

"If I could borrow some boots and a coat . . . I want to go walk around the campus at Radcliffe and Harvard." A sentimental journey.

"Would you like the car?"

"No. I'll take the subway. Thanks."

Kathleen gave Leslie boots, a down-filled coat, fur-lined gloves and a warm hat.

"When will you be back?" Kathleen asked.

"Before dark," Mark said firmly.

"I guess before dark," Leslie said, smiling. It was nice that he felt protective.

"That's perfect anyway. I think we all need an early evening tonight. I thought the champagne would start flowing at five," Kathleen said brightly.

"I'll be back by five."

After Leslie left, Kathleen led Mark to the study. Her heart pounded. Had she done too much? She didn't want to push him. She didn't care what he did. She only cared that he was happy.

The medical books were gone. The wooden shelves were filled with Mark's favorite books, the classic works of Shakespeare and Shaw and Joyce and Faulkner and Steinbeck. . . . Until that morning, most of the books had still been in boxes.

The framed documents that chronicled Mark's already distinguished career in medicine were gone. The Alpha Omega Alpha Honor Society diploma, the Doctor of Medicine degree—with highest honor—from the University of Nebraska, the Internal Medicine Residency certificate from the University of California and the California and Massachusetts licenses to practice medicine were gone, stored in a box in a remote corner of the attic.

Kathleen left his Bachelor of Arts degree — a degree in English — from the University of Nebraska on the wall, and in place of the medical documents, Kathleen had hung the picture of the Carlton Club.

"It's wonderful."

"I kept the diplomas. I gave the books to the public library."

"Already?"

"Is that all right?" she asked quickly, worried.

"Yes. Of course. How did you get them there?"

"By cab," Kathleen said simply.

"You are really amazing. I love you."

"Want to show me?"

"You bet." He began to kiss her. Then he whispered softly, "Kitzy."

Leslie stood in the middle of Harvard Square. The snow had begun to fall lightly, silently. Students trudged purposefully through the snow. She was the only tourist, the only one without a purpose.

But she had a purpose. She was retracing her steps. She was retracing the steps that had brought her here years ago, as a naive eighteen-year-old, wide-eyed and full of hope and energy. She loved the years she had spent here, and the next ones, the ones that trained her to be a doctor. Throughout that time, her steps had been sure, confident, buoyant, but somehow, the steps had led her astray, the footing had become false . . .

Because somehow the steps of her life had led her to Eric, to a wonderful limitless love that now — overnight — had turned into bitterness and hatred.

Leslie walked past the dormitory where she first made love and where she learned to recognize the smell of marijuana. She walked past the library where she had studied, eagerly, tirelessly pursuing her dream of becoming a doctor. She wandered by the lecture halls and the science labs and Harvard Square itself, where she had attended rallies and concerts and studied under the shady trees and laughed and kissed. . . .

As Leslie thought about her own memories—the happy memories of an innocent girl growing up—she began to feel the presence of other ghosts, other happy memories, other young, wide-eyed lovers.

This was the place of Charlie and Eric. They had loved each other here. And hurt each other here. This was where they had walked hand in hand talking of love and marriage . . . and where they had been when Victoria called to tell Eric about her pregnancy.

Had Charlie ever stood in this spot in Harvard Square—the spot where Leslie stood now—waiting impatiently for Eric to get out of class? In her mind's eye, Leslie saw Charlie, her cheeks rosy, her spun-gold hair tossed by the wind and her smile full of love as she waited, eager to throw her arms around Eric. To kiss him and tell him how much she missed him.

How much she missed him, Leslie thought. How much I miss him. But I don't even know him. The Eric I miss never existed, and I was never a part of the Eric Lansdale who does exist. Never as important as Charlie. Or Victoria. Or Bobby.

Never really important at all.

Leslie shivered. Was it from the bitter-cold winter day? Or the bitter-cold reality of her relationship with Eric?

At five o'clock Mark uncorked the bottle of champagne that had been chilling for the past thirty minutes. He filled the three crystal champagne glasses.

"A toast," Leslie said, lifting her glass of honey-colored bubbles.

"To what?" Kathleen asked, her eyes laughing, radiant. She and Mark had found each other and their love again.

513

Maybe this time it was theirs to keep.

"To happiness," Leslie said. *To your happiness.*

Mark took a small sip then sighed.

"Wish me luck," he said soberly.

"Why?" Leslie asked.

"He's going to call his father."

Leslie and Kathleen more than sipped champagne as they waited anxiously for Mark to return. He was upstairs. They couldn't hear him.

Mark returned in twenty minutes. His face was white. His jaw muscles rippled.

Kathleen's violet eyes scowled with worry and anger as she waited for Mark to speak.

"Bad, huh?" Leslie asked, breaking the interminable silence.

"Bad," Mark said heavily. He took a deep breath. He had to tell them. He had to tell Kathleen. And Leslie was there. He had to say it now, to get it out. He said slowly, bitterly, "He said it would be better if I were dead."

Leslie gasped.

Kathleen's eyes darkened. Then she began to giggle.

"Kathleen!"

"My God, Mark! He's such a poor excuse for a father. He's a joke," she exclaimed. A pathetic, malignant horrible joke. He had already harmed Mark enough.

Slowly the color returned to Mark's face, and the jaw muscles stopped moving.

"He's also a bastard," Kathleen said hotly.

"Now you're talking," Mark said, smiling a little.

"Have some champagne, Mark," Kathleen said. *And forget about your father. Please. I know how hard this is, but we don't need him or his approval. We have each other.*

The phone rang.

Mark grimaced but didn't move. It was probably his father calling to deliver the final shot. But how could he improve on wishing his son were dead?

514

"I'd better not talk to him," Kathleen announced.

Leslie stood up.

"I guess it's my turn to deal with Papa Doc," she said. "You just left for the evening, right?"

"Or the weekend," Kathleen said. "Or forever."

Leslie answered the phone in the kitchen. Mark followed her.

"Leslie?"

"Eric."

Mark touched her lightly then left, pulling the door behind him, giving her privacy.

"I tried to call you last night at the hospital. The on call resident said that you were in Boston."

"I am." You know Boston well, Eric, she thought grimly. You and Charlie spent three years here together. Leslie was amazed by the flatness of her own voice and by the way her heart ached at the sound of his, gentle, caring.

But he hadn't cared. Not really.

"When are you coming home?"

Home? Never. Back to San Francisco . . .

"I'll fly back sometime this weekend," she answered vaguely. She would leave in the morning. Kathleen and Mark needed to be alone, and she needed to get on with her life.

"When can I see you?"

His voice sounded so hopeful. Leslie blinked back tears.

"Never, Eric. I . . . it's . . . over."

"Over?"

"I needed to know about that part of your life, Eric. It was so pertinent to us. To my career. To our future."

"I was going to tell you in Maui, but then I found out about you and James."

"I don't understand. . . ."

"It tore me apart. You know that. I couldn't tell you about Charlie then. I didn't want to do that to you."

515

"What about any time in the past two months?"

"I didn't want to hurt you."

"What about Bobby, Eric? Bobby. Victoria. Your revulsion to hospitals." Leslie's pain erupted into anger, forcing words from her lips that she didn't really believe. Or did she? She didn't really know Eric Lansdale. Anything was possible. She continued, her voice like ice, "Did you actually hate me, Eric? Because I was a doctor? Did you plan to punish me all along?"

"Leslie," Eric interjected, horrified. "Leslie, I love you. I love you more than anything in the world."

"I can't believe that, Eric. I can't believe anything you say because I know that you *don't* say the things that are the most important."

"Leslie, let me see you. Please."

"There is no point."

"Maybe it's just too soon."

"No." With each hour that passed Leslie forced the Eric that she loved out of her heart and replaced him with the real Eric, the man she had never known or loved. *That* Eric would be easier to forget.

"I would have told you, Leslie."

"When? The day I told you I wanted to have children?"

"You are so bitter."

"I trusted you, Eric," Leslie said heavily. "Did you want me to stop being a doctor? Was that going to be part of our future? Or was there ever really a plan for the future?"

"You were—are—my future, Leslie. I would never ask you to stop being a doctor."

I might have given it up for you, Eric. If you had told me. If you had given me a chance to understand. You were more important to me than anything. Ever.

"You just would have spent your life, our life, being uncomfortable every time I told you about my work? Every time we saw a little boy? What were we going to do about children, *our* children?"

516

"Before I met you, I never thought I would have a future with anyone. I never even considered having children . . . another child. I was going to tell you, Leslie. I was just putting it off because I knew it would be so painful. For both of us."

Tears spilled down her cheeks. *I miss you. I hate you. I can't go back to you. I can't live without you.*

"Leslie?" he asked gently.

"Good-bye, Eric." *Sayonara.*

"Leslie, wait! I love you darling, I tried not to hurt you and it backfired. It hurt you more. It was a *mistake,* Leslie. Because I love you so much."

"It hurt me too much, Eric. It was too big a mistake." Her voice was ice cold. Like her heart: cold and empty, except for the ache that wouldn't leave. "Good-bye."

At eleven Monday morning, Charlie walked into James's office. She didn't stop to knock.

"Come in," James said, arching an eyebrow.

"What's wrong with Eric?" she demanded.

"Nothing as far as I know."

"Have you seen him today?"

"I just spent an hour with him."

"And he seemed fine?"

"He seemed businesslike. As usual. Why?"

"I just spoke to him over the phone. I'm on my way to his office now. He sounded terrible," she said.

"Angry?"

"No. Upset." *Despondent. Like when Bobby died.*

"Let me know. If there's anything I can do—"

Charlie was gone. Moments later she walked into Eric's office without knocking. She saw it in his eyes. Sad, empty icebergs. His eyes reflected only the tip of the deep pain.

"Tell me," she said softly.

Eric told her, slowly, painfully, his voice full of loss and regret.

"Victoria is such a shrew!" Charlie exclaimed as Eric told her.

"No she isn't. She never was. This was all my fault. My own stupidity."

"Were you going to tell her?"

"Of course. Sometime. Sometime when she was rested and I was rested and we had some time together."

"That sounds like never."

"I was going to tell her, Charlie," Eric repeated firmly.

"Well, anyway, now she knows. Is she angry?" Charlie still hadn't learned anything that could explain the look on his face or the tone in his voice.

"She's hurt and angry. She won't see me. She says it's over."

"It doesn't make sense."

"It makes sense to Leslie. And she's the only one who counts."

"Why?"

"She says she can't trust me. She says that by not sharing something so important I made my relationship with her unimportant. She says that she doesn't know me."

Charlie thought about the blood-framed blue eyes that glowered at a prying television camera. Proud, astonished, indignant eyes. Leslie had her own standards, her own rules.

"What are you going to do?" Charlie asked carefully.

"There is absolutely nothing I can do," Eric said, his voice empty, defeated. "Except to hope that some day she changes her mind."

Charlie waited for three weeks before telling Robert. Charlie was waiting to see if Leslie came back. She didn't.

She isn't going to, Charlie thought. How do I feel about it?

When she knew the answer to that question she told

518

Robert.

Charlie telephoned him at his home in Philadelphia on a Wednesday evening in February.

"What are you doing?" she asked as she always asked. She loved his answers. He usually said he was thinking about her. Or them. Together.

"I was wondering if I could pass the California Bar."

"Really?"

"Really. What are you doing?"

"Calling to tell you that I miss you. And to tell you about Eric and Leslie."

Robert knew from her tone that the news about Eric and Leslie wasn't good. He listened, without interrupting, until she had finished.

"How long ago did Victoria tell Leslie?"

"Four weeks," Charlie said. Then she added carefully, because he had to know, "I've known about it for about three weeks."

Charlie waited for him to ask the question: Why didn't you tell me, Charlie? There had been plenty of opportunities in the past three weeks for Charlie to tell Robert. They had spent all three weekends together and talked to each other almost daily.

The silence was so long that Charlie finally answered the unspoken question.

"I didn't tell you right away because I didn't want to worry you. I thought Leslie might come back."

"I wouldn't have worried about Leslie and Eric," Robert said firmly. *Not nearly as much as I would have worried about you and Eric*. Would Charlie want to try one more time with Eric?

Charlie knew what Robert meant. And she knew that the fact that she hadn't told him right away meant that she was uncertain herself.

Charlie knew that she had to be certain before she told Robert, and she was telling him now.

"Do you know what I was wondering?" she asked

softly, finally, after several moments of silence.

"No," he said sharply.

"I was wondering if I could pass the Pennsylvania Bar."

"You have to be very sure, Charlie," Robert said. *I will not compete with my son.*

"I am very sure. I love you, Robert. I love *you*."

Chapter Forty-one

"Where are you, Mrs. MacMillan?" Ross asked, relieved to hear Janet's voice. It was six-thirty in the evening on the last Saturday in March. He had been at the theater all day. She called fifteen minutes after he returned to their condominium on Sacramento Street.

"At the house," Janet said quietly.

"The *house?*" Two hours away. Why was she there? "Is Leslie with you?"

Ross knew that Janet had planned to spend part of the day with Leslie.

"No. I only saw her for a couple of hours."

"How is she?" Ross asked. *How are you? Why are you so far away?*

"She's terrible," Janet said with a sigh. "But she won't admit it. When the going gets tough, I guess Leslie turns into solid steel. She won't talk about it. She says she's fine—"

"But?" Ross asked gently. *Leslie's not fine. And neither are you. Why?*

"She's devastated. And so *restless*. She's like a hummingbird. She has to keep moving."

"She needs to talk to Eric."

"I know," Janet said. Then she added, "But I don't

521

think she ever will."

Ross waited. There had to be more. There had to be something to explain why Janet had gone to the house by herself. The house, the green hills, the blue ocean . . . Janet's retreat. It was where she went when she needed to be alone.

"Janet?"

"Did you know about Mark?" she asked bluntly.

"Mark?" Ross hadn't spoken to Kathleen since October. "No. What?"

"He quit medicine," Janet said flatly.

"Oh," Ross said. Then he asked sharply, "Don't you think that if I knew I would have told you?"

"I wasn't sure."

"You should be."

I know I should be, Janet thought. But I'm not sure of anything right now. Too many changes.

"When did he quit?" Ross asked, feigning interest. He wasn't really interested. *Especially* if this was what had separated him from his wife.

"Over two months ago. Leslie has known, but she didn't want to tell me until—"

"Until what?"

"Until she was sure he was OK, I guess. Until she was certain he would make it," Janet said. Leslie had sounded certain.

"Why wouldn't he?"

"I don't know. Anyway, she says he's fine. Happy."

A long silence followed.

"What's wrong, Janet?" Ross asked finally.

He heard her sigh. A long heavy sigh.

"Life just feels so precarious to me at the moment. Too disrupted. Too many changes."

"Like—"

"Like Leslie and Eric. It seems so senseless that this has happened to them," she said. "And Mark. Even though he's finally done what will make him happy, I'm sure it's painful for him. Just thinking about those wasted years.

522

Years of torment—"

"But *we're* happy, Janet," Ross interjected confidently. *There is nothing precarious about us, is there?*

"Yes," Janet said, her voice soft but distant. "Ross?"

"Yes?" *Tell me, Janet.*

"Do you think we'll ever have children?" she asked quietly.

"We've never talked about it, have we?" he asked gently.

"No. Do you want to have them?"

"Do you?"

"I think so."

"There's no hurry, is there?" Ross asked carefully. He sensed that this was an impulsive reaction to the precariousness Janet felt, a need to create something constant and lasting, but she had something constant and lasting already. She had his love.

"No. No hurry. I just wondered," she said softly. Then she repeated the question she had asked before. "Do you want children, Ross?"

"All I want is you," Ross said. "I want you now and you're two hours away. So I'm on my way—"

"No, Ross. I know that you have script rewrites to do, and I'm exhausted. I need a good night's sleep starting about now."

"Janet . . ."

"Really. I'll stay here tonight and drive down in the morning. I'll probably be there before you wake up."

"Are you OK?"

"*Yes.* Just a little sentimental or maudlin or something theatrical," she said, trying to sound amused at her own silliness. "I'll be fine in the morning."

"Well . . ."

"You're looking at the stack of script pages you brought home, aren't you?" she asked lightly.

"You know me so well."

"I'll see you in the morning," she whispered. "Goodnight, Ross."

"Sleep well, darling," Ross said.

This isn't right, he thought. This isn't right at all.

Janet closed her eyes and thought about the events of the day. Seeing Leslie, watching Leslie suffer, made her sad. And hearing about Mark, even though the news was wonderful, made her nostalgic. But it was her own news that made her drive to the house in the country. To think.

At ten in the morning she had called the doctor's office to get the result of the blood test that had been drawn the afternoon before. It only confirmed what she already knew, what she had known for the past three months. She was pregnant.

How had she known? It wasn't because she felt ill or missed a period or noticed her breasts enlarging. There were no external signs at all. But she had known, almost immediately. She had known almost the moment the tiny being inside her had been conceived. She *felt* its presence, a new and wonderful part of her.

Janet wondered if most women felt the presence of the new life as early as she had. Or was it because this baby was so special?

Janet had come to the house in the country to think about the new life that was growing inside her. What would its life be like? Janet wanted her child to be happy, free of pain, always. But how could she guarantee that? Would all her love really protect her child against life's sadnesses?

What if her baby was like Leslie? A beautiful happy girl with sapphire-blue eyes and shiny dark hair and a loving heart? Loving and trusting until, one day, her dreams were destroyed and she was forced to suffer. Needlessly. Endlessly.

Or what if her baby was a little boy who, like Mark, believed that he had to be the best? A little boy whose father, Ross, believed in being the best, and whose mother was the best even though she didn't care. How could the child escape the pressure? What if his life was almost destroyed — as Mark's almost had been — by that pressure?

Janet sighed. Oh, little one, she thought, I will do everything I can to make your life happy. I will give you all my love, but you know that, don't you? You already feel it. Just as I feel you.

What about Ross? *All I want is you,* he had said. What if Ross didn't want the baby? Why hadn't she told him? When was she going to tell him?

I have to tell him, she thought. I have to tell him *now.*

Ross arrived at the house in the country at nine P.M. The house was dark. Janet's car was gone. He drove to the cottage, but she wasn't there, either. He returned to the house to wait.

Where is she? he wondered. The worry that had made him — within moments of ending their conversation — grab his car keys and drive, too fast, to their country home increased as he waited in the empty house. Where is she?

At nine-forty-five the telephone rang, startling him.

"Hello?" he answered quickly.

"Ross," she said. Her voice was soft, loving, distant.

"Where are you?" he asked as relief pulsed through him. Then he realized, the only way she can know that I'm here is if . . . "Are you at the condo?"

"It's sort of *Gift of the Magi*-esque, isn't it?" she asked. He could hear the smile in her voice.

"I think we're making progress," he said gently. He had known it was wrong for them to be apart, and he had gone to her. She had known it and gone to him. The signals weren't crossed; they were intertwined. The way they should be.

"I know we are," she said. "Except that you're there and I'm here."

"Because we love each other. Because even when something is wrong we need to be together," Ross said. He was so happy, elated, that Janet had decided to go to him.

"I love you," she said. Come to me so I can tell you

525

about our baby, she thought.

"I love you, too. Now you stay put and I'll be there in two hours," he said amiably. He wasn't tired, just happy. He added carefully, it was only a guess, "You both stay put."

"Both?" she asked weakly. "Ross, how—"

"Am I right?"

"Yes," she breathed. "Ross, is it all right?"

"Yes. Of course. I love you both," he said tenderly. "I love you both."

"Are you sure you don't mind?" Mark asked.

"You know I don't," Kathleen answered lovingly.

He *did* know that she didn't mind because he knew how much she loved him. Just as Kathleen knew how much Mark loved her.

It was Saturday, May seventh. Friday's mail had brought an acceptance letter for Mark from Harvard University into the graduate program in English. For the past three months, Mark had been auditing graduate seminars in English literature at Harvard. In that time, Kathleen had watched his wariness and uncertainty about quitting medicine transform into joy and enthusiasm for his new life.

Now he had been admitted into the program at Harvard, and he wondered if Kathleen minded if they stayed in Boston a little longer. . . .

Of course she didn't mind. Despite the lingering worries—despite the uneasy memory of the epilogue of Mark's short story—the past few months had been the happiest in Kathleen's life. She and Mark had fallen in love. Again. Better. More deeply. More securely, because Mark's life, his dreams, were more secure.

"You think you can stand three more years in Boston?" he asked as he kissed her neck. They were in bed. It was ten in the morning. It was something else that Kathleen loved about the past few months, the luxury of having him with her.

"I'll love it," she said enthusiastically. "This year I'm going to learn how to drive in the snow."

Kathleen's style—the energy and vitality that was her style—had blossomed again, nourished by Mark's love and his happiness.

"I'll teach you," he said.

"Do you think you could tell Harvard that you'll accept their offer *contingent* on an agreement that your earliest class of the day is noon?"

"What?" Mark asked, laughing. "I don't think Harvard sends negotiable offers. Why?"

"Tell them that your wife needs you *in bed* in the morning," Kathleen said. "Tell them you have to make love with your wife every day before you can even begin to think about Shakespeare."

"Every day?"

"Every day," Kathleen said dreamily. She was getting used to—*addicted* to—the long wonderful hours in bed with her sensual, romantic husband.

"I *will* tell them that you are my inspiration," Mark said seriously. *Because you are.*

"Do you know what I would like you to do?" Kathleen asked, suddenly turning to face him, her violet eyes thoughtful.

"Yes," he teased gently. "I thought I just did it, fifteen minutes ago."

Kathleen was silent, thinking. Maybe she shouldn't mention it. Everything had been so perfect.

"What, Kathleen?" he asked, concerned by the sudden seriousness in her eyes.

"I'd like you to learn how to swim," she said quickly, before she lost her courage. *So you can't ever fall off a boat and drown. By accident or . . .*

"Oh, Kathleen. I wish you had never read that damned epilogue," he said. He wasn't angry, just concerned. "I wrote that part for myself. I needed to. It was part of the process. I had to think about all the possibilities."

"I know," she said. But . . .

527

"I am so happy now. I have never been this happy. I never thought I could be this happy. Don't you know that?"

"Yes . . ."

"But you want me to learn how to swim," he said amiably, kissing the tip of her nose.

Kathleen nodded then smiled seductively.

"So when we vacation in Martinique next month you can make love to me in the turquoise-blue water."

"*That's* the reason?" he teased. He would take swimming lessons, starting Monday, because he didn't want her to worry ever again.

Kathleen started to nod, then slowly shook her head. They both knew the real reason.

"But it's a wonderful dividend, isn't it?"

Mark nodded. Then he frowned, wondering if he should tell her what *he* had been thinking about, worrying about.

He should, he decided. It was the way they were going to spend the rest of their lives. Together. *Including* each other in their dreams and sharing their worries. For better or worse.

"What, Mark?"

"I've been thinking about writing to my father," he said.

There had been no communication since the snowy night in January four months before when Mark's father told him it would be better if he were dead.

"Why?" Kathleen asked. But she knew the answer. It—Mark's unresolved relationship with his father—was a long, troublesome, loose thread.

"Because it still feels awful. It's probably worse for him than for me. I've made it. I've escaped and I'm happy."

"You've made your own happiness," Kathleen said. She did not have generous feelings about Mark's father. She added, "In *spite* of him."

"He never wanted me to be unhappy, Kathleen," Mark said, his voice gentle and sad. "He was just a man who wanted everything—the best—for his son. He thought that what he wanted for me *would* make me happy. That's not so bad, is it?"

"But he drove you," Kathleen said. Was Mark's father pushing Mark for Mark's sake? Or for his own?

"He was as much a victim of his hopes and dreams for me as I was," Mark said wistfully. "I actually feel sorry for him."

"So," Kathleen began, then paused. So Mark is an incredible, kind, generous man, she thought lovingly. But I know that.

"So I am going to write to him, explain it to him if I can."

"And?"

"And hope that now, or someday, he understands."

And all is forgiven.

Chapter Forty-two

Toward the middle of May, Leslie realized that she needed to find an apartment in Palo Alto. She would be moving at the end of June. She set aside time on Saturday to drive to Palo Alto to look.

She needed to be near Stanford Hospital. She would take calls from home but had to be available, close by, for emergency cardiac catheterizations and patients with acute myocardial infarctions and arrhythmias. The rentals near Stanford Hospital were almost exclusively large apartment complexes inhabited by young single adults.

You *are* a young single adult, she told herself. Even if you want nothing to do with other young single adults. Or anyone.

Joylessly Leslie signed a six month lease for a corner apartment in a beautifully landscaped complex complete with tennis courts and a swimming pool. It was walking distance to the hospital. Clean, neat and safe.

She should have been thrilled. But she wasn't.

The ache that reminded her constantly that she and Eric were no longer together, had lost their forever, only intensified as the days turned into weeks and months. She dreamed about him—terrible tormented dreams—and sometimes woke up with tears in her eyes.

At work she could focus her mind away from him, even

though the aching emptiness was a constant companion. Leslie worked long hours, spending extra time with her patients and with the more junior residents, interns and students. She started to study for her Internal Medicine Board exam and spent hours in the library reading about cardiology so that she would be amply prepared for her fellowship at Stanford.

Time heals all wounds, she told herself, but she had no evidence that it was true. What if the wounds were too deep? too gaping? too raw? What if they healed with bulky, deformed scars? What if they never healed?

A hundred times, Leslie reached for the phone to call Eric, but she never dialed. She didn't know the man at the other end of the phone. He was, had always been, a stranger.

Leslie returned from her successful apartment-hunting trip to Palo Alto in the early evening. She had driven back to San Francisco along the coast highway. It was a flawless spring day. A warm gentle breeze carried the fragrance of lilacs and eucalyptus. The ocean beaches were crowded with swimmers, surfers, sunbathers, kite flyers and frisbee tossers. It was a day for Beach Boys' music, hot dogs, laughter and love. Leslie was a spectator, uninvolved with the humanity but still dazzled by the blue sky and yellow sun and azure sea.

Ten minutes after Leslie returned to her apartment, the doorbell rang.

"James," she breathed with a sigh.

"Hi. May I come in? I was just in the neighborhood —"

"Are you building a resort? Parnassus Palms?" Leslie asked sarcastically.

"Hey," he said swiftly. "I'm not the enemy."

"Did he send you?"

"Leslie, I came to see you. I've come before. This is the first time you've been here."

"I spend as little time here as possible," she admitted.

531

Her voice softened. It was nice to see James.

"Leslie," he said gently. Too gently. It reminded her of being loved.

Tears filled her large blue eyes.

"Oh Leslie," James said, wanting to hold her. She was so hurt. So vulnerable. So alone.

She had lost weight. Her shiny chestnut hair fell halfway down her back. Her huge blue eyes were tired, haunted and wary, as if on the lookout for someone who might hurt her again.

She was so beautiful.

"Sorry, James. I'm still a little emotional," she said as she wiped the tears that wouldn't stop.

He put his arms around her and held her tight. It felt so good. He felt so good. She needed to be held and loved. James used to love her. It could happen so easily again with James. . . .

Leslie stiffened.

"You're so tense," he whispered, his lips brushed against her hair.

You're strung so tight if I touched you you'd twang. The clever words of a fellow intern thundered in her mind. The intern had been referring to her inner tension. Her rigid critical standards. Her perfectionism. Was she too rigid? Did she expect too much from everyone? Did she expect too much from herself?

"James," she said finally. "It's too hard for me to have you touch me."

"Why?" he asked, releasing her but not moving away.

"I need—" *Something.*

"You need Eric," James said flatly.

"No."

"Leslie, look at yourself. This is tearing you apart," James said. Then he added softly, "Just like it's tearing Eric apart."

"I don't want to hear about him," Leslie said quickly.

"Well you just did. He looks about the way you look. He's pushing himself as hard as you are pushing yourself.

The company has never been more successful," James said seriously.

"James, you know what he did!"

"I know what he *didn't* do. He didn't tell you about another woman because he knew it would hurt you. He didn't tell you about his experience with hospitals and medicine because he knew it would make you question your career. And he didn't tell you about a little boy who died because he knew it would make you sad," James said, his voice breaking slightly.

"Did you know?" Leslie asked.

"I knew there had been something with Charlie. I didn't know the rest until recently. Charlie told me, not Eric. Eric would never tell me about Bobby." *Because of Michael.*

"You didn't *need* to know, James. I did. It had such a direct impact on our life together."

"Maybe he didn't want it to. I know he would never have wanted you to give up medicine because of him."

"But I would have," Leslie said thoughtfully. "I wouldn't give up Radcliffe for Alan or my internship for whoever it was in medical school. But for Eric . . ."

All those years ago I would have given up going to Radcliffe to be with you, James. And now I would have given up everything to make a life with Eric.

"I don't think he wanted you to give up anything. Not your career. Not children. He must have been struggling with how to convince you of that once he told you. That may be why he put off telling you."

"Because he wasn't sure himself?"

"Until he met you, he never thought about having another child."

"He told you that?" Leslie asked weakly. Eric had told her that himself, the night he called her in Boston.

"He told Charlie."

"Charlie, Charlie, Charlie. Maybe now Charlie and Eric will get back together. It seems right somehow," Leslie said, remembering Victoria's words.

"Love doesn't work that way," James said. Not by *default*. "Eric loves you."

"I don't even *know* Eric," Leslie persisted. Why was James defending Eric? Why wasn't he helping *her?* "The most important part of his life was hidden from me—"

"Leslie, when a man loses his child that *is* part of his life, every minute of his life, for the rest of his life," James said emotionally. "Whether or not Eric told you the words, you knew that part of him. He couldn't hide it."

That was true, Leslie realized uneasily. Bobby had been there. In his eyes, in his gentleness, in the way he loved her.

Have I been wrong? Too rigid? Too unforgiving? I don't know. I don't know.

Leslie lapsed into silence.

"Leslie?" James asked finally as he watched new tears flood her eyes.

"This is your fault, you know," she sniffed bravely.

"My fault? Because of Maui? Because he would have told you then if—"

"No. Because a year and a half ago you became the gold standard," she said carefully. The gold standard for loving and for trusting.

"Even though it ended?" he asked gently. Then he said what they both knew. "It didn't end, did it? We just stopped seeing each other."

James looked at her for a long moment. He would always love her. That was why he was here now. Because he loved her. Because he knew she was suffering, and he wanted her to be happy.

"After it was," Leslie began, finally, awkwardly, unable to hold his gaze. "After we stopped seeing each other, I decided that the relationships that followed would be like the ones before: pleasant, comfortable, *safe* liaisons that didn't threaten my career or really intrude on my life or my privacy. Relationships that didn't consume me."

"In other words, relationships without love," James

534

said.

"I had the memory of love." *The memory of you. And it wasn't bitter or sad.*

"And then you met Eric. And you realized that what we had . . ." James's voice trailed off. *What we had was—is—love, but it doesn't compare with what you found with Eric.*

"I knew that I could fall in love again. It wasn't a realization; it just happened, and now my memory of love isn't so lovely anymore. It's painful and angry and bitter. Now that it's over."

"It's not over, Leslie. No matter how much that smart, rational mind of yours tries to end it, your heart won't let it happen. Maybe Eric made a mistake. Maybe he broke some of your rules."

"James." She wanted him to stop. He was confusing her. He was telling her that she was too rigid. That when you loved someone the rules changed.

James didn't stop.

"You've broken some rules yourself, Leslie," James said quietly.

You had an affair with a married man. Because love changed the rules. Because it felt right despite the rules.

On the first Friday evening in June, three weeks after James's visit, Leslie dialed the unlisted number at Eric's penthouse. Until that moment, she hadn't thought specifically about calling him. But, she realized as her trembling fingers dialed the number she knew so well, for the past three weeks she hadn't thought about anything else.

The phone was answered on the second ring. But not by Eric.

"Hello! Hello!" the voice bubbled, a cascade of joy. "We're almost ready. Except Eric is pretending to have misplaced the wedding rings!"

Charlie. Leslie recognized the voice. *Wedding rings.*

Leslie stared at the receiver for a moment then returned

it to its cradle. The ache in her heart made her want to scream.

"Who was it, Charlie?" Eric asked. He had overheard Charlie's words and watched her puzzled expression.

"I assumed it was Robert wondering what was keeping us. But it wasn't. Whoever it was hung up."

"Before you answered?"

"No. Five or ten seconds after I stopped talking. Maybe it was a wrong number," Charlie said. "You *have* the rings, don't you?"

"Of course," Eric murmured distantly. He had never gotten a wrong number call before. His number was unlisted so he didn't get calls for other Lansdales. It was possible that someone had misdialed, but it had never happened before.

What if it had been Leslie after all these months? Leslie would have heard Charlie's words, hesitated a moment, then hung up.

But Leslie wasn't going to call him. Not ever.

But what if she had?

Eric stood motionless in the living room, his mind bombarded with what ifs, his heart pumping with uncomfortable energy.

"Eric?" Charlie asked.

"I have to make a phone call," he said, surprised at his own words. He had made a decision. He couldn't lose more than he had already lost.

"Now?"

"Yes. Now," he said.

Eric left a stunned Charlie in the living room. He went to his bedroom and shut the door.

I can't answer it, Leslie thought, startled by the telephone ring. It was so loud, so intrusive. I can't talk to anyone right now.

Five rings.

Leave me alone, whoever you are.

Ten rings.

Please. Give me time to understand. To recover. To get

536

back to hating him again. It should be so easy this time. . . .

Fifteen rings.

She answered it, finally, on the eighteenth ring. She answered it to make it stop ringing. The loud insistent noise made her ache even more.

"Hello?" she was surprised that she could make her voice sound almost normal.

"Leslie."

Eric. Leslie closed her eyes. *He's calling to explain to me about Charlie. I can't listen to it.*

"Leslie?"

"Yes."

"Did you just call me?" Eric held his breath.

"Yes." *I have to hang up.*

"Leslie, let me explain," Eric said quickly, sensing that she was withdrawing.

"There's nothing to explain. I understand." *I understand perfectly.*

"Leslie. Charlie and I are not getting married."

What did that mean?

Leslie waited.

"Charlie is marrying Father."

"Robert?"

"Yes. She thought it was Robert who called."

"Oh." *Oh.*

Eric waited. There was silence at the other end.

"Why did you call me, Leslie?" he asked carefully.

"I missed . . . miss . . . you." Was that why she had called? Just to tell him that? She didn't know. Except that now, hearing his voice, she knew there was more.

"I miss you, darling," he said gently. *Every minute of my life.*

He didn't sound like a stranger. He sounded like the man she loved. The father of a beloved little boy who died. Another woman's husband. Another woman's lover. They were all part of the loving voice that spoke to her. They always had been.

"That was it," she said weakly. "That was my whole prepared speech."

"Will you open the floor to questions?" he asked lightly, his confidence, his hope kindled by the warmth of her voice. And by the fact that she had called, finally, after almost five months.

"Sure," she said. Ask me the tough questions, Eric. I think I can answer them, she thought, her heart pounding. The emptiness and the aching were quickly retreating, and in their place was a familiar joy. A joy she had only known since Eric. Because of Eric.

"Can I see you?"

"Yes."

Can I kiss you and hold you and love you?

"When?"

"Now. Whenever." *Always.*

"The rehearsal dinner is this evening," Eric said. *I could miss it. They would understand.*

"You need to be there."

"I need to be with you more."

"I could . . ."

"Could you? Come with me?"

"Yes."

It meant that she knew what he knew. That they were already together. The love was there. Strong. Confident. They didn't have to search for it. They didn't have to spend long private hours trying to recapture what they had. They had to talk, to plan their life together, but they didn't have to find the love. It was there. It always had been.

"I love you, Leslie," he said, his eyes wet with happiness.

"I love you, Eric," she said as warm tears spilled onto her cheeks.

"I'll be over as soon as I drop Charlie at the Fairmont."

"Is that where the dinner is?"

"No. That's where Father is. The dinner is at a lovely place for weddings," he said softly, his voice full of love and happiness. *A lovely place for our wedding.* "A place with white lilacs and pink roses and canopied beds."

"Where," she breathed. She knew. And she knew he was talking about them.

"You know."

"The Carlton Club."

CATCH A RISING STAR!

ROBIN ST. THOMAS

FORTUNE'S SISTERS (2616, $3.95)

It was Pia's destiny to be a Hollywood star. She had complete self-confidence, breathtaking beauty, and the help of her domineering mother. But her younger sister Jeanne began to steal the spotlight meant for Pia, diverting attention away from the ruthlessly ambitious star. When her mother Mathilde started to return the advances of dashing director Wes Guest, Pia's jealousy surfaced. Her passion for Guest and desire to be the brightest star in Hollywood pitted Pia against her own family—sister against sister, mother against daughter. Pia was determined to be the only survivor in the arenas of love and fame. But neither Mathilde nor Jeanne would surrender without a fight. . . .

LOVER'S MASQUERADE (2886, $4.50)

New Orleans. A city of secrets, shrouded in mystery and magic. A city where dreams become obsessions and memories once again become reality. A city where even one trip, like a stop on Claudia Gage's book promotion tour, can lead to a perilous fall. For New Orleans is also the home of Armand Dantine, who knows the secrets that Claudia would conceal and the past she cannot remember. And he will stop at nothing to make her love him, and will not let her go again . . .

SENSATION (3228, $4.95)

They'd dreamed of stardom, and their dreams came true. Now they had fame and the power that comes with it. In Hollywood, in New York, and around the world, the names of Aurora Styles, Rachel Allenby, and Pia Decameron commanded immediate attention—and lust and envy as well. They were stars, idols on pedestals. And there was always someone waiting in the wings to bring them crashing down . . .

Available wherever paperbacks are sold, or order direct from the Publisher. Send cover price plus 50¢ per copy for mailing and handling to Penguin USA, P.O. Box 999, c/o Dept. 17109, Bergenfield, NJ 07621. Residents of New York and Tennessee must include sales tax. DO NOT SEND CASH.

JANE KIDDER'S EXCITING
WELLESLEY BROTHERS SERIES

MAIL ORDER TEMPTRESS   (3863, $4.25)
Kirsten Lundgren traveled all the way to Minnesota to be a
mail order bride, but when Eric Wellesley wrapped her in his
virile embrace, her hopes for security soon turned to dreams
of passion!

PASSION'S SONG   (4174, $4.25)
When beautiful opera singer Elizabeth Ashford agreed to care
for widower Adam Wellesley's four children, she never
dreamed she'd fall in love with the little devils—and with their
handsome father as well!

PASSION'S CAPTIVE   (4341, $4.50)
To prevent her from hanging, Union captain Stuart Wellesley
offered to marry feisty Confederate spy Claire Boudreau. Little
did he realize he was in for a different kind of war after the
wedding!

PASSION'S BARGAIN   (4539, $4.50)
When she was sold into an unwanted marriage by her father,
Megan Taylor took matters into her own hands and black-
mailed Geoffrey Wellesley into becoming her husband instead.
But Meg soon found that marriage to the handsome, wealthy
timber baron was far more than she had bargained for!